A Tender Tomorrow

A Tender Tomorrow

CAROL KING

iPUBLISH
at Time Warner Books

For information address iPublish.com, 135 West 50th Street, New York, NY 10020.

 A Time Warner Company

ISBN 0-7595-5009-3

First edition: June 2001

Visit our Web site at www.iPublish.com

Contents

Prologue

CAPE MAY, NEW JERSEY
1896

For Robert Moffat it is a matter of a goddess, though he is unable in his simplicity of reasoning to conceptualize such a notion. He imagines his goddess, not symbolically as a lodestone— a ruling passion in a blind hierarchy of moldy tradition, but literally. He strokes his great graying beard as he peers across the bay. From his vantage in the topmost room of the Cape May light, where he eats and sleeps, he can see the house, a mansard-roofed smear against the moon. It stands on a spit of land at the tip of a bluff over which the sea darts and swells and sometimes soars, and he watches it till the fog thickens sensibly and the moon fades and then vanishes beneath a wilderness of clouds. Except that he is standing upright, Robert no longer knows what is up or down, east or west. He turns from the tall, many-layered windows that rattle in the wind and lumbers up the circular iron stairway to light the tower lamp and to signal the arrival of the fog with one-two- three long blasts of the horn. What might seem like comfort to some only mourns the emptiness and loss of those in pain. Robert descends and pours himself a large draught of whiskey and lights his pipe. Glancing toward the windows, he is relieved he can no longer see the house. Again, he turns away and seats himself before his fire. He lays his head back. His reflections wander in shadowy, shifting currents of awareness, and he finally comes to a central truth: It is not fitting that a man should see so far or be so high. A sensible man stays in the thick of things, where he knows the world as it really is, not as he wishes it to be. Up here with the sea birds and the angels, a man might imagine all kinds of things—stubborn, wayward things he should not be thinking. A man should not place himself so high.

Robert has not attended his telescope in some minutes, and he rises tiredly to do so. He appreciates his work and his isolation, but more and more, he finds himself approaching the work, at least, with a fair amount of disinterest. He observes that Delaware Sound, silvered by the soft light from the tower lamp, is clear of sails as far as he can see, then trains his glass north and eastward on the intracoastal waters and southward to the open sea. Robert checks his compass. His headings are correct. He swings the glass and his view sweeps the bay. No sail is visible on the rising, wind-dashed waters. This is good, he tells himself. This is good. No vessel should be a'sea on a night like this. He logs his observations and resumes his seat and his whiskey. Robert gazes into his fire and finally picks up the neat parcel of notes, wrapped in ribbon, which he keeps always on the table near his chair. He does not read them though, preferring this night merely to hold them. Before long he finds himself dozing. And his dreams are of her, the authoress of those pretty testimonies.

She comes to him from across the bay, from across time, arms beckoning, and she calls his name, and smiles and laughs and gazes into his eyes in such a loving, knowing fashion that his body trembles and his heart tips in his breast. He allows her love to fill him, for if he tries to grasp it, he will become pained and terrified of its loss. And so his goddess caresses his soul and purifies his senses.

The horn! He has not signaled the fog for who knows how long. Robert lurches awake. He climbs the circular staircase and pulls the heavy cord attached to the signal. Two and then three times it sounds. Robert descends again into his small parlor. He re-lights his pipe, then leans down, picking up the bundle of letters that had fallen at his feet. He smiles at how quickly we abandon sweetness when duty calls. And Robert Moffat knows his duty. He looks once more toward the windows that overlook the bay. The glass echoes many layers of a fire-lit reflection, and each layer is the same—a ghostly old man with a great graying beard, a smoldering pipe, and a packet of ribbon-tied memories.

Chapter 1

Her name was Autumn Thackeray. She was gently bred, tranquilly raised, and always treated with open-handed kindness. Autumn had traveled by coach, a rackety public vehicle, from Philadelphia to Cape May, New Jersey. She had taken her leisure, such as was allowed in the course of her journey, in public rooms, eaten public food, and slept fitfully, sitting up, only when she could no longer keep her lids from falling. And now she stood on a public road, abandoned by even the uncertain protection of her traveling companions and the harsh-mouthed coachman. It was night. The air was washed in blown spume and fog, salty with the sea that thundered somewhere beyond. She glanced down at the trunks, baskets, and boxes scattered at her feet, the aggregation of a life. Her gaze lifted and traveled upward to a series of glowing lights in the distance. That, the coachman had informed her, was her destination, Byron Hall. She drew her muffler more securely around her shoulders, placed her hands firmly into her sable muff and began a brisk walk toward the lights. She had proceeded about halfway between the road and the house, when a woman's shriek rang out. Autumn stopped, stunned, waiting. Again, she heard the chilling scream. It came from where the lights were. She could not see the house, but her gaze was riveted in that direction. Hearing a third scream, more a screech this time, she bolted toward it. She set aside her fear and the fact that she was running practically blind; if someone was in danger, she must help. She came abruptly to a halt. The house was before her, its massive front door flung open, flooding the darkness with a yawning, bloodless light. A young woman, shawl flying, hair streaming, flew from the house as if she'd been thrown, shrilling curses, more angry it seemed than afraid. "He's a monster, he is," she shrieked at Autumn as she hurled herself into the fog. Autumn looked back toward the house. The door hung open. Against the illumination from inside, there appeared the alarming, dark figure of a man. Catching her breath, Autumn stared. The man was tall, of a muscular girth and rough-seeming. He shouted a curse into the night. Autumn swallowed and licked at her lips. They stood, the two figures, he framed in light, she at its fringes. He seemed to glare, though she could not see his eyes, seething in a silhouetted rage, in her direction. She wondered if he noticed her and if she should proceed or wait for an invitation. The thought almost made her laugh. Such a man did not issue invitations. She pressed her hands against the frenzied palpitations of her heart. She had come all this way, had weathered unimaginable discomfort. She would not await an invitation. A decision made, she pressed on, up to the house. The man at the door loomed menacingly, and the nearer Autumn got to the house the more ruggedly dangerous he appeared. He was dressed in lean-cut riding breeches and a lawn shirt, the sleeves of which were rolled up on his forearms. He snapped a riding crop against his long booted leg.

"Are you Miss Thackeray?" he called to her. The sudden resonance of her name spoken in this place by this odd and terrible man startled her.

"Yes," she replied, disallowing her voice to entertain the absurdity of a quiver. She must not appear timid or strained before this proudhearted individual. Throughout the long, humiliating days of the past year, she had poised herself constantly for attack. She lifted her chin, set her shoulders, and approached the house. "I had been in hope that someone would meet me at the coach stop," she said coolly, with found courage. "My luggage is lying willy-nilly in the road, soaking up all this wet." The man did not speak. As she mounted the porch steps and stopped before the door, she noted that his perusal of her was unnecessarily intense. "Your question indicates I was expected," she said. When again the man did not speak, she resumed. "My correspondence stated precisely the time of my arrival." Impatiently, at his further silence, she looked beyond him into the house. "Might I be admitted? It is awfully damp out here." In reply, the man nodded tersely. Autumn proceeded past him into the entryway and noted its contrast to the figure of the man who had—for lack of a better phrase—greeted her. The hallway was a spacious chamber with a thick gold-patterned carpet, muted wallpaper of a tasteful yellow hue, and a glimmering crystal chandelier that lit a grandly curved rosewood staircase. Spanning the height and breadth of one wall near the entry was an oil painting of a distant tall ship heeling on a gold-tinted sea. The painting's carved wooden frame caught the light of the candles above. "It is a Hassam," she said reverently.

"One of his seascapes," the man offered. "He comes down now and then to paint our bay." Autumn looked at the man who seemed so abruptly civilized. He swung the great door closed and unknotted the scarf at his neck. He used it to wipe unceremoniously at his forehead. She immediately amended her judgment.

"You're young," he observed.

"Some might say so."

"Not twenty, I'd wager."

"Nearly that." She lifted her chin a notch. "In any event, I wonder that my age is your business, sir. Though you know who I am, you've not identified yourself to me." A smile threatened at the corner of the man's lips, but did not reach the depths of his onyx gaze.

"Insolent, too," he said. "And you recognize art." He swiped once again at his forehead, displacing a tangle of rude black curls that hung loosely, and at the moment, glistened with perspiration. To Autumn's horror, he tossed the offending cloth onto a brilliantly polished center table and extended his paw of a hand. "I'm Cain Byron."

"How do you do," she managed, making her own hand available. "Is it *Doctor* Byron?" The man nodded. This then was the person with whom she had so daintily corresponded for the past two months on the subject of his mother's need of a companion. From his letters, Autumn had formed a very different picture. She had envisioned an aging man, an elegant and learned man, tidy in his habits and appearance—in short, a doctor. She averted her eyes, hoping her new employer would not perceive the disappointment, the disapproval, and the despondency in her heart.

Still grasping her hand, he said, "Come with me." Autumn found herself being towed along, nearly stumbling, down a lengthy corridor and into a room closed off by a pair of thick pocket doors. Once inside the room, having gained her balance and her hand, she noted that, though lit only by a flickering hearth fire and a few candles, the room was cozy and decorated with a lightness of hand. The hearth, which she could see plainly, was of white painted plaster and gold leaf. The mantel was crowded with a display of framed photographs, probably of family members. The walls were papered with a deep green neo-Grecian design and a tasteful ceiling border in the popular "Plume" pattern. A plush Oriental carpet had been placed in the center of a polished, parqueted floor. Autumn took in the outlines of side chairs, slipper stools, and a round center table draped with layers of velvet and lace. Her drifting gaze halted at the unexpected sight of a figure lying huddled on a couch outside the circlet of light provided by the fire. It moved as Autumn stepped toward it.

"Who is it?" asked a voice chafed with dryness.

"It is me, Mother," said Cain Byron. His voice was edged with annoyance. "Where is Mrs. Inman?"

"She . . . went to get me . . . something, I suppose. Oh, how the hell do I know?" Autumn's eyes widened. She glanced at the doctor, but he seemed unfazed by his mother's rude language. For all the coarseness of her speech, there was a vague, frail quality in her voice. Her head rolled to one side as though she had been fatigued with the effort of speech, and she exhaled with a soft, audible sigh. She was swathed in a thick draping of woolen fabric.

"How long have you been alone?" Cain Byron persisted. Beneath the heavy blanketing, the woman might have shrugged. Dr. Byron uttered a curse. "Stay with her," he ordered Autumn and strode from the room, slapping the riding crop against his thigh. Unsure of what ailed the woman—Dr. Byron's correspondence indicated that she had a "nervous disorder"—Autumn knelt beside her.

"Can I do something for you?" she asked uncertainly. There seemed so much that might be done for her. "Mightn't we untangle some of these blankets?" Receiving no answer, Autumn took the initiative. She began to adjust the coil of woolen fabric that entrapped the woman. Looking down into her face, Autumn saw that the woman was not old, middle-aged perhaps, no more than fifty, her face unlined, even pretty, though pale and sunken around her eyes and cheeks. Her head drifted from side to side.

"So sleepy," she whispered. "Always so . . . damnably . . . sleepy." She sounded more defeated than ill.

Abruptly the room erupted with light and sound. The doctor had returned. He carried a lantern and was followed by a heavy-breasted woman dressed in a prim cap and an apron, her hands folded before her.

"And there she was," Cain Byron was saying, "lying there with no comfort, no solace." Mrs. Inman's manner was as starched as her apron and cap.

"If I don't get up them preserves, doctor, the fruit'll rot in the bin—"

"The fruit be damned, woman," he returned. "Look at her!" He directed his light toward his mother's form. "Is this the way you care for your mistress?"

"I beg an apology," the woman returned in a rolling Irish lilt that sounded not in the least apologetic, "but since you run off Alma Louise and all the other girls, I'm just the one here—"

"By the gods, Careem Inman," Cain interrupted, "if this happens again, I shall dismember you and toss you into the sea, you blathering Celtic witch." Autumn's mouth fell open, but Mrs.

Inman simply rolled her eyes and moved to her charge. Helping her to her feet, she shepherded the invalid from the room. "You," he said to Autumn, "follow me." He led her to another room, which seemed to be the doctor's private parlor. This room was plushly decorated in the Turkish mode, with deep jewel-like colors. Chairs and couches were covered in thick, tufted crimson velvet, and heavy draperies were tasseled with gold fringe. A brass and green Tiffany floor lamp shed a dark emerald wash over the room. Autumn supposed the effect was meant to be restful. A small fire crackled on a hearth that was made of black marble. Above it was the startling sight of a framed portrait of an older, more handsomely dressed Cain Byron glaring into the room. Dr. Byron noted the direction of Autumn's stare. "My late father," he said, then directed Autumn to seat herself in a chair made, oddly, of animal horns. She did so hesitantly. She watched as he lit a slim cigar. He did not sit down, but paced the room like a restive leopard.

"You must understand, Miss Thackeray, if you are to acquire this position in my household, there will be no allowance for laxity or negligence. My mother is very ill. Her medicines must be administered faithfully, and she must be watched constantly. I shall brook no delinquency." The doctor bent a cutting gaze on Autumn. His words had come, she thought, not so much out of loving concern for his mother, but out of an apparent desire to control his environment. And he had said "if." Had they not corresponded these last months and had they not agreed ultimately that she *would* be hired? "My mother," the doctor was telling her, "suffers, as I mentioned in my letters, from a nervous disorder. She is under the care of my colleague, Dr. Winslow Beame, a most capable specialist in women's problems. He practices in

New York, but has kindly deigned to accommodate me in this case. We were at Harvard together, Win and I, and he is a most congenial fellow." Autumn's pale brows drew together. She wondered what the man's personality had to do with his competence as a doctor of medicine. Still, amending her expression, she asked about Mrs. Byron's treatment.

"A combination of medication and complete rest," Dr. Byron answered. "She must be absolutely shielded from any disturbance of body or mind. If you are to be placed in the position of her caretaker, you must, Miss Thackeray, be prepared to devote yourself to that purpose. Can you promise that?"

Autumn nodded. She needed no second thoughts to make such a vow. In shielding Mrs. Byron from the harshness of the world, she would also be shielding herself. She glanced up at her inquisitor. He lifted a dark brow in anticipation of her response.

"It will be my pleasure to protect your mother from the cares of the world, Dr. Byron. I will enfold her as I would my own dear mother," she said, adding hastily, "*if* I should be fortunate enough to obtain this position." In truth, it galled Autumn to make that qualification. Had she not traveled all this way for that very purpose? Had he not agreed in his last letter to hire her? Manipulative exhibitions of power had always angered her. She dimpled her most appealing smile, however, and lowered golden lashes over an amber gaze. Autumn needed this job.

"Dr. Beame visits once a month, Miss Thackeray. It is imperative that he find my mother composed. Otherwise, he threatens to take her back to New York for treatment. Win runs Belle Vue, a woman's sanitarium in the city. I am told it is a pleasant place, but mother is terrified of being confined there. So you see, it is most important to me that she be prepared for his examination."

"When will he visit next?"

"He arrives tomorrow," answered Cain Byron. "It is with some urgency, then, that I ask you to make this commitment to me."

To me! "Of course, Dr. Byron," Autumn said, standing and smiling. "I shall see that your mother is arranged most appealingly for Dr. Beame's visit. *Should* I be fortunate enough to deserve the position." Clearly the man needed her, but Autumn took no chances. His arrogance was such that he might send her packing out of spite. He had apparently run off others and selfishly had consequently left his household in a despairing state of disorder.

Cain Byron took a last draw on his cigar and then snuffed it out. He took in the confident figure before him, and Autumn realized that her confidence might imply a strong will. Her smile faded and her shoulders fell just a note, and she lowered her eyes. "You have the position," the man informed her.

"Thank you, sir," Autumn said with a small curtsy. She even allowed a bit of relief into her expression. "May I take it that my things will be brought up from the road?" Cain nodded.

"I am curious, Miss Thackeray," he said after a pause. "You are obviously a lady of some quality. Why would you seek out such a position?"

Some quality! "As I mentioned in my first letter to you, Dr. Byron, my family has suffered financial reverses. I would rather not discuss the subject, however, for it is most embarrassing."

"So you have been forced to take this position," he stated.

Autumn nodded, then attempting lightness, she said, "But you mustn't think I am not prepared for subservience. I have been around servants all my life—"

"In the posture of mistress," he mentioned quietly, finishing her unspoken thought.

"Of course," agreed Autumn. "But, it is precisely because of that exposure that I am capable of understanding the obligations of those in service." For the second time that evening, a smile threatened Cain Byron's stern countenance. His black gaze seemed to absorb her as the black hearth tiles absorbed the firelight. In his eyes, she saw herself reflected: The neat dimensions of her brown velvet carriage suit, the arranged upsweep of her pale tawny curls, the tilt of her bonnet, and the small plumes that decorated it. She perceived, moreover, the slim dimensions of her form and realized her own vulnerability in the face of this man's towering conceit. She swallowed audibly, covering the sound with a small cough. "Might I be shown to my room?" she asked. Lifting her chin in defiance of her abrupt realization, she regarded Dr. Byron evenly. "My long travels have exhausted me, sir." The man's returning gaze might have signaled admiration, but he turned abruptly and savagely pulled at a long brocaded cord.

"Mrs. Inman will see you up to your room," he said. "I shall see that your bags are brought in." With the words, he withdrew.

Autumn felt her whole body relax. She could barely credit the tension she had been feeling. She took a long breath and came to the realization that a posture of servility was going to be more difficult to maintain than she had imagined. It was one thing to be humble if one's employers were kind—as she had been to her servants, when she'd had them—but it was another to be expected to shrink into submissiveness in the face of deliberate hostility and intimidation.

"Will you follow me, miss?" Autumn turned to find Mrs. Inman behind her. She held a lantern. "You'll be up on the third floor." Autumn followed the woman from the room, glad to be quit of its lavish decadence. The two passed along the corridor, around a corner, through a gallery off which was the kitchen, buttery, and several other rooms, and finally, up a narrow wood staircase. This, Mrs. Inman assured the younger woman, was the staircase she was expected to use at all times. The front staircase was never to be utilized by the servants. Autumn took in the foot-worn steps and the small fluted gas fixtures that brushed the wall with the barest illumination. At the second floor landing, they passed beneath a huge overarch of ornamental fretwork, the same decoration that adorned all of the archways, both upstairs and down. They crossed a wide, carpeted gallery where tall pocket doors closed off what Autumn could only imagine were exceptionally beautiful chambers perhaps facing the sea and ascended a second flight of stairs to the third floor of the mansion. "Your room is up here," Mrs. Inman told her, "next to Mrs. Byron's. There's a connecting door, don't you know, for you must be available to her at all times." The woman moved aside as she pushed open a thick door. Autumn stepped into the room. As Mrs. Inman lit the candles that stood in tall pewter holders about the room, the meanness of the chamber was revealed. The ceiling was low and slanted, and there was only one window—a small darkly tessellated one, at that. At Autumn's stricken expression, Mrs. Inman offered, "I know it don't seem like much, but the tester's clean, the bed ropes have been tightened, and I had one of the boys air the mattress and the carpet this very morning." An unaccustomed sympathy crept into the woman's tone. "'T isn't easy, is it? A girl like yourself having to come to this."

Autumn glanced at her.

"You know my circumstances?"

Mrs. Inman nodded sagely.

"'T is easy to see, miss, you're not servant stock. Why, just look at yourself." She led the younger woman to a darkly veined standing mirror. "It isn't only in the dress, though that's patrician enough, it's the whole picture." Mrs. Inman pronounced the word "pitcher." "'Tis easy to tell you're an aristocrat." Autumn did not feel much like an aristocrat as she gazed at the distorted, lantern-washed reflection. "You've got good bones—*fine* bones, I like to say. And that hair of yours might've spun out from an autumn moon. And them eyes, miss! They're like the topaz crystals that hang from the chandelier in the front parlor. Wait'll you see *that!* It's something to behold."

Autumn smiled. "Why Mrs. Inman, you are waxing positively poetic."

"I'm a poet and don't know it, but my feet show it," said the woman gleefully. "They're lo-o-o-ng fellows!" It was a popular joke about the poet who had reigned over a good part of the mid-to-latter half of the nineteenth century and was in currency in prim drawing rooms and taverns up and down the eastern seaboard, but it became for Autumn an almost drown-ing release. She doubled over with unrestrained laughter, and Mrs. Inman, happy that her little jest had been so well-received, joined her. Together, the two women fell into the thickness of a small sofa near the hearth and enjoyed for some moments the pleasure of their amusement. It was in this unguarded pose that they were found by a young groom who brought Autumn's luggage to her room. The fellow halted just inside the door and smiled.

"Having a party, Mrs. Inman?" he asked. Mrs. Inman re-peated the joke, and the young man chuckled. "That's an old one," he observed. "Still, if it brings you a smile, what's the harm?" He divested his broad shoulder of the largest of Autumn's trunks, and set down another.

"The harm," said a voice from the dark hallway, "is that all this hilarity is bound to disturb my mother." The people inside the room sobered, and Cain Byron stepped across the threshold. He regarded them all coldly, his arms filled with hatboxes, cases, and baskets. He dropped his burdens unceremoniously where he stood. "Had you planned, Miss Thackeray, to relocate your entire household to mine?" Autumn stood.

"I only brought what I felt might be necessary for my entrance into an important household, Dr. Byron." She had no desire to inform him that his household had, unfortunately, become hers. She had nowhere else to go.

"I can assure you," the man returned icily, "your society will be with my mother only. There will be no dallying for you, miss. You will spend your time in this room or in my mother's. So you might as well have left most of this frippery in Philadelphia." He turned and stalked from the room. Autumn heard the echo of his booted feet long after he had passed from the hallway, and she remained speechless. Her silence, however, masked a roiling anger. Mrs. Inman touched her shoulder hesitantly.

And the young man, who followed his master from the room said solemnly, "This won't be a party for you, miss."

"I'll fetch you a tray," Mrs. Inman said as she, too, left the room.

The door closed. Autumn's repressed fury exploded. She tore at the pins that held her bonnet and hurled them and the hat to the floor. She ground her heel into its soft velvet, crushing the little plumes and rendering the once pretty accessory shapeless and mashed at her feet. Tears came to her eyes as she muttered an inarticulate curse. She turned in search of something else to fling to the floor, into the unlighted hearth, or at the wall. She gulped sobs as she picked up a candlestick, intending to hurl it at that ugly excuse for a mirror, but halted abruptly as she saw her own mad reflection, glowing ghostlike, arm raised, teeth bared, eyes hollowed, in the candlelit distortions of the glass. She realized with a crushing horror that she had no right. She had no right to destroy someone else's property, no right to feel resentment. She had no right . . . to feel. Her tears unchecked now, Autumn slowly, cautiously, set down the candlestick and sank back onto the sofa. Hopelessness encased her like a shroud as the realization of her circumstances overwhelmed her. She put her head into her hands, aware of the ache of a horrible truth. Autumn Thackeray, the once-proud heiress of a once-proud family, was nothing more than a servant. She had no home now—no place to think comfortably about "going back to." She had put herself willingly into this circumstance—never mind that she'd had little choice in the matter. And now, the consequences of her decision must be faced. Autumn Thackeray must live and think and feel—or rather not feel—as a humble, grateful recipient of the benevolence of others.

She pushed herself to a standing position and moved, suddenly overwhelmed with fatigue, to the bed. Without drawing back the counterpane or removing her clothes, she sank into its feathery softness. Lying there, eyes heavy with tears, she drifted, her anger exhausted, in a liminal wilderness somewhere between reality and dreams. Beyond her room, the sea thundered somewhere, a cadent lullaby. A foghorn murmured, one- two- three times. And Autumn slept . . . at last.

୧ଓ ଓ୨

The little girl, golden and pink, is wakened gently by sun-scented breezes and birdsong. She stretches lazily, idly reflecting, with the confidence of the deeply cherished, on the day's anticipated joys. She tumbles from her bed, slips into cozy slippers, and splashes her face with cool water from the flowered ewer. Refreshed, she scampers into her pinafore and hurries down the great staircase to a breakfast of scones and tea. She is spoiled, well nurtured, and loved.

Chapter 2

Autumn hearkened abruptly, her eyes popping open, to the restive tolling of a bell. She sat up with a start, wondering where she was. And that bell, its merciless resonance destroying her slumber, kept up its clamor. She rubbed the sleep from her eyes and swung her legs over the side of her bed—or was it hers? She scanned the low-ceilinged room. The hearth glowed with the dying embers of some fire she did not remember making. What had once been perhaps a wealth of heat was now only a tepid reminder that she was in some cold, unsympathetic climate. A parti-colored light that glimmered through the dark mosaic of the only window in the room told her it was morning.

The bell's insistence unnerved her. Observing that she was dressed only in a chemise and bloomers, she wrapped the counterpane carelessly about her and drew herself from the bed. Rushing to the door, she flung it open to find herself peering into a dark uninhabited corridor. She glanced back over her shoulder. The only other door in the room caught her attention. She bolted to it and slung it wide. She found before her a cavernous chamber, heavily draped against the morning light. Stepping barefooted into the shadowy room, Autumn suddenly recalled her mission. The ragged edges of denial evaporated and she padded to the huge silhouette of a tester bed, thickly curtained, which was situated at the center of the room. Parting the hangings, she saw the partially prone figure of the lady she'd met last night. Mrs. Byron was, with lean fingers wrapped around the handle of a bell, tolling her little instrument of torture furiously. Its relentless jangle sounded even louder within the confines of the velvet canopy.

"Mrs. Byron," Autumn ventured. "Please stop." The lady might have awakened from a dream. Her eyes, closed till now, opened abruptly.

"I have a headache," she complained, still tolling the bell. Autumn placed her hand gently on the older woman's, and both hand and bell fell to the thick folds of the coverlet. A merciful silence ensued.

"Mrs. Byron," Autumn repeated with concern, for as bell and hand relaxed, the lady's head lolled sidewise, and she issued a small sob. "Did you say you have a headache?" The graying head nodded lethargically. "I shall get some help," Autumn assured her. "Just . . . don't ring the bell, Mrs. Byron," she added hastily. "It will only make your headache worse." Autumn's own head throbbed now with the urgency of the past moments and the roughness of her awakening. She gathered her uncertain covering around her and hurried from the room. Racing down the stairways, obediently taking the back flight to the first floor, she made her way to the kitchen. Wrapped haphazardly in her counterpane, hair pouffed and tousled, Autumn burst into the room and winced at the sudden glare of sunlight. Blinking away the unexpected morning glitter, her eyes tearing, she stopped in the doorway.

"Good morning, Miss Thackeray," said a resonant masculine voice from somewhere in the room.

"Good morning," she returned, her tone abrupt and mechanical. She realized to her horror that the voice came from the master of the house. He stood, leaning against the iron sink, holding a mug of coffee. "Please pardon me, Dr. Byron," she said, "it is only that . . . You see, I would never venture from my room in this condition, except that Mrs. Byron has awakened—"

"Here's her breakfast," Mrs. Inman said, holding out a tray.

"I beg forgiveness, but Mrs. Byron is unwell," Autumn blurted. The doctor's brows furrowed.

"What do you mean—unwell?" he demanded.

"'Tis a condition of her daily waking," Mrs. Inman put in. "She'll be fine once she has her medicine."

"She complains of a headache," Autumn said in earnest. "And she seems quite . . . indisposed." Mrs. Inman merely nodded. The doctor, however, set down his coffee and strode past both women.

Mrs. Inman shook her head sadly and said, "Just give her this." She held out the tray. Autumn took it and hurried after the doctor. Making her way unsteadily up to the third floor with the heavy, unwieldy tray, Autumn at last reached Mrs. Byron's chamber. She found Dr. Byron there, seated at the edge of his mother's bed. He looked up as Autumn entered the room.

"This is appalling," he said over the low sobbing of the older woman. "From now on, you are to attend my mother at the moment of her awakening, Miss Thackeray." He chafed his mother's wrist gently. "She is not to be for one moment without her necessary morning medication."

"I didn't know, sir," Autumn offered, horrified at her own negligence. "I was not told of my responsibilities. I wasn't even
shown your mother's room—"

"No more excuses, miss," he interrupted. He looked back
down at his mother and his black gaze softened. "I shall send up
some headache powders, Mother," he said softly. He rose and
rounded on Autumn, saying in a fierce whisper, "You, lady, will
attend me in my parlor as soon as you are finished here. And do
try to have yourself properly appointed for our meeting." He
paused and regarded her keenly. "There will be no more chances
for you, Miss Thackeray. Please try to remember why you were
hired."

Dr. Byron made a striding exit from the room. Autumn's emotions were a mixture of guilt and resentment. How could she
have known what she was never told? Mrs. Byron's sudden
lamenting moan brought Autumn's attention back to the problem
at hand. The older woman was in great discomfort, and Mrs.
Inman had said it was a daily condition of her awakening.
Autumn resolved as she moved to the bed that from this day forward, she would be up and dressed before Mrs. Byron found it
necessary to wield her desperate bell. Autumn lifted the offending instrument and set it aside. On this morning, at least, it had
served its purpose, but its rude signal would not again be welcome—or necessary.

With trembling fingers, Mrs. Byron took the mug that
Autumn offered her and lifted it to her lips. The liquid was eagerly consumed, and Autumn detected, oddly, the vague odor of
spirits. Setting down the mug, Mrs. Byron seemed to relax visibly.
Though Autumn encouraged her, the woman dawdled over her
breakfast, insisting she was not hungry. She lay back against her

pillows, newly fluffed by Autumn, and sighed. Within moments Mrs. Inman appeared. She skillfully poured liquid between two glasses and handed Mrs. Byron one of them. Wordlessly, the servant lifted the tray from Mrs. Byron's bed and would have left the room had Autumn not detained her.

"Mrs. Inman," she whispered, "would you come into my room, please?" The lady grudgingly obliged.

"What is it, Miss Thackeray?" she asked impatiently. "I really must get on with my duties."

"It is *my* duty that concerns me, Mrs. Inman. I think I should have been informed that I would be expected to attend Mrs. Byron first thing in the morning and that she would be ill. You said the headache is a daily complaint. I was caught completely unawares." The Irish woman stared at Autumn for some moments.

"I meant to inform you, miss," she said quietly, "but you were asleep when I returned to your room last evening."

"Why didn't you waken me?"

"You were dead to the world. As it is, I built you a fire, undressed you, and got you tucked into bed." Her voice was rising. "I won't do it again, though, if you're going to be so high and mighty."

"High and mighty!" Autumn said on a breath. "I am only suggesting that you might have explained—"

"I got no time for explanations," returned Carrie Inman. "I got enough work in this house for ten women. I'm only the one, you know. When I come to this household ten years ago, there was a dozen of us girls, plus a cook and a butler, a gardener and a pot boy and a footman. Now there's just me to take care of the doctor and his mother and all the stable hands. He runs off the girls as soon as he hires them."

"Are you speaking of Dr. Byron?"

"Who else?" Autumn recalled the girl she had seen the previous night who had been all but thrust from the house. She asked Mrs. Inman about her. "That was Alma Louise. She was as good as you get from the docks today. She accidentally left one of the stable doors open, and one of the doctor's horses got out. Why you'd think she'd committed the Original Sin, the way he went on."

"He didn't use physical force, did he?" asked Autumn cautiously. Carrie Inman shook her head.

"No, but he might's well have. He upbraided that girl till she finally quit him, and I don't blame her. The yelling and accusations that went on in this house before you come was frightening, miss. I almost left meself."

"Why didn't you?"

"Because . . ." The woman's voice and assertive manner waned abruptly. She set down the tray and folded her hands before her. Eyeing Autumn levelly, she continued. "I come here, miss, right off the boat ten years ago. I've been here since I was sixteen years old. Much like yourself, I put myself in service willingly as Mrs. Byron's personal maid. And I seen that woman go from a vibrant healthy lady to—practically—a corpse.

"Now I don't make claims to a charitable heart, but I think, if I was to be asked, that I'm needed here. I'm all Mrs. Byron's got who remembers her when. That's real important to a sick woman. But, I'll tell you this, when she goes, so do I."

"Is she dying?" Autumn asked, her voice catching.

"If it ain't death she's facing, then I don't know what." Autumn's brows furrowed. She reminded Mrs. Inman that people simply did not die of nervous disorders.

"Beyond that," she added, "her physician is coming today. Surely he——"

"A lot of good he is," Carrie Inman said indignantly. "If you ask me——"

A call from the other chamber caught the attention of both women, and Autumn rushed past Mrs. Inman and into Mrs. Byron's room.

"What is it, Mrs. Byron," Autumn inquired solicitously. She parted the hangings to find the older woman sitting fully upright. She regarded Autumn testily. "Who are you?" she snapped. Autumn smiled and began to straighten the counterpane. "Stop rooting around my bed."

"I am Autumn Thackeray," she said calmly, as she tied the hangings back. Mrs. Inman interrupted the exchange to inform the women that she was headed back to the kitchen.

"You get me a fire going, Carrie," Mrs. Byron demanded. Mrs. Inman glanced at Autumn and mentioned that she would see to the fire. As she started to leave, Mrs. Byron stopped her with a stentorian oath. "It's goddamned cold in here!" Autumn's mouth fell open, but Carrie Inman merely rolled her eyes and withdrew. "I said," Mrs. Byron repeated, "it's goddamned cold in here. I want a goddamned fire." Autumn could hardly credit the woman's blasphemous language. More to stop it than anything, she hurried to the hearth. "And why are you dressed in a blanket?" An unnatural, almost diabolical energy seemed to have taken hold of Mrs. Byron.

"I just awakened," said Autumn, feverishly trying to coax a fire from nearly deadened embers. "I've been hired by your son to——"

"Don't I get any food?"

"Of course," Autumn said. "I'll bring you something. You didn't seem interested in your——"

"I want something to eat, goddamn it!" Appalled, Autumn hastened to finish her task, as with a horrible abruptness, the woman dissolved into tears. "They're starving me," Mrs. Byron said piteously, then laid her head back on her pillows, closed her eyes, and unimaginably, began to snore. Autumn moved to the bed tentatively.

"Mrs. Byron?" she questioned. "Are you awake?" There was no answer as the woman began to breathe evenly. In her store of experience, Autumn had never seen such swings of mood. Despite the fire that was now blazing behind her, she felt a cold chill beneath her flesh. She could give no credence to Mrs. Byron's accusation that she was being starved. Autumn recalled the heavy tray of food she'd brought up. The woman was obviously in the care of people who were devoted to her—certainly they would never abuse her. Mrs. Inman was an obdurate enough lady, but she had professed a deep well of feeling for her mistress. And there was no question of her devotion, though she sometimes lacked the outpouring of compassion that would affirm it. And Dr. Byron was a conscientious son, if not a warmhearted or affectionate one. There seemed no reason for Mrs. Byron's impeachment. She was not being starved.

Recalling that breakfast tray, Autumn was reminded that she had not eaten since early the previous day, and her own hunger gnawed. She made her way, glancing back at the slumbering Mrs. Byron and assuring herself that the lady was, for the moment, at peace, back to her own chamber and splashed her face with water from the flowered ewer. She dressed hurriedly, putting on her traveling outfit, minus the little hat, which she picked up sadly from the floor. Autumn shut her eyes against the scene that replayed itself in her mind, against the image of herself in the darkly veined mirror. Surely she had gone temporarily insane. She set down the hat and searched for her hairbrush. Her things were still scattered about the floor, but she found the brush. Working quickly, she pinned her hair into as neat a coif as she could manage. She made a last hasty inspection of herself in the mirror. Her carriage dress was a bit wilted from travel, but it retained, by virtue of the fineness of the material, a certain respectability. Finally, dissatisfied with her appearance but aware of her employer's impatience, she left the room. Passing the kitchen on the first floor, she glanced in. Carrie Inman was there kneading bread dough.

"There's coffee, and there's muffins on the shelf above the stove," that lady said sullenly.

"Mrs. Inman," Autumn said gently, "I am sorry I upset you earlier. We needn't be bad friends." Carrie shrugged a heavy shoulder. Autumn took some coffee and a muffin. "These look wonderful," she said. A bell, one of several lined up above the entrance to the kitchen, jangled resolutely, and both women came to attention.

"That'll be the doctor," Mrs. Inman said and began to wipe her hands on her apron.

"I'll see to it, Mrs. Inman," Autumn told her. She took a quick gulp of coffee and a bite of the muffin. "I suspect Dr. Byron will be wanting me anyway."

"No hard feelings, then?" Carrie asked.

"None," Autumn responded with a smile. "But I must tell you, I have had enough of bells to last me a lifetime." She proceeded from the room smoothing her hair and clothing and followed the hallway to the front of the house. She stopped before a double pocket door and composed herself. Taking a calming breath, she knocked.

"Come." Autumn took another breath and slid open the doors. Cain Byron, seated at his massive desk, glanced up. "Oh," he muttered, "it's you."

"Yes, sir," Autumn said, sliding the doors closed. "Mrs. Inman was busy in the kitchen, and I presumed that you wanted to see me in any event—"

"You presumed correctly, Miss Thackeray," he intoned, going back to his work. Autumn stood before the desk, hands folded primly before her, waiting for the doctor's attention. At last, he looked up. Rather than speaking, he stood and came around to the front of the desk. He did not remove the thin cigar that was tucked in his teeth. Folding his arms across his chest, he leaned back against his desk. "How is my mother?"

"She is sleeping at the moment, sir," Autumn replied, startled at the mildness of his tone. Perhaps, like the mother, the son, too, had inconsistent swings of humor.

"Sit down, Miss Thackeray."

"I dare not stay long," she ventured. He splayed a hand.

"I will not keep you." He removed the cigar and snuffed it out. His demeanor seemed less rattled, more serene, than it had the night before, or even earlier this morning. Even his clothing, though he wore the same style—buff jodhpurs and loose-collared shirt—seemed tidy and tucked. His boots were polished and his hair combed. He was not the shaggy brute she'd previously met, though his manner was still curt. "Apologies do not come easily to me, Miss Thackeray. But I am a reasonable man. I've taken some time this morning to write out your duties. It was not fair of me to expect that you would automatically know how to handle this most difficult assignment." He reached across the desk and retrieved a sheet of paper with carefully penned instructions.

Handing it to her, he resumed. "Please have Mrs. Inman look this over, as she has been my mother's primary caregiver. I am certain she will be glad to assist you in any way she can."

Autumn might have mentioned that Mrs. Inman seemed overburdened as it was with household duties, but she checked her comment and said, "This nervous disorder from which your mother suffers, may I know something about it?"

"Dr. Beame himself is often mystified, Miss Thackeray. He has treated many female patients, and he asserts that the constant swings of mood and the behaviors that form this disorder continue to bewilder him. And my mother is a particularly resistant patient. But he and I have every confidence that his treatment will eventually bear fruit."

"How long has he been treating Mrs. Byron?"

"For nearly three years."

"And what started all this?"

"That," he said, "I shall not discuss." At the flash of disappointment that crossed her face, he amended his tone. "I cannot discuss it, Miss Thackeray. It would prove an embarrassment to my mother." He lit another thin cigar. "As you will not speak of your financial reverses, I shall not speak of this." Autumn nodded, faintly unsettled. She looked down at the paper. Perusing the list of instructions, she was not altogether certain that, without understanding the details of Mrs. Byron's illness, she could conform to her treatment. The dictates of the lady's confinement seemed harsh.

Mrs. Byron was not allowed to go outside; she was not allowed to listen to music; she was not allowed to read; she was not allowed to engage in discussions of any sort; she was to remain in her room, with only the occasional visit to her parlor. Autumn

did not have time to read the rest of the prescribed treatment, but
if it were as austere as what she had read, it would be difficult to
maintain. She expressed as much to Dr. Byron.

"It is not for us to decide, Miss Thackeray. I will concede that
I was myself hesitant to agree to this type of rigid treatment of
my mother. She was an active and strong woman. But, I can assure
you that Dr. Beame has enjoyed great success with his female patients over the years. It is no fault of his that my mother has not
improved under his treatment. The fact is, this excessive, seem-
ingly harsh, regimen has only been necessary in the last year. The
problem, as I mentioned, is that she fights her treatment.
Winslow feels this . . . combativeness of her nature may have exacerbated and unnecessarily prolonged her illness."

"I am sorry to hear such a thing," Autumn said. "I can assure
you that I shall do my very best to see that these rules are followed. It would be a great joy to me to see your mother well."

"I am glad to hear you say it, Miss Thackeray. The fact is,
though, Win sees little hope for that. He insists, as I mentioned
last night, that mother needs a more confined environment." He
regarded her keenly. "But I shall not give in. That is the reason I
hired you. When I saw your advertisement in the *Cape May
Republican*, the idea occurred to me to retain the services of a gen-
tlewoman, a lady of breeding, to care for my mother. She has
been surrounded by careless indigence. Girls from the town come
here to care for her, and they do so with a stunning lack of good
will. They are interested only in the few coins they can gather
from their efforts." Autumn winced inwardly. Her own motiva-
tion was distinctly financial. "And," he added, "in the gossip they
can take back to their cronies."

"Has she no friends?"

Cain Byron shook his head. "She necessarily gave up her friendships long ago. I insisted on such a course. The nature of her disorder made that necessary. Society, as you may know, Miss Thackeray, is woefully judgmental. There were a few ladies around the town who used to call from time to time, but I have not allowed mother to receive them. As you have seen, her condition is grave, and . . . I must say, most unattractive. I will not have her reputation damaged by gossip. As far as anyone knows, she is being treated for a respectable disorder, one suffered by many women of her class."

"And what of family?"

"There is just me. My father passed on nearly ten years ago, and my four sisters are married and have moved with their husbands to various parts of the country. They have families of their own—each sister having numerous children. As executor of this entitlement, the house, the lands, the Byron fortune, it is my obligation . . . my *happy* obligation to care for my mother. Unfortunately, I know so little of the vagaries of women's thinking . . ." He took a long draw on his cigar. "The fact is, Miss Thackeray, I am counting heavily on the notion that my mother will respond more willingly to her treatment if it is ministered by someone of her own class. But that one must also be discreet. I want no hint of scandal to befall her. I am, you see, doing the best I can."

Given your limited patience and sensitivity. "I do understand your position, sir."

"Mother has lived by a definitive code her whole life. She has lived a life of social stability; she is a flower of gentility." Autumn thought briefly of the woman's not so genteel language of the morning, but she kept a solemn eye on the Turkish carpet.

"Despite your family's current financial embarrassment, I believe you, too, have lived such a life." He stepped back behind his desk and drew from the center drawer a sheaf of letters, tied with a length of twine. With some astonishment, Autumn recognized the pale blue stationery as her own. "This," he said, "is the correspondence of a young woman who understands advantage as well as adverse fortune. I respect that young woman. She is courageous and honest. She is gracious, and most importantly, kind." He slid the letters onto the desk. "I do not mean to shock you with a display of passion, but I must tell you, Miss Thackeray, you are my last hope." Autumn looked up.

"I shall not disappoint you, Dr. Byron," she said hesitantly. She stood. "If you will excuse me, I really must get back to Mrs. Byron." Cain held out his hand and Autumn took it. Without further word, she left the Turkish chamber of the master of the house.

Autumn had scarce time to pen a quick letter to her mother before beginning her duties in what would prove to be a most significant first day in the Byron household. She riffled through her belongings for her stationery and sat finally with pen in hand, wasting precious moments, she scolded herself, while agonizing over what to write. Best for her mother's peace of mind if she depicted a thoroughly positive image—one, sadly, Autumn only wished were true.

"Dearest Mother," she wrote hastily and with no bow to accuracy, "I have arrived safely in Cape May, have, in fact, spent a most assuredly comfortable first night and morning in my first situation away from home.

"My, my, how friendly the people are, how warm, how generous.

"The lady for whom I am to care, Mrs. Byron, seems a grand person indeed. I shall not have very much to do except to keep her company and to see that she is comfortable, and, as you might imagine, there is more than a sufficiency of help in such a magnificent household. You mustn't worry one whit about me; I am quite sitting in the very lap of luxury . . ." Autumn glanced briefly about the tiny, gray chamber, cast a disheartened eye on her rumpled bed, then, averting her gaze, continued the letter. "Naturally, I miss you terribly. One day, we must arrange a visit for you here. In the meantime, I remain your obedient and loving daughter." Autumn signed her name quickly, before a change of heart and the need for a sympathetic ear bade her write the absolute truth of her situation. She stuffed the note into an envelope and sealed it. Within the space of several days, Isabel Thackeray would have a most pleasant, most cheering, if not authentic, picture of her daughter's new circumstances.

She is as prettily turned out as a sunflower as she moves among the guests, curtsying, her smile as bright as their glowing approbation. She sees her father at the far end of the room, and suddenly bolting, she runs toward him. Her tiny foot catches a bit of loose carpeting and she totters, but the tall father leaps forward and prevents her fall. He lifts her in strong arms and presses her to his chest, laughing at her sweet exuberance. He smells of tobacco and cinnamon. Tea will be served presently, and she will receive an extra cake for her near misadventure.

Chapter 3

The clock in the lower gallery tolled the three o'clock hour, and Mrs. Byron's room was a pandemonium of scattered gowns, undergarments, and heirloom jewels. Scarves and shawls, fans and feathers were examined and discarded, flying about the chamber like drunken birds. Mrs. Inman had joined Autumn in the laborious task of making Mrs. Byron presentable for her doctor's visit. The man would arrive for tea, according to his letter.

"We'll never have her ready," Mrs. Inman informed Autumn as the older woman prepared a hot sponge bath for the patient.

"But we must," Autumn replied. She brushed feverishly at a silk file gown of watered mauve and attempted to revive the wilted rosettes at its shoulders and bodice. "Dr. Byron fears that if his mother isn't well turned out today, Dr. Beame may insist she travel with him to New York City and submit herself to institutionalization. We must see to it that she is as presentable a lady as any that ever walked the streets of Cape May." She glanced at the silent center of all this confusion. That woman lay snoring quietly in an upholstered chair. "She sleeps a great deal, does she not?" she observed. Mrs. Inman nodded.

"That's how it's supposed to be, miss," she said as she brought the ewer to a table and carefully poured warm water into a bowl. Carrie had proven more than helpful during Autumn's occasion-filled first day in the Byron household. But her generosity had its threshold. "Do you think you can handle things here, love?" she asked as she patted Mrs. Byron's arms and face down with a soft cloth. "I've got to get me back to the buttery. They'll be sending me off to one of their institutions if I don't get up a proper tea." She swiped at her upper lip with the hem of her apron.

"Oh, of course, Mrs. Inman," Autumn replied guiltily. "I've kept you from your work far too long. On the other hand . . ." she lamented before the lady could make her exit, "this gown needs a good pressing." Mrs. Inman eyed the younger woman incisively.

"Is it the *only* one she can wear?"

"It is the only one that isn't soiled," Autumn replied earnestly. "I'll get her clothes in order as soon as I have some time, I prom-ise, but in the meantime . . ."

The housekeeper *cum* laundry maid took the dress and hurried out before another task befell her. Autumn looked to the woman in the chair. If only there were some sort of cooperation, she re-flected. Lacking that, Autumn was determined to do her resolute best to make the woman at least appear as though she cared about herself. First, of course, Mrs. Byron had to wake up.

At precisely four o'clock, Autumn accompanied the freshened lady down the third floor hallway. "Now, remember," she in-structed as they slowly made their progress, "you must listen very carefully to Dr. Beame. Answer his questions as precisely as you possibly can." It was difficult to know whether or not Mrs. Byron was heeding Autumn's advice. She kept her eyes on the carpet, carefully placing her ivory walking stick ahead of each step. "You do recall," Autumn questioned her, "my telling you that your son desperately wishes you to stay here at Byron Hall, don't you? And that Dr. Beame might insist upon your leaving." The woman eyed her quizzically. "You do wish to stay here in your home, don't you, Mrs. Byron?"

"I do," she answered softly.

"Then you must try to be as bright and proper a lady as you know yourself to be—even though you don't feel very bright and proper right now. I shall be there to encourage you. There is a great deal at stake, Mrs. Byron." They negotiated the stairs with caution and at the entrance to her parlor, Mrs. Byron paused. She cast Autumn a solemn regard.

"You know," she said tenuously, "I have been so very lonely for so long a time." She took a breath, as though the mere speaking of words tired her. "One would think I would welcome company, and yet, I do not welcome company. This company, at any rate." Autumn nodded and gave the other woman's arm a small squeeze.

"I quite understand, Mrs. Byron. But the interview need not last long." Autumn tried to breathe optimism, but the woman's next words stilled her heart.

"They don't like me very much, you know, the men—my son and Dr. Beame."

"Your son loves you, Mrs. Byron," Autumn stated emphatically. "And your doctor has your best interests at heart." She paused, hoping that her words would instill confidence and knowing that Mrs. Byron's chilling instincts were probably correct. Before they entered the room, Autumn hurriedly smoothed the lady's gown once again and checked her hair and her lip rouge.

"One more thing, Mrs. Byron, do try not to fall asleep, and do try, if you can manage it, not to curse."

As Autumn slid the doors wide, the elder woman stepped inside. In queenly fashion, she greeted the two men. Autumn could not suppress her pride as Mrs. Byron was ushered to a chair. She looked well, though pale and inordinately thin. She was a more than moderately attractive woman in any circumstances, but dressed in high fashion, jeweled as befit her status as dowager of a great family, and neatly coifed, she made a striking appearance.

The men seated and complimented her in a pageantry of elaborate courtliness, and Mrs. Byron accepted their attentions gracefully, smiling, nodding, and answering their lightly posed questions. Autumn, from her position near the doorway, deemed the interview to be going well. Her mind wandered idly to her own appearance. She wished that she had made more of an effort on her own behalf. She had still not brushed her hair, and it curled wildly about her face, carelessly arranged in the confines of pins and combs. Her traveling dress, which she had still not changed, had been left unrefreshed. Her boots were mud stained, though she'd given them a light swatting with her handkerchief. Still, she too wanted to make an excellent impression on the doctor from New York. She wanted his trust.

Suddenly, unbelievably, Mrs. Byron was sobbing. Her graying head was hidden in her hands. She'd thrust down her walking stick and was twisting away from the offered ministrations of the helpless men. Autumn had not been following the conversation; she had no idea what was happening.

"Leave me alone," Mrs. Byron was saying. "Leave me, for God's sake, to my horrors." Cain Byron looked quickly to

Autumn, who rushed to the woman's side. Kneeling there, she addressed her cautiously.

"They are trying to help you, Mrs. Byron," she condoled. "Won't you speak with them a little longer?"

"Take me away," the older woman pleaded, grasping at Autumn's sleeve. "Won't you please just take me away from them?"

"You had better accompany her upstairs, Miss Thackeray," Dr. Byron said finally. "I shall ring Mrs. Inman. She will prepare her medication."

"And . . . Miss Thackeray, is it?" said the other doctor. Autumn looked up. "Won't you attend us when you've seen Mrs. Byron upstairs?" Dr. Winslow Beame was regarding her from above. His request did not seem a request, but a command. Autumn nodded and made her way from the room with Mrs. Byron.

It was a long time before Autumn was able to attend the doctors. By the time Mrs. Byron was undressed, had her medicine urgently administered, and fallen securely asleep—no longer moaning in unimaginable torment—more than half an hour had passed. Guiltily, Autumn ushered herself into the presence of the men. She apologized for the delay, but the doctors were solicitous and gentle with her.

Dr. Beame was the first to address her. He was a tall man, almost as tall as Dr. Byron, and like him, well shaped. Both men were pictures of sterling good health and robust intellect. And yet they were quite different, these two college friends. Dr. Beame had a head of neatly combed chestnut waves and long, puffed side whiskers, which gave him a mature, distinguished appearance, while Dr. Byron's ebony curls, once combed, struggled boyishly from their confinement to hang over his forehead. Winslow Beame seemed, from his pale and elegant appearance, to live a life of the mind, quite satisfied to be indoors with his books and his research. But even in formal attire, Cain Byron seemed more a man of the natural outdoor world. As they spoke, Autumn noted that Dr. Byron loosened his stock and collar, while Dr. Beame remained rigidly ceremonious. He held a brandy snifter, but set it down on her entrance.

"How is she faring, Miss Thackeray?"

"She is asleep, doctor."

"And her sleep seems . . . undisturbed?"

"I think so." The exchange was soft and solemn and urgent as though someone had passed away. Dr. Beame ushered her to a chair and paused over her as she sat down. He feathered his thick mustache with his index finger, inspecting Autumn carefully.

"And you, Miss Thackeray? Are you alright?"

"Quite, sir."

"I can only imagine how upsetting this must have been for you. Dr. Byron tells me you arrived only last evening." Autumn nodded. "If you are in any way overwrought please do not hesitate to acknowledge it. You needn't suffer one moment, Miss Thackeray, with tension or nervousness. Not," he added, smiling benevolently, "with two doctors in the house."

"I am quite well, doctor," Autumn affirmed. In truth, she was a bit off balance, but she attempted to retain her composure. She wished very much for the two doctors to have confidence in her ability to handle any situation.

"You understand, Miss Thackeray, that having observed Mrs. Byron for several moments only, I obtained no picture at all of her general health. I need to discover how she seems to others in the household on a daily basis." Autumn nodded studiously. She felt the warning gaze of Cain Byron upon her and cleared her throat in anticipation of Dr. Beame's questions. His picture of Mrs. Byron's general health was certainly not an accurate one—it had taken her and Carrie Inman hours just to get her pressed and polished and ready to be seen—but Autumn's loyalty belonged to the Byrons.

"I shall try to answer your questions accurately, Dr. Beame." She regarded the man evenly.

"That is all that can be expected," he said indulgently. His tall figure moved away and he returned, drawing a chair to the side of her own. Sitting down, he struck a casual pose. "From what I saw, Miss Thackeray . . ." He paused. "Mayn't I call you Autumn?" he asked, placing his hand gently on her arm.

"Of course, sir," Autumn replied, though this sort of familiarity, which she had met before in the medical community, annoyed her.

"Autumn, then," he confirmed with a smile. "What I did see of Vanessa Byron unsettles me very much. Her physical appearance has certainly improved since my visit last month. She had color, her hair was coifed, her clothing . . . well, she was quite immaculately turned out. Last time I came, she was wearing a stained and wrinkled dressing gown."

Lip rouge, an agonizing hour of hair-dressing, and a good pressing.

"She seemed to have cared about her appearance for our interview, and that was most refreshing. A woman's physical appearance is one of the first clues a doctor has of her overall health, Autumn. This is a well-approved medical fact. Now, all that aside, the sudden burst of emotion gives me pause." He stood and began to pace. "Tell me about this morning."

"This morning?" Autumn asked, recalling the horrors of the tolling bell, the foul language, and her own befuddlement.

"That is hardly fair, Win," Cain broke in. "Autumn only arrived last night, and this morning—"

Winslow Beame glanced at him. "No need to be defensive, Cain," he said easily. "I'm asking the girl a simple question. If you are intending to censor me . . ." His voice trailed off and his smile deepened as he returned his regard to Autumn. "Never mind that bucking stallion in the corner," he said jovially, with a small wink. "We shall send him from the room, if necessary. Just tell me the truth, my dear."

Autumn swallowed and attempted to ignore both men. She would speak of that hectic morning, but she would slant the events just a bit and soften the more truculent aspects of Mrs. Byron's behavior. "Mrs. Byron," she began tentatively, "was somewhat agitated this morning, but," she added with a quick look to Cain Byron, "that was my fault. You see, as Dr. Byron mentioned, I arrived late last evening and was deeply fatigued. I slept far past the hour of Mrs. Byron's awakening, and I, by my own tardiness, upset her morning routine. It was an unfortunate beginning to both the day and our relationship." She glanced at Cain Byron and saw the quick flash of a smile cross his face. He sobered immediately as Winslow Beame cast him a knowing look.

"So you would say, then," Beame asked mildly, "that I have not had a fair picture of Mrs. Byron's overall comportment?"

"I should say that, yes," answered Autumn truthfully. In truth, she had no idea how Mrs. Byron began her days, but she would, in the future, see that mornings were much more organized. She told Dr. Beame as much, and he nodded sagely.

"Now tell me of the rest of the day, the hours before my arrival. Had she had any untoward excitement? Had she received callers, listened to music, read mail?" Autumn could barely credit the questions; the activities he detailed were so dissimilar to any she could envision Mrs. Byron capable of handling. A momentary chill washed over her. This man had no idea of his patient's true condition.

"No, sir," she answered.

"I really think, Win," offered Cain Byron, "that you ought to remember that my mother has been under some stress during this last twenty-four hours. I don't blame Miss Thackeray, I blame myself."

"How so, Byron?" asked Winslow Beame, sitting and crossing one leg over the other. He leaned back in his chair and regarded Cain benignly. Autumn realized that Dr. Byron was as intimidated as she by the celebrated medical man.

"Well," said her employer, "I might have prepared them both more properly for their first meeting." He stepped forward, regarding Autumn regretfully. "I really am sorry, Miss Thackeray," he told her. "I should have taken more care of this situation." For the first time since they met, Autumn was in complete agreement with Cain Byron.

"Don't blame yourself too much, sir," Autumn said, her tone tinged with sympathy with a bit of mischief at the edges. "You seemed . . . distracted last evening when I arrived."

"Distracted?" asked Beame quickly.

Cain's regard of Autumn narrowed almost imperceptibly. "Yes," he said, "thank you for reminding me, Miss Thackeray." A knowing moment, small and silent, passed between them before Cain Byron turned his attention fully on his colleague. Autumn might have smiled but for the doctor's apparent lack of amusement on the subject. "It was nothing, really, Win. One of the girls left the stable door open, and my finest brood mare, Regan, escaped. I had to fire the wench—the girl, not the horse." Both men laughed easily.

"And . . . there was something of a disturbance over that," offered Autumn innocently.

"Yes," Cain conceded tightly, "there was a . . . disturbance."

"You did get her back, didn't you?" asked Beame. "I mean, naturally, the horse, not the girl."

"Yes," Cain said, refilling their brandy snifters. "But I spent a good part of the night doing so. The animal was an unholy mess by the time I retrieved her. I finally found her at O'Neill's place, down by the west shore. I can only pray she was not defiled by that licentious bay of his. That hellish stallion has been—" Winslow Beame cleared his throat delicately, and Cain looked up. "Oh, yes, of course," he averred, his eyes coming to rest on Autumn. "Did you need to speak any further with Miss Thackeray, Win?"

"I think not. She has been most helpful." He smiled and patted her hand. "You may go now, my dear."

"Thank you, sir," Autumn said as she rose. Her gaze drifted to Cain Byron. "Was there anything else you required of me, Dr. Byron?" she asked. Had he detected triumph in her tone?

"I think not, Miss Thackeray," he answered, his lips twitching with a threatened smile. He enjoyed a verbal duel with a pretty woman. "I would say you've told Dr. Beame quite enough for one day. You are dismissed."

"Thank you, sirs," she said offering a prim curtsy. "Then I shall go back to Mrs. Byron." With that, trailing a cloud of doe-colored velvet and tendrils of autumn-infused hair, she exited the room.

"You let her get away with quite a bit, Byron," observed Winslow Beame, watching the girl's withdrawal.

"I beg your pardon?" Cain's black brows came together.

"And you said 'Autumn' arrived last night. You called her by her first name."

"As did you."

"That is one of the privileges claimed by doctors. It puts the patient at ease, makes them feel safe. But it is highly irregular for an employer to refer to a servant in his house by her first name."

Cain regarded him in disgust.

"I called her Autumn in the heat of the moment, Win," he said. "You needn't make so much of it."

"I wouldn't think of doing so, old fellow," returned Winslow. "I am a gentleman, after all."

"And I'm not?" Byron asked archly.

Winslow Beame smiled contentedly. He'd always been able to bait his combustible friend. He recalled their college days and Cain Byron's legendary temper. He laughed, wondering just how far he might proceed. "She is rather a singular lady," he continued. "Adorable, really. She seems part vixen, part nun. For my taste she is just the right combination of siren and angel. Those cool, icy, aristocratic wenches have never held any appeal for me."

"As a matter of fact, Win," said Cain patiently, "she is something of an aristocrat. Her family are the Thackerays . . . of Philadelphia." He smiled obliquely at his friend's astonishment.

"*The* Thackerays?"

Cain nodded. "*The* Thackerays," he repeated. "Her father was Emmett Thackeray and her grandfather was Cornelius."

"Then, in heaven's name, how did she come to this?"

"She advertised," replied Cain dryly.

"I cannot credit such a thing," said Winslow, uncharacteristically awed. "Why that family—my father knew Cornelius personally—had an impeccable lineage. They were among the first bankers in Philadelphia. I believe," he said, pausing reflectively, "the mother could be traced back to the Hanovers. Why, as I recall, it was rumored she was a relative of England's Queen Victoria."

"Such rumors hold little significance for Americans."

"Nevertheless," replied the other man, "I should think such a child would have her future insured. And she is a child, Cain," he added, lifting a chestnut brow. "Never mind her bold display of independence. Advertising, indeed!" He shook his head derisively.

Cain Byron merely laughed. "Have no fear for the girl's virtue. Despite my former reputation as a rutting stag, Win, I have not defiled a virgin in several minutes."

"You always were an irreverent blackguard, Byron," said Dr. Beame with a tolerant smile. He toasted his friend, who lifted his own glass in return. "Still, if these young females insist upon extricating themselves from the protection of their families, they have little hope of decent treatment on the part of a less than benign society."

"As I understand it," put in Cain, "Autumn Thackeray had little choice in the matter."

Winslow's brows furrowed. "What are you talking about? This is 1896. We are a civilized world. No modest girl can be forced out into the streets, no matter her particular misfortune. And I should assume there was misfortune. She is not one of those appalling bluestockings, is she?"

"I would doubt that very much," replied Byron mildly. "She seems a most refined and feminine lady."

"Delectably so," agreed his friend. "Then her story must be a sad one." Cain shrugged his answer. Winslow laughed shortly. "You *have* become a gentleman, sir." Again they toasted.

"The truth is," Cain Byron said, "Autumn has asked me not to discuss her situation. And, though I've naturally done some checking on the matter, I must respect her wishes."

"'Autumn' again," remarked Beame, staring into the swirling amber of his brandy.

"That's her name," said Cain Byron shortly. Changing the subject and amending his tone, he added, "I believe she will be very good for my mother—a gracious influence." When Dr. Beame did not answer immediately, he went on. "Win," he said, hesitating briefly, "I know what you saw today has been disquieting. And I believe that, as is your habit, you will insist my mother be sent on to Belle Vue. But, again, I tell you she would not be happy there—"

"Happy," stated Winslow Beame. "Ah, Byron, you are an idealistic fool."

"Is it foolish that I afford my mother every opportunity for recovery?"

Beame splayed a hand.

"No, *doctor*, it is not." He went on, though he paused and became quite serious. Leaning forward, he said gently, "When we were in medical school, Cain, we were taught that a certain distance must be maintained between physician and patient. You know, in the depths of your doctor's mind, that your mother is desperately ill. Your heart, however, sends you another message. Heart and mind, Dr. Byron, are always in conflict in the field of medicine.

"You speak of happiness. I remind you, sir, that your mother has not been happy for a very long time. Happiness and health go hand in hand. Before we can make her happy, we must restore her health. Try to be logical, Cain. Explore the messages of your mind. Repress that heart-whole tenderness long enough to see the truth. Your mother needs to be in a place where I can watch her, restrict her. Has she ever in her life been so thin, so pale? Have you ever seen her so depressed? Has she ever before suddenly burst into tears for no apparent reason? These are signs of very ill health, Cain." Winslow Beame sat back. "I have seen this in women of your mother's age more times than I care to remember. And though my heart goes out to them, I know what's needed—what must be done. Their behavior must be modified, supervised on a daily basis by professionals in order that they may be able to perceive their own troubles. Healing can occur only when they begin to understand that behavior must always be justified. They cannot be allowed to continue to place themselves at the mercy of their emotions." He lifted a hand and smiled. "Oh, I know the prevailing opinion that women are flighty creatures, prone to bursts of emotive humours, and I accept that. If your mother were of childbearing years, we could attribute her behavior to, for instance, post- or even pre-partum mania, but that is not the case, and your mother's behavior is extreme." He glanced away from his friend. "I needn't remind you of how all this began." Cain shook his head and moved to refill his glass.

"Please don't," he said.

"We are supposed to tolerate those temporary states of womanly passion," continued Beame. "It is our man's fate—and sometimes our pleasure—" he added with a wink, "to cajole these pretty treasures of ours, to maneuver and manage them through the muddle of their emotions. But the fact is that when their tempers become unmanageable, it is our duty to guide them back to the proper course. This involves—sometimes sadly so—a certain . . . toughness of character. Strength, we must call it, Cain. Now, I am not suggesting you are not strong," he added hastily. "I suggest only that you must rely on your logic in this case, though it will be difficult, and not on your feelings. She is your mother, but she is also a woman. You have a man's obligation to her. Consider it deeply, Cain. It is no small thing to be a protector." Cain lifted his drink slowly to his lips, and Winslow continued in a soft mesmeric monotone. "It gives me no pleasure, Byron, to make this diagnosis. Vanessa is very dear to me, too. I remember joining you during our college days here at Byron Hall for spring breaks. Your mother was the closest thing to a mother I had. Don't forget, my own mother suffered at the time from this very complaint, and Vanessa was a cheerful counterpoint to that horror. She played tennis and croquet with us, and she and Maggie baked us chocolate cakes. It's a vivid memory for me, Byron, one of the best of my life. Certainly, you don't imagine I would suggest anything that might harm Vanessa. I want only the best for her."

Cain Byron set down his drink slowly. "You make an excellent case, Win," he said. "I can see now I've neglected my obligation toward my mother for much too long." He glanced at his friend. Winslow Beame drew out his pipe and filled it. Each move he made was cautious, wary; he did not wish to upset the balance of Byron's thinking. He was on the verge of a decision—a conscientious one—at long last. "You know," said Cain after a pause, "she cries each time I mention sending her away." Winslow nodded in understanding. Cain continued. "It takes days to calm her after such a discussion." Again, the nod.

"I have seen this more times than I can recount," Winslow said, taking a long draw on his pipe. "But it really is the only answer in some cases."

"Still," Cain eventually resumed quietly, "the question bears some thought."

"The thought of a man of medicine," warned Beame, "not of a son."

"For better or worse, I am the lady's son, however."

"And a doctor," returned Winslow firmly. In order that he might sway Cain's thinking now that the decision was practically made, he added, "You know there is much work being done in New York. Some interesting drugs are being developed all over the world, Cain, and New York has become rather a focal point for exciting new treatments. Neuralgic medicine and psychology are enjoying a certain interest, not that I have any respect for the efficacy of the latter, but I point it out for the purpose of letting you know how much science is changing. We are exploring all sorts of horizons. We are, after all, on the verge of a new age, Cain, a new century." As if the thought was new, he declared, "Why don't you come along with your mother and me. We could visit the university hospital, hear some lectures, delve into the mysteries of new-sprung practices—"

"You know I have no interest in the practice of medicine," Cain interjected caustically.

"I know, of course, that you have chosen not to practice, old fellow, but surely your interest in the world of medicine has not been abandoned. And might I remind you," he added knowingly, "New York City has more to offer than academic pursuits. I speak particularly of Miss Antoinette Fraser who still pines, I am told, for the pleasures of your last visit."

Cain laughed. "Does she?" he said wryly.

"Indeed. And though I have offered solace, I fear it is you after whom the lady hankers."

Cain threw back his head and laughed deeply. "This mockery of lament is quite unnecessary, Win. The proudhearted Nettie Fraser hankers after my money, and you know it as well as I."

Winslow nodded, joining in his friend's mirth. "And we both know, too, that Nettie Fraser gets that after which she . . . hankers." They toasted the lady, and then Winslow resumed more seriously. "I do honestly believe, Cain, that Miss Fraser would be most amenable to a sincere suitor." Cain lifted a dark brow.

"And what makes you think I am interested, Win?"

"You ought to be. We are both reaching an age where we should be considering that fateful plunge into matrimony. You could do worse than Antoinette Fraser."

Cain nodded amiably. "I could do worse," he agreed.

"And she already dotes on you. I saw her only last Saturday, and she inquired about your health. We attended a play—a naughty play, I might add, Shakespeare's *As You Like It.*"

"What made it naughty?" inquired Cain.

Winslow Beame leaned forward. "Lillie Langtry," he said confidentially. "She played Rosalind."

"Ah," said Cain in understanding. "Jersey Lily in men's breeches."

"Now doesn't that fire your interest in traveling to New York? Think of the excitement we could cause in her magnificent bosom if we two went backstage after one of her shows and introduced ourselves. Actresses love doctors, and she just might be tempted to extend us an invitation to her dressing room." He sat back contentedly.

"You amaze me, Dr. Beame," Cain commented in amusement. "One moment you are the reverent man of letters, speaking of universities and medicine, and the next you are talking like a lad fresh out of normal school, lusting after a peek at Miss Lillie's breasts." They both laughed. Finally, they shared a toast. "Nettie Fraser and Lillie Langtry aside," said Cain, "I shall make the trip, Win. I've not been out of this city in months. I look forward to it."

"And I," said Winslow Beame.

❦

Her round cheeks flushed, her golden gaze wide and tear-filled in the dark, she calls out. Candlelight interrupts the blackness of her terror and she is scooped into comforting arms. "There are no monsters," her mother soothes. "Nothing can hurt you." But the demons are there, writhing in the flickering candlelight. She is rocked, the little girl, rocked and cradled in comforting arms till her breathing evens and she falls into a fathomless sleep.

Chapter 4

"But, Dr. Byron," Autumn was saying, her tone impassioned, "you must give our situation a chance. I do not beg this for myself, but your poor mother has exhausted herself with tears."

Winslow Beame had been in the house for two days and had seen for himself the extent of his patient's debilitation. That it was exacerbated on the day of his arrival by the announcement that Vanessa was to be moved to Belle Vue impressed him not at all. In truth, he still did not have an accurate picture of the lady's true condition. This was the focus of Autumn's argument as she faced the two men in Cain Byron's study. She pointed out that Mrs. Byron had not experienced a moment's peace in nearly three days.

"And what of the weeks and months before that?" asked Cain. "What of the days when she had no will to survive, no desire, even, to rise from her bed?"

"That is precisely why you hired me, sir. And now, without following through with your original plan, you would uproot the distraught lady, pack her off to an institution, and place her among sterile strangers. I can help her, Dr. Byron, I know it."

Autumn knew nothing of the kind. But it seemed the more confidence she displayed, the less dogmatic he became. Not so Winslow Beame.

"You, young woman," he said, regarding Autumn darkly, "are a menace to this household. I have been trying for months now to convince Dr. Byron to commit his mother. I do not appreciate your interference in this matter. After all, you have been here but three days—"

"*Only* three days, Dr. Beame," Autumn said earnestly.

"Yes! *Only* three days, by heaven," he thundered. He smashed his fist down onto a table, and Autumn flinched. "What gives you the temerity to attempt to dissuade the master of this house from a course he knows—and, more importantly, *I* know—is right?"

"Win," interjected Cain, holding up a steadying hand, "calm yourself." He turned a questing regard on Autumn. "The question has been put to you, Miss Thackeray, and it stands: What gives you the right to interfere in this?" Autumn paused, barely able to form an answer. She licked at her lips and tried to moisten her dry mouth.

"You see," she began, addressing first one man and then the other as she spoke, keeping her voice steady purely by force of will, "Mrs. Byron is sorely strained just now. I am sure she is at her lowest ebb, imagining she will be taken from her home. Of her previous mental and physical condition I have no knowledge, it is true, but I am convinced that, whatever her troubles, they have been intensified by the threat of this move to New York City. She fears it deeply, speaks of it constantly. It is a horror to her. Let her rest for a time. Let her heal from this latest terror. Then, in time, once she is fit to be judged, judge her."

"You have not answered the question," said Cain Byron. Though his tone was harsh, Autumn retained the hope that he was not totally unconvinced.

"I know that, Dr. Byron," she admitted. "I suppose it is because I know that I have no right to interfere." Discerning from his silence the emboldening notion that her words had carried weight, she continued. "I know I seem insubordinate—"

"You are positively mutinous," put in Dr. Beame.

"—but I cannot express too strongly," Autumn went on without pause, "my belief that Mrs. Byron deserves at least one small chance to recover. And you so want it for her." She regarded Cain. "You told me that yourself."

"What we want, young renegade," Beame intoned, "is not always what we may have." Autumn rounded on him with a surprising vehemence. Her wide gaze narrowed to sparkling gilt.

"What we want, sir, may not be what we get, but we can still want it. No one has the right to control the part of us that feels and thinks." She paused, taking a rationed breath. "We may act as we are expected to act, but there is always a private part of us that remains true to who we really are. If that were taken from us, sir, we would be brutes. No man or woman faces life without obstacles. It is how we face those obstacles that determines character." Autumn stopped abruptly. Her voice trembling, she resumed, amending her tone. "I apologize for my boldness, but I do not apologize for my plea. All I ask of either of you is the grace of a little time for Mrs. Byron. Give her the opportunity to recover from the provocation of these past few days. If it is mutinous of me to want such a thing, then I am guilty of mutiny." She placed her regard squarely on Cain Byron. "You, doctor, must make the final decision."

Cain considered her in silence. Some unguarded piece of him was in awe of this slip of a girl, who had the courage to face what would normally be an intimidating situation and still compose a compelling argument. As a rule, he did not admire such conspicuous acumen in women, but this argument seemed a particularly challenging one, and it was delivered in defense of his mother.

"Win," he said quietly, "I must reason that Autumn, young as she is and uninitiated, certainly, in this business, is at least potentially correct. You, of all people, know how uncomfortable I have been with the thought of sending my mother to an institution."

Winslow nodded. "So uncomfortable," he commented bitingly, "that you would risk further damage to her already delicate state of mind." He raked Autumn with a withering regard. "You do see what you have done here, don't you. You do see the damage you have caused, the uncertainty you have generated." Shame rose up like a flame in Autumn's breast. Her face reddened, and her heart tripped.

Still, she said staunchly, "I believe Mrs. Byron's present problems lie in the circumstances of my arrival and the threat of being trucked off to an institution in New York. How would you, Dr. Beame—how would anyone—react if someone told you that you were going to be sent to what amounts, in Mrs. Byron's imaginings, to a prison?"

Beame's gaze flared. "How dare you," he intoned. "Belle Vue is the most respected women's facility in the world. How dare you refer to it in such a disgusting fashion."

"I should appreciate it if you would not twist my words, sir," Autumn answered him. "I said the sanitarium *seems* like a prison to Mrs. Byron, and she is naturally afraid of it."

"Oh, come now," Winslow Beame returned. His manner was beginning to become dismissive. If the girl continued exploring this vein, and he hoped that she would, he would surely triumph. "In the Lord's name, girl, do you think I would send women to a prison? Why the very word conjures filth and neglect."

"Exactly. A woman's home is her sanctuary, and a woman in Mrs. Byron's condition sees only the darkest outcomes in being torn from it. Everything outside her home seems alien and grim."

"And yet, Miss Thackeray," Cain Byron reminded her, "you managed to leave your home. Have you found anything here that is alien and grim?"

Autumn skimmed the Turkish motif of the room with her eyes, taking in the numerous animal heads staring glass-sighted from the walls, the copper figurines of cobras and ancient god-like men, the paisley wall hangings that were twisted and tasseled, and the more than several embossed friezes depicting such scenes as jungle hunts and the Rape of the Sabine Women. Her regard rested for some moments on the patriarchal image above the fire-place before it returned to her employer.

"My circumstance, sir," she said steadily, avoiding a direct answer, "is different from your mother's. I am of a sound mind and a sturdy constitution. And I was fortified by necessity—not helplessness. My decision to come here was my own and not the result of manhandling." There, thought Autumn, it had been said. In many ways she was relieved. She looked pointedly at Dr. Beame, and that man's attention returned to Cain exclusively.

"Do you see to whom you are entrusting your mother's care, Byron? This venomous child dares to refer to confirmed medical practices as 'manhandling.'" Winslow Beame was no longer dis-missing Autumn's comments, and she was glad, but she wondered momentarily if she had gone too far. Men were notoriously savage when threatened by women's intellectual muscle. She tried to hedge.

"I only meant that the pressure being exerted here seems harsh, Dr. Beame. I am only asking for a little time."

"What you meant, young woman," returned Beame furiously, "could be interpreted as an accusation of medical frivolity. If you were a man, I would be at this moment filing suit in a court of law or calling you out onto the field of honor. In any event, your statement is intolerable; at the least it is born of ignorance and at the most of viciousness. I will, being a gentleman, assume the former." He addressed Cain once again. "She is right about one thing, Byron. The final decision is yours." Both people awaited his response. Cain Byron lowered his head and ran his fingers through his dark curls. He lit a small cigar and paced to the other side of the room.

"Would a few weeks really make such a difference, Win?" he asked.

Glancing in disgust at the person to whom his friend had so shamefully yielded, Beame responded. "Allow me to propose a compromise, Byron. I can arrange a visit for you to Belle Vue. Come with me to New York tomorrow. We can leave your mother here for now—with very strict instructions for this girl to follow. Our plans need not change a whit. You can ease your mind, see your friends, and then, when we return, if circumstances are not immensely altered, we will do as I have prescribed." He paused. "I must tell you I am not entirely comfortable with this, Cain, but I see that I must yield on this very emotional issue. And I yield in deference to our long friendship. But I shall say this. We will give this experiment exactly one month. If, at the end of that time, your mother has not notably improved—and I shall accept no excuses or mitigation regarding her behavior—I will, as an ethical man of medicine, take matters into my own hands. That, I know, would cause an unfortunate but necessary breach in our friendship. Therefore, I must insist on your word that you will agree to the terms of this compromise." Cain turned to him and offered his hand.

"You have my word, Win." They both glanced then at the cause of this very significant moment.

"You, young woman," said Beame, "will spend the next hour with me. You have a prodigious responsibility, and I intend to see to it that you carry it out to the letter. May we have the room, Cain?"

That man nodded curtly, and without the smallest glance at Autumn, he withdrew. Autumn girded herself for what was to come. She had bought time for Mrs. Byron, but at what price? Autumn understood precisely the implications of what had been decided. She knew that she had challenged the authority of not only this particular doctor, but of the medical treatment of a generation of women. She felt Beame's loathing for her as a palpable presence. Winslow Beame did not wish her well. He began his lecture, instructing her in Mrs. Byron's care and warning her darkly of the consequence of deviations from his prescribed treatment. As he droned on, Autumn was aware of spectres of her memory, shades of women of her mother's age and acquaintance. Aberrant women; absentminded, confused, aggressive women. Women whose houses were closed to callers. The days, the weeks, the months and years of their absence from society were followed by their return with lusterless faces, empty smiles, and nearly wordless encounters with their neighbors. They were women who had been "in treatment" it was whispered—some in places far from their homes—and their comportment was much improved. The improvement to Autumn's mind was arguable. The ladies had seemed pale imitations of their former selves. On the other hand, they had their old lives back; their husbands and children and friends were happier with them; their servants no longer whispered of "Madame's 'off' behavior"; and the ladies themselves seemed content to fit at last into a society that recoiled from variations from the norm.

Autumn suspected that Dr. Beame's treatment of Mrs. Byron was not unlike that of so many other doctors of so many other women. She was prepared at this moment of probing instruction to fulfill the requirements of Mrs. Byron's treatment, but she suspected Dr. Beame perceived her ambiguity. It was probably for that reason that he went on so. His voice came to her out of the pale mists of her memory.

"I shall write out my instructions before I leave tomorrow morning, Miss Thackeray, and you shall follow them to the letter. Is that clear?" Autumn nodded afresh, as she had nodded for the last hour at each of his stern dictations. "My women patients trust me. My reputation, as well as Mrs. Byron's health," he added, it seemed, as an afterthought, "are at stake. If anything happens to either, I will hold you personally accountable. Is *that* understood?"

"It is, sir," Autumn said. "Most assuredly." Beame's eyes narrowed. Autumn lowered her own. This was not the time to be confrontational. "I will do exactly as you say, Dr. Beame."

The morning of the men's departure loomed gray and doubt-ful. Autumn watched through a gap in Mrs. Byron's heavy bed-room curtains as the doctors mounted their horses and rode away. They disappeared at a pounding gallop into the thick fog of the frosty mid-November morning. As she stepped back from the window embrasure and carefully secured the draperies against the day's uncertain light (she often wondered why Dr. Beame would not allow those velvet barriers to the morning to be opened), she heard the first soft moans of Mrs. Byron's awaken-ing. Autumn hastened to the bed and parted the hangings.

Sitting at the edge of the soft mattress, she lifted Mrs. Byron's hand in her own. Autumn had determined that the lady's waking would be filled with tenderness. She inclined her head as Mrs. Byron's eyes fluttered open.

"Miss Thackeray," she whispered. The name was the first she uttered and had been since the second day of Autumn's arrival. The bell had been abandoned. It now sat, dull brass finish barely visible in the darkened room, on a table far from the bed.

"I hope you rested well, Mrs. Byron," said Autumn gently. "I have your breakfast tray warming on the hearth. May I fluff your pillows for you?" The lady nodded weakly. "And then I'll bring the tray with your morning medication." It was the first rule that Autumn had broken. Enjoined by Dr. Beame to fire a battery of questions at Mrs. Byron upon her awakening, Autumn had de-cided that she would delay the questions. Mrs. Byron was neither prepared for, nor interested in, discussing how she felt at just this moment. It was a small but worthwhile sin, for Mrs. Byron seemed most calm.

The morning routine was simple and not too much of a de-parture from that directed by Winslow Beame. The patient was fed, gently washed, her bedclothes changed. As always, Mrs. Byron drank her morning medicine eagerly, and, as always, Autumn found herself less than pleased by the enforcement of that particular regimen. She had discovered that the drink consisted of two parts fortified wine, one part laudanum powder, and another part cider for taste. It unsettled Autumn to serve spirits to a lady so early in the day. But she reasoned that the mixture had been prescribed by Dr. Beame, and that it must, therefore, serve a very specific healthful purpose. In truth, it seemed to calm any agitation Mrs. Byron might have been inclined to suffer in the mornings, though Autumn felt that her own presence and gentle treatment of the lady might have served the same calming purpose. Still, indoctrinated as she had been by Dr. Beame's warnings, Autumn followed his rules unstintingly.

Mrs. Byron's afternoons were taken up with luncheon in an armchair in the bedroom, more medication, and a long nap. In the evenings, after dinner in her room, Mrs. Byron was allowed to be robed and escorted to her parlor on the first floor. Autumn saw no harm in offering Mrs. Byron her stitching for a brief period. She watched carefully to see that the woman did not become aggrieved with complicated needlework, however, and strove to help immediately if tangles intruded on her peace. More often than not, Mrs. Byron drowsed by the fire, and her sewing lay in her lap. When awake, she was often cold or hot, unsettled—or more disturbingly, to Autumn at least—bored.

Conversations between the two women were limited to Mrs. Byron's complaints. Autumn had been told to ask certain questions of the woman several times a day, such as did she have pain, did she experience dizziness, and had she dreamed when she slept. The questions were always answered with a simple negative.

After less than a week of this routine, Autumn found herself—most annoyingly because Dr. Beame had warned her it might be so—restive. For several days after that she forced herself to adhere to her duties without question, but the battle was lost, and soon she began to cast about for reasons for her restlessness and ways to assuage the feeling. Surveying her little room one morning, Autumn decided that she and Mrs. Byron were literally cloistered, with not even prayer, as nuns had, to distract them. Autumn awakened in her little, nearly windowless room each day, went in to Mrs. Byron, and there they lived together in a dim gaslit world with only the occasional diversion of an evening sojourn to the parlor. This was not natural, Autumn determined, and though Dr. Beame had forbidden it emphatically, she asked Mrs. Byron one day if she would mind if the draperies were drawn back for an hour or so in the afternoon. Mrs. Byron hesitated but agreed.

It had begun to snow, and the two women watched the sky from Mrs. Byron's third floor windows. It was as if nature had planned the resplendent panorama of soft, swirling crystal just for them, and Mrs. Byron fell asleep that afternoon in her armchair that was now facing the window. The hint of a smile curved her lips.

Making her way down to the kitchen to prepare medication for her charge, Autumn's feelings were a mixture of guilt, exaltation, and despondency that such a small thing as looking out a window could cause her so much pleasure. Still, when there was such a dearth of pleasure in one's life, the smallest diversions were priceless treasures. In the kitchen, Autumn was greeted happily by Mrs. Inman, who told her that she'd stewed a fat hip of beef for their supper.

"I doubt that Mrs. Byron will be much interested," Autumn told her, but at that woman's sudden disappointed silence, she amended that she would certainly enjoy the treat. She sighed. "I grow fat, Carrie," she said, sitting down at the thick board of the kitchen table, "while Mrs. Byron withers."

"I know, Miss Autumn," the older woman said, shaking her capped head. She was folding linens in the tiny utility compartment off the kitchen. "This is no life for a young woman like yourself. It's no life for any of us, really. Vigorous souls need the company of society." Autumn traced her finger through a few grains of spilled flour on the table in the otherwise spotless room.

"I have seen no evidence of society in this house, Carrie," she observed idly.

"That's because of the trouble," returned the servant. She came into the kitchen carrying a pot of unpeeled potatoes. Seating herself in a chair opposite Autumn, she began to prepare them for the stew. "Once this house was a hive of elegant peacocks." She laughed. "Each of them was tryin' to outdo the other. They'd come swarmin' in, jabberin' their dandified jabber—the ladies in their silks and feathers and jewels and the gents in their frock coats and high hats. Oh, it was a gay time when I first come into this house. It was all color and fluff and so much excitement."

"And then, the . . . 'trouble' happened?" asked Autumn, curious. Carrie Inman nodded emphatically. "And what was the trouble?"

Mrs. Inman hesitated. Her attention became studiously riveted on her potatoes. She peeled them with assiduous care. "I don't know as I should go on, Miss Autumn," she murmured. "It ain't my place." Slowly her attention drifted back to the younger woman. "If you ask me, miss," she said confidentially, "the doctor should of told you himself. It ain't fair, makin' you responsible without givin' you one whit of information."

"I agree," said Autumn cautiously. When Mrs. Inman went back to her work, the younger woman continued. "You told me once that Mrs. Byron had been quite a vigorous woman, Carrie," she probed. "I can only assume that the trouble of which you speak had to do with something that happened to her." Carrie nodded but remained tight-lipped. Autumn could understand her reticence. As a servant, one was expected to remain ardently protective of the secrets of the household. And yet gossip was the life's blood of the underclass—as it was of the gentry. It seeped through the social fabric of Victorian-era America, trickling down and pooling, forming great ponds into which the serving classes dove heartily. Having now been on both strata, Autumn approved Carrie Inman's desire to remain loyal to her employer. At the same time, she was experiencing a decidedly indelicate curiosity. Even beyond these two warring perspectives, however, Autumn felt that, as the housekeeper had pointed out, she had been unfairly excluded from Mrs. Byron's history.

"Carrie," she said earnestly, "I respect your discretion." The woman looked up. "Sincerely I do. I have always agreed that those we trust with our secrets ought to remain trustworthy. But I am troubled by so many things concerning Mrs. Byron. The restrictions placed on her seem harsh, and I have been told that I must enforce these restrictions to the letter. Do you know," she said, reaching out and taking the older woman's hand, "that today I opened the draperies in Mrs. Byron's bedroom? It was such a little pleasure and so remarkable a joy that I nearly burst with happiness, and yet I felt so guilty. Perhaps if I understood the nature of her illness, I might be more amenable to the solution."

Carrie Inman regarded her solemnly. "Maybe you would, Miss Autumn, and then again maybe you wouldn't." Her brows furrowed. "But you deserve the right to make your own judgment. You ought to know the truth—at least as much of it as I know."

"Thank you, Carrie." She stood and paced the room. Feeling the need to explain herself, she went on. "I have never been one to follow dogma blindly. Institutions such as politics and religion demand bedazzled faith, and that is why I have nothing to do with either of them. If I cannot debate a question to my satisfaction with reasonable people, I leave the question to heaven and go on about my business." She glanced at Carrie, who was regarding her blankly. Autumn laughed. "My mother looks at me the same way sometimes, Carrie." That woman offered a slow, bemused smile. "In any event," Autumn resumed, "this situation with Mrs. Byron requires my involvement, so I should be most appreciative of your enlightenment."

Thus Autumn felt she had lifted the burden of a conscientious servant's guilt at telling a family's secret sorrow. Carrie's face displayed her relief. But before she could tell her story, several young men burst energetically into the kitchen. They were stablemen from Dr. Byron's carefully selected crew, and they were tanned, strong, and exuberant. Their very presence, reeking of nature and youth, filled the kitchen with warmth and vitality.

"Won't you throw us a crumb, Carrie?" said one of them as he eyed Autumn admiringly. "We haven't had a bite since lunch." His even teeth gleamed dazzlingly, exceeding the brightness of the streaming daylight that washed the kitchen. With his golden curls and beaming smile, he might have been the sunlight erupting from the clouds on that snowy winter's day. Autumn hastily

averted her eyes, reining her unguarded interest, and went to prepare Mrs. Byron's afternoon medication.

"You'll get your supper soon, old lad," stated Carrie Inman with
a twitching smile and an unconscious swipe at the curls that peeked
beneath the brim of her cap. "Can't you wait an hour or two?"

"I can wait a week," said the boy with a sly glance at Autumn's
trim back, "if I know something good's a-coming." He checked
the reactions of his smiling pals and offered Mrs. Inman a hearty
and knowing wink. That woman dismissed their foolery with an
emphatic wave of her hand.

"There's a basket of rolls in the buttery and cider on the back
porch," she said with an indulgent laugh. "Get y' to it, and don't
bother this kitchen again till supper." The youths bundled from
the room, laughing, taking the sunshine with them. Autumn had
prepared Mrs. Byron's prescription and turned to the older
woman. They regarded each other with smiles for a long moment.
They shared knowledge of something unsaid, and they soon
shied from their daring peek into the other's soul. Their smiles
evaporated. At an impasse, the two women hastily occupied
themselves with other urgencies. Carrie moved to the sink, carrying her pot of potatoes. "We'll talk soon, miss," she said pumping water from the spout to wash the vegetables. "Like I told you,
it's only fair." She paused, continuing her work, but keeping her
eyes downcast. "Tonight, my man Henry's comin' in from the
farm he tenants for Dr. Byron, so I'll be busy," she told Autumn,
with not a hint of suggestion in her tone, "but if you could come
to my room tomorrow night, after Mrs. Byron's tended, I'll tell
you all I know."

"Thank you, Carrie," said Autumn and made her way from
the kitchen, disheartened in some inexplicable way that she and

Carrie had missed an opportunity to share some womanly truth. Surely, Autumn was not the only girl who had ever felt oddly moved by men. Surely, she was not the only one who had noticed that unexplained and profound synergy that existed between men and women. The knowable but never-discussed symmetrical quality of a perfect design should not go unexplored, and yet Autumn had never talked about it, even with her mother. Autumn Thackeray was eighteen years old; she was a product of a repressed and unenlightened society, a child of a world both fascinated and repelled by the relationship between man and woman. And her own feelings on the subject were as confused and ambivalent as those of the society from which she had sprung.

That night Autumn was restless. Her bedcovers stifled her, and the very air of her tiny room felt confining and claustrophobic. Very late, she dressed and wandered downstairs and out to the stable yards. A thick snow was beginning to fall over the moonlit landscape as she approached, and several proud animals whickered softly as she entered the gates. She moved along the stalls and gave each an affectionate pat. Autumn was beginning to understand Cain Byron's protective attitude toward these lovely big-eyed creatures and why he had become so angry with the girl who had allowed one of them to escape. It was not often a tender world for the unprotected.

Autumn was startled by a footfall behind her in the yard, a simple crunch of gravel. She pulled her shawl tightly around her shoulders and squinted into the dim, snow-shrouded distance. At the far end of the fence stood one of the boys she had met that afternoon.

"Can I help you, miss?" he asked.

"I was just . . . petting the horses," Autumn replied. "Is that alright?" The lad moved slowly toward her, his blond head bright, pale as the moonlight that lit his path.

"Just so long as you don't leave one of the gates open. We caught hell the other week for . . . Well, but you must know that story by now, miss."

"Yes," said Autumn mesmerized by the man's approach. "It was, I believe, Alma Louise who . . ."

"But you see, we lads are the ones responsible."

"Yes," Autumn said. He stood directly before her now, smiling. Her heart fluttered, and she knew suddenly with a terrible realization what Alma Louise had been doing in the stable yard. "She . . . should have been . . . more . . . careful."

"That she should have been, Miss Autumn." His voice was soft, caressing. "But, like I said, we boys are responsible." Autumn nodded. The fluttering in her breast had risen to her throat and she could not form sounds. She turned suddenly in the direction of the house. The young man took her arm, stopping her gently. "Wait, miss," he said softly. "It gets awful lonely out here." Again, Autumn nodded. "We sleep in shifts, and there's nobody to talk to."

"I understand," Autumn choked out, gripped by an inexplicable fear. "Please let me go." The boy's smile deepened and he released her arm.

"Come again," he said. Autumn flew from the stables across the lawn and into the house, slamming the door behind her and locking it, for what reason she knew not. She knew the lad would not break in. Perhaps she locked it against herself, to keep herself from going back outside. She made her way feverishly up the back staircase, and her lonely bed beckoned. It had been wrong, so wrong of her, to have sought out that which coerced her from the lowest, most unexamined, and artless depths of her being. She had been wrong, yet compelled by that terrible and obscene stratum of her soul. She swaddled herself in her bedclothes, protecting herself like a child from monsters that haunted her, monsters she could not possibly understand.

The foghorn sent its lonely call across the bay. One-two-three long warnings in the night.

❧❧

The little girl, hair tossed like liquid pearls, is flushed with exertion. She has run all the way from the orchard where she has chosen only the prettiest apple blossoms for her bouquet. She dallies in the lilac grove and in the green garden, dewy with impending rain. She follows her course with sunny willfulness, though her nanny calls from the house, and gathers new-blossomed irises to compliment her arrangement. Her mother will forgive her, for the florets will adorn her tea table most prettily . . .

Chapter 5

"Miss Autumn," Mrs. Inman was saying. Autumn started.

"I'm sorry, Carrie," she said. "Were you speaking to me?"

"I was, miss. I was wanting to tell you the eggs is all but boiled to the pot."

"Oh, Carrie," Autumn breathed. She ran to the stove.

"No need to hurry. I took them off."

Autumn paused, her fingertips flying to her temples. "Thank you," she said softly. "I'm afraid I was daydreaming."

"Are you alright, Miss Autumn?"

"I'm fine, Carrie. It's only that . . . Oh, I don't know what's wrong with me. I'll just get Mrs. Byron's lunch for her." Carrie Inman stopped the girl, placing a hand gently on her shoulder.

"You need to get out of this house, miss," she said. "Like I told you yesterday, this ain't no life for such a one as you. Now you listen to me," she insisted, taking the lunch tray that Autumn had retrieved from the table, "I was going to send one of the boys to the market with a list. Why don't you go instead?"

"Oh, Carrie, could I?"

"Of course you could. Why, the town's not two miles down the road, and my list is light today. No reason in the world why you couldn't. I'll get one of the lads to drive you."

"No," Autumn said a bit more hastily than was necessary. "I should love to walk. I'll just fetch Mrs. Byron's lunch—"

"I'll do that, Miss Autumn," Carrie told her sternly. "You just get yourself wrapped up warm and go." She took a folded piece of paper from the pocket of her apron. "Here's my list. Just get yourself to Mr. Fletcher's Food Emporium on Ocean Street; it's your second left turn off the main road. Anyone can direct you there should you get lost, but I can't imagine it." She smiled broadly as Autumn expressed her gratitude, gave her a quick embrace and a peck on the cheek, and hastened up to her room to prepare for her outing. "Dress warm, my girl," Mrs. Inman called after her. "It's a might chilly out there, and—" But Autumn was gone. Carrie shook her head in understanding. One minute the girl was wasting away, bored and distracted, and the next she was exuberant with expectancy. Carrie understood the cyclical energies of girls and women. Had she not perceived Autumn's sweet unguarded response to the groomsmen yesterday? Had Carrie not shared that secret knowledge of women's needs with the girl? And she was a girl who was fast becoming a woman. Too bad, thought Carrie, that she must endure such a monumental transition so far from her mother's careful guidance. Perhaps Carrie could help; she knew of a woman's wantings. Her own cherished Henry had left that morning after his monthly visit. He'd gone back to his work on one of Dr. Byron's tenant farms, and he'd left his wife, for all his virile attentions, with still untended yearnings. He'd been there, after all, only one night. Surely, it took more time to educate a man to the nuances of a woman's needs. And Henry, reflected Carrie wistfully, was teachable. Someday, when their finances allowed it, they would be together for long periods of time, and he would learn, in time, those secret subtleties of pleasuring a woman. Carrie Inman smiled despite her mortification at such unseemly ruminations. Well into her twenty-sixth year, she was thinking like a schoolgirl. On the other hand, she reflected with a certain sly pride, schoolgirls did not really know the rewards that could be gotten when a woman made it her business to educate a man.

∽ᗡᗷ﹀

After the previous night's thick snowfall, a welkin radiance covered the world. It adorned the branches and boles of trees and blanketed the shapes of distant hills. This was no ordinary outing—a young servant trudging dutifully to market. As Autumn traveled from Byron Hall to the populated town of Cape May, she imagined the empty road canopied with snowy trees as a diamond-white grotto where she might find unimagined treasures. Autumn cherished every sight of snow-drifted luminescence, exulting in every breath of frosted air.

She avoided the first left turn of the road, as Carrie had instructed, and took the second, down Ocean Street. Walking briskly, she noted that signs of civilization became more prevalent as she progressed. Houses began to dot the roadside in abundance, and a wooden walkway was now available to her. Horse-drawn carriages, wagons, and jingling sleighs made their way on the rutted dirt road and across perpendicular byways. There was a corner park where children built snowmen and forts for snowball battles. She saw storefronts and a church—and even a circulating library. In her excitement, Autumn did not bother to look for Mr. Fletcher's Food Emporium. Instead, she wound her way to the center of the town and finally to the unimaginably wondrous place where snow-draped city met ice-clouded ocean. Autumn stood on a street lined with grand hotels and a winding board-walk that followed the coastline as far as she could see. People strolled by, ladies with prams and busy shoppers carrying baskets of bread, imported fresh vegetables, and waxed cheeses, unaware of her awe-filled presence. Autumn was pleasantly aware that today she was the observer and not the observed. She gazed out onto the sparkling vista of snowy beach and icy water. Seagulls soared and landed, congregating on sandy patches and ice floes, searching for food. Their searches were mainly in vain this time of year, for the beach and boardwalk were empty of vacationers. Autumn noted that the porches and balconies spanning the heights of the colorful hotels that lined the other side of the street were abandoned yet still alive with elegant splendor. Even in their emptiness, these painted wonders of Victorian architec-ture resembled fancy women, dressed and decorated, jeweled and waiting with endless patience for the party to begin. Their drap-ings of snow might have been lush ermine cloaks, and the crys-talline icicles hanging from their eaves the finest diamond ear bobs. The warm bright colors they wore, their lacy gingerbread trim and lofting windows of stained glass, might have been gowns of the most sophisticated design. And their graciously curving carriage steps eloquently promised the refinement and grandeur that would be found within. Patterns unique to this time and this place of turrets and gables, lovingly ornamented, offered themselves as symbols, monuments to a gilded time. In other times, Autumn herself might have enjoyed their splendid hospitality.

The cold ocean smell drew her down toward the boardwalk that girdled the beach. She raised her parasol against a misting spume and made herself a picture of graceful isolation as she stood along the rail looking out to sea. In her solitude, her mind drifted like ice floes on viscid water. She ruminated on the circumstances of her presence in this world-famous resort town, idle now, dressed in its winter cloak, awaiting the attention of the summertime affluent. In other times, Autumn might have come here with her family; her pretty mother in her wide-brimmed, beribboned straw hats; her strong and rigidly confident father, willing in the heat of summer to loosen his stock and remove his dark stuff waistcoat; and the jolly contingent of servants that accompanied them everywhere they stopped. And Autumn would have been turned out in her laciest frocks, her sun-gilt curls wound with bows and flower garlands. Domestically picturesque, the family would have strolled the beaches, Autumn barefooted and running ahead to collect the prettiest shells for her little bucket. They would have idled on lawn chairs. And they would have played croquet, that new and dubious lawn game, which most of society thought too raucous for good taste, for they were a liberal and free-spirited family. When the bells rang from the hotel, they would have scurried into their cotton bathing suits and run down to the water to play, the ladies and children first, and once they had emerged, the gentlemen. Then they were three and joyously cherished by one another. They were rich and free. But that was then.

Over the years, Autumn had seen worry and consternation darken her father's beloved countenance and with it, Autumn's life had become irretrievably altered. Her mother abandoned her beribboned hats, the servants disappeared, the family home had gone on the market, and the furniture sold. Inconceivably, Autumn's father had committed the one sin that neither God nor society could forgive. He had taken his own life. Autumn's heart swelled and her throat knotted with the knowledge of the despair that must have led him to this ultimate act of abandonment. She and her mother had moved into a mean apartment where they lived for a time on the pittance they had received as dependants of a successful banker, but that little money had disappeared like her father, and the women were left without resources, without protection. Autumn was at an age at which young debutantes were expected to announce an engagement, but her suitors were few, and those who remained had no thought of marriage to a young lady bereft of money and societal stature. Autumn was horrified to learn that the men who courted her entertained visions not of weddings, but of "arrangements." She understood finally that she must find some sort of employment if she and her mother were to survive. They could not go on pretending elegance—fanning themselves delicately in summer heat, playing cards and mending their ever more threadbare clothes before a dwindling fire on winter evenings, averting their eyes modestly from the questing gazes of rejecting, disdainful, former friends on the street. Their diminishing finances could not be ignored. They could not, for all their pretenses, afford to remain together. Autumn's mother, Isabel, had taken a position in the home of a discreet local artisan as housekeeper and seamstress. The family could not afford, however, to hire Autumn, or to offer her their hospitality for more than a few weeks, and so she advertised her willingness to take on any situation suitable to her gifted upbringing. She could not bring herself to apply in Philadelphia, where she and her mother would be subjected to that noxious and insulting tribute, pity. Newspapers in several surrounding cities therefore discreetly announced that a young lady of breeding and taste who could stitch an elegant border, play the pianoforte, sing, speak French, write poems, arrange flowers, and make entertaining conversation was available for employment. In short, this advantaged young lady could do everything but make herself a living. The letter from Cape May came as a lavish gift, and Autumn had accepted the invitation to companion an elder lady with surprise and relief.

One day she might begin to explore the feelings, currently suppressed by her young heart, of anger and resentment at her father's abandonment. For now, the weight of necessity pressed, and Autumn's gratitude at being allowed to sustain herself without burdening her poor mother consoled her. It was enough for now that she lived among refined people, had access to merciful anonymity, and that she might someday acquire the resources to lift her mother and herself from life in one room in someone else's home. She could address the pain of her father's loss, but not the bitterness inflicted by his deliberate desertion.

Autumn had remained on the boardwalk for some time, and she was beginning to feel a chill. She glanced about, wondering what someone passing would think of her senseless loitering; she was, after all, not on holiday, but a dedicated servant in a refined household. It was then that she noticed a man, far down the beach, watching her. He was a rather ragtag gentleman, though she could not see him clearly. He had a great graying beard and he wore a seaman's woolen cap and a pea coat. He held a long, curved pipe in his teeth. Though it was true Autumn could not analyze his expression, she had no doubt that he was observing her. The way he stood, hands in pockets, gray puffs of smoke trailing in the light ocean breezes, feet planted in the sand, gave him the appearance of a sentinel. Autumn took down her parasol and hastened from the boardwalk. More frightening than the idea of his watching her for nefarious purposes was the thought that he was observing—and judging—her idleness. As the sun lowered she made her way back to Ocean Street to locate Mr. Fletcher's Food Emporium.

On the byway, as she traveled back to Byron Hall, Autumn noted with dismay that the man appeared to be following her. Her bundles tucked firmly beneath her arms, she hastened her step. Did his step quicken behind her? She glanced over her shoulder several times. The man seemed to walk no more slowly nor any faster as her own pace changed. His pose was casual, and he seemed to trail her at a discreet distance. At one point, he stopped as he came nearer to her and drew the pipe from his teeth. He stood for several moments, tamping down the tobacco and relighting it. When Autumn had gained some distance, he began to walk once again. At last, unable to bear the bewildering presence and with Byron Hall comfortably in sight, Autumn stopped and turned. The man stopped, too.

"Why are you following me?" Autumn called to him, more indignant than afraid. Slowly, the gentleman approached. He was larger than he'd seemed from her perspective on the boardwalk. He drew the pipe from his lips and held it in the cradle of his big hand. As he neared, his shoulders loomed wide above her, and the barrel of his chest blocked her view of the vermilion ribbon of the sunset. He stood over her finally, very near. She could see she had been right about the graying beard, but what she hadn't perceived was the laughing, sea-glass blue of his eyes, the sparkle of his even teeth, the crinkle of many generations of smiles that lightened his weathered face.

"I hope I did not frighten you, little one," he said, his rumbling voice a warming caress in the chilled twilight. Autumn's mouth fell open. Here was a wonder of a man—surely as old as her father had been—even older—and of mythic proportion and charm.

"No," she managed, "you did not frighten me, sir." Beneath her incredulity loomed an inkling of resentment, however, and she added, "But you have perturbed me, and you now leave me quite puzzled." She furrowed her brows in a display of injury. "I must ask again why you are following me."

"I wanted to see where you lived," the man told her easily.

"Why?"

"That I would rather not say." He smiled and set the pipe firmly between his teeth. "I take it that you are heading for Byron Hall." Autumn hesitated only a moment before replying.

"Yes I am," she conceded. She saw no reason to hide her destination; the man could easily watch her go there. Still, she was troubled that he'd had the audacity to ask such a question in the first place. There had been no proper introduction. She was unsettled, too, that she'd been left little choice in the matter of her response. A lady was always offered the preemptive of falsehood if she chose it. "I must demand that you tell me what interest that fact is to you, sir," she said, lifting her chin and catching the man in a withering golden glare. He nearly laughed. Autumn's eyes widened at the man's effrontery. "You, sir," she affirmed, "are no gentleman."

"I have rarely made claim to such a title, little one," he said,

and now he did laugh. Autumn spun away from him and made a
brisk retreat up the private road to the house. She did not look
back and wondered with every step whether or not he would follow. More soberingly, she wondered who he was and what he
would do with the information he now possessed. By the time she
reached the house, her sober reflections had been overshadowed
by anger. She stormed into the kitchen and flung her parcels furiously on the table.

"Miss Autumn," Carrie said, "what on God's green earth has
gotten into you?"

"A man," Autumn shot back. The two women stared at
each other for a brief astonished moment, then realizing the
implication of Autumn's pronouncement they dissolved into
gales of irreverent laughter. "Oh, Carrie," Autumn said when
she'd contained her mirth, "I meant to say that a man followed
me home." Carrie Inman's smile faded instantly.

"What's that you say? You was followed? My lord, are you alright?"

"Oh my, yes," Autumn assured her. "I am just fine." She took
the older woman's hand and sat her down at the table to explain
the events of the afternoon. "I suppose," she finished forlornly,
"it was my own fault for making myself so visible there on the
boardwalk, but I was fascinated by the ocean, and I'm afraid, lost
in my own thoughts."

"An' what the devil is wrong with that?" asked Carrie, assuring
Autumn that a woman's "thinkin' time" ought to be respected.
"That was the very purpose of your outing; you've had little
enough time to yourself. 'Tis a pity and a shame," asserted Carrie,
"that a lady can't walk the streets without bein' mauled."

"Well, I was hardly mauled," Autumn demurred.

"It's one and the same, miss," Carrie returned heatedly. "It's a God-awful world it is," she stated, pounding a chubby fist on the board, "that lets a man think he can approach us just because he's got a whim to." She cast a narrowed glance at Autumn. "From now on, my girl, you'll take the carriage."

"Maybe that would be best, Carrie," Autumn said, gauging her response to soothe the woman's wrath. She dared not mention, at least for the moment, that she'd actually spoken to the gentleman, and that she'd not felt in the least threatened or intimidated by him. As she thought on it now, Autumn recalled that she'd realized a certain amiability in the man. Whether it was his maturity that consoled her or his straightforwardness in finally approaching her, she did not know. There had been nothing calculating in his posture; even his unwillingness to speak of his reason for following her held a certain frankness that Autumn, upon reflection, could respect. The only fault she could truly attribute to the gentleman was a determined arrogance. He was, no doubt, a rogue—but he was a charming one. Naturally, she reminded herself, the charming ones were the most dangerous.

Changing the subject, Autumn inquired as to Mrs. Byron's well-being, and Carrie assured her that the woman had spent a quiet afternoon, as usual, sleeping most of the day. Ever troubled by this, Autumn reluctantly began to mix the medication her patient required, and she and Carrie made up a supper tray.

"May we meet later?" asked Autumn, recalling their conversation of the previous afternoon.

"I'm lookin' forward to it. You an' me, we'll have a real sociable evenin'."

❧ ❦

The house was dark and silent as Autumn slipped down the back stairs to Mrs. Inman's first floor room. Carrie greeted her knock with a bright and hearty welcome and led Autumn to a comfortable upholstered armchair. The room was furnished pleasantly, and Autumn commented on the fact that Carrie enjoyed the amenity of two windows, while Autumn had barely one. The women giggled over the insensitivity of some employers, and Carrie played hostess.

"I got me some wine, Miss Autumn," she said, "or would you prefer tea?"

"Wine would be welcome, Carrie. Mother and I enjoyed an occasional glass in the evening . . . when we could afford it."

"I know how you must feel, Miss Autumn, bein' so far from the one you love." She poured two glasses, offered one to Autumn, then nestled herself into a pile of decorative pillows on her bed.

"I am sure you understand, Carrie. You must miss your husband terribly."

Carrie nodded, but commented that they had been lucky to find their situation. "Henry tenants one of Dr. Byron's farms. He's got land all over New Jersey—horse farms and crop farms and dairy farms and who knows what else all. You see this place but it ain't nothin' to what's out there." She waved a chubby hand at some vast expanse of property that existed "out there" somewhere. "But one day we hope to buy a place of our own. We're savin' our money, and it won't be long before we can start a family."

"One would think Dr. Byron would *give* you a farm, Carrie," mused Autumn, sipping her wine. "He is one of the richest men in New Jersey, so I hear."

"That he is, miss, but my Henry's a proud man. You see the farms and the money—everything—came from *Mrs.* Byron. *She* was the one brought all the wealth into the family. Naturally, once she married, all the money and property went to her husband." Her voice faded. "Anyway, it's a complicated business all around, it is," she resumed, taking a long sip on her wine. "For one, the property, this house, most of the money, was left to Mrs. Byron. I mean it's hers, except she can't do anything with it, 'cause she ain't fit. There's some law, or somethin'."

"It sounds like a very stupid law," Autumn commented.

"It may be, miss, but there it is. So the doctor has to . . . um, *execute* the whole estate. It's confusin' to me, but Henry says he won't be takin' nothin' from a woman. That's the way of the old country, Miss Autumn, and here, too, apparently. Men are so proud." Autumn nodded.

"Tell me about the house, Carrie, and how it was before Mrs. Byron became ill."

"Oh, that," said Carrie, rising and pouring more wine, then resuming her seat. "You see, the grandfather built the house with the help of the people in town. For their help, he promised them he'd be their doctor forever, and that all his heirs—male heirs, that is—would be doctors, too, and that they'd serve the town." She was warming to the tale. "Well now, the father, Dr. Byron's father, kept to the agreement, and Dr. Byron, too."

"I see no evidence of a medical practice," Autumn put in.

"That's 'cause there ain't none," Carrie returned. "I mean the present Dr. Byron went to medical school, but once he got out— more important, once his father died—he just walked away from the house, from the people, from his grandfather's promise. You see that's why the money and all was left to Mrs. Byron and not a pittance for the son. I suspect the old master knew his son was a bit of a proud heart, if you know what I mean. Why from what folks say Cain Byron had every girl in town salutin' him with her skirts. But that's gossip," she added hastily. "So the father put it in his will that his son couldn't inherit nothin' till he started a medical practice."

"Still he . . ." Autumn searched for the word Carrie had used, "*executes* the estate," she observed.

"That's how it is, miss. Like I said, it's a complicated business." Carrie poured a dollop more wine into each glass. "All I know is that since we was kids together, young Cain Byron was always in some kind of trouble. He was always ridin' his horses through the town, busy as it is, with an arrogance that just riled everybody's bones. And there was nothin' could stop him, either. The constable was always up here, I remember. And me, bein' a serious-minded girl just off the boat, didn't appreciate the high jinks. It was just as well, far as I was concerned, that he got himself sent off to that Harvard College. It stopped the fightin' between him an' his father anyway. No father and son should be so at odds."

"And Mrs. Byron?"

"She couldn't do much, miss, except be the angel that she was—consolin' the young Dr. Byron and givin' him and the father all the love she could give. If it wasn't for her there wouldn't've been no love at all around here. Oh, she was a grand lady in them days and a real elegant strutter. Not that she was full of herself, oh, no. But she could've been, if she'd wanted to be," Carrie rhapsodized. "She and the old master gave the most elegant parties. Why this house was a regular palace, with the guests all decked out and music playin'. They had their own little orchestra that used to come in most every weekend. Why me an' the other girls'd just get the place cleaned and polished from one party, and we'd start all over for the next. It was more excitin' than you can imagine." Carrie became lost for several seconds in smiling reflection.

"And then the 'trouble' happened," prodded Autumn. She was feeling a glowing curiosity. She folded her feet beneath her in the comfortable chair.

"The trouble." Carrie nodded and drew herself up to pour more wine. She settled herself once more on the bed and seemed to pause as she collected her thoughts. "The trouble," she repeated. "Now that didn't happen till after the old master died. See, the old master passed on, and it seemed like things happened."

"I understand," Autumn told her solemnly. "What things?" she asked as an afterthought.

"Oh, things," said Carrie giving the word a dangerous emphasis. "Like, Mrs. Byron forgot things. She forgot bridge games and even supper parties. And," she added with significance, "she seemed happy. Well, I mean, a widow lady shouldn't be happy, should she?"

"No," agreed Autumn. "A widow lady should not be happy."

Carrie nodded, confirming her observation, and continued, "She was happy. Flighty kind of. And she would go on little trips on her own. A few days, a week. And then Dr. Byron come home from New York one day, and he brought this Dr. Beame with 'im, and he was a kind of specialist, or somethin'—in women." She began to laugh uproariously. "Imagine it, Miss Autumn," she said through her mirth. "He went to college to study up on women!" Autumn found much humor in Carrie's observation. She accepted another helping of wine and found the taste becoming more and more agreeable to her. "So anyway," continued Carrie on a serious note, "there was these two doctor lads askin' questions, and all of a sudden we get to thinkin' about things, we girls. 'How'd she act today?' they'd ask and 'Where'd she go last night?' And we'd start goin' to the doctors with our stories for fear Mrs. Byron was really sick. I think," she confided to Autumn, "that some of the girls made up things just to get closer to the doctors." Carrie gave a sage wink and Autumn nodded knowingly, though she could not for the life of her remember what she had just in that previous moment known. "But anyway . . ." Carrie continued, pausing for a moment to recall her drift, "that was the trouble." Autumn's brows furrowed.

"What was?" she asked after a moment.

"What I said," Carrie informed her. She drew up her knees, and they both sipped their wine in reflection.

"So," recounted Autumn, putting her thoughts in some sort of muddied order, "Cain Byron thought his mother's happiness unhealthy." Carrie nodded emphatically. Autumn's mind drifted with the puzzle. Questions darted into her consciousness and as quickly disappeared. She wanted to say something, but found it difficult to form the words. "Just one second . . ." she said slowly, cautiously, lifting a detaining finger lest Carrie should attempt to interrupt. "I'd like to understand."

Her thoughts trailed off. She tried to recall what she'd been about to ask. She took yet another sip of wine, for her mouth felt dry. "Was she sick?" she asked finally. The words had not come out correctly. Carrie, however, seemed to have no difficulty understanding her. She bowed her head.

"It's a God-awful world," that lady pronounced. Tears formed

on her lashes as her face crumpled. "Once she was so happy . . .
We was all happy once."

Autumn reached into the pocket of her houserobe and laboriously drew out a handkerchief. She handed it to Carrie, who took
it and dabbed at her eyes. Autumn suddenly felt, watching the
other woman, an infinite sadness. *It was an awful world.* Tears puddled in her own eyes, blurring and distorting her vision. Carrie
blew her nose heartily into the hanky, and Autumn dabbed at her
own with the hem of her robe. "What's the use?" she asked.
Again, the words had not formed themselves properly, but again,
Carrie seemed to understand.

"We go on and on . . . tryin', tryin', tryin'."

Autumn nodded. She understood her friend perfectly and
agreed with her sentiments. Before she could express her acknowledgement, however, she noted with some disinterest that
Carrie's empty wineglass had fallen onto the carpet. Lifting her
tear-glazed eyes, she stared blankly at the sleeping older woman.
Poor Carrie, Autumn reflected. Poor, poor, Carrie. Poor, poor,
everybody. Pushing herself up with some difficulty from the
chair, Autumn thought to withdraw to her own room. However,
the floor beneath her feet had suddenly turned gelatinous. She
sat back down with surprising abruptness. The world spun
darkly. A bright spot of sunlight beckoned, and then everything
was nothing.

✑❧

*She is twirling. She is laughing. She is graduating in one week from Miss
Merriman's School for young ladies of quality. She is trying on the dress she will
wear, made for a lady not a little girl. It is satiny white. With one gloved hand*

she holds up the hem, with the other she holds down the crown of baby's breath and seed pearls placed carefully atop her head. She has learned everything—and perhaps nothing—about life. But she is free. She is going too fast! Too fast! Too . . . fast. She falls, giddy, breathless, onto a settee. Her dance, her life, has begun.

Chapter 6

Upon awakening next morn, Autumn considered praying for her own demise. But of course one did not pray for such things; one only wished for them. She struggled to wakefulness, managed somehow to physically crawl through the initial agony, but her cow-hearted mental state unnerved her. All morning Autumn had felt a sense of helplessness, hopelessness, and unreasoned fear. Combined with those, she was overwhelmed with a feeling of guilt. She lay on her bed for some time after lunch remembering that earlier she had done the unimaginable; she had snapped at Mrs. Byron. That poor, helpless creature had refused her lunch as usual, and Autumn had, as usual, admonished her—rather harshly, now she remembered it. Mrs. Byron had cursed, and Autumn had, unbelievably, cursed back. "You sound like me," Mrs. Byron had told her dully.

Autumn attempted to sit up, but the sudden sharp throbbing in her head bade her lie back down—very slowly. She and Carrie had agreed that there was some pernicious infirmity in the air, for they both, upon their awakening early that day in Carrie's room, experienced the same nausea, headache, and listlessness. Whatever it was that ailed them, they resolved, they must protect Mrs. Byron from contracting it. And so it was not without some gratitude that Autumn had kept to her room for the most part throughout the morning. She'd risen long enough to give Mrs. Byron her breakfast, which she did not eat, and her lunch, which she had refused with horrible consequences. Autumn flayed herself with the memory of that awful moment. Angered beyond reason at Mrs. Byron's customary and willful disdain of food, Autumn had reminded her that one could not live without nourishment. Mrs. Byron had eagerly downed her medication, the smell of which sickened Autumn and brought to her mind the excess of wine she'd consumed the night before. Setting down her mug, Mrs. Byron had pointed out to Autumn that her own breakfast and lunch had gone untouched, and Autumn had reminded Mrs. Byron that *she* was the patient. It was at that point that Mrs. Byron had cursed. And it was at that point that Autumn had dismayed herself by cursing back. Another employer might have dismissed such a flagrantly disrespectful servant on the spot, but Mrs. Byron had simply sat back, her gaze vague and drifting, and told Autumn that she sounded like her.

You sound like me . . . You sound like me . . . You sound like me. The words echoed like a dull and painful heartbeat in Autumn's mind. *She should have dismissed me,* Autumn reflected. Any self-respecting mistress would not have allowed such insolence, to say nothing of such indelicacy, in a servant. But of course Mrs. Byron had no self-respect. . . .

Autumn sat up abruptly, almost toppling herself in the process. Her eyes were wide with a sudden recognition. "You sound like me," she uttered aloud. Shocked, horrified, Autumn struggled from the bed. She raced into Mrs. Byron's room and grabbed her empty mug from the tray. Steeling herself, she sniffed it. *That was it! Of course! It had to be!*

She glanced quickly at the slumbering Mrs. Byron; she looked so like Carrie had looked last night. Hers was not the sleep of peace and wound-knitting dreams; it was the sleep of oblivion. In that sleep there was no healing; there was only nothingness. And from such a sleep, Mrs. Byron could only awaken to remembered horrors and the raveled fears that had never been given the opportunity to mend. *Good God!*

Autumn sank heavily into the armchair where Mrs. Byron had eaten—or, rather, not eaten—her lunch. Her own stomach roiled, rejecting even the concept of food. The same terrible feeling of helplessness that had been with her all morning washed over her. She attempted to shake it off. She had become, in one day, a hopeless pessimist, a mindless coward, a weary grappler at the bottom of a fear-muddied pit. She looked down at the mug that lay overturned in her lap. *You sound like me.* Slowly, she lifted her gaze. Mrs. Byron's troubles, then, were nothing more or less than the product of a pernicious cycle: An excess of spirit and its horrible effects, the elimination of the horror with more wine, which caused more horror. Autumn's eyes widened with the knowledge of what she must do. Rising carefully, she began to clear up the dishes from the afternoon meal. Dismissing the dull pounding of pain behind her eyes, she made her way from the room and down to the kitchen. That very day, Autumn would begin, deliberately and cautiously, to wean Mrs. Byron from the drugs that had savaged her mind and body. No matter the consequences, she reflected—and the consequences could be grave—Autumn was determined to do the thing she instinctively knew was right.

As she slept that night, the two doctors loomed up before her, blocking her determination with distortions of what she knew absolutely to be true.

My mother's fate is in your hands, Miss Thackeray. You must follow Dr. Beame's instructions to the letter.

My women patients trust me, Miss Thackeray. I would never do them harm.

But this is right, her heart argued. No one, man or woman, should be rendered mindless, without the ability to make choices or even understand that choices exist. No living thing should be tortured by horrors they cannot hope to understand.

Torture, Miss Thackeray? This is medicine! If you were a man, I would call you out onto the field of honor.

You are my mother's last hope, Miss Thackeray. Please remember why you were hired.

I was not hired to drive a woman to madness!

Autumn sat up, sleep leaving her like a heavy cloak. She was perspiring, and in her uncertainty, sobbing mournfully. She was making her own choice; if it were the wrong choice, a bad choice, a harmful choice, she would never forgive herself.

❧ ❦

It was nearly four weeks before Autumn had completely estranged Mrs. Byron from the hold of her wine and laudanum. With great care she had decreased the dosages, adding more and more cider to the medication and less and less of the prescribed amounts of the drugs. She had substituted tea later on for the morning dosage and then tea again for the afternoon. Only two nights ago, she had eliminated Mrs. Byron's evening medication altogether. She had confided none of this to Carrie, for she wanted no one but herself to be responsible for the results, whatever they might be.

Though at first Mrs. Byron had been insensible to the changes, she had become puzzled with newly discovered energies. She questioned Autumn concerning long-forgotten and finally abandoned interests, such as conversation, a desire to get out of bed, to be read to. Her appetite had been restored. And finally, Carrie noticed the changes, and she questioned Autumn, too. But Autumn remained firmly unwilling to discuss her own involvement in Mrs. Byron's apparent recovery. One night, however, Carrie found the two of them in the music room, with Autumn rendering for Mrs. Byron's pleasure the popular tune of the day, "Poor Little Butterfly," on the pianoforte. Her pretty, light soprano filled the house, and Carrie was reminded of the days when gaiety and fun ruled Byron Hall. The two ladies applauded Autumn's performance and that lady took many bows, assured by her audience that her talent was worthy of the stage at the Adelphi Hotel in downtown Cape May. It was a silly moment at best, but one that drew the three women close. The sharing of harmless mischief strengthened the already blossoming friendship between them, and Autumn thought it time that she allowed them in on the secret of Mrs. Byron's "recovery." Their discussion was solemn, with Autumn beginning by reminding them that everything she had done over the past weeks was a direct contradiction of Dr. Beame's orders and Cain Byron's expectations. Though she had managed to console herself that Mrs. Byron was improving, she had no idea what long-term effects her very *unmedical* deviations might produce. Certain that what she was doing was right, she'd managed to ignore or forget or simply willfully evade the matter of accountability. She was sure that once observed, the results of her efforts would be applauded by both doctors. Carrie and Mrs. Byron agreed. Still, Autumn wondered if she had not undermined some larger plan.

"You see," she struggled on, focussing on Mrs. Byron for the next portion of her discourse, "little by little, step by step, I have taken away the drugs that I felt were doing you a great deal of harm." The older woman nodded. "For now," Autumn continued, "for the time being, it seemed enough that you were gaining emotional and physical weight, and you seemed a very different person than the one to whom I had been introduced the night of my arrival at Byron Hall. That is all I was thinking about. Now, though, I wonder if at some future time, some terrible result might show itself. I am no doctor, and I cannot foresee your future."

"Neither can the doctors, Autumn," returned Mrs. Byron with the easy grace that now characterized her conversation and every move. "Carrie," she said quietly, "may we have some tea?" That lady, eager to be of service to her newly awakened employer, hastily agreed and withdrew.

"Mrs. Byron—" Autumn began, but that woman splayed a hand.

"I've asked you to please call me Vanessa," her employer gently reminded her.

"Vanessa," amended Autumn, but once again she was stopped.

"Do you think me an idiot, child?"

"Oh, no—"

"Let me just say a few words in your defense, since you seem incapable of giving yourself any credit. It occurred to me about three weeks ago that something wonderful was happening to me. Winslow's plan—his treatment—" she gave the word a questionable significance, "may or may not be medically sound, but I would rather become a raving lunatic than succumb ever again to his so-called cures. And if I should at some future time become, in fact, a raving lunatic, I shall have you to thank for it." She noted Autumn's involuntary shudder. She smiled and continued mildly, "What is lunacy, after all, but a certain unpredictability, an unexpected energy—foolishness, folly? You have given me the power, Autumn Thackeray, to say that I shall never again give anyone, not Dr. Beame, and not my son, permission to deprive me of my folly."

꧁꧂

"We've had a letter from Dr. Byron," said Carrie cheerily as Autumn entered the kitchen one morning. "He says, with the good news about his mother and all, he'll be bringin' guests down for the holidays. He wants me to have three rooms prepared. I always loved the holidays here at Byron Hall—"

"Carrie," Autumn interrupted her, "will one of the guests be Dr. Beame?" The servant nodded.

"Wait'll he sees what you done for herself, miss," Carrie said triumphantly. "He won't believe it."

"That is just what I'm afraid of, Carrie," Autumn returned, running her fingertips shakily over her suddenly perspiring brow.

"Now don't you be worryin'. You done a miracle—all by yourself. Now," she continued, scurrying around the kitchen searching for paper to make a list, "we're going to need to hire extra girls, three ought to do it, and we'll order in extra food. And we ought to decorate." She looked up at Autumn who was regarding her blankly. "For Christmas," she said in explanation. "This house

ain't been decorated in years. Will you help me, Miss Autumn?"
The younger woman nodded and offered a courageous smile.

"Of course I will, Carrie," she replied. "We shall make
everything festive for the homecoming." As Carrie went about
scribbling notes, Autumn arranged Mrs. Byron's tray. Her
thoughts were not on gleeful preparations, however, they were absorbed in dour possibilities. First she must inform Mrs. Byron of
the doctors' arrival, and then a plan must be designed to break the
news of what had transpired over the past few weeks. Autumn
could not simply present her patient inexplicably cured to the men.

"And we'll get ourselves to town for some ribbon and a good
length of lace for the tree," Carrie was saying, but Autumn was
gone.

She found Mrs. Byron nestled in an armchair by the undraped
window in her bedchamber. She was reading, one of her favorite
pastimes, and she looked up as Autumn entered the room. "I'm
enjoying that new volume of poetry you brought me," she said.
"It's the book by that reclusive lady from Amherst."

"Emily Dickinson," Autumn affirmed vaguely. Each time she
had gone into town over the past weeks, she had indulged Mrs.
Byron's insatiable yearning for new reading material. Books were
stacked and scattered haphazardly about the chamber. Autumn's
brows knitted.

"We ought to keep these in some kind of order," she said irri-
tably. "We have no way of knowing which ones we own and
which are from the circulating library."

"We really should have some shelves brought up," Mrs. Byron
observed cheerily. She watched Autumn keenly as the girl set out
food for the two of them. She seemed distracted and uncustom-
arily tense. "I have a better idea," Vanessa Byron resumed,

attempting a soothing tone. "I shall take my old room on the second floor. It has built-in bookshelves, and there is a room next to it for you—with *lots* of windows facing the sea." She paused, noting Autumn's sudden look of dismay. "Is there a problem?" she asked.

Autumn hesitated, then straightened and folded her hands before her. "Mrs. Byron," she began.

"Won't you call me Vanessa?"

"Vanessa," Autumn said firmly. "I don't think it a good idea for you to move to the second floor. Dr. Beame specifically assigned you to this floor."

"Since when," commented Vanessa, "have you been concerned with what Dr. Beame has prescribed?" She had intended the observation as a light jest, and was not prepared for the girl's response. Autumn's face crumbled and tears came to her eyes. Vanessa was up immediately and held Autumn in her arms.

"You see," Autumn sobbed, "Carrie has just informed me that the men are coming back. Your son and Dr. Beame are coming here for the holiday," she rushed on. "I don't know what we shall tell them."

"We shall tell them that I have recovered," Vanessa told her firmly.

"But how? *How* have you recovered?"

"I suppose," Vanessa mentioned, wiping away Autumn's tears with her own handkerchief, "we can't very well say it was Winslow's fine medicines that cured me." She gave a dry chuckle. "Come, Autumn," she urged the girl, "sit down." She led them both to a small sofa. "Listen, child," she said calmly, "Winslow Beame will ask me questions and I will answer them." Autumn looked up in horror. "I will answer his questions," the woman assured her firmly, "but like our Miss Dickinson, I shall slant the truth—just a bit. 'The truth must dazzle gradually/Or every man be blind.' Someday, perhaps, Winslow will be able to understand my true assessment of his treatment of me. He is not a fool, but he is a man, and worse, he is a man of medicine. That makes his opinions doubly intractable."

"And what of your son?" Autumn said, sniffing loudly. "I fear he will send me away."

"I shall not allow that, my girl," Vanessa assured her. "You will not leave here until you are ready to leave." She stood, and from the vantage of her superior height, she regarded the younger woman tenderly. "Cain will be made to realize how important you are to me and how important your continuing presence will remain." She paused briefly. "You've no idea what you've done for me, have you?" she said quietly. Autumn glanced up. "You have emancipated me."

"But what of your . . . 'nervous disorder'? Has that simply gone away?"

Vanessa paced away and stared out the window for several moments. "My nervous disorder," she repeated, and her voice was reflective, a murmur on the quiet air. "It is only fair that you know, Autumn, that several years ago I did challenge everyone's definition of what is commonly referred to as sanity." Autumn's brows furrowed, and Vanessa, glancing toward her, waved away her concerns with long, tapered fingers. "Oh, I did no one any harm. I didn't prance naked in the garden or set anything on fire as did Charlotte Brontë's mad Bertha Mason. But I did display an indifference to long-embraced traditions."

"Is that all?" asked Autumn earnestly.

"Quite enough," Vanessa assured her. "You see, Cain believed that I was doing harm—to myself. And, finally, he was able to convince me, too. And then he brought Winslow into the picture to convince me further that my behavior was not only unconventional, but dangerous to the very foundations of our life. They became certain that I needed to be isolated from . . . people who meant me harm."

"Your friends," stated Autumn.

"Yes, certain . . . friends. The two young doctors became angry with me when I refused their ministrations. I was never one for confrontations, and so I attempted to humor them for a while. After a time," she said on a sigh, "it just seemed easier to go along with their so-called treatments. But I continued to rebel in small ways, and that is when Winslow became determined that I must go on to Belle Vue. He was adamant. But for my—and then my son's—resistance, I would be there now. It was at that point that Win became convinced that I needed radical treatment, but he allowed me to receive it here at home. I suppose Cain's being a medical doctor had a great deal to do with that concession. Most women do not enjoy the advantage of having a doctor in the house." Vanessa managed a small laugh. "And so I was spared the humiliation of incarceration. But there have been so many other humiliations, Autumn." She turned to the younger woman. "One day I may tell you about them. One day," she added, "I may tell the world. For now, I shall say only that the 'nervous disorder' about which you've inquired was caused by something—a gift—that I was given several years ago. It will never come back, and it will never leave me."

"What was the gift?" asked Autumn.

"I was given," she paused and smiled in remembrance, "the gift of wonder."

Chapter 7

The night of Dr. Byron's return to Cape May, Autumn took some time to organize her thoughts before descending the stairs to inspect the preparations. Sitting quietly before the hearth fire in her new second floor bedchamber, she made an effort to write her mother a cheery Christmas greeting. In this far more pleasant environment, she could almost manage a sense of true optimism.

"Dearest Mother" she wrote, "I wish you all the gaiety of the season. I have sent a small remembrance, and I hope it has arrived. If not, I shall spoil the surprise and tell you it is a set of antimacassars. You should know my tatting lessons with Mrs. Gainor were not in vain.

"Do you recall the Christmas when I was fourteen? I think it was the best Christmas of all. Daddy (God keep his soul) presented me with a pony—a roistering little thing. I named him Pegasus and rode him in Fairmount Park every Sunday thereafter. The boys always challenged me to races, and I would always win, though you and daddy firmly advised me that I ought to lose sometimes. Oh, Mother, I fear I was rarely the demure daughter of your dreams, but I truly believe you secretly liked me the way I was! Don't deny it, for I cherish your not-so-hidden smiles of pride each time I announced another victory.

"At the moment, I am awaiting the arrival of Dr. Byron and his friends. He has been away, and I hope we have made the house special for him, and of course, his houseguests.

"I love you and miss you. Happy holidays."

Autumn signed her name with some reluctance. She longed to write more, to tell her mother of Mrs. Byron's progress and of her own role in the recovery, but she thought it better to wait until they were together. Autumn could not express that triumph without writing of her accompanying uncertainties and fears. So far, she had managed to keep Isabel ignorant of those. And tonight, especially, she did not wish to wallow in her uncertainties. This night, she vowed, was going to be a festive one.

❦

The dining hall archway was festooned with a garland of fresh greens and silver plate and crystal graced the lace-covered dining table. Carrie scrambled to put the finishing touches on the welcoming meal.

"They'll be here by supper; that's what it said in the letter, Miss Autumn," she announced as she bumped her way in from the kitchen. "And the pea soup's barely bubblin'."

"It'll bubble, Carrie," Autumn said, laughing. "It'll bubble and steam and do exactly what it's supposed to do." She finished lighting all the candles in all the sconces and candelabrums throughout the room. The women had decided that candlelight should augment the gaslight that would be dimmed for the occasion. From the lofting windows, a twilight glaze faded, casting the room in a softly glowing aura of rose-gold. "Oh," Autumn said, "that we could keep this light forever." She turned her attention to the girl who was laying the fire, while Carrie arranged place cards at each table setting.

"Now I hope I got them names right," she muttered.

"It ought to blaze invitingly," Autumn was telling the woman at the fire, "but it oughtn't overshadow the decorations." The girl nodded her capped head wisely. They both watched as the tinder sparked and a little flame took hold.

"You think that's right?" asked the girl after a time. Autumn considered the blaze thoughtfully.

"I think it is perfect," she pronounced. The girl smiled gratefully, then withdrew to join Carrie in the kitchen.

Autumn regarded the room with pride. In fact, the whole house had become, in the last five days, a monument to cleanliness and order. Three girls from the town had been hired. They had been assured the master of the house was not in residence, and when he returned, they were also assured, his guests would keep his infamous temper in check. With their aid, Carrie and Autumn had worked feverishly, removing dustcovers, airing carpets and feather-bedding, polishing furniture and silver, and in general, preparing a house—one that had not been so prepared in a long time—for guests. Ornate moldings had been brushed, fretwork dusted, draperies retasseled. And decorations had been strung on every archway, fresh fruit arranged in bowls, mantels adorned with ribbons. It had been a titanic effort, but the house was a magnificent one and responded to a woman's loving ministrations. Vanessa Byron had pronounced the house "resplendent" as she toured the rooms. Autumn smiled at the recollection of her own and Carrie's self-congratulations as they at last presented their crowning glory—the Christmas tree—a splendid fir set in the entrance hallway. All three of them had immediately seen to its decoration. With bits of lace, pieces of costume jewelry, and some remembered trinkets hauled up from the cellar, they had managed to create a frothy winter jewel box in the center of the stately hall. And now, with the house sparkling, the decorations artfully displayed, the pea soup most assuredly a-bubble on the stove, there was little to do but wait for Dr. Byron and his guests. If the doctors did not throttle her first, they would surely approve her efforts on behalf of both the house and Mrs. Byron. Autumn shuddered involuntarily. She knew she had done the best for everyone, the only thing she could have done, and Mrs. Byron was now thriving, but . . . and it was a very large "but" . . . would the men approve?

Restless, Autumn went into the kitchen and took up a basket. Drawing on her shawl, she told Carrie that she was going to step outside and gather some pinecones for the dining room hearth.

"Can you get along without me for five minutes?" she asked Carrie.

"Not for five seconds," Carrie assured her with a broad smile. The other young ladies laughed. The bond of friendship that had developed between the women of Byron Hall was congenial, openhearted, and affectionate. They'd worked together and laughed together with equal energy.

As Autumn stepped outside the warm kitchen, the night encloaked her. It was cold and deeply hushed as a feathery snow began to fall. Autumn could smell the ocean. A light wind came up and ruffled her hair, and she resigned herself that she might have to redo her upsweep before the guests arrived. She surveyed the pearly opalescence of the garden and made her way to a pine tree in the distance. Before she reached it, however, she was aware of another presence. One of the stable boys? she wondered. And her heart tipped in her breast. Someone stepped into her path.

"You!" she said on a breath.

"Hello, little one," he greeted her. He held out a small package wrapped with tissue and twine. Autumn stared up at the gray-streaked beard, the curved pipe held securely in strong white teeth, the moonstruck twinkle of sea-glass blue eyes. "Will you take it to her?" he asked.

"To whom?" Autumn questioned him. But she already knew. Her heart fluttered as he took her hand and placed the gift in her palm.

"Thank you," he said, and his voice was a caress. Again, as before, the man was not threatening, only boldly determined. He turned then and strode away. Autumn's fingers closed on the crudely wrapped parcel, and she held it to her breast and watched as the man vanished in the thick, cold, deepening darkness.

A sudden resonance of sound broke the stillness of her thoughts. From the front of the house, Autumn heard the approach of horses up the drive, the magical jingle of sleigh bells, the quick bright evidence of arriving humanity. She gathered her composure and ran up the back steps and into the kitchen. Throwing down her basket and tearing off her shawl, she told Carrie that Dr. Byron and his guests had arrived.

"Oh, m'gawd," the woman responded, straightening her cap and brushing at her apron. The other girls tensed, but Carrie and Autumn murmured assurances to them as Carrie gave the soup a last stir and Autumn hastily checked her appearance in the tiny kitchen mirror. There would be no time to adjust the wild curls that tangled about her forehead and flushed cheeks. Already, the hollow reverberation of footsteps sounded on the wide sweep of the wooden front porch. Both women flew through the house to the front entry hall and nearly skidded to a halt at the massive door. It was opening even as they reached it. The great room erupted with buoyant life. Gay as larks, the guests, led by Dr. Byron, traipsed into the hall, brushing themselves, laughing, complaining good-naturedly about the cold and the length of the trip. Carrie and Autumn greeted them as individually as possible as the men handed over their scarves and greatcoats and top hats and the lady unwrapped herself from her long fur cloak. Autumn watched the singular female with awed disbelief; she was undoubtedly the most arresting woman she had ever encountered. She was tall, statelybreasted, and she had a lavish display of blue-black curls piled artfully atop her head, making her seem taller than she was. She had bright green eyes that were laughing and keen as knife points at the same time.

Antoinette Fraser responded indifferently as she was introduced to the two women who greeted her, then swept into the grand parlor. Autumn stood, nearly toppled by the weight of thick winter garments and watched the pocket doors close behind the lively withdrawal of the guests. Suddenly the great hall was empty. She glanced at Carrie briefly and in some consternation as grumbling, she made her bundled way to the entry closet. Together, laboriously, the two women hung the coats upon hooks and set the hats on stands that lined the top shelf.

"We'll brush 'em later," Carrie said hurriedly. "The fire's goin' and the brandy's been set out. I'll just get the tea and the hors d'oeuvres." She rushed off down the hall. Autumn glanced toward the closed pocket doors, more than mere oaken barriers muffling the sounds of gaiety from within. Her pale brows furrowed. She wondered for a fleeting moment what she'd expected of this homecoming. Near the gracefully curving staircase stood the Christmas tree, shimmering now in magnificent isolation. No one had even noticed it. Autumn shrugged off her own sense of isolation and headed for the back stairs. Surely Mrs. Byron had heard the voices. She would be anxious to join her guests.

"You look positively grumpy," said Vanessa as the younger woman entered her room. Whatever grumpiness Autumn had felt evaporated at the sight of that lovely woman, standing so regally, so confident in her newly found fine health. Her only concession to her recently acquired strength was her ivory walking stick, which she held but rarely leaned on.

Autumn smiled regretfully. "I suppose," she admitted, "I was just a little . . . disappointed by the homecoming. They didn't even notice our tree."

"And we worked so hard." Vanessa offered an almost mocking solemnity. She laughed and placed a gentle finger beneath Autumn's drooping chin. "Remember one thing, darling, we do what we do for ourselves alone. We must ever be content with our own thanks. If someone offers theirs, we are doubly blessed." Autumn attempted to absorb the new thought. "You wanted everyone to be impressed," Vanessa said kindly and with a small laugh. "That would have been most rewarding. But no one, apparently, was impressed. If it is any comfort," she added quietly, "I am most impressed—with you." Autumn looked up. "Just look at me," Vanessa said encouragingly. "Did you ever see a grander *grande dame*? And it's all your doing." She postured before the full-length cheval glass, and both women laughed. But

Autumn sobered in admiration as she studied the older woman's reflection. Her lustrous graying hair was piled becomingly and caught with tortoise shell combs. Her gown, high-necked and fastened with self buttons, draped her stately figure handsomely. Her luminous eyes, the same deep indigo of her gown, danced with intelligence and humor. "All this," she told her young companion, "I owe to you. You, and you alone, are responsible for the rebirth of that lady." She pointed with her stick to the majestic creature defined in the mirrored glass. She turned to see the flush of Autumn's cheeks and her demurring smile.

"All I did, Vanessa," ventured Autumn quietly, "was to make some adjustments in your treatment which I believed to be valid. I might add that I am aware those adjustments have no validity in medical circles."

"Are you practicing for the men?" asked Vanessa, laughing.

"I suppose I am," conceded Autumn. "But it is true that we are both likely to be soundly admonished when the facts come out."

"Let them admonish us," stated Vanessa with a lift of an elegant brow. "We mustn't care two pins. Let them perform their bloody medical miracles on somebody else; I have my own miracle maker." She reached out and touched a sweetly curved tress that clung to Autumn's cheek. "I shall not allow you the indulgence of humility, my darling Autumn. We shall tell those witch doctors downstairs what you've done for me. Let them rail and brawl. We'll sit quietly and be very proud of you."

Autumn smiled. "Shall we not . . . slant the truth a bit in the manner of our Miss Dickinson?"

"Well, for now. Just a bit."

"Vanessa," Autumn said seriously, "would you mind awfully if we didn't tell them right off about what I've done? It's only that," she added hastily, "I am not anxious to be reproved in front of . . . of . . . everyone." Autumn was thinking most specifically of that beautiful and proud lady who now graced the front parlor. She appeared, from Autumn's brief scrutiny, to be a lady of the world, sophisticated, cosmopolitan, and most likely schooled in clever disparagement. Autumn had no idea how she had perceived so much in that very brief moment of introduction, but she had. Perhaps it was the woman's lynx-eyed, almost predatory, examination of her that had aroused such an uncomplimentary impression. Perhaps it was the dismissive way the woman had tossed her gloves onto the pile of coats in Autumn's arms. Autumn had met such women, had even, in a sense, admired their essentially narrow power. Such conceit was a kind of thorny protection; though it might prick the sensibilities of some, it guarded the wearer and elevated her to an impenetrable ascendancy over the mere personal opinions of those to whom she felt superior. Autumn eyed the woman before her. Vanessa Byron had some of that conceit, but hers seemed born from within, not superimposed on a lesser presence. Autumn's ruminations were abruptly cut short as Carrie burst into the room.

Eyes widened, she said, "Dr. Byron wants to see you both. I told him I'd come up and get you. I didn't want him to know, for all the world, that you'd switched your rooms to the second floor." The last words were gasped. Carrie was still awed and unsettled by the fact that the ladies had taken over the second floor library and the adjoining chamber as their bedrooms. Her eye roved restively about the cheerful, book-lined chamber, tall windows adorning the lofting, delicately patterned walls. And, while she approved the transfer from those dingy third-story rooms, she shared Autumn's knowledge that the doctors would not approve.

"We shall be down presently, Carrie," said Vanessa Byron soothingly. "And thank you." The three women glanced at each other, knowing full well that the hour of judgment was at hand. They could delay, obscure, and withhold information for only so long. The truth would eventually seep out; truth, slanted or not, always does. And for all Vanessa's imperious assurance she, too, knew that, once discovered, there would be hell to pay for the insubordination that had taken place over the past four weeks at Byron Hall. Still, she smiled and waved Carrie off. Autumn took a moment to stand before the glass and smooth the curls from her cheeks, but Vanessa stopped her. "You look adorable. Remember that nothing, dear child, must be too perfect." She took Autumn's arm. In truth, Vanessa was looking forward to enjoying her grand entrance and the astonishment in the eyes of her son and her physician when they saw her—a whole and substantive woman for the first time in many years. "Let us go, Autumn," she said grittily. With a lift of her chin, her pearl-draped neck elongated gracefully, her shoulders drawn back, her dancing eyes on the path ahead, she made her way down the stairs. Carrie was waiting at the parlor doors, and with some pride, she swept them open, then drew them closed as the ladies entered. She could not check the small, triumphant smile that curved her lips as she very nearly skipped back to the kitchen.

Vanessa Byron advanced into the parlor on Autumn's arm and was not disappointed by the reaction she received; her son and her doctor were properly thunderstruck.

"Mrs. Byron," Dr. Beame said, gaping, "you look . . . well . . . very well, indeed."

"Mother," Cain said approaching her. "I can barely believe my eyes." Autumn relinquished Vanessa's arm to her son. She backed away from the general greetings. "This," Cain said, once he had kissed his mother's cheek, "is Miss Antoinette Fraser of New York." That lady stood and extended a hand.

"Mrs. Byron," she said in a cultured, though excessively breathy voice, Autumn reflected wryly, "I have waited just *forever* to meet you. Your son has mentioned you often and in such devoted terms. He is very naughty not to have brought us together sooner."

"And this," Cain continued, indicating a young gentleman, "is Mr. Damien Fraser, Antoinette's brother." That man stepped lazily to Vanessa and took her hand, bowing over it.

"How do you do, Mrs. Byron. It is a pleasure to be welcomed to your home, especially at such a festive time of year." Everything about the young man, though he was not yet twenty, spoke of a quiet, almost secret, composure. A flicker of a smile seemed to play on his lips constantly. Autumn was uneasily aware that, though he was greeting Vanessa, he was looking more than occasionally at her.

"I don't know if you've met Miss Thackeray," Vanessa said, noting where the lad's attention had settled.

"Antoinette and Damien," Cain assured his mother, "have already met Autumn. She is Mother's companion," he explained to the others. How unceremoniously Autumn's status had changed. From friend and miracle worker only moments ago, she had been reduced to hired companion. Still, she smiled and nodded at Antoinette's bare acknowledgment of her. She glanced hastily at Damien and then away. His smile had deepened imperceptibly as he offered Autumn a leisurely inspection. He most likely imagined her nothing more than a little serving girl to be plucked and played with, and then, appropriately impressed with his cosmopolitan charms, conquered, as it were, and tossed onto the cinder barrel. Well, the man had quite another thing coming, Autumn resolved. She sat primly on a nearby chair and folded her hands. She vowed she would not notice the young guest for the rest of the evening. She was hard-pressed to keep that vow, however, as his veiled scrutiny never seemed to leave her.

"I can hardly believe what I see, Mrs. Byron," Dr. Beame said. "I daren't allow myself too much optimism, however," he said with a hearty laugh.

Vanessa looked obliquely up into his eyes. For all his apparent delight in her metamorphosis, he studied her with a technician's dubious concern. "Perhaps," she said wryly, "you are expecting me to convulse and return to that broken, mad creature you left here some weeks ago." Her last words were clouded by disdain. Winslow Beame's eyes widened in astonishment.

"Why . . . heavens, Mrs. Byron," he groped, stunned by the lady's forthrightness. "I would not think of such a thing, I daresay."

"It's exactly what you were thinking, Winslow," returned Vanessa. She smiled toward Autumn who was, at the moment, wincing visibly.

"Now, Mother," soothed Cain anxiously, "Win wasn't thinking anything of the sort." He glanced apologetically about the room. "And we do have guests. We may wish to discuss this later." Antoinette Fraser's regard hung determinedly on an object far from Mrs. Byron, and even Damien's eyes shifted to the carpeted floor. "Carrie brought in tea a few moments ago," Cain continued. His onyx regard fell on Autumn as he wordlessly entreated her aid. "Would someone care to pour?" he asked.

"I should be honored," Autumn said hastily. Vanessa must consider her words carefully now, she reflected as she made her way to the sideboard. Her sense of irreverent fun needed to be checked now more than ever. Both doctors would naturally be inspecting her carefully for any signs of the returning disorder. Impiety and an indifference to accepted deportment were the first signs, as Vanessa herself had pointed out, of an unstable female mind. As Autumn passed among the guests with the tea tray, she worriedly eyed the older woman. It was one thing for the two of them to have a bit of fun at the expense of the rigid behavioral expectations of the day, but it was entirely another for Vanessa to dispense with propriety and mention publicly a very private, and less than seemly, matter. Such things as madness and "nervous disorders" were not pretty topics for discussion. Etiquette demanded a certain reticence. One did not say just anything that popped into one's head, or one might be considered, well . . . mad.

"Autumn is such a pretty name," said Antoinette Fraser as she idly stirred her tea. Autumn looked up, startled. She had not expected to be addressed and certainly not by the lordly Antoinette. Perhaps she had misjudged the lady.

"Why thank you." Autumn's gratitude was genuine and unguarded.

"However did your mother and daddy think of it?" Before Autumn could answer, she continued. "It is my experience that the working classes seem to come up with such colorful cute and childlike names. I had a little maid once—a darling girl, really, though she did attempt to steal a pair of gloves from me and I was forced to dismiss her—whose name was Utica, like the city. Everyone called her Utie. Isn't that cute? And then, once, we had a buttery girl whose name was—" she paused, pondering prettily. "Now I must get this right. Oh, yes," she said brightly. "Her name was Wisteria Mae. Remember her, brother? Her friends called her 'Misty'." Antoinette laughed indulgently. "It was rather a reverse combination of her two names, don't you know. And she was such a love! She was always ready to just pop up and help with any old thing that needed doing, just like your little Autumn." Her gaze, green and glittering, drifted to Cain Byron. Autumn set down the tray, now unburdened, more heavily than was necessary, onto the sideboard, and Antoinette's eyes lifted in studiously adorable bemusement.

"Actually," Autumn said, turning to the guests and dimpling her sweetest smile, "my mother is . . . a Gypsy. Oh, mummy is such a piece of work! You shall meet her one day. In naming me, she followed an old Hungarian custom. Once a lady has given birth, she goes to the door of her tent and looks outside, review- ing the scene before her. Then she names the child for the first thing she sees. As it turns out, once freed from the throes of childbirth, mummy looked outside and saw the most beautiful autumn morn. And that's how I got my name." The words were said with a small challenge. Childbirth, like madness, was an un- welcome topic in polite society. Antoinette stared at her blankly. Vanessa burst into appreciative laughter, followed by Cain and then, reluctantly, Winslow Beame. Damien offered an amiable chortle. It was only his sister who remained unmoved.

"May we assume," Antoinette asked stonily, "that the story is a fantasy?"

Autumn returned to her chair. "It is," she said easily.

"My," commented Antoinette, "aren't you the original one."

"That she is, Nettie," Damien reported. Everyone glanced in his direction.

"My name is not *Nettie*, brother, and don't you dare call me that." The lad swiped at the feathery fuzz that decorated his upper lip and smiled.

"Would you mind, Dr. Byron," he asked as he stood up, "if I poured myself more brandy? This rather stately gathering has suddenly become a party." Without awaiting the approval of his host, Damien moved to the sideboard. Setting down his cup and saucer and still smiling in Autumn's direction, he poured himself a brandy. His sister eyed him darkly.

Returning her attention to Cain, she said with forced brightness, "You must remember that lady I introduced to you at the Monarch Social Club, Cain darling. She makes up stories like that—for a living, if you can imagine such a thing. Her name is Mrs. Eldora Weaver and she pens the most extraordinary penny romances, drivel really, for the masses." Antoinette's gaze drifted to include Vanessa Byron and Dr. Beame. "She comes from nothing, but she fancies herself a descendant of Miss Jane Austen of England," she continued, lowering her tone. "I shouldn't boast of such an aberrant background, if I were she."

"Nor would I," Winslow Beame agreed, feathering his chestnut colored mustache reflectively. "It is a well-known medical fact that intellect in a lady is a dangerous thing. Add to that imagination and you have a lethal combination. Miss Austen had too much imagination and too cutting an intellect for her own good. She died, as I remember, quite young, and," he stated with pointed significance, "—unmarried."

"However did Mrs. Weaver get into the Monarch?" asked Vanessa with wide-gazed innocence.

"I believe," replied Antoinette seriously, "she *married* into it. Her husband is the very well-known architect, Mr. Jacob Weaver, don't you know. And, for all their wealth and social status, they are now living on the West Side of the city with all the musicians and painters and even actors. How dreary! It is no wonder they are childless."

"I have treated Dorie Weaver for a number of years," stated Winslow Beame. "And, without breaking any confidences, I shall tell you that I have firmly advised her to give her indomitable imagination a rest. In a female, a most dangerous thing—imagination." He glanced fleetingly at Autumn. That young woman stared boldly back.

Imagination and intellect, she thought, lacing her fingers more tightly in her lap. *Dangerous.* She almost laughed, but she knew that she was on dangerous ground as it was. She regarded her employer through veiled lashes, wondering what he had thought of the exchange that had just taken place. Surprisingly, he was looking at her, and the smile in his eyes was threatening the hard line of his mouth. Autumn knew there would be no more smiles for her once the facts came out about Mrs. Byron's treatment, and so she reveled in this temporary approval. She smiled back. At that moment Carrie drew open the doors and announced that dinner was served. Dr. Beame immediately stepped to Vanessa Byron and offered his arm. With Cain escorting Antoinette, Autumn had little choice but to accept Damien Fraser's companionship.

"You are, I take it, sitting down with us, little Gypsy," he said. Autumn hid a smile and nodded.

She noted Antoinette's arched inquiry and accepted that it must seem strange to such a refined lady that a servant should sit at table with honored guests. "Mrs. Byron insisted, I fear," she offered lamely. Still, despite her uncertainties about the arrangement, it was with a sense of triumph that she took Damien's arm.

"You know," said he, as they proceeded to the dining room, "I was not looking forward to this holiday, but I think, dear improbable servant, I am going to enjoy it after all."

"Did you say improbable?" Autumn inquired.

"Oh, yes, Miss Thackeray. You are quite the patrician, if delicious little *bonne bouche*." Autumn glanced briefly at the questionable compliment. She decided to be generous.

"Mr. Fraser," she said, dimpling a smile, "I have heard it is quite impossible to amuse a *bonne bouche*. You, it would seem, have achieved the impossible."

❦

Dinner was over, and Vanessa rose from her chair, begging the pardon of the men. She led the two younger women to her parlor for after dinner coffee.

"Do join us soon, gentlemen. We shall simply die without you," Antoinette chimed out, then glanced at Autumn. "Are you coming, too, Miss Thackeray?" she asked sweetly.

"Yes," said Autumn distractedly. She noted that Carrie, who was already serving the men, seemed a bit rattled. "Why don't you go on, ladies, I shall get our coffee." Carrie glanced at her gratefully, and Autumn went through the serving door to the kitchen.

"Such a helpful child," she heard Antoinette croon to Vanessa as they made their way across the hall.

"'Such a *helpful child*,'" Autumn repeated in a syrupy burlesque of Antoinette's so-called cultured voice. "'Such a helpful *child*.'"

She slammed cups down onto a tray and filled a silver pot with coffee. The serving girls looked on, a bit awestricken at Autumn's uncustomary show of temper.

"Now, Miss Autumn," said Carrie as she backed into the kitchen with a tray loaded with the remnants of the meal, "what's got you so worked up? If it's that tinsel-hearted Lady Jane out there, then I'm ashamed of y'." She offered an arched smile. "Surely you ain't jealous of such a creature."

Autumn took the time for a long, calming exhalation. "I am sorry," she apologized generally. "You see, once I was quite good at exactly what Miss Fraser has been doing out there for the last two hours."

"And just what has she been doin'?" asked Carrie. "Why she's just been playin' at bein' female and gettin' everybody's attention in the bargain. But that ain't the kind of attention *I* want. And you shouldn't want it either, Miss Autumn. You're too smart for that." She waggled an imaginary fan and minced about the room. The serving girls laughed as they unloaded the tray.

"Oh, Mrs. Inman," said one of them, "you do that real good."

"Anybody c'n do it, even you." She grabbed the girl's hand and positioned it on her hip. "Now," continued Carrie, "take the other hand and wiggle it under your chin. Now flap your lashes, swing your hips, and curlicue up your lips into the tightest, brightest smile you can imagine. Now," she said imperiously, "walk on your tiptoes." With the girl's efficient rendering of a *femme fatale*, all the women burst into giggles. Carrie turned at last to Autumn. "Now you do it, Miss Autumn, and see how much better it makes you feel." Through her amusement Autumn regarded Carrie warmly.

"Touché," she said softly.

"To-what?" asked Carrie.

"It means," replied Autumn, "you have made your point. And a very exacting point it is, too, Carrie. If you don't watch yourself, you will be accused of having imagination *and* intellect."

"I don't know what you're talkin' about, Miss Autumn," said Carrie laughing, "but I'll tell you this; I believe you was good at all that flirtin' and fussin' over the boys—I was good at it, too. But I'm hopin' neither of us was *that* good. There's names for the likes of that one," she added pointedly, with a jerk of her thumb toward the parlor.

"I must admit," Autumn conceded with a smile, "I was never quite as extravagantly female as Miss Fraser is."

"I think," said one of the serving girls shyly, "you're twice as pretty as her. I had a peek at her in the dining room," she added confidentially, "and I sure wouldn't like to get her mad at me." Autumn smiled warmly at the girl. Her thoughts were interrupted, however, by the scraping of chairs in the dining room.

"Oh, Lord," she said, "the men are finished with their brandy and cigars and I haven't even served the ladies." She hastily finished arranging the tray.

"Is this anything?" asked one of the girls. She had lifted from the counter the little package that Autumn had received earlier from the stranger outside. Autumn stared at it in bemusement.

"It was given me by someone in the yard."

"Who?" asked Carrie.

"I'm not sure," said Autumn, "but he said it was for . . . it was a gift. He asked if I would present it for him. I suppose I should bring it in."

"Probably one of the stablemen," Carrie offered. Autumn decided against telling her it was the same man who had followed her home; she dared not risk rekindling the woman's wrath over that incident, and so she only shrugged and agreed that it could have been one of the stablemen. The girl put the little gift on the tray. "We'll finish clearin'," said Carrie, and Autumn moved off with the tray.

Upon her entrance into Mrs. Byron's parlor, the gentlemen stood and Damien approached her to help with her burden. Antoinette was answering a previous question put to her by Mrs. Byron.

"New York City is indeed an exciting place to live, but as everywhere, the servant problem is growing daily." Her green gaze slid to Autumn, who was becoming a bit wearied by the constant attacks. Antoinette went on. "People take no pride in serving others these days. Everyone imagines themselves too good for domestic work. There is a growing population of middle-class families in the city who will simply not train their children for service. All one can find these days are little brown guttersnipes off the boats—and you know they are impossible to train. What the future holds, I shudder to imagine."

Autumn brought coffee to the ladies. "I am terribly sorry it is late," she murmured. "Everyone was so busy in the kitchen." Antoinette smiled thinly.

"Are we just a bit understaffed?" she asked Autumn condolingly.

Vanessa Byron laughed as she put in, "Not understaffed so much as overwhelmed. We haven't enjoyed the company of guests in this house in many years, Miss Fraser. I'm afraid we were not quite prepared for my son's announcement that he was bringing company home—and *New York City* company at that." She stirred her coffee tranquilly. "We know that you and your brother are used to the best of everything. I only hope you can put up with our inadequacies for a while. Our little efforts are sincere, if not always completely sufficient. We are just country folk, after all." Antoinette's eyes widened, and Autumn averted her gaze. Was there just the slightest quaking of Autumn's shoulders? Was she hiding amusement?

"Actually, Mrs. Byron," said Antoinette through her embarrassment, and with a narrowed perusal of Autumn's slender back, "I was not criticizing the excellent accommodations of your household. My comments concern the indifference of servants, not the luckless circumstances of well-intentioned hostesses. We, after all, are only the hapless victims of a rather distressing social phenomenon."

"It is quite true," commented Winslow Beame expansively. He accepted coffee from Autumn and barely looked at her. He, at least, was unaware of Antoinette's very specific target. "We rich must be ever wary of the rising influence of the working classes," he continued. "My God, it strikes me that their confrontational potential smacks of the worst excesses of the French Revolution. We all know," he said solemnly as he stirred his coffee, "what that little uprising led to. A very good king lost his head in the bargain."

"A queen did, too," offered Autumn.

"I beg your pardon, Miss Thackeray?" Dr. Beame inquired, irritated at the interruption.

"A queen lost her head in the French Revolution," Autumn repeated. She smiled generally before allowing her gaze to rest on Antoinette. "It was said she had no sympathy for the underclass and so they chopped off her head." She glanced serenely at her employer, who had, it seemed, been studying her throughout the evening. And, as always, a smile lurked just beneath the surface of his expression. But for his almost wordless composure, he might have laughed and even been easy with her. He, however, Autumn reminded herself, had other thoughts. He was no doubt anxious to discuss Vanessa's recovery and hear some explanation for it. Autumn glanced at Damien, who was still perusing her, but his seemed a harder sentiment. Damien Fraser might laugh *at* someone but never with them. Winslow Beame regarded her with simple derision.

"You have effectively supported my point, Miss Thackeray," he returned narrowly. "A simple love of luxury brought the wretched Marie to a violent end. And she wasn't even French. It is a frightening thing when our ladies cannot enjoy their little pleasures—clothes and jewels and leisurely gossip and such— without being accused of excess."

"I think her pleasures might have been more acceptable had she not stepped on the bones of the poor to accomplish them," returned Autumn.

Winslow lowered his gaze in a pointed display of concern. "I do wonder where you picked up such information."

"About the French Revolution?" asked Autumn.

"Indeed."

"Well . . . I'm not sure. I suppose in a book."

Beame shook his head sadly. "Why would a pretty young girl want to read about such a bloody and mean-spirited historical event?" he asked rhetorically. "As I've told many of my women patients, books are evil things in the hands of those who have not the capacity to understand their messages." Autumn decided not to intrude on his thick despairing silence. She glanced at Vanessa, who was having difficulty hiding her amusement, and recalled the present that had been left.

"Before I forget," Autumn said, "I was given a package earlier." She picked up the small tissue and twine wrapped present. "A gentleman left it."

"Who?" asked Cain, his brow furrowing.

"Carrie," Autumn replied hastily, "suggested it was one of the stablemen."

"Oh, yes," said Cain Byron, visibly relieved, "the men are often generous this time of year."

"He wanted me to . . . present it. Why don't you open it, Mrs. Byron?" She brought the package to Vanessa and placed it in her palms. A moment of knowing certainty passed between them. As Vanessa slowly unwrapped the gift, a visible shudder passed through her stately frame. She held up the offering for all to see. It was a snow globe. Inside was a lighthouse with tiny shells strewn about on a little beach. She shook it gently and snow swirled and sparkled about the miniature environment.

"It is," she said softly, "a most lovely remembrance." Tears came to her eyes and fell on her cheeks. "It is . . . a wonder." There was silence in the room as everyone watched Vanessa. She offered a smile to each of her guests. "I am fine," she assured all of them, "just deeply touched."

"And probably very tired," offered Dr. Beame, once again the courtly physician.

"Yes, Mother," agreed Cain, "it has been a big day for all of us. I must insist that you retire immediately."

"I shall escort her up, Dr. Byron," said Autumn quickly, but Cain stopped her with a glare. She was not anxious that Vanessa's recently altered location be revealed, especially in light of Dr. Beame's comment on the evils of books, but there seemed no hope of delaying that discovery. Dr. Beame was already taking Vanessa's arm.

"You," said Cain, "will remain with me." He stood and rang for Carrie as Winslow Beame helped Vanessa to her feet. Cain looked to the other guests. "Carrie will see you to your rooms." As the evening seemed officially over, everyone shifted and rose from their seats.

"I, for one, welcome the suspension of our conversation," said Antoinette. "I am quite exhausted from the day's journey, not to mention the conversation regarding the killing of queens named Antoinette." She stretched delicately and glanced at Autumn, offering her a small, sidewise smile. "It seems, Miss Thackeray, that you are some distance from relief." Touching Cain's cheek, she bid him goodnight, then took her brother's arm, and at Carrie's entrance, the two of them withdrew.

"I shall be back momentarily, Cain," said Winslow Beame, as he exited with Vanessa on his arm. Vanessa and Autumn exchanged glances. Dr. Beame was about to make the first discovery that would displease him, Autumn reflected.

"Are you amused by something?" Cain Byron inquired, lighting a small cigar.

"No, sir," said Autumn in reply, "I don't believe so."

"I detected the beginning of a smile," he observed. Had she been about to smile, Autumn wondered? Perhaps she was just a bit amused by the thought of the confrontation that was about to ensue between Dr. Beame and the now formidable Vanessa.

"Actually, sir," she said seriously, "there is something you should know." She took a breath and licked at her lips. "You see, it's only that . . . you see, your mother and I decided, in your absence, and as she was feeling so much better, that, quite frankly, the rooms we occupied on the third floor were so depressing that we removed ourselves to the second floor." Autumn wondered if she had made any sense at all. Cain's onyx gaze riveted her.

"And this amuses you?" he asked.

"Only in the sense," Autumn admitted, "that Dr. Beame had not ordered your mother placed elsewhere and I fear that his reaction will be quite harsh. And Mrs. Byron is not one to accept a scolding without some . . . dispute."

"You are so right, Miss Thackeray," Cain agreed and reminded Autumn that his mother's disputatious nature had been the reason that she had become so ill. He added that he was indeed anxious to believe in her recovery. "In truth, however," he maintained, "her problems were so severe that this turnabout in so short a time strikes me as curious. And then," he continued, pacing before the fire, "there is the matter of that little gift you presented this evening." He turned to Autumn and his figure against the flames reminded her of the portrait in his parlor of that stern and terrible patriarch, his father. "Where did you get it?"

"As I mentioned," Autumn reminded him, "a gentleman gave it me."

"What *gentleman?*"

"He came into the garden. I did not recognize him, but he seemed a pleasant soul."

"Did he say the present was for Mrs. Byron particularly?"

"No," Autumn answered, recalling that he hadn't needed to. Cain reverted to a thoughtful silence. "Dr. Byron," Autumn put in, "is there something I should know?"

"There is nothing you should know, Miss Thackeray." A muscle worked in his jaw and again there was the silence. "It is only that," he resumed, "my mother's struggle has been a valiant one. I should hate to think it was in vain. You see, I worry that—"

"And you have every right to worry, sir," boomed the voice of Winslow Beame. He entered the room, and his hard glare bent on Autumn. "You were charged, young miss, with the care of a very sick woman," he stormed, "and you have failed miserably in your duties." He faced Cain and pointed an avenging finger at Autumn. "This person," he ground out, "has taken it upon her-self—her *uninformed* self—to allow your mother to relocate her-self to a most disturbing environment—in the middle of the house, books strewn everywhere. It was not for nothing, Cain, that she was moved to the third floor in the first place. You will remember—"

"I remember, Win," said Cain Byron. They both looked at Autumn.

"The room was so bare," she offered.

"That is exactly the point!" Beame exploded, advancing on her. Autumn was sickened by the narrow focus of his fury. "It is not for the likes of you to question my method, girl, nor any doc-tor's method. There are prescribed treatments for women in Mrs. Byron's condition."

"But her condition changed, Dr. Beame."

His mouth screwed into a sneer. There was danger here. Autumn backed from him. "That is my judgment to make, not yours," he grated, following her retreat. "How dare you?" He stood over her. "This insolence is not to be tolerated." They both looked at Cain. That man stood quietly, watching the confrontation.

"She is right, Win," he said. Beame stiffened.

"How dare *you*, Cain?" There was a hard silence. "Am I to take it," Beame finally inquired, "that you are siding with a hired ser-vant against your mother's own physician?"

"The fact is, Win, an amazing transformation has occurred. I don't intend to fire Autumn until I learn how it came about."

"Do you mean to tell me, Cain Byron—*Dr.* Byron—that you would allow yourself to be influenced by this . . . chattel?" Autumn's own gaze narrowed and glistered menacingly.

"I am not chattel, Dr. Beame," she said, pent rage releasing itself. "I am a human being. I shall tell you something about Mrs. Byron's recovery and how I accomplished it. You had her living— or dying really—under the influence of sleeping powders and spirits, tucked away in that tomb on the third floor. She was a godforsaken ghost of a woman when I met her, and realizing the cause, I took it upon myself to remove it." Autumn advanced on the two men. "Like it or not, Mrs. Byron has recovered from your unholy doctoring. She is not receiving the benefits of your treatment, nor will she while I am present in this house. And if anyone imagines they might remove me they will have to step on the bones of Vanessa Byron. I am under *her* protection now." Winslow Beame gasped audibly. It was a death rattle.

"Am I to understand you discontinued the medication I prescribed?"

"You are, sir," Autumn returned. "I have weaned her from that garbled botch of drugs and powders that held her poor mind and body captive. She is no longer your lethargic, insensible, sluggish little patient. For better or worse, Vanessa Byron is an open-eyed, sometimes troublesome, often singular person, just like the rest of us. And I shall tell you this," she pointed her own avenging finger, "if you or anyone dares to interfere, if you attempt to take away her uniqueness as a person, I shall stop you, my man, in any way available to me." With a peremptory glance at an apparently impassive Cain Byron, Autumn straightened, swung away from the two of them, and left the room.

Once in her room, trembling wildly, Autumn sought the comfort of her writing desk. She drew a sheet of paper from a drawer and took pen in hand. The time had come, she realized, to finally confide in Isabel and seek her council. Autumn knew she had reached a point of turning—or of no return. She had challenged the very foundations of male authority. She did not know what the consequences would be or whether she would have the strength to carry out her threats and promises to the men. Isabel had taught her independence and esteem for the person she was, but even her mother's example had not prepared Autumn for direct confrontation with the established traditions of an unforgiving societal prerogative. Even Isabel had never locked horns with the men. A knock on Autumn's door startled her, and she looked up uncertainly. She was not emotionally prepared for another stand.

Still, she said, "Come in." The door opened and Cain Byron stepped across the threshold. With a hard click he closed the door behind him. He stood just inside the room, perusing her with more interest, she perceived, than anger. Autumn stood slowly. Cain leaned back, his wide shoulders effectively covering the width of the door. Autumn studied him, wondering whether he was intending to cuff her or verbally reprove her; either, it seemed, would be done passionlessly, for he appeared at the moment unwilling or incapable of expressing emotion. He pushed himself from the door and crossed the room to a tall window. Staring out into the black night, his reflection, tall, wide-shouldered, and proud, gazed back at both of them.

"I pride myself on being a reasonable man, Miss Thackeray," he said quietly. "Throughout my adult life some dark corner of my mind has always told me how things ought to be." He turned to her and the brooding reflection turned its back. "Something remarkable happened here tonight. I am speaking not only of my mother's recovery, but of something else, too. Somehow, a light has been shed on that dark corner of my mind. What *ought* to be has changed. You have asserted yourself in ways I don't understand and should not have tolerated. And yet, Miss Thackeray, I have tolerated it. Something is telling me I ought to tolerate it."

"I have not acted without compunction or deep consideration and concern. Your mother's well-being means a great deal to me. In a way—I know it will sound odd for me to say it—I love her. And I flatter myself that she returns my affection."

"It does not sound at all odd, Miss Thackeray. I have heard that love is a much underrated remedy for many ailments."

"I have heard that, too," she said. She wondered that this doctor, trained at the best medical school in the country, would espouse such an unorthodox philosophy of healing. He turned again to the window.

"I find it necessary to mention one more thing. Winslow Beame has demanded an apology." Autumn fought a compelling impulse to refuse. Her fleeting outrage became puzzlement, however, for her employer had not demanded the apology, but only mentioned that Dr. Beame had. She battled with herself for some moments.

"I shall apologize," she said, "for acting the shrew in the parlor tonight. I should not have raised my voice. That, of course, is not the apology Dr. Beame demands, at least not the full one, but it is all I am prepared to offer." Cain Byron turned to face her once again.

There was a twinkle in his onyx gaze that reminded Autumn of his mother's. "For now," he said, "he must be satisfied with that."

Chapter 8

Christmas morning was celebrated with a fox hunt. Autumn had been invited along, but she had demurred, disapproving as she was of hunting down and killing little furry creatures. Instead, she chose to spend the morning with Vanessa. They sat across from each other in Vanessa's cheery, book-lined bedchamber. Autumn had given her a heavy shawl knitted of rug yarn, and they both laughed, for the idea of it was a holdover from Vanessa's bedridden days.

"You really don't need this," Autumn said, as Vanessa held up the intricately designed but bulky garment.

"It is very pretty," Vanessa assured her. "And who really knows what one will need, or will not need, in the future." Autumn studied her reflectively.

"What does your future hold, Vanessa?"

"I do not honestly know, Autumn. But, I can tell you one thing: I shall not stand for another moment of scrutiny by that officious Winslow Beame. If he counts the pulses of my heart one more time, or asks me one more question about my feelings I

shall scream." Again both women laughed. It was desultory laughter, however, and soon—so very soon—they were eyeing each
other dispiritedly. "If he really knew what I was feeling," Vanessa
said quietly, "the poor man would have a stroke." She glanced
quickly away.

"*I* wouldn't have a stroke," Autumn told her, "if you told *me*
what you were feeling."

"I wish I could," responded Vanessa earnestly, leaning toward
her friend. "Oh, how I wish I could." Autumn looked into her
eyes, offering release.

"Does it have to do with the little gift you received last night?"
There was a pause during which Autumn knew the older woman
was deciding. "It isn't fair that you must bear this burden alone,
Vanessa," she encouraged.

"Fair," repeated Vanessa harshly. "What is fair, my darling
Autumn? Microbes grow on babies' faces. Is that fair? The universe is *notoriously* unfair." She stood suddenly, pressing her
hands together, entwining her long fingers, and turning her
regard upward. Tears coursed down her cheeks. Autumn went to
her immediately, taking her hands and pressing them to her own
breast.

"Sometimes," she said solemnly, "we must make do with what
the universe decides, Vanessa, but in the end it is really up to us.
We *can* manage what seems unmanageable. We are not powerless,
you know."

"I know," conceded Vanessa, bowing her head. Autumn offered her hanky, which Vanessa accepted gratefully. "I have never
been one to acquiesce to the vagaries of fortune without protest,
Autumn. It is only . . . in this case . . ." Her voice trailed off. She
smiled as she dabbed at her tears. "You mustn't imagine that I

have fallen back into my hopeless, helpless despair, love. Please forgive me."

"There is nothing to forgive, Vanessa." She led them back to their chairs. "I suppose now, with the men back, certain . . . circumstances seem to be replaying themselves." Vanessa nodded tiredly. "But that is temporary," Autumn assured her. "In the meantime," she added with a wry smile, "I shall not ask you again about your feelings. I am becoming quite as tiresome as Dr. Beame."

"He was hard on you last night, was he not?" commented Vanessa.

"I don't believe he was any harder on me than I was on him," Autumn returned, forcing lightness. "After all, I defied the very foundations of his authority. Still, he sincerely believes that his treatment, and no other, is the reason for your recovery—or so he says. *I* believe," continued Autumn with a piquant dip of her pale lashes, "I shook his confidence, and in the bargain, may have given our arrogant New York City doctor something to think about."

Vanessa laughed softly. "I have heard that's what Gypsies do." Autumn lifted her brows.

"Gypsies?"

"Gypsies. Free spirits, anyone who doesn't follow the rules. They defy convention. They give people something to think about."

"A silly joke," said Autumn, lowering her eyes, half ashamed at her impulsiveness the previous evening.

"Cain enjoyed it."

"Did he?" asked Autumn, looking up. There was a pause.

"Yes," said Vanessa thoughtfully, "he did." She searched

Autumn's countenance for several moments. "You care very much what Cain thinks, don't you."

"Of course, Vanessa. He is your son and my employer—"

"I mean as a man."

"I don't really know him as a man."

"Yes you do, Autumn," Vanessa said softly. "Cain has been touched by your presence in this house, and you sense that."

"And how could you know such a thing?" asked Autumn, attempting playfulness. "Are you a Gypsy, too?"

"Only a watchful mother. I fear I am not in your class." They laughed together companionably. Finally, as the younger woman's laughter waned, Vanessa resumed. "I will not press you, dear Autumn. We seem to be causing each other all sorts of discomfort today. Instead, I shall ask you to read what is in my future."

Autumn extended her hand playfully. Her eyes closed and her voice became low and modulated as she said, "Cross my palm with silver, wealthy lady, and I shall tell you the secrets of the ages." To her surprise, Autumn felt the cold weight of something in her hand. She opened her eyes and looked down. In her palm lay a small silver band with a turquoise stone in a molded setting. She looked up. Vanessa smiled.

"You wanted silver, Gypsy woman. That is the only silver I own." Her smile deepened. "Keep it, Autumn dear. I've wanted to give you something, and that is a little treasure of mine." Autumn slipped it onto her middle finger, for it was too big for her ring finger. "It is a Caribbean stone, given me by a friend—a very dear friend."

"Then you must keep it, Vanessa."

"No. I want you to wear it. It is time for me to part with it."

Gazing down on the exotic ring, Autumn murmured, "It is

lovely." She lifted her regard, and said seriously, "I shall wear it with pleasure and reverence, for I have the feeling it means a great deal to you." Vanessa lay her head back against the tufted chair in which she sat.

"Oh, yes," she said softly, "a great deal. Once it represented every dream I ever imagined. But dreams are the province of the young. And I am not young, Autumn." She lifted the little snow globe from the table beside her and stirred its contents with a small revolution of her hand. The snowflakes inside swirled across the sand and obscured the tiny lighthouse. "What have dreams to do with me?"

వ§ళ

Autumn made her way down to the kitchen to clear up the dishes from Vanessa's breakfast tray. She was disturbed and dejected over the older woman's turn of mood. In the first flush of her recovery, Vanessa had revealed an optimism and a buoyancy of character which Autumn perceived was the woman's true nature. Now, she had descended into a pervading depression. Autumn had imagined her in sterling, young middle age, presiding at parties, strolling though the town greeting friends, attending the theater. But there had been no indication that any of those possibilities interested Vanessa. There seemed an abiding sadness in her that Autumn resolved to explore. Perhaps, she reflected with some pique, her observation of the morning was true. Perhaps the presence of the men had dampened Vanessa's spirits. Dr. Winslow Beame, with his dire attentions, could surely drag any woman into the depths of pessimism. His solicitations were filled not so much with concern but with foreboding.

He'd warned Autumn, in the midst of her apology to him earlier that day, that Mrs. Byron was weak and susceptible to fluctuations of mood. "Didn't you see," he asked, "how she was affected by that silly novelty gift? A simple little favor made of glass sent her into a pensive melancholia. This is female neurasthenia at its worst. Her hysteria has caused a weakening of her constitution," Beame had told her. "In your ignorance, young miss, you say she is cured. I, as a man of medicine, say the cure has just begun. We cannot be too careful. There is no telling what dangerous or even disgusting path this illness may take. One must learn," said Winslow Beame with lordly gravity, "to follow orders without question or the necessity of interpretation." This, Autumn supposed, referred to her rearing in a privileged home. He had also suggested hotly that she learn to curb her tongue and her temper. Her behavior toward him had been most high-handed and, more importantly, he lectured, unladylike. All these comments, though irritating and unnecessarily dismal, remained with Autumn through the morning. While she did not believe for a moment that Vanessa Byron was heading for "dangerous" or "disgusting" behavior patterns, Autumn did realize that something profound had once befallen the woman. This event, whatever it had been, had caused the men to deem her mentally ill—or at least unconcerned with convention, rebellious, and willful—and it had caused Dr. Beame to prescribe the abominable treatment that had savaged Vanessa's very soul. He could do it again, Autumn thought with a shudder. Winslow Beame could, conceivably, with his convoluted medical terminology and urgent doomsday predictions, turn Vanessa once more into a wasted spectre of a human being. Doctors were doing it every day. Women in their care were being ravaged, body and soul, by the medical profession with society's blessing. There was a bright spot in Autumn's thinking; Cain Byron would not again give his blessing to such treatment. Winslow Beame would have a powerful adversary in Cain. Of this Autumn was certain. Last night he had proven himself an advocate for both his mother and for her. That was a comfort, a blessing not to be discarded. In this world of men and their arbitrary rules concerning women's behavior, male advocacy could be an important tool. In that sense, Vanessa's earlier pronouncement was true. Autumn did care what Cain Byron thought. She cared very much that he approved her handling of his mother's recovery. She cared that Cain Byron was willing to concede that in some way Autumn had made a difference in their lives.

She looked up from her work to find Damien Fraser just inside the entrance to the kitchen.

"Lost in thought, little Gypsy?" he asked blandly.

Autumn smiled apologetically. "I was, sir," she answered. She quirked her brows at him. "Weren't you off with the others, hunting down that poor little fox?"

"I was," he replied. "But, like you, I am not all that enthralled with the chase. Actually," he said, drawing a fluted glass from behind his back, "I only attend these fox hunts because they give you champagne for breakfast." He brushed a tangle of light, feathery tresses from his pale forehead. "Do you know where they keep it?"

"The champagne?" Autumn inquired.

"The champagne," he affirmed with a thin smile. Autumn divined that he'd had quite enough spirits for one morning and told him that she did not, in fact, know where the wine was kept. It was a lie, of course, but a worthy one. Already she was breaching

Dr. Beame's suggestion that she free herself from interpreting the requests of her "betters." "Ah, well," Damien said with a small sigh, "I suppose I shall have to wait for lunch." He stepped forward and placed the glass on the wooden table that separated them. As he did so, he leaned forward, resting his weight on his hands. "I should like to pluck you, little Gypsy flower," he said thoughtfully.

"Would you?" Autumn remarked, turning away and pumping water into the iron sink. The wine, she thought, had gone to the man's head. "Well, I am afraid, sir, that I am not interested in being . . . 'plucked' by you or anyone, for that matter."

"Why not?" asked Damien, feigning affront. "Am I not the handsomest of men?" Autumn nodded and smiled as the young man struck a classical pose.

"You are, good sir."

"I am also rich. I could take you away from all this." He waved an arm, taking in the entirety of the kitchen. Offering her a cocked perusal, he continued, "You are used to something better than servitude, I perceive." Autumn lowered her gaze.

"That is why you referred to me as an 'improbable' servant."

"It is," returned Damien seriously. "I know quality when I see it, and you, Miss Autumn, are quality personified. I suppose," he added thoughtfully, "that is why my big sister is jealous of you."

"Jealous," said Autumn, lifting her pale brows. "Antoinette jealous? Of me? I cannot credit such a notion."

"Credit it well, for jealous she is."

"How could you possibly have come to such a conclusion?" asked Autumn, rolling up her sleeves in anticipation of washing the dishes.

"Antoinette," said that lady's brother, "is an arrogant vixen in the best of circumstances; she holds herself above all females in the art of seducing a man. But when she's jealous she positively exudes a siren song. I've seen it before." Autumn slipped into an apron and tied it.

"Have you?" she asked, turning to the sink full of dishes.

"Indeed. It goes something like this," he said, pacing, his pale poetic face intent. "She becomes as alluring a creature as any Lorelei. She is helpless, awestruck, passionately trusting in a man's protection. She hangs on his every word, his every action, as though she will accept a cuff or a kiss with equal gratitude. She is docile, compliant, satisfied merely to stand in the glorious presence of a glorious male. She is, in short, every man's ideal woman. She becomes irresistible."

"With all that effort," remarked Autumn wryly, "the huntress deserves her prey, especially," she added more thoughtfully, "if the prey is foolish enough to be dazzled by such an obvious trap."

"But the men don't know it's a trap, you see. Just like sailors on the ocean, they imagine that distant chimera, that longed-for ideal to be not a trap but a haven."

"Then they are sorely misinformed," stated Autumn, tiring of the game. She sponged off her dishes and, pumping mechanically, rinsed them under the spout. "In any event, Mr. Fraser, if your sister has her sites set on Cain Byron, it seems to me she has a right. They have had a long-standing relationship as I understand it. And she has no reason to be jealous of the likes of me. As you point out, she is every man's dream."

"But her charms are false, and yours are not," Damien said, striding to her. Autumn looked up in surprise. Damien stood above her. "You are a perfect May-time blossom, trembling 'neath the morning dew. Antoinette is a lushly ornamented tropical bloom—with poison at its center."

"Oh, come now, Mr. Fraser," scolded Autumn. "Is that any way to talk about your sister?"

"It is the only way I know how to talk about her. Wait and watch, little Gypsy. Dr. Byron has been praising you all morning to Dr. Beame, and Antoinette is irritated to her bones. She will attempt to destroy you." Autumn moved away from the sink and took a towel from a hook.

"I am afraid she has chosen the wrong competitor," she said quietly. "I am not schooled in the female arts. And even if I were, I would not claw my way to a man's heart."

"My very impression," Damien told her honestly. "That is why I dared approach you, dear little patrician. I am not anxious to have my heart clawed." Autumn laughed. This Damien was a sweet creature. His sometimes snide exterior masked the soul of a scared little boy. He was laughing, too, a gentle, abandoned laughter.

"I take this hilarity to be a sign that your morning duties are accomplished, Miss Thackeray," said a rough voice from the entry to the kitchen. Standing tall, outfitted in a splendid riding suit of black velvet, Cain Byron eyed the two. He snapped his crop against his thigh.

"I was just finishing up your mother's breakfast dishes," Autumn offered, hurrying to the sink.

"And I was looking for the wine, Dr. Byron," said Damien easily. "But Miss Thackeray didn't know where it was kept. We were speculating on the possible locations of the wine cellar." Cain's perusal narrowed. Autumn perceived accusation in his gaze, for he knew very well that she knew exactly where the wine was kept.

Without a word, Cain turned and went into the buttery. He returned with a bottle and extended it to Damien.

"Thank you," Damien intoned with a lingering smile. He glanced at Autumn. "And . . . thank you, Miss Thackeray for the lively speculation." He excused himself with a small bow and left the kitchen.

Cain Byron regarded her with a question. "Was the lad bothering you, Miss Thackeray?"

"Oh, no, sir," she said. "It was only that I felt that Mr. Fraser had had quite enough of spirits for one morning, and I—"

"What have you against spirits?" Cain interrupted.

"Why . . . nothing, sir. It is only that a certain moderation ought to be exercised . . ." Her voice trailed off because Dr. Byron was smiling. As always, that rare expression on a countenance so suitable to smiles and so bereft of them gave her pause. "It will not happen again," she murmured.

"Oh, yes it will, I fear," said Cain moving to her. He set his riding crop on the table. Standing above her, he repeated, "Oh, yes it will." He lifted her chin with a leather-gloved forefinger, so that her amber gaze rested on him. "Miss Thackeray," he intoned, "it has been said more than once, you are most unsuited to servitude." Autumn, looking into that darkly, inexplicably tender, regard felt a sudden melting in the area of her knees.

"I shall try harder, sir," she managed.

"I know you will . . . Autumn," came the response. Her name on his lips became the focus of her world. It was only the sound of footsteps on the back porch that brought her back to the kitchen at Byron Hall. Autumn stepped quickly away. The back door swung open and Dr. Beame and Antoinette, in their fashionable riding ensembles, bubbled into the kitchen.

"Cain," Antoinette said in extravagant wonder, "where do you suppose that little vixen got to?" She drew off a flowered scarf and flourished it in the air. Smelling of fresh breezes and perfume, she swept across the room. "I could have sworn we had her in sight."

"They are beastly sly little devils," Dr. Beame pronounced as he watched Antoinette lay her arms on Cain's shoulders. "We must ever be wary of them," he added with an indulgent smile.

"I am so disappointed, Cain darling," Antoinette said, pouting prettily. Autumn's attempt to withdraw caught her attention. "Why hello, Miss Thackeray," she exclaimed. "I didn't even see you hiding there. Whatever are you doing skulking in the shadows like that." She glanced back up at Cain and seemed to gasp softly. "Oh, darling, I haven't interrupted another scolding, have I?" Concern etched her clear brow. "If so, I do apologize." She touched a gloved fingertip to his lips, and Autumn winced. Those were, after all, the lips that had just spoken her name with such heavenly tenderness. "You really must," Antoinette went on, "try to be a bit more patient with that poor little creature. Look at her." They both turned and bent their gazes on Autumn. "She is such a downtrodden old thing. She looks like a rag that has been left out in the sun too long, tattered by the winds." Autumn's eyes widened. She suddenly felt like that grimy, faded, and battered rag. Unconsciously, she began to roll down her sleeves and to smooth the folds of her apron. Antoinette laughed. "See how she attempts to make herself presentable. She *is* trying. You really oughtn't to be such a bully," she scolded and thumped Cain's shoulder lightly. "Don't you pay him any mind, Miss Thackeray," she soothed. "Men can be so cruel, especially where overworked and underpaid serving girls are concerned. They think they own them."

"You needn't worry, Miss Fraser," said Autumn, squaring her shoulders and lifting her chin, "Dr. Byron wasn't scolding me." She said the words with more confidence than she felt. "And I am not, I can assure you, overworked. Neither am I underpaid. Dr. Byron is most generous with his servants—*especially* the girls." She offered a bright and knowing smile. Antoinette paled, and Winslow Beame feathered his moustache distractedly. Cain Byron managed to hide his own smile.

"Actually," he said, "I was asking Miss Thackeray if she and my mother would join us for luncheon. She has not given me an answer," he added, his eyes searching Autumn's.

"I'm sure Vanessa will be happy to join you, sir," Autumn replied. "And I would enjoy it as well. I'll just be busy here in the kitchen for a few more minutes. I promised Carrie I would help her with the table preparations. She's outside lopping off the heads of some lovely partridge at the moment. It's a bit like fox hunting, except the little prey have feathers instead of fur, and, of course, you can eat the birds. In any event, Carrie will be in soon, and luncheon should be served up in no time." Again she offered Antoinette a perky smile. That lady eyed her darkly.

"Such a helpful child," was all she could manage. At Cain's not-very-well-hidden smile, Antoinette took his arm. "We really must be off," she announced. "Come along, Win darling," she called over her shoulder. "We all need to freshen up after the morning's exertion." Autumn watched them troop from the room and knew, with a sudden stunning realization, that she would, in plain fact, be willing to compete for the attentions of Cain Byron. Naturally, the thought of "competing" with the likes of Antoinette Fraser was laughable. Her charms may be false, but they were highly effective.

❦

Luncheon over, as they all lingered in the parlor, it was suggested that they attend the Adelphi Theater that evening. It seemed a flyer had arrived earlier, announcing that the famous seeress and advocate of free love, Victoria Woodhull, was touring the provinces. She was giving a special Christmas reading.

"I've read about her in the New York City papers," Antoinette said. "She was even in jail once. The evening should prove at the very least amusing," she urged everyone. "I hear she says the most deliciously offensive things."

Vanessa declined, but insisted that Autumn attend with the others. Carrie assured her that Mrs. Byron would be well looked after. There was a good deal of help in the house these days, what with the three serving girls hired for the holidays (the master had been enjoined not to rouse their fears with his dark looks and thunderous tones—and he had complied), and Carrie herself would keep company with Mrs. Byron until everyone arrived home.

Autumn dressed for the occasion in her finest array. She wore a soft green creation of watered silk, smocked delicately at the wide bodice and flounced at the hem. Beneath the flounce was a border of deeper green file. The long, sheathing sleeves were piped in emerald velvet and fastened with tiny pearl buttons. Autumn's jewelry had been sold long ago, but Vanessa offered a string of seed pearls and ear bobs to complete the outfit. She also offered a pair of combs made of luminous abalone. Autumn's hair was piled artfully atop her head in a cushion of curls.

"You are a picture rare and wondrous," Vanessa pronounced, as Autumn inspected her reflection in that lady's cheval glass.

Autumn half agreed, but it was not long before that assessment faded in her mind. The dazzling appearance of Antoinette Fraser in the entrance hall challenged even the glittering luster of the Christmas tree. This, then, Autumn acknowledged, was the reason Antoinette had insisted they attend the showcase at the Adelphi. She knew her gloss and polish would undermine any effort that Autumn might make.

Every head turned as the party entered the lobby of the theater. That grand palace, its columned passages brightly lit, its lofty ceilings and wedding-cake moldings painted in jeweled colors and gold leaf, was the perfect setting for Antoinette's glamour. She wore a gown of crimson velvet, its voluminous skirt shirred, caught with rhinestones, and trailing a heavy train. In her raven curls, swept dramatically to one side, she wore the bright plumage of some exotic bird. Her lips had been brightly rouged and kohl lined her glittering green gaze. She and Cain, Autumn noted with a rush of regret, made an elegantly handsome couple. Both tall, dark-maned, intelligent-eyed, they advanced through the thronged entrance and up one side of the sweeping double staircase. Autumn and Damien followed, arm-in-arm, an ascetic and drab counterpoint to the brilliant couple, almost an afterthought to Cain and Antoinette's radiance. Dr. Beame followed with them, approving the animated attention of the admiring crowd. In their gold-draped box, high above the orchestra, the party became the center of an upward-directed perusal, watched by everyone, envied by all. Opera glasses were lifted, speculations whispered.

"I suppose," Cain said with ingratiating good humor and not a little embarrassment, "they wonder if my mother is in attendance. This box has not been used in years."

"It could not be," ventured Antoinette, feigning injury, "that they might just be admiring us." She offered Cain a piquant glance and then an equally piquant smile. "We make quite a splendid couple," she added. "Don't we, Cain darling?" That man nodded noncommittally.

"You really do," put in Winslow Beame.

"You are too kind, Win," Antoinette responded. She glanced expectantly, awaiting another compliment, at her brother. Autumn might not have been present.

Damien smiled apathetically. "You are the most stylish lady here," he assured his sister, hoping the adjective would suffice.

"Thank you, Damien," she said with satisfaction. Having been approved all around, Antoinette turned her attention to the stage as the house chandeliers were dimmed. The chairman of the theater clacked his gavel announcing each act; first a pair of jugglers, then a mentalist, a comic singer, and a Chinese magician. At last it was time for the main attraction.

The stage's apron was lit by small torches, and from the hollows of the wing a tiny, immaculately dressed and coifed woman emerged. She was Victoria Woodhull, the notorious seeress, feminist, and once presidential candidate. At her throat she wore her signature white rose. Her speech was soft, her manner enigmatic. She assured her audience that she had prepared nothing for her talk, that her "spirits" would guide her words. Her subject this night, she told her audience, was the advocacy of the same sexual standards for both men and women.

"Some women seem to glory over the fact that they never had any sexual desire and to think that desire is vulgar," she began. "What! Vulgar! The instinct that creates immortal souls vulgar?" Winslow Beame shifted audibly in his seat. "Who dares," she continued, "stand up amid Nature, all prolific and beautiful, where pulses are ever bounding with the creative desire, and utter such sacrilege? Vulgar, rather, must be the mind that can conceive such blasphemy. No sexual passion, say you . . . Bah! . . . It is not the possession of strong sexual powers that is to be deprecated. They are that necessary part of human character . . . they are the foundation upon which civilization rests."

Her speech lasted no more than fifteen minutes, and during that time fans fluttered, throats were cleared, and whispers rose to a heated rhetoric. No applause rewarded the infamous lady as she left the stage. The great hall was silent. At last, a small sound, the sound of one person's approbation, echoed hollowly in the cavernous hall. Unimaginably, the sound came from the up-until-now abandoned Byron box. Cain, Antoinette, and Winslow Beame looked on in amazement as Autumn stood. "Brava!" she called out. Damien soon joined her, and it was bare moments before, one by one, other members of the audience, mostly women, stood and applauded as well. At last, Mrs. Woodhull made a second appearance. She curtsied modestly to the now thunderous applause of more than half the audience. She thrust out her arms and said above the approving crescendo: "Be of good cheer, my darling ladies! We are winning!"

After the show, a private room was obtained for the Byron party at Mrs. Rainey's Imperial Restaurant, and a supper of fresh oysters and cold salmon was served by Mrs. Rainey herself. Winslow Beame observed that he now understood why Mrs. Woodhull had served time at that notorious and most dreaded prison on Centre Street in New York City called the Tombs. The newspaper account said that the reason for her trial and ultimate sentencing had something to do with a scandalous accusation made against the godliest of men, Henry Ward Beecher, pastor of the respected Plymouth Church, and some lady—or several ladies. In any case, observed Beame, warning against female imagination and intelligence, a woman like Mrs. Woodhull should not be given a public forum.

"Such incendiary notions, in the words of the Bard, deserve a madhouse and a whip. A speech such as the one she gave tonight—spirit-written or not—just might give some susceptible lady ideas to which she should *not* be introduced." He regarded Autumn pointedly. "We must be ever wary of what we approve in this life," he stated. Antoinette argued that, though she agreed entirely with Dr. Beame's criticism of Mrs. Woodhull's position on sexuality (Antoinette used the phrase "what is appropriate behavior for ladies of quality"), the notion of spiritualism fascinated her. She hastily amended her opinion when it was greeted with an amused silence by Dr. Beame and her escort. Supper over, the party drove home, and again, before bed, Cain and Autumn were sequestered for some moments in his study—ostensibly to discuss Vanessa Byron's condition and the events of the day.

Antoinette sensed that Cain's growing disinterest in her had something—if not everything—to do with his odd and very apparent devotion to that pallid little creature, Autumn Thackeray. Now was the time, she determined, to do something about it. She had no idea how long she could stretch this visit to Byron Hall, but somehow she must make it count. Antoinette had waited far too long for the attentions of the very eligible Dr. Cain Byron to gel into a firm commitment. She was, after all, nearly twenty-four, and she'd turned down too many—far too many—offers of marriage. He must hold himself responsible for that. It was his lavish courting of her in New York that had raised her hopes in the first place, made her abandon some very essential proprieties, and placed her on the verge of spinsterhood. Antoinette resolved that if he would not hold himself responsible, he must be made to see that responsibility. Tomorrow she would pen the letter that would seal her fortune. Dr. Byron would learn that his obligation to her could no longer be ignored.

Chapter 9

Mr. Hamilton St. John Fraser, of the New York Frasers, arrived rather startlingly at Byron Hall just three days after the new year had begun. Antoinette had told no one, including her brother, that she had summoned their father. The household became galvanized at the unexpected appearance of such a distinguished gentleman. He named his visit "a mere whim" and apologized to Vanessa for any inconvenience he may have caused.

"The plain truth is, I longed to see my children and to greet the gentleman my daughter has been doting on lo! these many, *many* years," he stated, as he took tea in the parlor. There was a warning in this. "A new year always inspires a conscientious father to contemplate the notion that our young 'uns are growing up. Sands of time and all that, don't you know." Another warning. "Time," he lamented grandly, "it does create change." He chuckled comfortably. "And we, as parents," he said, addressing Vanessa, "must accept those changes. What?!!" Again, he chuckled and, unimaginably, patted Vanessa on the knee. She flinched. "Oh," he apologized, "so sorry, my dear. I forget myself. I'm just

the friendliest of creatures, you understand. Just an old redneck
from the bowels of the city. Clawed my way up, don't you know.
Gave those old boys on Wall Street quite a start, I did. Made a
fortune. But I'm still just a country boy at heart."

Damien watched his father's performance with equal parts of
admiration and disgust. He confided later to Autumn that
Hamilton St. John Fraser was a master at getting people to un-
derestimate him. He also expressed the knowledge that his father's visit was no "whim" and no accident.

"Antoinette sent for him," he said one evening as he and
Autumn strolled outside after supper. "It is quite plain. She
hopes—and trusts—that he will exert some patriarchal pressure
in the matter of her relationship with Dr. Byron." Autumn remained silent as they took the path through the gardens down to
the sea. "There is no one," asserted Damien Fraser dryly, "who
can exert patriarchal pressure better than our father." Autumn
glanced up at her companion.

"Does he mean for them to marry?" she asked.

Damien shrugged beneath his heavy cloak. "I can imagine
no other explanation for his arrival. Antoinette and Dr. Byron
have had what New York folks cheekily refer to as a 'friendship' for years. I believe," he added shrewdly, "he was her first,
if not her last, if you catch my implication." Autumn glanced
away. She very definitely understood Damien's implication. He
caught up her hand and placed it in the crook of his arm. "In
my opinion, if I know my father—and I do—Antoinette and her
reluctant suitor will be wed before this year is out." They walked
on in silence. The night was clear and cold. At last Autumn gave
voice to something in Damien's discourse that had struck her
particularly.

"You mentioned that Dr. Byron is a reluctant suitor," she noted.

"Oh, indeed," returned Damien.

"How do you know he is reluctant?"

"He exhibits all the signs. Haven't you noticed? Why he's hardly spoken a word to her since we've been here. It wasn't his idea, you know, that Antoinette should visit."

"Really," said Autumn. They stood now at the shoreline, and she feigned interest only in the black waters of the sea.

"Oh, no," Damien told her. "The plan was that Dr. Beame should visit for the holidays. My sister rather invited herself along—and me." He paused and regarded Autumn solemnly. "I am very glad I came." Autumn drew her hand away.

"We are all glad that you came," she said turning from him. He moved to her and took her shoulders in his hands, pulling her back against him.

"There is really only one person—"

"We should go back, Damien," Autumn said hastily as she extricated herself from his caress.

"Oh, my," he remarked blandly after a pause, "I had no idea. Well . . . I shouldn't say quite that. Let me be frank, Miss Thackeray. You might as well give up any fantastic dreams you may have had about Cain Byron."

"I don't know what you're talking about, Damien Fraser," she returned.

"Don't you?" asked the young man. He laughed bitterly. "Do you imagine I have not noted those excrutiatingly yearning looks you cast on the good doctor when you think no one's looking? Have I not noticed those little conclaves you and he hold every evening?"

"Those are meetings about his mother," Autumn said firmly. "He is most anxious because she seems to be digressing from her former good health."

"Be that as it may," Damien cut in, "when my father—the imperious emperor of the Fraser household—wants someone out of the way, they might as well just evaporate. My mother is quite the perfect example of that. She became a bit too feisty for father's taste and now she's rarely seen."

"Feisty?" Autumn inquired.

"Yes," said Damien emphatically, "feisty. She had entirely too much nervous energy; so saith Hamilton St. John Fraser. In truth, my mother was a bold woman. Chained herself to the gate in front of City Hall one day to protest women's lack of suffrage. She was arrested along with some other ladies. They were all released within the hour, and mother and I had a good laugh about it, but father deemed the incident a scandal. And mother was put to bed. Father called in your Dr. Beame, and mother was never arrested again. She was also never again fun, or frisky, or . . . irritating to anybody. She wasn't, as a matter of fact, *anything* ever again." Autumn looked up. Damien's eyes were glazed in the moonlight with tears. For all his show of sophistication and worldly dispassion, he was really just a boy who'd lost his mother. Autumn placed her hand back into the crook of his arm. Her heart went out to him. She imagined that his mother and he had been very close. Perhaps they even looked alike. With his soft, pale hair, his gentle beauty, he was quite the antithesis of the robust Antoinette and their full-blooded sire. "In any event," said Damien, swiping at his eyes and reestablishing his veneer of detachment, "one doesn't want to get too close to someone to whom my father might take a dislike. They might just disappear. Father, despite his 'good-old-boy' façade, always gets what he wants, particularly if his adversaries are weak." He glanced briefly at Autumn. "I am not for a moment suggesting that you are weak, dear Gypsy, but Cain Byron is. His weakness lies in his rock-hard commitment to our societal sensibilities. It is that very commitment that will bind him to my sister. He shall never marry you."

"Believe it or not, Damien," said Autumn firmly, "not every woman is on the prowl for a husband. I have no romantic hopes concerning Dr. Byron. Such hopes would be futile . . . whimsical. And I do not kowtow to my whimsy. I cannot afford to. A young woman in my position could place herself on perilous ground if she suddenly decided to make herself available to the master of the house—or his guests." Damien eyed her slyly. "You receive my message well," she assured him. "Let me ask you this; when you informed me some nights ago that you would like to 'pluck' me, were you offering marriage?"

The young man's mouth fell open. "Wh . . . why, Autumn, I don't know what to say."

"Of course you don't, Damien. You were flirting, merely that. And I suppose I should have been flattered. But I must be wary. My particular position does not allow me even the harmless luxury of a small flirtation. Someday, when you are nearing thirty and considering marriage, will you think of the likes of me? A servant? I doubt it. You will want a woman who has something to offer you, a woman of your own financial and social caste. That is the way of the world, and I accept it. I do not, for one moment, imagine that Dr. Byron—or you for that matter— would have even the slightest interest in marrying me. And I would settle for nothing less." She patted his arm. "Let us go back to the house."

"Wait," said Damien as Autumn turned to the path. "You have delivered a challenge, and I accept."

Autumn looked at him in surprise. "I have done no such thing," she protested.

"I accept," he repeated and strode past her up the path in the direction of the house. Autumn watched him, his cloak flaring behind him, before fully realizing his intention. She called out his name and when he did not respond, she hurried after him. The young couple erupted into the kitchen. Carrie eyed them in surprise. "Where is everyone?" Damien demanded.

"In the parlor, I think," responded Carrie, "I believe they're playing whist."

"Good," said Damien pointedly. "There is nothing like a game of cards to put Father in a docile mood." Autumn regarded him worriedly.

"Damien," she said as she drew off her cloak, "if you mean to prove some silly point, I would advise you—"

"I do not intend to prove a point, little Gypsy," he told her excitedly, "I intend to marry you." With that, he disappeared from the kitchen. Carrie gaped after him.

"Are you going to marry that young fellow?" she asked Autumn.

"I certainly hope not, Carrie," she stated in some dismay. By the time she reached the parlor, it was apparent that Damien had delivered his news.

"Are you insane, brother!" Antoinette was gasping. "You are not seriously considering that dim little creature as a wife. Can't you even, for heaven's sake, get yourself a *real* woman?" Autumn stepped into the room and Antoinette silenced herself immediately. She attempted to cover her clumsy insult with a giggle. Her father eyed her darkly in the ensuing embarrassed silence.

"So," he said, regaining his composure, "here is the dear little lady who has captured the heart of my little boy." He chuckled spiritedly. "You might have told a fellow, Damien," he said addressing his son. His tone was amiable, but his words were followed by another disapproving glare at his daughter. When would the twit learn, he wondered, that there were far less ham-handed ways of showing one's disfavor? She was a graceless creature and surely the most coarse of women. It was no wonder, he reflected briefly, that he'd been forced to come down to this godforsaken province to intercede in the matter of Cain Byron.

"We've only just decided ourselves, Father," put in Damien. He glanced at his sister dismissively. "And despite the recent thoughtless outburst, my feelings for this very *real* woman are very real."

"Well, then," piped Antoinette, "I suppose congratulations are in order." Hamilton St. John Fraser might have sighed audibly, but he did not. Instead he smiled thinly at his daughter.

"I believe, *Nettie* dear, we might save the congratulations for a later time." He looked back at Autumn with an indulgent regard. "Have you a parent or guardian with whom my son and I might speak, my dear?" he asked.

"My father, sir, is not alive," replied Autumn hastily, "and, anyway—"

"Any anyway," Damien interrupted, "her family are in Philadelphia. We shall simply have to write them and apprise them of our plans—"

Hamilton Fraser raised a thick, dark brow. "You are not of the Philadelphia Thackerays!" His voice was nearly a growl.

"I am, sir," Autumn replied.

"I had a great respect for your grandfather, Miss Thackeray."
Implied was the fact that Hamilton Fraser had no respect for the
chance-taking and overextension of investment revenue funds
practiced by her father. His arched brow and stern demeanor told
of his contempt for such liberal business practices. The man's
suicide had been a scandal but surely no surprise to knowledge-
able men.

"My grandfather was a great man, Mr. Fraser," Autumn was
saying, "and so was my father." Her countenance held a determination that silenced Fraser's further consideration of this most
embarrassing subject. He wished no confrontation with the indigent daughter of a failed maverick financier. He smiled with
forced warmth.

"Both men great in their own sphere," he agreed. "I never
could count myself in their class." He stood and took a cigar
offered by Cain as that man eyed Autumn keenly. At last the
older man took his ease in a chair by the fire. "Oh, these children of ours," he said addressing Vanessa, "they do keep us young
and on our toes, Mrs. Byron," he said composedly. That lady
shifted uneasily.

"Yes, Mr. Fraser," she agreed, "they surely do keep us on our
toes." She glanced at Autumn and then at Cain.

"Now, Damien," said Hamilton Fraser, turning his attention
to his son, "you will allow some discussion on this matter, I presume." He smiled benignly in Autumn's direction. "A marriage is
not to be entered lightly. All sorts of preparations are necessary.
Naturally," he added, "the protection of the lady is of primary
importance. We cannot have our feminine treasures entering such
a serious and abiding contract willy-nilly." Assuming Damien's
assent, he rose. "I should think tomorrow will be time enough for

that." Hamilton looked to his daughter. "Won't you accompany me upstairs, Antoinette," he said. It was not a question.

"Of course, Father," she murmured, with no hint of the shudder that raced up her spine. She knew she was in for a browbeating for her graceless reaction to her brother's announcement.

"And you, dear son," said Hamilton mildly, "please join us." He bid the rest of the company good evening, and followed by his children, he left the room.

Before anyone could address the bemused Autumn, Cain Byron rose from his chair and impaled her with a black regard.

"I wish to see you in my study, Miss Thackeray." Obediently, with only a discreet rolling of her eyes in Vanessa's direction, she withdrew in Cain's striding wake.

"Well," stated Winslow Beame, dismayed, "I should say that's the end of whist for tonight."

ళ్ళ ళ్ళ

Autumn reached Cain Byron's study to find him leaning with both arms on the mantelpiece. His gaze was riveted on the flaring hearth fire. His hard jaw in the dancing light was marked by a deep line of concentrated vexation. He turned his gaze as she entered and anchored it firmly upon her.

"You will, of course, not marry that feckless lad," he said. His tone was surly and forbidding. The Fraser siblings, it seemed, were not the only ones in for a browbeating this evening.

"Damien Fraser is not feckless," Autumn responded, drawing the doors closed. "He is young."

"Yes," said Cain. He pushed himself away from the hearth and took a cigar from a box on his desk. He lit it, and with the same match, lighted the lamp that hung above his desk. The room became sheathed in a dusky golden lamplight. Cain regarded Autumn with penetrating shrewdness as he blew out the match. "You have not answered my question."

"Did you ask me a question?" Autumn's defenses were firmly poised.

"I asked if you were going to marry Damien."

"You did not 'ask,' Dr. Byron. You made a declarative statement." Cain might have smiled but for the weight of his impatience.

"I am attempting," he stated, "to discover your feelings toward the boy. You said nothing in there, while he was all enthusiasm and decision. Your face, in truth, displayed bemusement. Did you expect his proposal? Did you accept it?"

"There was no proposal," Autumn said calmly.

"That tears it," Cain growled, almost to himself. "I have not trusted that youngster since he entered this house." He stopped suddenly. "Unless," he intoned, regarding Autumn cannily. "Have you encouraged the boy to assume you would consider him?" Autumn knitted her brows.

"I cannot think what you mean, Dr. Byron," she replied.

"Oh, come now, Miss Thackeray, most men do not up and propose marriage on a whim."

"As I mentioned, sir, Damien did not propose."

"Then you must have done something to cause him to make such an announcement. Women have ways of making men assume they would make willing wives."

Autumn flushed, her anger becoming apparent. Still, she kept her voice calm. "I will not dignify that comment with a response," she said, adding, "and how dare you make such an accusation." She turned, intending to leave the room.

"I make it, lady," Cain growled, striding to her and grasping her arm roughly, "because that boy is a guest in my house, and because you, as my employee, owe me an answer."

"As your employee," Autumn returned, her eyes flashing golden sparks as fiery as those in the hearth, "I owe you the services for which you pay me. Now unhand me." The words were ground out. Cain loosed his hold, stunned by her vehemence. Autumn swiped at a curl the lout's manhandling had displaced and turned once again to leave.

"Wait," said Cain Byron. "Just . . . wait."

"For what am I waiting, sir?" asked Autumn, pausing before the door.

"I'm not sure," he said, his gaze downcast.

"Am I waiting for an apology?" Autumn inquired.

"Yes. Yes, I do apologize," he answered quietly. Hard won, the expressed regret extended both Autumn's decision to stay and her curiosity. Cain's explanation for his brutality would speak directly to the nature of the man. "I have a temper," he resumed, "which I am hard-pressed to control." Autumn may have made an obvious rejoinder, but she reined that impulse. "Up to now, I've had no check upon my angry responses. But I am most sincere in my efforts to control them." He stopped, then finally continued. "I am hoping to get to the bottom of your feelings for young Fraser—and his for you."

"Mr. Fraser's feelings are his own, sir," Autumn said evenly, "I have no access to them. As to my feelings, you have no right to ask me about them. Be about your own business, Dr. Byron." Cain looked at her directly. In his regard she saw . . . what? Confusion? Conflict? Everything but the characteristic confidence he usually conveyed. He rolled his head back and raked his fingers through his dark curls.

"Autumn," he said wearily, "don't you know that *you* are my business?" The words gave her pause. She regarded him steadily. "Don't you know?" *Know what?* "If you are in love with Fraser, I shall speak not a word against the marriage. If you are not, you must tell me." He again riveted her with his regard, and Autumn saw that his eyes were not black at all, but a clear, unclouded indigo.

"I . . . am not in love with Damien Fraser," she said evenly. "And I have extended him no encouragement."

"Then, why? Why, Autumn, did he make that announcement tonight—and why did you not refute it?" Before answering, Autumn made her way to the little horned chair and sat heavily.

"Damien has been making flirtatious gestures toward me since he arrived," she began. "I suppose I was flattered at first. But, tonight, I told him that he must stop. I told him that a young lady in my position could not afford to succumb to even a harmless flirtation, lest she be considered . . . available. I explained to him that a wealthy man does not make overtures to a female servant with the intention of marriage—and that I would consider nothing less. Damien thought that I had issued him a challenge. That is why he barged into the parlor with his wild and ill-considered announcement." She looked up to find Cain Byron watching her intently.

"Is that how you feel, Autumn?" he asked. "I mean about wealthy men." She nodded.

"It is."

"And if a wealthy man, even one with whom you shared a certain affection, made overtures to you, would you deny him?"

"I would, sir," Autumn responded solemnly, "especially if that man were about to become engaged to another woman."

"I see," said Cain, defeat clear in his tone. "But what if," he asked, rallying, "the wealthy man were *not* engaged to another woman?"

"Oh, sir," Autumn said after only a moment's consideration, "if the man were free to love me, I would dog his every step. My heart would be his—if the man were free." She glanced away, allowing him to absorb her words. Her gaze was drawn back to his own, and they regarded each other meaningfully. Time became suspended in their knowing silence.

"If the man were free," repeated Cain softly.

"If," affirmed Autumn. At last she stood, slowly, rigidly. "I will leave you now, Dr. Byron," she said. His eyes hardened to a jet density.

"Will you, Autumn?" he asked.

"Yes. I must."

Upstairs Autumn hastened across the second-floor gallery, Cain's brooding image strong in her mind. She heard muffled voices from behind the closed door of Hamilton Fraser's suite. She knew very well what that conversation was about. *If*, she reflected, her heart twisting painfully. As Autumn was about to enter her own room, she heard Antoinette's strident voice lashing out over the darker tones of the men:

"She's bewitched both of them, I tell you! She is a Satan-loving Gypsy!"

Despite her pain, despite her anxiety over an uncertain future, Autumn could not help but smile.

Chapter 10

The next morning saw the departure of Winslow Beame. He would be back in a month, he told Cain, and he further stated that his prognosis was not optimistic. Vanessa's tears over that silly bit of trinketry on Christmas Eve worried him. Her listlessness and apparent detachment from even the lively society of the Frasers concerned him as well. This was only the beginning, Winslow had said, of a downward spiral to mental incapacity. He had seen it in his women patients time after time. The word "cure" could only be applied when a lady had returned to her fullest mental capacities—minus, naturally, the "nonconformities." He was grateful that Vanessa had not attended the Woodhull debacle—and Cain knew why, he said. The idea, he said, of women actually enjoying sexual relations was as repugnant as any of the new notions now abounding in this permissive age. Something had to happen, and very soon, too, Winslow opined. The one bright spot in the holiday, according to Winslow Beame, was that something was going to be accomplished in the matter of Antoinette Fraser.

"It took a visit from her father," he said expansively, "to force you to do the right thing by the girl, Byron. High time, too. She's a catch, is Nettie," he added with a sly wink. The "other matter" he said, would take care of itself. "The little Thackeray wench has hooked herself a big fish." Even the old father could not refute a direct proposal and an announcement in front of witnesses. "But I would warn young Fraser," said Beame seriously, "that he has a tiger by the tail." In any event, he said, they would all be rid of that meddling and troublesome miss before the year was out. Cain was not sorry that he was leaving.

Upstairs, a morning meeting was underway. Hamilton St. John Fraser had requested that Damien and Autumn meet with him in his apartment after breakfast. Damien's secret, all-knowing smile had vanished. He tapped his fingers nervously on a side table and attempted to look relaxed. A filled brandy snifter within his reach was emptied rapidly and refilled and gave the lie to his pose.

"You see, my dear," the elder Fraser was confiding to Autumn, "my son has failed to see the ramifications of his . . . impulsive gesture. He is, quite simply, not prepared to marry you—or anyone for that matter. Why, he has not even completed his education. I have decided, therefore, that it might be best if the two of you . . . postpone the wedding. Just for a year, or perhaps two. Marry in haste, repent in leisure, as the saying goes. Too, there is precedent in the Fraser family for the eldest son's attendance at Jesus College at Oxford. Heaven knows, we would not wish to deprive our young roustabout of *that* advantage."

"I agree," said Autumn quietly. Hamilton Fraser's brows lifted.

"You do?" he asked warily. Autumn's intention was to end this

conference as quickly as possible and with as little hurt to
Damien as she could manage.

"Yes," she said emphatically. She regarded her young suitor
with a wide, liquid gaze. "Damien," she addressed him gently,
"we must both be reasonable. Our youthful haste must be tempered by mature consideration." The young man merely cocked
his head. "Think on it, Damien," resumed Autumn, going to him.
"Your father is offering you something wonderful. An education,
Damien, at one of the finest colleges in the world."

"Do you know what he told me last night?" he asked. Ignoring
his father's menacing glare, the lad continued. "He said if I married you he would cut me off without a penny." He rose, the
canny smile returning to his lips. "You see, Father," he said easily,
"I have the courage not to be bribed." He went to the sideboard
and refilled his glass with a generous supply of brandy.

"You call it bribery," Autumn said, thinking hastily, attempting to reason with the lad before his irate father interjected with
some stupid and demeaning comment, "I call it an unparalleled
opportunity. Do you know what I would have given to be sent to
such a college? I was sent to a charming boarding school for girls
that taught me deportment and stitchery. And French! None of
which has ever served me in the real world. I longed for books
and mathematical problems and scientific discoveries to challenge
me. You shall have all those challenges, Damien. You shall have
knowledge of the finest, most elevating sort."

Hamilton St. John Fraser's thick brows furrowed, and he fin-
gered his side-whiskers uneasily. On the one hand, the girl was
making his argument for him, but on the other, she was making it
with a most distressing revelation of her own quite unfeminine
desires. The family would be well-rid of this puzzling and, no

doubt, troublesome wench. "A very fine point, my girl," he said.

"I am not finished, sir," Autumn interrupted resolutely. She was rather enjoying the older man's discomfort. "You and I are both so young, Damien," she went on, "we've hardly tasted life. And life has so much to offer the young. I, at least, expect to taste and touch and smell every joyous aspect of it. In the meantime, let us both resolve to know life fully. Let us resolve to experience every joy it has to offer." Slowly, she removed the brandy snifter from his hand. "Let us become drunk with every imaginable opportunity with which we are presented. Let us in our youth and exuberance offer ourselves to the world, and let it give us all the ecstasy it has to offer. When time has passed, a little time to be sure, we will be ready to meet again. And when we do, we shall have so much more to bring to each other. We shall be fuller people then, Damien. We shall have lived in the world. Only then can we give the world to each other. Someday, when you are ready to marry, to settle into a comfortable life of obedience to tradition and counting your gold, you may think of me. I shall be thinking of you always with tenderness, Damien."

Hamilton cast the girl a hooded gaze. He looked then to his son. Did the boy understand, he wondered, what he had almost gotten himself into? Thank God the creature had capitulated. Life with her and her fanciful and irritating and, God save us, "ecstatic" talk would be unbearable. She was, in truth, one of the scariest women Hamilton Fraser had ever encountered. Damien was smiling.

"You paint a pretty future, Autumn," he said.

"Yes, yes. A pretty *future*," intervened Hamilton with, in his consideration, some necessary haste. "Sands of time and all that," he said inanely. Not only was the girl penniless, and apparently, quite a proud little chatterbox, she was, Hamilton perceived, imaginative. Winslow Beame had warned him of the wench's whirligig-like mind. She had managed, in her slyness, to secure her own future, while seeming to acquiesce to the father's dictates. In the bargain, she had gained the son's admiration. *Oh, Lord!* This was just the sort of nightmare woman who had caused all that trouble up in Seneca Falls in '48 with talk of a bright future when men and women might come together on *equal* terms. A frightening thought. Hamilton would see the boy in school and safely engaged to some docile New York City belle before the season was quite over. He would not allow any more chatter. The matter settled, he rapped the curving wooden arm of his chair and grinned. "It won't be so very long," he said to both young people. "You shall see. In the meantime, I suggest that all commitments between the two of you be considered moot . . . for now, of course." He looked at Autumn. "You understand, my dear, that if, as you say, you and Damien are to allow yourselves to, one might say, 'taste life fully' you must be *free* to do so. You must not feel entrapped by the formal commitment of an engagement."

"I agree," Autumn responded.

"And would you agree," inquired Hamilton, "in a . . . formal statement?" He would not have her coming back at some future time with a back door breach-of-promise suit beneath her belt. She had witnesses, after all, to his son's foolhardy announcement—and distinguished witnesses as well. Two medical doctors had been in the room to hear Damien's promise of marriage to the girl.

"Of course," Autumn told him. Hamilton reached into his coat and produced a folded sheaf of papers.

"Oh, Father," protested Damien, "is this absolutely necessary? Autumn has agreed, and I, God save me, have not the strength to fight you."

"Leave this to me, son," said Hamilton. He knocked on the adjoining door, and Antoinette appeared. "Go downstairs, daughter, and send up Drs. Byron and Beame. They will be our witnesses." Antoinette hurried obediently from the room. "Now," he said, contentedly eyeing Autumn, "you shall have your taste of the 'real world,' as you describe it, dear child." Autumn's heart constricted. Cain Byron would, in fact, be witness to this humiliating ceremony. She reasoned, however, that he would also see that she had been sincere in her protestation that she had no intention or wish to marry Damien. But what, she wondered, was her alternative?

Before long, the two doctors had been ushered into the room. They stood solemnly, understanding their function, as Autumn signed the document emancipating Damien from any promise to her. Hamilton Fraser offered brandies all around, once the witnesses' signatures had been obtained, but only Winslow Beame accepted. Cain Byron had withdrawn immediately.

"Cruel business," said Damien as he and Autumn retired to another part of the room.

"Not so cruel," said Autumn gently. "It is for the best all round, Damien. But, I do thank you."

"Thank me, little gypsy? For what?"

"For thinking for a moment that you wanted to marry me. A lady might consider that the highest compliment a man could offer."

"A lady might," he agreed, smiling. "Will we meet again?" he asked her after a pause.

"Damien," said she, "our future is always a mystery."

"Not mine," he affirmed quietly, sadly. "Father will have me in school and then married off in no time." Autumn placed her hand tenderly on his.

"Do not take my words of before lightly, Damien. Accept the opportunity for an education—and use it wisely. Take the time to make your own choices."

"I shall try, little gypsy." They parted with a handshake.

In her room, Antoinette practiced for the meeting that was to take place directly after luncheon. Odd, she thought, as she gazed at her mirrored reflection, that this day should contain both the elimination of a marriage contract and the making of one. And how bitter a circumstance that her own future should be entwined with that of the implausible little servant, Autumn Thackeray. Antoinette wondered how the betrothal had been thwarted, but decided to think on other, happier, things. The fact was, when Hamilton St. John Fraser wanted someone eliminated it simply happened. Antoinette had every confidence that his powers would work in reverse. She rehearsed the vacuous smile she'd been told to assume for the meeting with Cain, but it came back pinched and anxious. The loathsome Autumn's hand could be found in this, too. At first, Antoinette had only disdained the girl, but now she feared her. Somehow, the twit had managed to dampen Cain's long-standing and well-established ardor. For a brace of years, he had been the most ardent of suitors, bringing her little presents and not so little ones. She looked down on the remarkable bracelet of emeralds Cain had given her—"damning evidence," her father had called it, without for a moment suggesting its significance. Antoinette looked up, attempting her smile once more. She sighed discontentedly. "Autumn Thackeray be damned," she said aloud, and lifted her chin, forcing upon herself her brightest, most piquant and alluring manner. She had seduced Cain Byron before; she could do it again. And if all else failed, Antoinette had her father's facility for manipulation *and* her emerald bracelet in her arsenal. Autumn Thackeray had exactly nothing in her favor.

After lunch, Antoinette was ushered into Cain Byron's parlor where he and her father had been talking for some moments. Hamilton Fraser bowed indulgently at her appearance.

"Take a chair, my dear," he murmured. "We are so glad you could join us." Once seated—in an unlikely chair made, oddly, of animal horns—Antoinette placed that bland and practiced smile on her lips and prepared herself to say absolutely nothing and to hold no opinion on anything that happened in the room. "Dr. Byron and I," Hamilton was saying, "—but let us not be so formal—Cain and I," he amended, "were just discussing your visit here. I was telling him that I was reluctant to allow you to come on this holiday. However, when I realized that Damien and Dr. Winslow Beame, whom I highly respect, were also invited, I relented. Do you recall my resistance, darling?" Antoinette nodded obediently. She was well coached, was Nettie, reflected Cain. Hamilton's satisfaction at his daughter's vapid response was evident. "With such chaperones to protect my little girl, I said to myself, how could I refuse her this most consequential visit? It is no small thing," he reminded Cain, "for a man to invite a young lady to his home for an extended holiday. This, I reasoned, is the natural progression in a long-standing relationship. Though in my time," he noted with a small chuckle, "ladies and gentlemen did not indulge in such intimacy until they were engaged. In fact, such a visit *announced* an engagement." He glanced pointedly at Cain. "And, in truth, the times, I said to myself, have not changed so very much. A long-standing relationship is a very good thing, just as it was when I was a youth. And I appreciate your reserve, Cain. You saw what happened with my own son. His very impulsive gesture caused nothing but disquiet. Fortunately for us all, Miss Thackeray has wisdom beyond her years and saw that Damien's rashness was born of immaturity." Antoinette shifted uncomfortably in her chair, but quieted as her father's dark glare fell upon her. "Maturity, Cain," pronounced Hamilton, "that's the ticket. In a mature relationship, a mature gentleman always does the right thing." He waited expectantly for Cain to respond, but that man remained impassive. He was, Hamilton reflected, either a dullard or he intended to put up some resistance. No matter. Hamilton Fraser had followed his script exactly. He was practically at the end of his oration. "The right thing, Cain," he resumed. "The *honorable* thing. The honorable, long-standing relationship between a gentleman and a lady can have only one conclusion and that is a pledge of holy matrimony."

At last—at long last—Cain responded. "It does sometimes happen that way," he acknowledged.

"In an honorable relationship," put in Hamilton rigidly, "it happens that way—always. And, I assume, knowing my cherished daughter has been raised honorably, that she could be involved in nothing less than an *honorable* relationship." This time, Hamilton's silence was a demanding one. Cain reached into the small enameled box and drew out a slim cigar, offered one to Hamilton who refused it, and inhaled deeply as he put a match to its end. He eyed the two Frasers passionlessly.

"As you pointed out," he said evenly, "Antoinette's and my relationship has gone on for a very long time."

"Almost three years," Antoinette put in perkily. She was horrified to receive the weight of her father's dour, reproachful regard. She shrank back into the chair. Cain nodded his agreement with her outburst.

"I was barely out of university when Win brought me to New York and introduced me to your . . . cherished daughter." He smiled, but there was no affection or gentleness in the expression. In fact, if Antoinette was not mistaken, his gaze held a certain challenge. "Do you recall our first meeting, Antoinette?" Cain inquired. Antoinette looked quickly to her father. He regarded Cain steadily as he lifted a silencing hand toward his daughter.

"Reminiscences," he pointed out, "can be a jolly way to pass the time. Perhaps we can reminisce right now on promises made, on expectations supplied, on . . . tokens extended." He paused, noting with gratification that Cain's regard was now bent on Antoinette's bracelet. How clever of the girl to be toying with it like that. "Or would you prefer not to reminisce, Dr. Byron?"

"I was about to point out," said Cain levelly as he raised his eyes, "that in a long-term relationship, people and circumstances are subject to change."

Hamilton raised his brows. "Exactly my point, Cain lad. Exactly my point. Change is the very thing that vitalizes a relationship. It must change. It must grow." Cain realized his error immediately. He had to admire both the old man's determination and his ability to manipulate words to his advantage. Hamilton persisted. "The obvious change, then, in this very particular relationship, is marriage—wouldn't you say so, lad?" Rather than awaiting Cain's answer and risking another digression, he added, "It is the only reasonable—and certainly the only honorable—conclusion I can imagine. Do you agree, Antoinette?" She smiled and nodded mutely. "Antoinette agrees with us, Cain," said Hamilton expansively. "How fortunate! But secretly, I knew she would." He looked to Cain benignly. "She has always doted on you, Dr. Byron—or should I call you 'son'? And, I must tell you that she has made her devotion quite public. You may not realize it, but Antoinette has turned down many an ardent suitor on your behalf. It is well documented in New York social circles that she has awaited the attentions of that one suitor who would completely please her. That one suitor is you, my boy." He stood and extended his hand to Cain. "I approve of her choice with all my heart and give you both my most earnest blessings. Also," he added with a knowing wink and taking up Cain's hand in both of his, "I am prepared to settle on this union a most generous endowment. Antoinette has over three thousand a year, and I can add to that another thousand, with," he paused significantly, "a lump sum of ten thousand to start you off." He smiled broadly. "That," he pronounced, "should take the sting out of losing one's treasured bachelorhood." He laughed. Antoinette scowled inwardly; she dared not allow her grievance to show. Her father was using the most unseemly terms to describe her marriage. Still, she pondered, he had done the deed. She wondered that she did not feel happier. She had expected relief to well up inside her once the bargain was sealed, but relief was not at all what she felt. Glancing up at Cain Byron, she knew only a sense of dread. Cain, after all, had said almost nothing. He had certainly not agreed verbally to the marriage. Yet, at this point, and once that eccentric mother of his had been told, there would be no question of

Cain's compliance. *Compliance,* thought Antoinette dismally. The word itself implied resigned obedience—not the stuff of which impassioned lovers were made. Oh, for that urgency with which her brother had proclaimed his love for Autumn Thackeray. Antoinette paused in her ruminations. If there was any satisfaction in all this, it was that she, not that little witch, had won Cain Byron. Autumn Thackeray had been defeated; she could never have Cain now. Antoinette's brows knitted with a sudden apprehension: Men had been known to take mistresses. Resolution filled Antoinette's soul. She had bargained with the devil, and won Cain Byron. She would do no less to see Autumn Thackeray eliminated from their lives completely.

Hamilton extended his arm to his daughter. He thought it best if all three of them made the fateful announcement together. With a weariness that was not altogether unpleasant, and a sense of deep pride, he escorted Antoinette from the room. One marriage had been aborted, one had been ensured. It was not a bad day's work for a man his age.

Chapter 11

"Antoinette," Hamilton Fraser asserted, "you are making yourself a fool. Get up off your knees."

"But I must find it, Daddy." Antoinette was feverishly casting about on the floor beneath her dressing table.

"'Tis obvious the catch slipped. You will find it somewhere in the house no doubt."

"I have looked everywhere, Daddy," returned Antoinette, tears coursing down her cheeks. "The bracelet is nowhere to be found."

"Get up," ordered Fraser, beyond his patience. "It has done its work, and you must stop comporting yourself like a buttery girl who has lost her pennies."

"That bracelet meant the world to me," she murmured tearfully as she obediently rose.

"I know exactly what that bracelet meant to you, Antoinette," said the father wryly. He amended his ironic tone as the girl burst into sobs anew. "Now, now, Nettie," Hamilton consoled her. He patted her shoulder awkwardly. "Did you speak with the servants?"

"Only that grumpy Mrs. Inman," Antoinette said with a sniff. She swiped unceremoniously at her dripping nose, and Hamilton, with an upward roll of his eyes, offered his handkerchief. "She said she would speak with the other girls." Antoinette blew her nose noisily, and her father winced. "But, of course," added the girl, "nobody will admit to having stolen it."

"The bracelet was not stolen," stated Hamilton emphatically. He glanced uncertainly at his daughter. "Why would you make such an accusation?" he asked.

"What other explanation could there be? I've looked everywhere. Someone has stolen it and secreted it away somewhere."

"I can't believe that," Hamilton asserted, but his tone was less affirmative than he wished it to be. "We must speak with Cain and Mrs. Byron," he said after a pause. "If there has been a theft, they must know about it."

"I think so, too," agreed Antoinette. Together, father and daughter made their way down to the parlor. They found Vanessa and Damien at the card table. The two looked up as Hamilton and Antoinette, dry-eyed now, entered the room.

"Where is Dr. Byron?" inquired Hamilton.

"He is in his office," Vanessa informed them, "with Autumn," she added with no apparent significance. "I presume they are discussing Winslow's dire predictions regarding the state of my precarious health."

"I must speak with both you and Dr. Byron," stated Hamilton. Damien cringed. He pushed himself from the table and approached the hearth, wondering what new terror his father intended to inflict on this household. As Vanessa rose, he hastened to help her with her chair.

"It seems," intoned Vanessa, "there is one crisis after another today." Damien eyed her regretfully. "We shall finish our card game later," she said patting the lad's cheek. "Shall we join Cain and Autumn?" she said as she advanced past the father and daughter. They moved ceremoniously across the hall. Once admitted to the private conclave, Vanessa announced that Hamilton and Antoinette wished to make some communication. Autumn would have withdrawn, but Antoinette stopped her.

"I think Miss Thackeray should stay," she said pointedly. "She seems, after all, to have some authority in this household."

"I have not been in this room in years," commented Vanessa as she seated herself in the little horn chair. She gazed about the chamber with its depictions of chaotic violence. At last her regard lifted to the portrait of her deceased husband. "You still have that hanging there, Cain," she observed. "My, my," she said softly, "what a handsome gentleman he was."

"Yes, yes," commented Fraser disinterestedly. "Handsome is as handsome does," he observed for no apparent reason. He clamped his regard on Cain. Despite the mother's obvious distraction, Hamilton Fraser meant to make quick business of this ugly circumstance. "Dr. Byron," he said. "It seems there has been a theft." Cain lifted his brows.

"You mean the bracelet, of course," he responded. "Carrie has spread the word. But we were led to assume it had been misplaced."

"It wasn't misplaced," Antoinette stated. "I have looked everywhere for it. It was stolen." Vanessa's eyes lowered.

"Who do you think has . . . stolen it, Antoinette?" she asked.

"I've no idea," said that lady. "One of the servants, I suppose." Vanessa looked up sharply, the steel of her gaze settling on the acid of Antoinette's.

"What would you have us do?"

"What do you usually do in cases like this?" inquired Antoinette.

"To be quite candid, Miss Fraser," returned Vanessa, "such a 'case' has never come up."

Cain, realizing a confrontation was imminent, commented, "Our girls are the soul of honesty, and the stablemen have been with us for years."

"Well, one of your 'souls of honesty' has stolen my bracelet, Cain," said Antoinette flatly. "I would suggest a room-by-room search."

"Oh," put in Autumn, "but everyone would be mortified, Miss Fraser." That lady regarded Autumn icily.

"Methinks the lady doth protest too much. Perhaps we should start with her room."

"I don't mind a bit if you search my room," stated Autumn. "I protest only because the girls have done such a fine job here, and they have felt so comfortable in the house. I think it would be a shame to subject them to such humiliation."

"Humiliation or no," said Hamilton Fraser equably, "the bracelet must be found."

"It was Cain's first gift to me," Antoinette said, pouting quite purposefully. No one missed the innuendo in her tone. Cain shifted uncomfortably as all eyes fell on him.

"It is an expensive piece, is it not, Cain?" Hamilton persisted doggedly. Cain only nodded. "Then I think it well worth the search."

It was decided that Autumn, being both a member of the household staff and close to the family, should conduct the investigation. She put the news to the girls as respectfully as was possible with Antoinette and her father looking on dourly.

Vanessa had decided she would have nothing to do with the search and went back to her card game with an apologetic Damien, and Cain remained present, but silent, throughout the most uncomfortable business. Autumn allowed the girls to empty their own purses and dresser drawers. They were forced, at Antoinette's insistence, to unmake their beds, empty the pockets of each of their dresses, and spread out all their toiletries for inspection. After an hour's search, only Carrie's belongings were left to investigate. With a great deal of pride, an upraised chin, and a silent condemnation of the process that spoke louder than any verbal protest, she opened her door to the searchers. Autumn's own disapproval was palpable, but she dutifully conducted as thorough a fine-combing as she had in the rooms of the other girls. Autumn surreptitiously squeezed Carrie's hand as they left her room.

"I believe everyone has been searched," said Autumn stiffly as the party stood in the entry hall.

"Except you," Antoinette pointed out archly.

"Oh, come now," Cain interjected, "will you search my room next—or my mother's?"

Antoinette eyed him darkly. "How you do protect the drab little creature," she intoned. Cain might have spoken, but Autumn held up a detaining hand.

"Miss Fraser is correct, Dr. Byron. I am, after all, a member of your staff. My assurances would mean no more to Miss Fraser and her father than those of the others." She paused and offered a serene and general smile. "If you all wish to go on ahead, I shall meet you on the second floor. I, you see, take the back stairs." Shoulders squared, Autumn made her way past them and headed down the hall.

Cain's discomfort was obvious, and he growled quietly, "I shall take the back stairs, too." Once on the second floor, he called to Autumn. She turned to find him standing in the gaslit glow of the archway. "I am sorry," he said. The arrival of Antoinette and her father in the gallery made further words impossible. Autumn led them to her room and ushered them inside. Antoinette glanced about first in wonder and then in disdain.

"What a pretty room," she said, "for a hireling." She moved about the window-lined chamber, lifting objects and setting them down disinterestedly.

"Thank you, Miss Fraser," Autumn responded. "I am glad you like it." She went immediately to her dresser and began emptying the drawers. She took each of her dresses from the closet and shook them out, displaying the contents of any pockets. Dutifully she unmade her bed and, just as the other girls had, she spread out her toiletries. "Is there anything I've forgotten?" she asked. Her tone was without emotion, but she realized firsthand how humiliating the process had been for all the girls.

"We might check under the chair cushions," Cain suggested disgustedly. "And when we have found nothing, let us go out into the stables and waste yet another hour or so searching the bunkhouses."

"Now, now, Cain," put in Hamilton Fraser, "we must be adult about this. My daughter is deeply heartbroken over her loss. We must not mock her efforts."

"You knit, Miss Thackeray," said Antoinette, eyeing Autumn's work basket.

"Mayn't I see some of your creations?" Autumn was well aware that this was most assuredly a ploy, and resignedly she moved to the basket and took it up.

"This," she said, drawing out a length of delicate lace, "is a table cover for my mother. And this is a sweater I am—" She stopped abruptly, because suddenly at her feet, making the tiniest of sounds as it hit the carpet, was the emerald bracelet. Autumn looked up amazed. Cain's gaze narrowed.

"Oh, my," gasped Antoinette. She placed her hands delicately to her lips. Then stooping to retrieve her bracelet, she held it up in triumph. "We have found our thief!" Hamilton Fraser eyed Cain levelly, daring him to dispute Antoinette's charge.

"It seems we shall not have to search the stablemen after all," Cain said mildly.

"Dr. Byron," Autumn protested, "you cannot think that I—"

"That is quite enough, Miss Thackeray," he intoned. "I should like to see you immediately in my parlor." Antoinette arched a brow, smiling, but Hamilton Fraser took her arm more roughly than was quite necessary. Her triumph was short-lived, for her father hustled her straight from the room to his own suite across the gallery. Autumn followed Cain Byron downstairs to his parlor. They hastened inside, and Autumn closed the doors behind them. She turned to face Cain Byron. He was smiling broadly.

"What is it, Dr. Byron?" she asked. "Why are you smiling?"

"Oh, Autumn," he said, moving to her, "I suppose I am smiling at you most of all." Autumn cocked her head.

"At me?" she asked.

"You are a staunch little wench," he commented, taking her shoulders in his hands. "I admire you more than I can say."

Autumn's brows quirked. "You admire me for stealing Antoinette's bracelet?" she asked.

"You didn't steal that bracelet."

"Indeed I did not, sir."

"Antoinette's scheme is as transparent as glass." He gazed down at Autumn. "And you are the dearest of women. You have accepted each of the humiliations the Frasers have heaped upon you with dignity and grace. You are a wonder of a woman." Spontaneously, he drew her to him, holding her against his chest for moments. The thunder of his heart caused her own to beat wildly. Gently, Autumn pushed against him.

"Thank you," she said, her voice catching. She looked up at him, her gaze liquid. "I cannot thank you enough for your support of me." She was still in the circle of his arms and knew that another moment of contact between them would result in something neither of them could control. She lowered her eyes and extracted herself from his embrace. She spent several seconds gazing into the fire, attempting to regain her composure. "I wonder why she did it?" she said softly. Cain moved to his desk and retrieved a cigar. He lit it before answering.

"She planted the bracelet because she wished to be rid of you, Autumn."

She turned. "But why?"

"Because she knows the truth."

"And what exactly is the truth, Dr. Byron?"

"The truth, Autumn, is that I would kill or die for you." Cain's expression was solemn, earnest, his voice husky with emotion.

Autumn turned abruptly back to the fire, then her gaze lifted to the imposing portrait of Cain's father. "Tradition dies hard," she said quietly.

"But it does die."

Autumn shook her head slowly. "Not this day, I fear. You and Antoinette are betrothed."

"There is something you must understand, Autumn," said

Cain. "The betrothal is a sham. Everything between Antoinette and me is false. It has been from the first. I was a lad when I met her, inexperienced and vulnerable, despite my dubious reputation hereabouts. I had never met anyone like her. I took her attentions to me, her lavish flirtation, to be love. I blame myself entirely for the misunderstanding. Antoinette didn't fool me, Autumn, I fooled myself. I wanted love so desperately. But then I discovered, through Win's foolish gossip, that Antoinette was lavishing those same attentions on other men. Winslow believed her behavior to be harmless fun, but I knew what she and I had been to each other, and I knew that her behavior wasn't harmless—not to me, and probably not to the other fellows she was leading on. I suspect that Antoinette chooses her escorts most judiciously. She quite deliberately picks uninitiated lads who believe her charms are intended only for them, or hopelessly narrow-minded dupes like Winslow Beame, who cannot imagine women as anything but pure-minded, and quite bluntly, stupid and completely malleable. Either of those types are the easiest to betray." He paused. "You may wonder why, knowing all I did, I continued my relationship with Antoinette."

"*I* am not stupid, Dr. Byron," said Autumn quietly. "I suppose I know very well why you continued the relationship. What I do not know is why you are telling me all this."

"I am hoping," returned Cain, "that you will begin to understand that Antoinette Fraser and I will never be man and wife. Her true nature will come out, Autumn. And when it does, I shall be free."

"That is speculation."

"That is a fact. How long can she maintain a false front? How long can she go on playing the part of adoring fiancée?

Antoinette does not love me, Autumn, and she knows I do not love her. Eventually, she will have to admit it to the world."

"And if that happens," Autumn asked solemnly, "will it change anything? She may still hold you to your contract."

"Even Antoinette Fraser," said Cain confidently, "is not that devoid of emotion. How could she marry a man she has publicly admitted she despises?"

How, indeed, thought Autumn.

❦

The next day, less than two weeks after his arrival, Hamilton St. John Fraser and Damien left for New York. The elder Fraser never inquired as to the outcome of the supposed theft.

"His discretion," commented Vanessa, "to misquote the Bard, is the best part of his valor, maybe the only part," she added. "But then, with a daughter like Antoinette, the poor old man needs to exercise a great deal of discretion." Neither she nor anyone else in the household could imagine why Antoinette had opted to stay on for the rest of the month. "Surely she knows that, to a person, everyone in this house despises her," Vanessa commented further.

"I believe," Autumn said, "that she is trying to make amends." Vanessa lifted her brows.

"Can she hope to?"

Autumn shrugged a shoulder. "She seems to be trying. She has not directly apologized to me, but I believe there is some cause for hope."

"You are by far," Vanessa said, sighing deeply, "the most optimistic person I have ever met. You say there is hope. What do you

mean by it, Autumn? Hope for what? If she mends her ways—
and I doubt that scenario—but if she does and proves herself a
monument to righteous behavior, what then?"

"Then," said Autumn hesitantly, "she might realize that . . .
that her marriage to Cain . . . to Dr. Byron would be a disaster."

Vanessa, watching her struggle, understood the girl's pain.

"My dear," she said gently, "Antoinette will never release Cain
of her own volition."

"But," returned Autumn earnestly, "if she comes to acknowledge that the engagement is false, that there is no . . . love—"

"Girls of Antoinette's breed are not interested in finding love,
Autumn. They marry for convenience, *their* convenience. If
Antoinette Fraser is nothing else, she is a pioneer on that front. I
give her credit in many ways for doing what men have been doing
for centuries. I only wish," she lamented wryly, "she was not
doing it to my son."

ᶜ୨ ୧ᵓ

For Autumn, at least, Antoinette's attempts at friendship still
held the promise that she might come to realize the mistake she
had made in forcing Cain's compliance in the matter of their engagement. It was undoubtedly a false hope at best, as Vanessa had
pointed out, but it was all Autumn had. She knew now that she
loved Cain Byron, and she believed with all her heart that he
loved her. When he touched her, looked down into her eyes,
smiled, Autumn succumbed to a melting enchantment. She
dreamed that enchantment every night. In her dreams, Cain gathered her to him, pressing her to the throbbing power of his heart,
transfusing passion, hunger, ecstasy. A whispering need encloaked

her dreams. A raging desire awakened her. Perspiring, trembling, she would face the void of her reality.

Autumn made a habit of staying up late, stitching in Vanessa's parlor, hoping to tire herself into a dreamless sleep. She looked up one evening to find Antoinette bustling into the room in a cloud of perfumed satin.

"Where is Mrs. Byron?" she inquired.

"She has retired, Antoinette."

"Then I must depend on you, Autumn. Won't you help me with this one little thing?" There was always a wheedling quality in the woman's voice that irritated Autumn, but she would not allow herself to become irritated.

"What is the problem?" she asked, setting her stitching in her lap.

"It's right here," Antoinette replied in agitation, advancing on Autumn and holding out a thin catalogue. "Madame Colette has sent her brochure. There are a *hundred* gowns to choose from; I can't possibly make such a decision on my own. Won't you help me?"

"I have told you, Antoinette, these are your decisions to make." Antoinette had announced that it would be such "fun" if Vanessa and Autumn helped her plan her wedding. Vanessa had refused outright, but Autumn had demurred and was eventually persuaded by Antoinette's pleas. The enforced closeness to the woman's prenuptial enthusiasm, however, caused Autumn a wrenching anxiety.

"You did say you'd help," Antoinette reminded her. Autumn watched as she hooked the table lamp in the center of the room to the chandelier's gas line. She drew two chairs to the table. "Do help me, Autumn dear."

Autumn dear. The appellation was used constantly, and most annoyingly, these days. Autumn lifted herself resignedly from her chair and placed her sewing aside. Moving to the center table, she took a chair and watched as Antoinette leafed through the pages. At one point she wordlessly indicated a pretty design.

"Do you really like that one?" Antoinette inquired. Implied was the fact that she did not. Autumn nodded. "I don't think it suits me, though I must remember that these are only the most basic designs. Perhaps if we picture it with feathers—and sequins!"

She glanced at Autumn expectantly. "Don't you think that would be lovely?"

"Lovely," Autumn agreed. She would agree to anything, she thought, if only Antoinette would keep her plans to herself.

"Do you really think so?" asked Antoinette uncertainly. "You don't seem very enthusiastic about it."

"I think sequins would be quite perfect. Feathers, too." She noted a slight alteration in Antoinette's gaze. Her friendliness seemed to have many such layers, and Autumn did not trust it completely. There were times, however, when the woman seemed completely sincere. In many ways, Autumn wished she could give herself fully to Antoinette's elation. It would be fun to plan a wedding—if only it was not Cain's wedding to another woman.

"There are lots more to look at," said Antoinette fixedly. "I wouldn't want to make a mistake and pick the wrong gown." Autumn rose from her chair.

"In the end," she assured the other woman, "you will make a beautiful bride, no matter what you are wearing. You must know that."

"I do know it, I suppose," said Antoinette reflectively. Autumn regarded her keenly. Sometimes, though not often enough, the

woman seemed entirely vulnerable. Antoinette turned her regard
to the purling fire. "What I should really like," she said quietly,
"is to be truly lovely, inside and out." She looked up suddenly.
"Like you, Autumn. Cain admires that in you. I suppose it's why
I lost his admiration. I'm not lovely. Not as you are." Her hands
were folded before her, her fingers tensely meshed. She studied
them, it seemed, carefully. "I used the emerald bracelet to ensnare
Cain, and then I used it again to entrap you. I planted it among
your things, Autumn, assuming that you would be blamed for
theft. What I hadn't counted on is Cain's belief in your character."
She made a desolate little sound in her throat that might have
passed, on another occasion, for amusement. "My own father
couldn't believe you were a thief. I was hauled onto the carpet for
my little . . . erratum." She looked up. "Does that give you any
satisfaction, Autumn?" Autumn knew the tiniest rush of triumph
but it died as instantly as it took form. She shook her head sadly.

"No," she answered, "it does not. In truth, I—" She stopped
suddenly. Autumn was about to use the word "pity" but she
thought better of it. Pity was a noxious tribute; it had been hers
once in Philadelphia after her father died. "I regret that any of it
ever happened," she resumed. "I regret that you felt it necessary
to go to such lengths and involve the other girls in such a scheme.
But mostly I regret that I somehow caused you to imagine that I
was a rival. Nothing good ever comes of female rivalries,
Antoinette. The fact is, Dr. Byron is grateful to me for my care of
his mother, that is all. He is your fiancé, and he will marry you."
In all this, Cain Byron was emerging as the villain. Antoinette's
jealousy had been born of fear, of her deteriorating claim on a
man she had every right to believe ought to marry her. In truth,
Cain should not have allowed their relationship to linger all those

years. He should not have held Antoinette on a string, implying devotion where no devotion was intended. But as Autumn had pointed out, they were, in fact, engaged. It was a hollow victory, to be sure, to be chained to a man who had been forced to marry you. Autumn's tender heart swelled with sympathy for Antoinette. In a moment of decision, she said, "Let me see your catalogue again. We shall pick out the loveliest gown of all."

❧ ❧

Conflicted, her heart and mind roiling with an ocean of information she did not wish to possess, Autumn wandered out as the night settled into a soft, shadow-laden silence. On nights like these, nights when Autumn dreaded her bed, dreaded facing unwelcome and heart-shattering dreams of Cain, she would visit the horses. She held a special place in her heart for the most special of the animals. His name was Castillo, and he was a breeder of champions. Esteemed as he was, Autumn loved the great steed for his lesser greatness—his apparent deep affection for her. He greeted her each time she approached the stables with gentle whickers, playful pawings of the earth, and proud tosses of his black mane. Autumn was his special friend, the stablemen chided her, laughing. They wondered privately, however, how she had endeared herself to the obstinate charger. It was no secret; Autumn simply made certain that each time she came to Castillo she carried a piece of hardened sugar. And she treated him always with a calm but gentle hand, expecting only his best behavior, behavior that befitted his noble stature.

It was a clear night, the late winter moon shone brightly with no haze to mellow its luster. The distance from the house to the stables was less than a quarter of a mile, and Autumn could see the rambling structures of the stablemen's quarters as she walked, holding her lantern aloft. She hardly needed its dim illumination, for the path before her was well lit. Abruptly, a heart-crushing sight halted her. In the distance, the tall, dark-haired Antoinette was standing with one of the lads, the blond one, and she was talking with some animation. Of a height, the two were face to face with only the moonlight separating their muffled laughter. At last, the thing that Autumn had feared to see took place. The handsome heads came together in a kiss. Antoinette's arms lifted and lay over the strong shoulders of the young man, and he took her in a hard embrace. Autumn's gaze was riveted on them, paralyzed with a realization that sickened her. She could not look away. Horrified, she watched as their lips separated and the young man placed his arm on Antoinette's slim back and ushered her inside his residence. A wooden door slammed behind them. Autumn lowered her eyes at last, shutting them tight against the betrayal she knew was taking place behind the door. Her thoughts were of Cain. Of his confidence that Antoinette would betray her true nature. She had. "Cain . . ." said Autumn on a breath.

Then, a sound so terrible it made her heart jump implanted itself on her consciousness. She looked up toward the stables. The gate to Castillo's stall hung open. It creaked wildly in the mercurial night breezes, and the animal himself, a great shadow against the moon, charged across the yard. With a muscled ease, he leapt the fence and raced down the sloping hill to the road. As the sound of his powerful hooves died, Autumn could not believe her own vision. Surely, she had imagined some ghostly echo of reality. Still, the gate to Castillo's stall gaped unguarded. Tears blurring her sight, she cast her gaze about wildly, attempting to spot the figure of the horse. Would that he were somewhere nearby, idly munching on found grasses, pawing the ground, waiting for her to come and bring him home. But she saw no such form on the moon-washed terrain. Blood pumping, she raced down the hill, following the path that Castillo had taken. She recalled something about another horse—the brood mare Regan, who had escaped the night of her arrival. Cain had said something about a farm on the west shore. What had compelled the mare, she reasoned, might also—in the converse—seduce the steed. Rounding the corner of the house, Autumn skidded to an astonished halt. There, silhouetted in the moonlight down the road, was a horse, walking proudly in its aborted attempt at freedom, and led by a man. Autumn ran down the drive. It must be Castillo! It had to be. But who was the man? Gasping raggedly she met horse and man at the bottom of the drive. Autumn doubled over in relief as she recognized Castillo.

"Oh, thank you," she whispered, her words a prayer. "Thank you . . . thank you!"

"My pleasure to serve you, always." That caressing resonance in the man's voice gave her pause. She looked up. Before her was the mythic stranger in all his wondrous proportions, with his great graying beard and his laughing sea-glass eyes. "Are you all right, little one?" he asked.

"How did you stop him?" was all Autumn could think to say. "He was running so fast."

"He wasn't running all that fast," the man said quietly. "And my guess is, he wanted to be caught. Animals, like men, are instinctive creatures. As soon as they see an opening, they bolt, but maybe they don't really want to get away. They just think they do."

"Castillo is my favorite," Autumn told him, her confusion clear. "Why did he run? Why did he go?"

"As I said," the man repeated patiently, "they only think they want to run." He placed his arm around her trembling shoulders and, leading the horse, he walked with her up the drive.

"I cannot imagine allowing him to roam the countryside untended. Why, he might have broken one of his precious ankles, or hurt himself in some way."

"But he didn't," the man said gently as they walked.

"No," Autumn replied. "No, he . . ." Autumn stopped and looked up at the man. "Why are you here?" she asked. "Who are you?" When he did not answer, Autumn found a smile curving her lips. "Are you my guardian angel? Or Castillo's?"

"I am no angel, little one," he told her, his eyes laughing, "though I would gladly guard you and everyone in this house." The last was said reflectively. He paused a long time. "I walk sometimes on clear nights, when the harbor is safe." Autumn's head cocked.

"Won't you tell me who you are?" The big man succumbed to the earnestness in her voice.

"My name is Robert Moffat," he said. "I keep the light." With the words, the man strode off. Autumn said another silent thank you and led Castillo back to his stall. Once she had locked it securely, she glanced toward the stableman's residence, and wondered briefly if Antoinette had left. The door was still closed and a light burned dimly through a tiny window. Had the couple inside, engaged in their own little drama, any idea of the drama that had ensued without? Not likely, she thought. Her heart settling to a normal pulse, she looked up into the animal's wide, questing gaze.

"I, too, Castillo, wonder at the carelessness of men—and the perfidy of women." She caressed the animal's snout and reached into the pocket of her cloak, drawing out the lump of sugar she always brought for him.

"So that is your secret," intoned a voice from the stable yard. Eyes widened, Autumn jumped and turned about. Cain Byron was moving toward her. His stride was casual, his manner relaxed. Hands in the pockets of his jodhpurs, he stopped within several feet of her. "You bring him sugar *and* you speak his language."

"A winning combination," she said, her voice quavering. She forced a smile. Her only thought was that he must not know of Castillo's escape—or the reason for it. She glanced back to the rambling, ramshackle residences of the stablemen and turned deliberately away from them. "I was just going inside."

"'Tis a beautiful night," said Cain Byron. Autumn nodded.

"Yes," she agreed perfunctorily and hurried past him, hoping he would follow her to the house.

"Wait," he said softly and put a hand on her shoulder. "You're trembling," he observed. Again, she nodded.

"I have been out here awhile. I suppose I am chilled." She was not looking at him.

He turned her gently to face him, and asked, "Is it the cold you feel, Autumn, or is it possible you are experiencing some warmth . . . for me?" Autumn looked up into his moon-silvered gaze. Her heart swelled and tipped in her breast. Her eyes brimmed over with tears as sadness and sympathy overwhelmed her. She reached up and touched his face tenderly.

"My heart . . . Cain," she said, using his name deliberately, "is, and always will be, filled with warmth for you." He reached up, touching the hand that touched his cheek.

"Autumn," he said on a breath, "do you mean what you say?" She nodded, still steadfastly regarding him.

"I do," she told him. "I do," she repeated emphatically. With the words, she lifted herself up to his great height and kissed him reverently, impulsively on the lips. He gathered her into his embrace and suddenly, so very suddenly, her dreams were real. She felt the great heart throbbing against her breast, transfusing passion, hunger, ecstasy, and the warmth of him, the scent of him, enveloped her. And he was kissing her, caressing her with his lips. Somewhere in the distance, the ocean thundered, the surf swelled and soared. He whispered words—enchantment—into her ears. "I love you, Cain," she said. "And I shall love you forever. Of that you may be certain."

"And I love you, Autumn," Cain responded.

"I know," she told him softly. "It may be," she added, looking up into his onyx gaze, "the only certainty there is in the world."

"It is all we need."

"Is it, Cain?" she asked him seriously. He nodded and smiled and brushed a sweet curl from her perspiring cheek.

"Yes, Autumn. It is." She would have spoken, asked other questions, but Cain touched her lips with silencing fingertips. "Despite what you have heard, despite what you may have believed, I do not make idle promises. I promise you, my darling, that one day—and very soon, too—we shall be able to express our love as freely as the air, as the ocean tides. I am not afraid; don't you be. When love is in the air, everything falls into place." Autumn glanced toward the shack where the candle still burned dimly. Everything, she had to believe, must fall into place. But she prayed it might do so with as little hurt to Cain as possible.

Once inside the house, Autumn made her way across the silent second floor gallery. She entered her room, closing the door with a soft click, and peeked into Vanessa's room through the adjoining door. She saw that the woman was sleeping soundly, her breathing even and untroubled. Next to her on the night table near her bed the little snow globe caught a glint of moonlight from the unclosed draperies. Autumn smiled. That ornament was never far from Vanessa's reach. How odd and how sweet that an inexpensive bit of glass, offered at Christmastime by that lovely, gentle—and, tonight, most helpful—man, should hold such attraction for the dignified Vanessa.

Autumn returned to her own room and set down her lantern. She needed no other illumination. She undressed and, blowing out the light, slipped into her bed. Nestling beneath the smooth covers, she wondered if, again, she would dream of Cain. Tonight, she did not fear her dreams, for they had come true. She and Cain had kissed before they parted, and she had felt his urgency. She had known an urgency of her own. But they could wait, she assured herself. Their time would come. Cain had promised. Her brows drew together in a frown. Cain knew, as she knew, that she would settle for nothing less than marriage, and Autumn's heart was clawed by the uncertainty of his engagement to Antoinette. That woman, it was true, had revealed her true nature, but it was still concealed by a cloak of deception. Autumn tossed beneath her coverlet. Cain had promised her that everything would fall into place, and she must be content with that. Before sleep clouded her consciousness, she must clear her mind of doubt and think on the good things that had happened that night. She remembered Robert Moffat and Castillo and the disaster that had been averted. Treading time between awareness and slumber, she allowed words and phrases to drip like sealing wax on the empty paper of her senses. "I walk on clear nights," Robert Moffat had said, "when the harbor is safe." And, "I keep the light," she thought sleepily. An odd phrase. ". . . the gift of wonder . . . keeper of the light. Light and wonder." Autumn sat up suddenly, her movement in the dark more substance than sound. "Vanessa!" she whispered in amazement. Drawing herself from the bed, Autumn padded to the room next door. She opened the door and softly made her way across the carpet, around the bed to the little bedside table. Lifting the snow globe, she peered into it. The moonlight caught the glint of tiny windows at the top of the lighthouse inside. Shaking the little ball, she watched as snowflakes swirled, shrouding the scene in the wonder of a wintertime seacoast. Looking down at the sleeping Vanessa, Autumn could not help but smile.

Chapter 12

The Cape May light rose majestically over the harbor, a giant protecting sentinel, guardian of the night. Autumn stretched her gaze to the lighted top that nearly vanished among the stars. To be up there, so high, so distanced from earthly concerns, would be a rare and wondrous experience, she thought. And yet, the same experience might encourage impractical thoughts, unrealistic fantasies, capricious hopes. Autumn stood for long moments looking up, deciding. She had planned this visit for two days; she could not give up her resolve to timidity; she must be brave. She turned her attention to the surrounding landscape. The ocean, unbound from its winter chrysalis, swashed against the shore. Night creatures chirred, but Autumn saw no evidence of them. She was alone with the massive structure of the lighthouse, its unwavering illumination at the top, and surrounding that, the heavens. Shrouded in the sea-scented darkness, she made her silent way, wraithlike, up the path toward the entrance. The door swung easily on oiled hinges, making no sound, betraying no presence. As she stepped inside, an unearthly cold assailed her, and Autumn drew her cloak and hood tighter about her. Surveying the height of the sharply curved cone of the staircase, she knew a moment of hesitation. She must be prepared for anything, she told herself. The risk she was taking might prove to be worth any perceived danger. If she were right, a welkin world would open for Vanessa. If Autumn was right, Vanessa would know the bliss of an earthly paradise—a pure and perfect fulfillment. *If* Autumn was right. That was the dream. But first Autumn must conquer the reality, the brick-lined, unlighted shaft that housed an iron staircase. Her slow and cautious footfalls reverberated, sending clanging evidence of her presence to the lofting summit of the building. Because of the narrowing circumference of the lighthouse, she faced a more and more alarmingly constricted circular ascent. The window embrasures stationed at each landing became less and less thick, drawing her more chillingly near to the soaring height she was about to confront. Her flaring cloak often impeded her ascent, tripping her. She caught her balance time and time again. She shuddered against her own vulnerability. On the final landing a dizzying star-swept view of the sky, the world she now occupied, assaulted her and confused her sense of balance, her sense of up and down, her hold on reality. She felt giddiness overtake her as the spiral staircase turned, upended, whirled her with a reeling velocity into its plunging depths. She grabbed for the iron railing. The world swirled, towered, darkened, and stopped. Autumn felt strong arms envelop her. She clung to this new reality.

"Watch your step, little one," a resonant, caressing voice told her. Autumn opened her eyes and looked into a world of laughing sea-glass blue.

"Robert," she gasped. "I thought I had fallen. I thought I was going to die."

"You're not going to die," he said, smiling deeply, richly, "not for a while, anyway." He lifted her, sweeping her from her unsteady footing on the stair, and with a sure step he carried her the few feet up to a little round room at the very top of the lighthouse just beneath the light. He set her down onto a small wooden stool and held her as she leveled herself, regaining her equilibrium. "Feeling a little queasy?" he asked her. Autumn nodded. "You experienced a bit of vertigo, little one, that's all."

"'Tis high," Autumn managed.

"Aye," affirmed Robert Moffat. "'Tis higher than most people ever imagine being." He moved away and poured her a small draught of brandy. "Take this." She obeyed, sipping cautiously. The blazing, musky liquid seemed to ease her discomfort just a little. She handed him the glass and took several long breaths. At last she looked cautiously about at the surrounding windows. The night sky, clear and crowded with stars, was everywhere.

"You live here," said Autumn, amazed.

"Aye," Robert affirmed. "This is my aerie. 'Tis wondrous, is it not?"

"It is," Autumn agreed. Her amber gaze caught the dazzle of the sequined sky. She looked back at Robert. Here in this star-ornamented lofty world, he seemed different. He seemed like a great eagle. With no sea cap hiding his mass of steely curls, he looked even larger, if possible, than when she'd found him, earthbound, following her. Autumn studied him for a further moment. "You brought Vanessa here, did you not?" she asked evenly. He hesitated, then nodded his proud head.

"Aye, little one," he answered softly.

"And you gave this, not to the Byron household, but to Vanessa—to inspire her memories." She drew from her pocket the little snow globe, wrapped in tissue. She held it up between them and peeled away the protective layers of paper. He looked down on it. The stars were reflected in its watery depths. Autumn shook it gently, and snow and stars swirled together, producing for just a moment a heaven, an Eden of dreams. Robert forced his gaze away from the snow globe. He looked out into the night, hands folded behind him. His face was echoed in the star-slung world of the many-layered windows.

"You know our secret," he said.

"I do," Autumn told him gently. She stepped down from the stool and moved to him. "I should say, Robert, that I know some things but not all." The sea thundered and swelled beneath them. Like the floor of the heavens, it rose up to enshroud them in sound and spume. Vaporous clouds of blown foam separated them from earthly restraints, and together, Robert and Autumn soared free on the silver mists of truth. Robert turned to her.

"I can tell you of a love so grand it made the heavens sing, Autumn." He smiled. "Did Vanessa say anything of that?"

"Yes, Robert," Autumn affirmed, "in so many, many ways. More often, words failed her, but I know of that."

"And you came here out of . . . curiosity?"

"No," Autumn replied firmly, "not curiosity. My purpose is not self-indulgent." She lifted her hand and displayed the turquoise ring. "She told me that this was her treasure." Robert lifted her hand in his and his eyes danced. "She gave it to me as payment for telling her future. I could not do it at the time, but now I believe I could—if you will cooperate, Robert." He let go of her hand and glanced away uncertainly. Autumn held up the snow globe. "When she looks at this, and she looks at it often, and when she touches it, and that she does, too, a tenderness arises from her soul that reveals more than any mere words. She longs for you, Robert, with longings that only love can produce. I am not 'curious,' I am determined that whatever dream Vanessa imagines she conceals be made real." Robert turned and paced as much as the tiny room beneath the light would allow.

"'Tis impossible, Autumn," he said finally.

"If you think it so impossible, why have you been following me? Why have you made yourself visible at the Byron estate?" Autumn moved to him, facing him directly. "You do not believe in impossibility, Robert. No man who is familiar with this starry world believes in that. You condole with the planets; you are intimate with the stars; you are cordial with the sea. You are not confined by earthly restraints. You believe, Robert, in every possibility the universe has to offer." She paused, catching her breath, then resumed. "And what of Vanessa? She wants to believe. She longs for that. But she is trapped in a smothering world of systems and fashions and propriety. Is that what you want for her?"

"It is not what I want, Autumn. It is not what I want at all." He paused and lowered himself into his chair. He picked up the small parcel of letters and held it reverently as he spoke. "I shall tell you what I want, and I shall tell you why I cannot have it." He set the letters on his knee, lit his pipe, and poured himself a brandy. "It was nearly four years ago that I met her. She was beautiful, alone on the promenade, as you were all those weeks ago. For one breath of a moment, in truth, I thought you were she that day. She lifted her tiny parasol against the dampness of the sea, but I knew," he said, smiling in recollection, "that she was exhilarated by it. She came every day. And one day I approached her.

"You speak, Autumn, of systems and fashions and propriety, and you know whereof you speak. It is not the fashion for a proper lady, the widow of a wealthy doctor, to interest herself in a someone like me. And, to be frank, she resisted at first. Oh, she lowered her pretty lashes and gave me her shoulder," he remembered laughing, "but one day a tiny smile curved her lips, and I knew. And then another day, she spoke to me. Oh, that was a day, little one. She said—and I remember the words perfectly—she said, 'You are most persistent, Captain Moffat.' You see I had told her of my days at sea, of the years I had spent as captain of the *Thomas*, a whaler out of Gloucester, and of my desire to lead a quiet, contemplative life, and of my commission as keeper of the Cape May light. I don't honestly recall everything I told her in those hours we spent by the sea, but I must have said a great deal, while she, in silence, listened. For, once we began speaking together, she seemed to know a great deal about me. And though she had revealed nothing of herself, I knew everything that was important for me to know about her. Eventually, though, we exchanged the stories of our lives, sitting on benches on the promenade, watching the sea. It was a glorious time, little one. A glorious time." His voice trailed off, and he took a sip of his brandy. "We began to keep company, but it was a furtive company. We both knew, I think, even then, at the beginning of those dream-clouded days, that what was growing between us could never be. Rumors began. Embarrassed silences greeted Vanessa when she called on former friends or invited them to her home. She told me it didn't matter. She said her life as she had known it had been false, a ready-made existence she had never really wished for or wanted. All she cared about was me, she said. And then, one day, her son returned from college. She made the mistake of telling him of me." Robert smiled sadly. "He could only assume, given the details, that she was losing—or had lost—her senses. He did what any son would do under those circumstances. He took his mother under his protection."

Autumn's brows furrowed. "And Vanessa allowed this?" she asked.

Robert nodded. "There was little she could do," he replied. "Vanessa loves her son deeply. She respects his authority as a man, as the head of her household, and as her protector."

"And what exactly," asked Autumn flatly, "was he protecting her from?"

"From me," answered Robert. "From herself, I suppose. Belief systems die hard, little one. Both Vanessa and I understood that in the eyes of the world our love was, well, scandalous. Vanessa is a very rich woman and I am, in her son's eyes at any rate, a ne'er-do-well, a nobody. My motives could have been nefarious. And Vanessa's unspeakable."

"But they were not," stated Autumn. "One would think Cain would have taken the time to discover that."

Robert Moffat smiled. "When scandal threatens, little one, people—especially sons—do not take the time to examine what seems obvious to them. For Vanessa, I suppose it was easier to admit to insanity than to a wantonness of character."

"I wish I understood," Autumn observed, "why the choice must be made between insanity and wantonness. Are they the only explanations for Vanessa's relationship with you?"

Robert laughed fully, deeply, the rich sound reverberating in the tiny room. "It would seem so, would it not?" he said. He sobered at last and said gravely and with no tinge of bitterness, "That is the way of the world, and I must accept it."

"Why?" said Autumn.

"Because," answered Robert quietly, "it is the way of the world, the way people look at things, little one. We cannot change that. We can wish things were different, even dream that they are, but our wishes and our dreams change nothing. We are better off not wishing and not dreaming."

"I disagree," stated Autumn solemnly. "We must never stop dreaming, Robert, no matter what happens to us. We are not animals; we do not live by instinct alone. Our dreams are made of hope, and we human beings live on hope. Hope is what made you watch me on the promenade, what made you follow me home that day; it is what made you approach me in the garden with this little snow globe." She held it up. "Hope," she said, "is sometimes all we have, Robert. We must not lose it, for it comes from the soul. Our minds tell us that certain things are true, but hope is what tells us that they can change."

"I have all but lost hope," said Robert. He looked up to find Autumn's eyes filled with tears.

"Don't say that," she implored him in a whisper. "Please don't ever say that." Robert stood immediately and went to her. She looked up into his sea-glass gaze and clutched the rough wool of his shirt. "My own father lost hope, Robert. And when he lost that, he lost the will to live. What he did not realize was that those of us who loved him could have helped restore his hope. I can help you. Vanessa can help you—and herself. She loves you deeply, Robert, and she is strong now; she is stronger than she has ever been."

"Autumn," said Robert earnestly, "there are things you don't understand . . . about Cain . . . about everything."

"I understand only one thing," Autumn said, her passion rising, "you and Vanessa must be together. A public scandal may ensue, but the real scandal of one's life is to deny one's truest feelings. Promise me, Robert, that you will cherish your dreams and that you will not lose hope." Robert bowed his head. "Oh, please promise me that," she urged.

"I will," Robert said finally. "But I do not see how . . ."

"You must trust me." Autumn swiped impatiently at her tears. "I promise you," she said, managing a small smile, "that Vanessa will very soon realize that she must choose you over insanity." Robert smiled, too.

❧❧

It was very late and very dark as Autumn made her journey back to Byron Hall. Clouds had rolled in to shroud the starlight in a gauzy mist. Robert had accompanied her to the private road that led up to the estate. She lifted herself onto the tips of her toes to kiss his weathered cheek when they parted. She drew her heavy cloak more tightly around her as she made the climb up the drive. Moving past the house, Autumn could not bring herself to go inside just yet. She was too filled with the exhilaration of the events of the evening. She ambled down the shrub-edged path behind the house to the shore. She looked out over the rolling expanse of the water and waves, shimmering darkly. The words she'd said to Robert drifted like the lapping water onto the edges of her consciousness. She had been so bold, so certain, where Robert and Vanessa were concerned. But what of herself? What was to become of her hope?

"Hello, Autumn," said a loved masculine voice from behind her. She turned to find Cain approaching.

"You're back," she said softly. Cain had been away for several days, looking to his tenant farms. "I did not hear your horse."

"He is stabled." He moved closer to her. "I saw you come home," he told her. Autumn's heart tipped and began to pump wildly. He had seen! He knew! "You have a beau?" he asked, his voice hard and questing.

"A . . . beau?" Autumn could not imagine Cain's implication.

"I saw him walking with you down on the road." And suddenly, Autumn's mind cleared.

"Oh!" she said, the word a breath of relief. "Oh, no, Cain. How could you think such a thing? He is not my beau."

"Who is he, then?"

"No one," Autumn said hastily, her mind whirling with possible, plausible explanations. "He is . . . no one. Just someone with whom I was walking."

Cain shoved his hands deep into the pockets of his jodhpurs. "You kissed him," he said quietly. Autumn's breath caught.

"Yes," she admitted. "I did. I did kiss him. I was . . . thanking him." Cain's black gaze captured the starlight.

"Thanking him," he said evenly. "For what?"

"For walking with me." Beneath her cloak she clutched the little snow globe in a perspiring palm. Autumn, for all her facility with words, had never learned to lie. But she knew that right now she could not tell Cain the truth. "The truth is," she stammered softly, "he was the man who brought back Castillo."

Cain's brows formed a dark V over his eyes. "What do you mean?" he asked sharply.

"Castillo got out . . . some nights ago."

"How?"

"He . . . the wind. The wind must have blown open the gate to his stall." Autumn was thinking rapidly, her words coming in breathless gasps. She could not tell Cain that Antoinette's betrayal had led to a slackening of the stableman's attention, that because of her, Castillo's stall had been left neglected. The lie, piled upon another lie nearly stopped her heart. Still, she persisted. She knew her story must persuade. "That man, you see, was from another farm—one on the west shore—a stableman. And he brought Castillo back, Cain. He brought him back. And I never thanked him properly. And tonight, I went to thank him." She left off abruptly and left Cain staring at her in bewilderment and disbelief.

"Why did it fall to you to offer thanks?" he asked. "Where were our own men?"

"It was very late," she offered. "I was walking . . . standing by the shore. I was coming back to the house—"

"And the man was bringing back Castillo," stated Cain softly. Autumn nodded, swiping at her dry lips with her tongue. "And you went to thank him—" again Autumn was about to confirm Cain's conclusion, "—in the middle of the night." Autumn was only too willing to concur, but checked herself suddenly at Cain's dark, forbidding tone.

She said, "I . . . didn't want anyone to know. . . ." Her voice trailed off. Cain studied her for a long moment. She might have swooned beneath his stony perusal. It captured her uncertainty, held it, examined it, forced her to examine her lame explanation. She lifted her chin against her own self-accusation. Her fingers curled around the tiny glass ornament clasped to her breast. Disgusted by her double falsehood and determined to face his challenge, she ventured. "I was afraid of what you might do. I was frightened, Cain. I remember well the night of my arrival. I know how you feel about your horses; I know how protective you are of them."

"And so you—"

"I did what I felt I had to do. I sneaked out because I was afraid of you, afraid of your anger, afraid, Cain, *for* you." The last words came in a relieving rush. At last Autumn had said the absolute truth. Everything she had done—corralling Castillo, visiting Robert in secret, and finally lying about all of it—had been done to protect Cain.

At last he advanced to her. He looked down into her determined face. "Is that the truth?" he asked.

"It is," Autumn replied in a whisper.

"You did it for me."

"I did. Your anger, Cain, saddens me."

He lifted his hand and brushed a curl away from her cheek. "Does it?" he said softly.

"Yes," she answered. "And I want always to protect you from it." He smiled.

"You are the optimist, Autumn." He paused, and his smile faded. "No one ever cared about me as you do. I am most grateful for your concern. But, Autumn," he added seriously, "we cannot make ourselves responsible for the feelings and temperament of others. We must have no secrets from one another. No matter how painful, or . . . frightening a revelation might seem, we must face each other with our truths." Autumn lowered her head, and Cain lifted it with both his hands. "No secrets, my darling," he said and his head lowered. He took her lips in a kiss of divine purity. He pressed her to him. "Did you miss me, love?" he asked hoarsely, pressing his lips to her ear. She nodded mutely. "Say it," he commanded. "Tell me."

"Oh, yes, Cain, I did miss you. I miss you every moment that we are apart." She looked up into his hooded regard. His mouth moved to her arched throat, feathering kisses along its tender flesh, his hand cupped her breast and something blossomed inside her. She pushed against his chest, but he would not allow her the freedom of a moment's respite to question her response. He strengthened it, encouraged it, with each assault on her ripening passion. "Please, Cain," she implored softly, not knowing whether she was pleading for him to stop or to go on. Ecstasy flowed from an up-until-now unrealized source. Such euphoria exalted her, so much that she became suddenly frightened. Autumn had never experienced the intensity of pleasure she was feeling now, had never imagined such pleasure possible, and she knew it was horribly wrong. "Cain, no!" she said on a breath. "Please don't." He looked down at her, a question in his regard. "We cannot," she said.

"Why?" he asked. "Why, Autumn? I love you, and, the gods be praised, you have said you love me. Why may we not express our love in the most perfect way possible for a man and a woman?"

"Because we haven't the right, Cain," she told him gently, solemnly. Cain released her and turned away.

He paused a long time before speaking, then said quietly, "And what is 'right,' Autumn? Who decides what is *right*?" Autumn touched his arm and turned him to her.

"We do, Cain," she told him sadly.

❧ ❧

It was very late when Cain and Autumn made their way back to the house. He kissed her softly, secretly, at her door, and Autumn withdrew into her bedroom. As she shrugged out of her

cloak, the warmth of him still clung to her flesh. The command-
ing tenderness of his embraces heated her being from within. She
flushed, thinking of them together in the star-shrouded night.
She still held the little snow globe and looked down on it now,
studying it, and thinking on all that it signified. Autumn padded
into Vanessa's room and replaced the globe on her night table. *No
secrets!* The phrase echoed and swelled in her heart. Cain had said
there must be no secrets between them, but how could that be
when their very relationship was founded on secrets? Autumn had
never intended her life to be filled with so many secrets, so many
lies. Her eyes brimmed over with tears and she lifted her hand to
her mouth to stifle a tiny sob. She hastened back to her room.
She stood for long moments gazing out over the lawn and saw in
the star-silvered mist below Cain's lone figure moving down toward the sea. *Who decides what is right?* he had asked her. *We do,* she
had answered. "We must decide, Cain," she said aloud through
her tears. Having made those decisions, she reflected, we must
then live with them.

༺ ༻

*The young lady studies her features in the mirror. She sees refinement in the
face, translucence in the skin, a harmony of colors in the complexion. She has
been told there is a symmetry of proportion about her appearance: A well-shaped
head; a moderate length of neck; a clearly-defined nose; mouth not too large; and
all parts of her form equally and well-ordered. She has been told she must give
animated expression and vivacity to her manner—which she does. She has been
told she must be graceful in her movement—which she is. In this way, it has been
said, she will attract the best of husbands.*

Chapter 13

Autumn wrote her mother regular letters, but cold perspiration accompanied each attempt to apprise that lady of her daughter's life at Byron Hall. It was not a life of which Isabel Thackeray would be proud. And so Autumn filled the letters with unimportant, often misleading, and always cheery details of her daily routine. She told her mother of the bicycle she had found in the back of a shed, and that she used it to navigate about the little city of Cape May. Isabel would find that amusing. Autumn allowed her mother to know that Carrie Inman had agreed, after much cajoling, to let Autumn do the early morning shopping. This was not something she was forced to do, she assured Isabel, but something she wanted to do, as it afforded her some much appreciated exercise and fresh air. She had become, she said, a familiar sight on the byways of Cape May, and a popular curiosity, waving to the merchants and the walking school children. "If once," Autumn wrote, "they were startled by me, they are now most friendly and wave back all the time." The truth was that Autumn wanted desperately to be out of the house early.

She could not bear to see Antoinette coming to the breakfast table and fawning over Cain, and she could not bear Cain's corresponding silences. Antoinette's visit had spilled over into the early spring, and the tension in the house was palpable. Autumn no longer pretended friendship with Antoinette, and that lady no longer made her wheedling, whining gestures of kinship. Her entire focus was on Cain Byron. If open warfare had not broken out between the two women, there was at least a recognizable hostility.

Each morning, Autumn came downstairs to clear Vanessa's breakfast tray, and each day she would find Cain awaiting her in the kitchen. He stood, as always in the morning, sipping at his coffee, watching her with a keen, hooded gaze. As always, Autumn entered, fresh from dreams of him, and avoided that gaze. Her dreams over the past several weeks had taken on, naturally, a new reality. Mixed with her unfocused desire for the embrace of his strong arms, the lean length of him pressing against her body, was the breathless desire for the further intimacy between them that seemed both impossible and inevitable.

"You mustn't look at me so," she informed him in a stern whisper one morning. Carrie had retreated to another part of the house to tend her morning duties, and Autumn was clearing Vanessa's breakfast tray.

He lifted a dark brow and smiled lazily. "Mustn't I?" he intoned.

"No," she rejoined. "You are attempting to wear down my composure."

"And succeeding," he informed her.

"Not at all," she said haughtily.

"You have been avoiding me of late. Where do you go every morning?"

"Shopping," she said with a nonchalance she did not feel.

"I thought Carrie did the shopping." Autumn glanced at him.

"I asked Carrie if I might do it." She did not mention the bicycle, for she knew that Cain would not approve.

"Why?" Cain inquired.

Autumn rounded on him. "I do it because I want to get out of the house before you and Antoinette sit down to breakfast." She looked at him directly. "She imagines, I believe, that you and I have been . . . intimate." The last word came out with an accompanying blush.

"And what of that?" Cain inquired.

Her next words were whispered, but no less intense for their lack of volume. "We have not been intimate, Cain," she said. "And we will not be till we are wed—if that day ever comes." Autumn averted her eyes. He moved to her, and setting down his mug, he took her shoulders in his hands.

"Listen to me, love," he said cupping her chin so that she had no choice but to look up into his eyes, "Antoinette may imagine anything she wishes to imagine. It can have no effect on us."

"I am not so sure of that, Cain. She seems more determined than ever to win your affection."

"She does seem determined," he acknowledged.

"And if she is so determined that even in the face of your attraction to another woman she would throw herself at your head, then we must face the fact that you will have no choice but to marry her."

"But there is always Antoinette's true nature to rely on," he said with a smile. Autumn drew away from him. Antoinette's "true nature" had already been revealed—and skillfully hidden by both her and Autumn.

"Cain," Autumn implored, "you must try to understand that Antoinette's assumption—false though it may be—has succeeded only in making her desperate. She will attempt anything to win you."

"Are you suggesting, Autumn, that I *might* be won? By Antoinette Fraser? Are you suggesting," he asked, taking her shoulders and turning her roughly to face him, "that I am so foul-hearted a brute that I would profess my love for you and then allow myself to be seduced by the likes of Antoinette? Am I a prize bull, Autumn, a derby-winning stud who will bow its head and nuzzle whoever offers the largest hunk of hardened sugar?"

"No, Cain," Autumn shot back. "But you may be forcing the issue. You say that Antoinette will reveal herself—and I have no doubt that she will do so . . . in time. But what if she does? Her revelation might only be the response of a browbeaten lady who has been dealt with unkindly. We want the truth, Cain, not some manufactured response forced out of her." His regard altered. His face became a mask.

"Perhaps I would not need to force the issue," he said harshly, "if you would be sensible and shed that mantle of chastity with which you protect yourself. You want me as I want you, and yet you cling to some absurd, idealistic notion of a precious purity that may not be breached until a preacher sanctifies our union. One day, I warn you, your pose of maidenly virtue will come under my assault. And whether or not Antoinette has deigned to reveal her true self, you will submit to the truth of your feelings for me. I am no martyr to be sacrificed on the altar of your pride."

"And I, Cain," Autumn retorted hotly, "am no martyr to be sacrificed on the altar of your lust. Your obligation to Antoinette has not diminished simply because a willing wench may or may not allow you to bed her." Cain's face darkened.

"Is that how you characterize our love, Autumn? Is that how you dare to speak of what we are to each other?" His lips lowered and his mouth came down on hers in a brutal kiss. His tongue ravished the sanctity of her most carefully hidden hungers. She felt her heart twist, pounding in her breast. Her flesh thrilled, her passion spiraled. Cain's lips released hers, but he held her arched to him. "You are fooling no one, Miss Thackeray," he said, grinding out the words. "You are as powerless as I over what we share."

Her eyes closed against the raging swell of her need. "Yes," she said. "I cannot deny it, Cain. I do love you. I do want you. But I am bound as you are to—"

"To what!" he charged, his grasp tightening.

"To honor," she said. He loosened his hold on her, and she placed a hand on his broad chest. "To honor, Cain," she repeated. Her words came raggedly as tears puddled in her great eyes. "If Antoinette does not reveal herself . . . if you must marry her," she said, gasping, "will you make me your *doxy?*" The last word was clenched, and Cain's hold on her loosened even further. Autumn waited for his response, her heart fluttering, pausing with every beat. His gaze was hard, questing, as he looked down on her. He could throttle her, Autumn reflected briefly. She moistened the soft bow of her lips. His face was very close above hers, its planes rigid as bronze.

"Doxy," he intoned very quietly. Autumn attempted to swallow, but there was nothing there to swallow. Tears cascaded freely now from her terrified gaze. Yet she would not relent; she would have her say.

"You say that I deny you because I am proud. You challenge

me, telling me you will not be sacrificed on the altar of some idealized purity. Oh, Cain, I deny you because I believe in the sanctity of marriage—and in the sanctity of love. These are not idealized notions, they are my truths. You said we must always tell each other our truths." She paused, catching her breath, and then went on. "Don't you know how much I love you, Cain?" He straightened, awed by her passion, and drew her to him, pressing her cheek against his chest. He could feel her tears, hot and unchecked, through the lightness of his lawn shirt. "I cannot bear it that our love has been sullied, dirtied by lies, cheapened by deception. And, no matter how much I love you, my darling," she gasped out, "I was not born—and certainly not bred—to be any man's light-o'-love."

Cain's darkly maned head rolled back as he gathered her deeper into his embrace. What would he do, he wondered resignedly, with this adorable woman? She was part siren, part gamin, part tight-laced little Grundy, and in all parts, the center of his world. His heart swelled with his love for her. Her tirade had made little sense and yet he understood it more fully than he had ever understood anything before in his life. "Light-o'-love," he said, rocking her in his arms. "'Tis a pretty phrase." He felt a smile tug at his lips, but dared not allow it to display itself as she drew away from him and swiped at her eyes.

"You think such a thing pretty?" she asked indignantly. He splayed a hand.

"No, love," he said hastily, with found solemnity. "The phrase—" he attempted to explain lamely.

"Well, I do not think it one bit pretty, not one bit, Cain. My mother would be mortified if she ever even imagined such a future for me," she asserted. She was about to continue a wrathful scolding when Carrie bumped into the kitchen through the swinging door.

"Breakfast's on," she said brightly. "Miss Fraser's already in there. Is Mrs. Byron comin' down?"

"No," said Autumn without expression and perhaps a bit too hastily. Carrie regarded both she and Cain with a question. "No," Autumn amended, "she is not. I've already served her." Carrie noted the oddly gorged silence between the couple, but ignored it. There were many such silences these days, she mused, as Cain withdrew.

As she cleaned the dishes from Vanessa's breakfast, Autumn heard snatches of the dining room conversation, though the word "conversation" implied an exchange of thoughts. There was no true exchange, for Antoinette was doing all the talking. She spoke of the house her father had bought for her and Cain in Washington Square, of its proximity to "all the best people and places in Manhattan," to both a girls' school and "just across the Hudson" a boys' military academy. She talked of the plans that were being made for a grand engagement party in New York City and the one she hoped might be held in Cape May so that she might be introduced to "all the Byrons' friends."

"The Byrons have no friends," Autumn heard Cain comment. And then, mesmerized, Autumn listened as the terrible, true nature of Cain's and Antoinette's relationship combusted into hellfire. She might have been with them in the room, so histrionic and revealing was the conflagration. And, at last, Autumn was, in truth, witness to a "conversation."

"You really will make no effort on behalf of my plans," Antoinette said tartly. Cain's response was immediate and leveling.

"If you continue to carry on with this falsehood you call an engagement," he said darkly, "I shall continue to have nothing to do with it."

"You are not being fair, Cain," Antoinette shot back. "Plans have been made—expensive plans. Had you not dangled me on a string all those years, I could have been making them with some-one else."

Cain was up, nearly knocking over his chair. "Who dangled whom, Antoinette?" he demanded. "You promised love, lady. You promised devotion. I believed your promises, but I found you to be the most faithless of women."

"Rumors—" she interjected.

"Not 'rumors,' Antoinette. Rumors be damned." He hurled his napkin to the table. "Rumors would be bad enough, but I've seen your flirtatiousness, your insatiable need for attention, your coarse, cruel ways with my own eyes. I have seen what you are. I am not the same green lad who came bounding into New York seeking a partner in life. In those days, I was eager for a gentle love that you haven't the heart or the soul to give. I blame myself, Antoinette, for not seeing your true nature from the beginning. I blame myself for being so damned trusting. You showered such lavish attentions on me; how was I to know you showered the same lavish attentions on every man who caught your fancy?

"Do you recall the first time we met? I do. You told me I was the man for whom you had waited all your life, and I flattered myself that I was special to you. I wanted desperately to be spe-cial to someone. I think it is what we all want—men and women alike. And for a while, Antoinette, for a long, sad while, you were special to me." He paused, apparently overmastering a great hurt. "I shall say one thing in your favor," he resumed finally, "the years have changed my view of you, but you have remained quite constant. You are not kind; you never were. And you never loved me. You clung to me, knowing you would not find a wealthier man, but hoping somehow, I suppose, that you might find a more compliant one. When you did not, you decided to manipulate me into this bizarre and ugly charade of a marriage. And believe me when I tell you, Antoinette, it will be ugly." He paused, checking a powerful anger. "Now I ask you again; who dangled whom?"

Antoinette eyed him obliquely. When she finally spoke, her tone was both patient and snide. "Let me answer your question with one of my own. If all this is true, why have you continued our relationship? Believing as you have—for some time, apparently—in all my shortcomings, why have you remained with me?"

"I suppose up to now," he said reflectively, "I was treading time, waiting for my life to begin. I have been at loose ends for so many, many years, Antoinette. We were good company for each other when I came to New York. I assumed that you, feeling no love for me, would find someone else eventually and marry him." She chuckled derisively, drawing back her chair and rising.

"Poor foolish Cain," she crooned. "Does he really believe the world works that way? How sad for him. How ignorant and stupid he is. How pathetic." Her voice turned hard. "'Cain, Cain, the doctor's son/Stole a heart and away he run.'" She quoted the nursery rhyme in a sing-song yet menacing cadence. Then she laughed fully. "What a shame that you were truly convinced, in your *man's* ignorance, that when you tired of me I would simply go away. That is not going to happen, Cain."

He targeted her with a black regard. "Will you be happy married to a man you do not love, Antoinette?"

"And who does not love me," she reminded him. He nodded

curtly. "Yes," she responded with a comfortable smile. "Yes. I shall be happy. I shall have money, a pretty house in Washington Square, and," she added smugly, "I shall have a good name—your name, Dr. Byron. That is all a woman really needs. Let me add something to that, Cain. While you have been casting about, searching for your one true love—" the words were said with contempt "—I have been making my reputation in New York over the past year, not as a faithless woman, as you so ungallantly put it, but as a wronged one. If you do me ill in our marriage, as you have done for all the world to see in our courtship, you will loose the vengeance of society on your loutish head." She paused significantly. "I find it worthy of note, by the way, that your 'time treading' ended with the arrival of one Miss Autumn Thackeray."

Cain advanced on Antoinette swiftly. His teeth bared, he might have cuffed her. It was only with a great reining of his anger that she was spared. "For your own sake, Antoinette," he grated, "hold your viperous tongue. You have wounded that woman more than once. By the gods, will nothing slake your appetite for inflicting torment?" Antoinette glanced down at his clenched fists. She arched her brow derisively.

"Cain's gallantry, when it finally emerges, falls on sterile fields. That seed," she assured him, "will never grow." Her eyes narrowed and her next words were delivered in deadly earnest. "Hear this, Cain Byron: You shall never have her. That I promise. You may take your mistresses by the dozens if you so desire, and I shall have my paramours, but if you touch her, you will lose everything. I shall divorce you, Cain, and strip you of every penny of your fortune. Add this to that: I shall take this house, this estate, your precious horses, your lands, and your good name. The courts are notoriously sympathetic to wounded women, and I shall be the most wounded woman the world has ever seen. You and your bemused and bewildered old mother will be penniless." She ground out the last words with such venom that Cain, even in his own wrath, was taken aback. "Yes, dear betrothed, I shall leave you and your pathetic little family destitute. You shall have to take up doctoring—if anyone would trust such a debased human being to doctor him—to earn your supper. Think about that the next time you decide to display your gallantry in defense of that hired slattern." She paused. "In the meantime," she added, daring to touch his jaw with one poised and polished fingernail, "a marriage is in your future—a marriage to me. If there is any question of that in your mind, check the law books. I can just as easily revert you to poverty with a suit for breach of promise as send you to jail. It is all one to me, Cain dear, for you see, what you say is true. I do not love you; I never have, and I am convinced that I never shall. I suppose," she added mildly, mirthfully, "I am quite incapable of love. That suits my purposes very well." She turned and ambled from the room. In a perfumed froth, she made her way across the entrance hall and up the gracefully curving staircase. She ventured one smiling glance over a slender shoulder to see Cain storming from the house.

Autumn was stunned. The voices and the vitriol had resounded through the house. There could no longer be even a pretense of civility. But what of that? Antoinette had, indeed, revealed her true nature, her complete lack of morality—this time to Cain himself. But what of that? It was over. The marriage would take place. Autumn made her stumbling way up the back staircase, the aching realization growing in her heart. Her wildest dreams had not prepared her for this outcome. Cain's manly image, always strong in her mind, had been stripped, laid bare of all its defenses. Antoinette was, in fact, devoid of emotion, of any normal human response, and no one, not even Cain, for all his strength and confidence, could fight that. Autumn knew that both she and Cain had been idealistic fools—rendered even more foolish by Antoinette's depravity. They were puppets, merely that, dancing on her string. Damien had been right. Antoinette was a gorgeous tropical bloom with poison at its center. Up to now that observation had been merely a colorful metaphor. But those words had become reality. Autumn could not even cry, so profound was her amazement. She sat heavily on her window seat that overlooked the grounds beyond the house, and though the sun was strong and warm, she felt a cold chill. She watched the newly budded leaves of trees, planted a hundred years ago, shuddering in the ocean breezes. She looked down, and through the distortion of her disbelief, her incomprehension, she saw Cain striding toward the stables. She saw him speak to one of the grooms and she saw that man unstable Castillo. Cain mounted the unsaddled horse in one powerful motion, and the animal, spurred immediately to a gallop, reared, wheeled mightily, and pounded off. The scene riveted her. It was a display of action, of unchecked power and control. And Autumn knew that she, too, must take action.

She raced to her armoire and pulled out a light jacket from among the tumble of her clothing. Desperate in her desire to overtake Cain, she raced down the stairs, slammed from the kitchen, and flew across the back lawn to the stables. "Get me a horse," she called to one of the men. That man sprang to the task of saddling one of the animals. Autumn mounted with bare assistance and charged off. She did not, of course, perceive the narrowed green gaze that watched her from a second floor window.

The Byron estate was a vast holding. Verdant fields and cultivated farmland stretched out behind her as Autumn kept her horse to a steady gallop. She abandoned established paths to ride into wooded areas, only to find them empty of human inhabitance. She rode on, past a sparkling blue pond that reposed in the sun, and down through the dewy purple shadows of a lilac grove. Everywhere, Autumn found evidence of the earth's annual renewal. Buds burst forth, their delicate fragrances carried on blue breezes. New leaves lifted their virgin flesh to be nourished by the springtime sun.

At last, slowing her horse and entering a heavily foliated grove, Autumn spotted Cain. He stood, leaning back against the bole of a tree. His head resting against the bark, his arms folded on his chest, he seemed in repose. But Autumn knew that beneath that relaxed exterior there was anger and confusion, bitterness, and deep, deep pain. She dismounted noiselessly, tossing her horse's rein over a low-hanging limb and approached him. He shot a quick, wary look in her direction and straightened at the sound of her footfall. Autumn's lips curved into a soft smile. Before she could utter a word, Cain was upon her. His arms took her in a hard, acquisitive, not-to-be-breached embrace.

"Oh, love," he said, the sound almost a groan. He captured her mouth in a searing kiss. "Autumn," he whispered hoarsely on ragged breaths again and again. He swept her down onto the fresh grasses, cradling her in his arms. The sound and scent of him inflamed her senses, and Autumn knew that never again would she deny him. To deny him would be to deny herself. Now, knowing all that she knew, understanding the universe as it functioned now, in this present moment, Autumn gave herself fully to the mastery of her desire—and to his. She opened herself to Cain Byron, obeyed his every urgency as the tide obeys the compelling power of the moon. The ferocity of his lovemaking did not overmaster his consideration. He held her, stroked her, caressed her, and found the secret places where her deepest hungers resided. He fed them with succulent attention. Autumn's soul was yielded up on the surging sea winds of a need so powerful it transcended all earthly thought. He entered her with a tender force and Autumn cried out. Cain hesitated, but she held him fiercely. He gazed down into the liquid dusk of her eyes, a question in his own.

"Don't stop, Cain," she whispered, "don't ever stop loving me." A smile tugged at the corners of his lips, and his eyes were the color of a midnight ocean.

"I never shall, Autumn," he assured her. His lovemaking gentled and slowed as he watched the splendorous tableau of her rapturous response. Her whispered expressions of love and passion were rhapsodic music on the scented breezes of their perfect union. As his own desire mounted, he gathered her to him, his ardor swelling. They rose together to a voluptuous release, and they lay in each other's arms for what might have been eternity. Cain watched her, her lips dewy, her eyes shadowed by tangled golden lashes, her skin flushed with passion's innocence. He brushed a moist curl from her cheek. "I am the most fortunate of men," he said quietly. She lay back in the setting of his arms, a jewel touched by the sun.

"And I," she returned, "the most fortunate of women." She lifted her arms, entwining them about his neck, and drew him to her for a last kiss. They both knew that eternity must end. Autumn sat up slowly, surveying the wreckage of her clothes that were strewn about the moist grass. She smiled softly. How unnecessary were these remnants of civility in Eden, she thought. She glanced at Cain who was regarding her keenly.

"May I ask a question—or several questions?" he inquired, suppressing a smile.

"You may," she told him as she gathered her things. "But I can guess what they are." He waited, his smile deepening. "You wish to know why I came, how I came to find you, and what happened to my former restraint." She glanced at him archly. He was lying next to her, facing her, his weight held on one muscled arm. "You are quite smug, sir," she told him tartly. "You think yourself the most desirable of men, don't you? You imagine I was compelled to my wanton fall by your virility." Amending her attitude, she smiled and drawing her knees beneath her, she leaned toward him. Her hair fell in creamy, sun-touched tangles over her shoulders. "If you think that, Cain Byron, then you know exactly why I came here." They both laughed. "As to how I found you," she added, "I might say that I shall always find you. Just try to run away from me and you will discover the truth of that. I shall dog your heels till the end of my days—and possibly even after that. We Gypsies, you know, believe in ghosts." He drew her into his embrace and she lay contentedly against his lean length.

"And why," he asked, stroking her hair, "have you abandoned your former restraint?" Autumn stiffened imperceptibly. She would not have him know that she had witnessed Antoinette's humiliating assault. She would never allow him to know that, even though it had been the vehicle that had empowered her. Some secrets, she resolved, were a kindness to keep.

"I suppose," she replied, her tone light, her face betraying no guardedness, "it is because . . . light-o'-love really is a pretty phrase." Cain looked down on her, his gaze questioning but not doubting. His gratitude was in his eyes.

Chapter 14

The day of the engagement party for Cain and Antoinette dawned blue and breezy with only a touch of a sea-scented chill in the air. By mid-afternoon, the sun had warmed the earth, and a daffodil-tinted glow covered the world. Before the guests arrived, tables draped with pristine linen cloths were set in the side gardens of Byron Hall and were laden with bowls of fruit, trays of cakes, and crystal dishes filled with relishes and jams. The house was ablaze with springtime color. Tall vases of rhododendron, bleeding heart, and white lilacs brought the outdoors inside. Serving people swarmed between the kitchen and the parlors and the gardens, setting up tea tables, punch bowls, and conversation corners, filling every space with festivity.

Vanessa Byron, alone in her second floor chamber far above the ground-level bustle, put the finishing touches on her costume. She felt it was indeed a "costume." Vanessa compared herself to a puppet in a silly shadow box farce—manipulated into taking part in an entertaining, completely unbelievable, event. Standing before her mirror, she studied herself, lifted a steely eyebrow, and smiled thinly. She had decided earlier that day that she had had quite enough of the "patriarchal pressure" that had staged this whole manufactured mess. She intended to use a bit of *matriarchal* pressure to see it stopped. She had asked her son to attend her in her room. She heard his tentative knock and opened her door, greeting him warmly.

"We've not been alone in some time," she said, embracing him.

"You are quite right, Mother," he replied as he bowed her into a chair.

"We needn't be so formal, Cain," she said, though she took the chair and sat for several moments looking up at her son. He seemed ill at ease and decidedly restless. Vanessa was not at all surprised that this should be so. "Did you realize that we haven't had a party at Byron Hall in nearly ten years?" she ventured. Cain nodded tensely and paced to the bay of windows. "The lawns look so pretty, don't you think? With the hedges groomed and the flower beds—"

"Yes," Cain said impatiently. "Yes, Mother, everything looks manicured and fine. What did you wish to speak to me about?" He regarded her resolutely, and she smiled.

"I suppose it is necessary these days for me to have quite a good reason to summon you into my presence. It wasn't always so, you know. Once, you would come in here just to lie on my bed while I dressed for a party, and we would talk and laugh and alter the universe. But, of course these days you are so busy with the farms and the tenants . . . and your plans."

"I apologize, Mother," he told her. "Of course you do not need a reason. It is only that," he hesitated, "your summons seems so uncharacteristic."

Vanessa laughed softly. "I suppose I haven't taken much of an interest in this household of late, or in you. I think it is time I did." Their blue gazes merged in a long-remembered well of tenderness. "I am, after all, your mother. And believe me when I tell you, Cain darling, I am very interested in what happens to you." She paused and leaned forward. "This marriage," she began. Cain averted his eyes.

"What about it?" he asked. His manner was defensive, though he adopted a casual tone.

"I don't approve of it," stated Vanessa shortly. Cain turned to her, a question in his regard.

"You don't?"

Vanessa shook her head firmly and responded, "No. I do not." Cain crossed to her.

"Why not, Mother?" he asked.

"Call it a mother's instinct, Cain," she explained softly. "Call it the meddlesome observation of a woman who has spent entirely too much time alone. Call it what you will, but please do take note of my objection."

Cain managed a half smile. "I do note it," he affirmed. He paced back to the windows.

"And," asked Vanessa, "do you credit it?"

"Of course I do, Mother," he answered kindly. She watched the broad back, beloved, cherished once in her motherly arms. She stood, having long ago abandoned her walking stick, and moved to him, placing her hand on that now quite strong, quite powerfully self-sufficient back.

"Cain," she said gently, "why are you going through with it?" He turned to her and in the diffused light of the softly curtained window he examined her. She was lovely in her motherly concern. Cain smiled and gathered her into his embrace.

"I am going through with it, Mother, because I must."

"Must you?" she asked. Cain drew away from her and nodded.

"Why?" asked Vanessa. Before he could answer she went on. "Why must you persist in something that is so obviously being done against your will?"

"Mother," Cain said with kindness and concern, "you simply do not understand the situation."

"Don't I?" she replied narrowly.

"No," Cain told her. "You do not." With some difficulty, he explained. "Antoinette has been given every reason to believe that I would marry her."

"Has she," stated Vanessa evenly.

"Yes," Cain responded quirking his brows. His mother's attitude was puzzling and not altogether expected. He had misgivings about pursuing the subject with her at all. "Let it stand," he said patiently. "Your objection is duly noted, Mother. But I assure you that as long as Antoinette wishes it so, the wedding will go on. There is nothing I can do about it."

"The wedding," returned Vanessa flatly, "is the machination of a proud old patriarchal poop and his spoiled brat of a daughter." Startled, Cain regarded his mother in wonder. He had no idea that she harbored such strong opinions, and her language was colorful, if less than decorous. A smile curved his lips unchecked.

"Mother," he said mirthfully, "we really must not speak about Antoinette and her father in such terms—"

"Antoinette and her father be pickled in brine," remarked Vanessa dismissively. She moved from the window and placed herself before her mirror. Adjusting an errant curl, she commented, "You play the gentleman, Cain, most unstintingly. And that is admirable. Your father would be proud, if that thought gives you any consolation. But as your mother, I would remind you that a gentleman is first a man—a human being. And no human being should be made to endure a life with that venomous woman."

Cain's mouth gaped and his brows lifted in astonishment. "Mother," he intoned, "if your judgment is based on the incident concerning the emerald bracelet, you must understand that no matter how any of us feel about it, nothing can be absolutely proven. Antoinette attempted something that is unforgivable, but it is not grounds for—"

She turned to him, halting further comment. Her regard softened. "I heard, Cain," she told him gently. "I heard it all." Her son averted his gaze. How like a boy he seemed—this proud, aggressive, authoritative man.

"I am not sure I understand," he said hesitantly.

"You understand me well, son," Vanessa returned. "I had taken my breakfast in my room that morning, but I became restless and decided to go down into my parlor. You and Antoinette were at the dining table. I did not wish to eavesdrop, Cain, but your voices became so loud that I could not help but hear the argument. Antoinette does not love you—she admitted herself that she is incapable of love. Further, she has colluded with her father to engineer a marriage for herself, and I find that repugnant." She paused. "I never liked her in the first place," she sniffed. "But after the incident with the emerald bracelet—and especially after that morning—I could no longer tolerate her in my home. And I wouldn't have either, had you not been so relentlessly noble about everything."

Cain sighed softly. His proud shoulders drooped. He could not look at his mother as he said, "I have not been . . . altogether noble."

"Have you not," Vanessa said, her tone heavy with irony. Cain lifted his gaze.

"No," he said rigidly. "I have done things of which my father would not be proud." Vanessa was reminded of the times when Cain was a boy and had done something he was ashamed to admit.

"Listen to me," she said in sympathy, "you men make entirely too much of your supposed responsibility toward 'frail womanhood.' We are not so frail as you imagine, Cain. I blame myself for many of your assumptions about women; I have not been the sturdiest example for you. But, please believe me, we are stronger than you think."

"Mother," Cain said quietly, "I have caused myself an obligation to Antoinette—"

"Did you cause that obligation, Cain," asked Vanessa, "or did she? Did you take her by force?"

Cain regarded her in bewilderment and surprise. "Of course not, Mother," he said. "You surely know me better than that."

"I do, Cain," she acknowledged. "My question was rhetorical." Cain's interest was piqued. He folded his hands behind his back and listened further to his mother's comments. "Did you seduce her?" she asked. "Did you promise marriage, or anything else? Did you ask anything of Antoinette other than an intimacy that is—or should be—most welcomed by people who love each other? You approached your intimacy with Antoinette in the spirit of love. She did not.

"You men, and some women, too, see intimacy as a monumental gift offered by a woman in return for your protection. Believe me, my darling Cain, a woman is as feeling a creature as a man, and unless she is a prostitute, she offers intimacy freely and with no expectation of reward except that inherent in the moment."

She moved to him and continued in earnest. "I know I am speaking more plainly than you may wish or expect me to, but I desperately want you to realize that you owe Antoinette nothing.

"If she loved you, Cain, then or now, we would not be discussing this, for your obligation to her would be clear. It would be an honest one, born of mutual respect. But that is not the case. This obligation you feel toward her has been designed, imposed on your relationship by conventions so time-worn and so out-of-date that they fairly reek with their own decay and corruption. And those conventions are corrupting, Cain. They stifle honesty between men and women."

Cain did not attempt to conceal his admiration for his mother's observations. His mind grasped with enlightening clarity the contrast between the very true obligation he felt toward Autumn and the false one, the one designed for him by societal convention, that he felt toward Antoinette. However, it did not change the facts. "I am afraid Antoinette and her father would see this matter in an entirely different light," he said.

"I agree. They see it according to their own design. But their design need not be yours, Cain. It seems to me that our 'pathetic little family,' as Antoinette describes us, needs a small change in perspective." Vanessa paused and returned to her mirror. Straightening her bodice, she said almost casually, "I shall not pressure you or attempt to advise you any further, Cain, but I am quite certain of one thing. That self-centered little creature who is so anxious to marry a wealthy and sophisticated man-about-town would not be equally anxious to marry a provincial doctor." She glanced at her son, allowing the significance of her words to penetrate his, up to now, extremely narrow perception. "What if," she resumed, "I held you to the terms of your father's will? Do you recall those terms?" Cain's brows furrowed. "I shall remind you of them. In order to receive your full inheritance, you were to set up a medical practice here in Cape May. That was your father's promise to the city, as it was his father's before him. Your father may have been misguided, but he was in earnest, Cain. He wished the city to have a Dr. Byron to serve it in perpetuity. I never held you to the terms of your inheritance, because I never believed you motivated in that direction. But I do ask the question. What if I decided to do so? As importantly, Cain, what if you yourself decided to comply with those terms? And what if you announced your compliance at, say, a party here at Byron Hall? I should say your future would take on a completely different design. Wouldn't you?" Vanessa neither expected nor waited for an immediate answer. She knew her son well enough to realize that he needed time to examine and absorb these notions. And she prayed she knew him well enough to count on his making the right choice. "Now," she said, apparently satisfied with her appearance, "I shall leave it to you to design your own future, my darling." She held out her hand. "Will you escort your mother downstairs?"

Cain offered his arm and they proceeded regally—the queen and the handsome young prince—across the second floor gallery and down the grand staircase to receive their guests. The carriages were already arriving.

Antoinette had chosen the city's elite to people this most auspicious affair. On her father's exquisitely coated arm, she greeted Cain and Vanessa as they stepped down into the entry hall.

"We shall need you both right here," she called brightly, indicating the place to her father's left. "You must be first, Mrs. Byron, then Cain, then me, and then daddy." When Vanessa and her son had obediently taken their places, Antoinette dimpled a proud smile. "We make the handsomest receiving line in the world," she bubbled.

"Indeed we do," agreed Hamilton St. John Fraser, bowing gallantly and lifting Vanessa's hand to his lips. "Damien would have enjoyed sharing his sister's joy, but as you know, Mrs. Byron, he is at school in Europe."

"Now don't anyone spoil our lovely picture by not smiling," Antoinette instructed.

All through the afternoon the crème of Cape May society passed beneath the great entry arches of Byron Hall. Commenting cordially on this most unprecedented event, the mayor assured Vanessa that she was as beautiful as ever she had been, and he kissed Antoinette's hand warmly and told her that she was a welcome addition to the formerly reclusive household. Selectmen and their wives greeted Vanessa with barely suppressed curiosity and congratulated Cain on his good fortune in securing the affection of the distinguished daughter of Hamilton St. John Fraser.

From the kitchen, Autumn listened to the jocularity of the arriving guests, and she and Carrie and the many servants hired for the occasion prepared themselves for the most wearying of afternoons. It had been decided that Autumn would hire and then supervise the servants. She'd accepted the job gratefully, though Cain had protested. Autumn would have done almost anything to absent herself from the public rooms of the house that day; she had no desire to face this pronounced evidence of Cain's coming marriage to Antoinette. The thought of losing Cain to the triumphant and fierce-hearted Antoinette was painful enough, but the thought that she would be mistress and not wife—an appendage to Cain's life and not its heart—stung

Autumn's pride and played havoc with her self-perception. She had not been raised to be a mistress; Autumn was not sure she even knew how to be one. But mistress she would be, she had determined, if that were the only way that she and Cain could be together. Autumn had watched herself grow thin and pale and wondered at Cain's continuing desire for her. Surely mistresses were expected to be something more than wan slips of girls. Mistresses of Autumn's imagination were vivacious creatures, full-spirited and certainly full-bodied—like Antoinette, she thought wryly. She sighed inwardly and stuffed a tiny meat-filled pie into her mouth.

Adding to the stress of the day was another concern. Autumn had penned a very unofficial invitation to someone and had delivered it herself. Now she wondered at the advisability of what she had done. Every half hour or so, she made her way around the back of the house to the side garden off the front parlor to furtively examine the milling guests. Undaunted by the swarms of people, she made her circuit, searching relentlessly for the one she alone was awaiting. Each time, she came back to the kitchen disappointed and a little less hopeful that Robert Moffat would attend. Autumn could well understand his hesitancy, but she prayed, nevertheless, that he would find the courage in his proud heart to come. She felt that, seeing him once, Vanessa would set convention aside and perhaps seize some happiness for herself.

"The announcement's going to be made, Miss Autumn," said Carrie as she hurriedly made her way into the kitchen with an empty tray. "And Dr. Byron wants you in there. He told me." Autumn winced.

"Oh, Carrie," she moaned, "you can't mean that." Carrie affirmed the request—or order—with an emphatic nod.

"He does, Miss Autumn. He sought me out and told me to get you into the front parlor. Him and Miss Fraser's going to stand on the side porch. Folks are already gatherin' in the garden and the parlor. They left the French doors open so everybody could see." Autumn's brows drew together as she set about folding tea napkins with a vengeance.

"Well, if he expects me to witness that particular announcement, he's got quite another think coming," she muttered.

"But, Miss Autumn," Carrie persisted darkly, "Dr. Byron was real insistent—you know how he can be—and if you don't come, he'll think that I—"

"I shall let him know that you delivered the message, Carrie. I shall make it very clear," she added categorically, "that you are not at fault—" At that moment, Vanessa appeared in the doorway.

"Autumn," she said with uncustomary assertiveness, "I am in great need of your assistance."

"What is the trouble, Vanessa?" she asked worriedly.

"I've left my walking stick upstairs, and I am feeling very weak."

"But you haven't used your walking stick in weeks," Autumn pointed out as she went to her. Vanessa took her arm firmly.

"Today I need it," she responded flatly.

"I shall get it for you."

"No. Just take me to a chair." The two women made their way from the kitchen arm in arm. Autumn's hopeful gaze scanned the crowd. Had Robert come? Had Vanessa seen him and become weakened by the encounter? It was not until Vanessa had steered her to a chair near the tall parlor windows, not until Cain and Antoinette and Mr. Hamilton Fraser appeared on the side porch, that Autumn realized she had been manipulated. She shot an accusing glance toward Vanessa, and that woman, settling herself comfortably into the chair, merely smiled.

"You can't leave now," Vanessa told her in a low tone. Horrified, Autumn realized she was right. Everyone was gathering about the doors, spilling from the parlor out onto the lawn. They were smiling and murmuring expectantly and watching Vanessa for her reaction. Autumn's sudden departure would cause a stir— and quite possibly some unwelcome speculation. With a furious frown toward her employer, Autumn stood her ground next to Vanessa's chair.

"We all know why we are here," began Mr. Fraser with an air of merriment. "But nothing is ever quite official until it has been *officially* announced." He droned on for several moments about the joys and hardships of fatherhood, causing rippling and indulgent laughter. Autumn lost track of his words until she realized the guests had raised their glasses in salute and were offering a cheer. Her heart twisted in pain, and her hand instinctively went to rest on Vanessa's shoulder. Her hand lifted in response and took Autumn's gently.

"And now I have an announcement." Cain's voice resonated above the gay approval of the guests, and Antoinette and her father glanced at him in surprise. "As you know," Cain continued, "Antoinette and I had planned to live in New York City. My soon-to-be father-in-law has generously provided us with a house there, and I am most grateful. However, I am going to suggest to him that he sell that house." Antoinette's mouth fell open, and Autumn's brows knitted. Vanessa only sighed with relief. Cain went on in the attending silence. "It has been my observation that, since my father's passing, Cape May has been without a general practitioner. With your approval, I would like to serve you in that capacity." The crowd roared its appreciation. "It is my intention to set up my practice," Cain added above the din, "right here at Byron Hall. And to show my sincerity and my commitment to this endeavor, it is also my intention to turn over my inheritance to my mother. I will be one of you, serving among you for as long as you will have me!" Tears came to Vanessa's eyes then, and she felt the warmth of love encloak her. Her son, precious to her as gold, had not only taken her suggestion, he had taken it to another plane entirely. He had done her one better.

"We are returning to the days of your grandfather!" cried one applauding gentleman, who remembered those days well.

"I'll be your first patient!" called out an otherwise dignified lady delightedly, and everyone laughed. Autumn barely heard the shouts and the applause and the crescendos of laughter, so stunned was she. She watched as Cain led Antoinette from the porch and into the parlor. He held her trapped in the circle of one strong arm, and "trapped" was exactly the way her astonished expression made her appear. Her green gaze was wide and uncomprehending, and her lips were parted in unspoken disbelief as they passed into the crowd that fought to congratulate them on both their marriage and Cain's altruism. She did hear Cain's murmured exhortation to her as they passed.

"Smile, Antoinette," he intoned, "or you'll spoil everything." Autumn looked down at Vanessa. Both ladies' eyes were welling with tears.

Winslow Beame had drifted back through the gaily mingling guests to stand beside them. "Gracious," he said, "how long has your devil of a son been planning this surprise?"

"I haven't the faintest idea, Win," Vanessa responded almost giddily. "He never mentioned a word of it to me."

Chapter 15

"I did not attend the party, little one, because I could not."

"Why?" Autumn prodded. "I was so disappointed. I just know that once you and Vanessa see each other you will—"

"It is not that simple," Robert interjected tolerantly. "I know it seems so, but it is not. Your disappointment aside, Autumn," he said with a small quirk of his brow, "there are considerations that you know nothing about." Autumn lowered her lashes.

"Thank you, Captain Moffat. I am properly chastised." Robert laughed softly, and Autumn looked up. "I really did not mean to sound so selfish, but it took a great deal of thought for me to imagine how to get you two together."

"I know," Robert said, patting her cheek. "And I am most grateful." They stood together on the shoreline where it met the sea, the lighthouse rising crystal-flecked in the sun behind them.

"Please understand, Robert, I've watched Vanessa regain her health only to see her mental state decline steadily since the day I presented your gift to her. It wasn't hard to guess that she longs for something she feels she can never have." The man's gaze lingered on Autumn for long moments and then drifted out to the farthest swells of the rolling ocean. At last, he indicated a bench above the shoreline at the base of the lighthouse.

"Let us sit down, little one," he said. As they settled themselves, Robert leaned forward, his forearms resting on his thighs, and rubbed his big weathered hands together. Autumn waited for him to speak. She waited a long time. Robert seemed to be forming his tale cautiously. The soft wash of the glittering spume upon the shore seemed to capture his attention. "I told you some of what happened between Vanessa and me—but not all," he began slowly. "All those years ago, after we had lived for a time with our secret love, we gave each other the most complete expression of that love. We shared perfect nights in our perfect love." He bowed his head. The sun shone on his silvered curls and he raked his fingers through them. "I am ashamed to tell you this, little one. I do not mind for myself, but for Vanessa . . ."

Autumn touched his great shoulder, and said, "I am not so callow as I seem, Robert." She smiled softly at his regard. "In actual years, I may be young, but I know of love, believe me. And Vanessa is my friend. Among friends there is no need for embarrassment, ever. In truth, I anticipated exactly what you have told me."

"What you did not anticipate, however, was a particular night." His blue gaze hardened to an icy gray. "You did not anticipate learning that Vanessa's son found us in my little room in the tower beneath the light and that he beat me savagely to within a hair's breadth of my life." He stopped abruptly and his chilling words hung in the blue spring air like daggers. Like daggers they plunged into Autumn's heart. Her fingertips flew to her mouth and she suppressed a gasp. "Do you wish me to go on, Autumn? Do you wish to hear it all?" Autumn only nodded. "I did not dare defend myself," Robert resumed resolutely, "for fear that, in his rage, Cain Byron would make it a fight to the death. And one of us would have died, of this I am convinced. If it had been me, that boy would have faced a prison sentence and a scandal from which he and his mother would never have been redeemed; if it had been Cain, Vanessa would never have forgiven me—and I would not have forgiven myself. And so I couldn't fight. I allowed that boy to vent a monstrous wrath without raising a hand in my own defense. I dream of that night, and I wonder if, in the lad's mind at any rate, there was a defense for what I had done."

Autumn's hand slowly fell to her lap as Robert finished his story. She tried not to envision that hellish scene, but it played itself out in horror-filled images. Autumn closed her eyes against the images, but they overwhelmed her. She caught the edge of the bench, steadying herself against the sudden rolling of the world. Robert reached out to steady her. "I am sorry, little one," he murmured. "I would not have upset you for all the world. I should have softened the story for you—"

"No, Robert. No. Such a tale cannot be softened. I insisted . . ." Autumn looked up. Her amber gaze was tear-glistened. "I am so sorry I forced you to tell me all this." She lifted her hand and touched his bearded jaw. He smiled and covered her hand with his own.

"You mustn't cry for me," he said. "Though I live with that memory, I also live with another, and that one is sweet. I shall only add to what I have already told you—that Cain threatened another violent confrontation if ever I attempted to see his mother again. No matter how much she and I long for what we had, I know the price of gaining it would be appalling. I will never fight that boy; I will never raise my hand against him. I blame myself for all that has happened. Cain was defending his mother against what he saw as a threat to her. He is Vanessa's son, and therefore, beloved by me."

"Things may have changed, Robert," offered Autumn. "Perhaps Cain has rethought—"

"Oh, no, little one, I cannot take that chance. The risk of my own life aside, I could not risk Vanessa's well-being. Can you imagine what it must have done to her to see her son in combat with the man she loved?"

Autumn knew exactly what it had done to Vanessa. Tears filled her eyes anew.

"But there must be some way," she said. "Some way . . ."

"If you think of it, Autumn," he said softly, sadly, "please let me know." She looked up into his regretful blue gaze. She dared not say to this already wounded soul that the real blame for all Vanessa's pain, for all his own pain, lay squarely on the shoulders of Cain Byron.

⋯⋯

Autumn traveled the Shore Road back to Byron Hall with an unsettled heart. She wondered how she might intervene in Robert's behalf and cursed the terror that filled her soul each time the question entered her mind. She attempted to see the situation from Cain's perspective, but found it hard. Cain had changed, his perspective had changed, and Vanessa said that Autumn had been at least partially responsible for that change. He was no longer the troubled if charismatic youth of his college days; he was a man, confident and growing more and more enlightened. As difficult as it was for Autumn to reconcile Cain's past with his present, she knew it must be more so for Robert.

As she entered the kitchen, her mind troubled and searching for possible solutions, Autumn was not happy to find Antoinette apparently awaiting her.

"I believe this is yours," that woman said. She held between her thumb and forefinger an envelope. She held it as though it contained some repugnant thing. Autumn reached for it resignedly. As was customary each week, her pay envelope had been left on the kitchen table. Before she could take it, however, Antoinette snatched it away. She smiled. Her gaze narrowed and became a lurid, acidic yellow-green. "This, then, is the truth of your relationship with Cain Byron," she said. Autumn shuddered.

"You know nothing of Cain and me, Antoinette," she answered, lifting her chin and ignoring the cold chill that raced beneath her flesh.

Antoinette's brow lifted as she said, "I know everything, Autumn." Her voice was soft, almost consoling. "I know you are his kept woman." Autumn's lips parted, but no words came from them. She stood before Antoinette and held herself rigid—and silent. "And here's the surprise, Autumn—I'm not going to do anything about it." She laughed lightly and tossed the envelope onto the table. "At least I've never done it for money."

"Haven't you, Antoinette?" asked Autumn. "Hasn't everything you've done been about money? You've admitted yourself that you don't love Cain. You wanted him because he was rich. The day of your tirade in the dining room was the day I realized how far you would go—for money, Antoinette. And I realized that day how much Cain had been hurt by your greed."

"And you decided to . . . lick his wounds," Antoinette countered with a smile. "How commendable, Autumn. How generous of you. Like a little white knight you rode out on your Pegasus and saved him from the demon harpy." She laughed fully. "Let me tell you something, miss," she continued, her voice deadening suddenly, "you have chosen the wrong woman with whom to do battle. Cain Byron wanted to get rid of me, but he hasn't. I am leaving Cape May, of course. But I would not break out the champagne if I were you. There will be no celebrations in this house. You see I am not ending our engagement; I am *postponing* it. Think about it, Autumn. Cain will be tied to me for as long as I will him to be. You will never have him."

"Why are you doing this?" asked Autumn in earnest.

"I realized early on that no efforts of mine would deter him from his lust for you," Antoinette answered conversationally. "When a rutting stag wants a willing doe, it is said he will knock down ages-old trees to get to her. But stags do not mate for life. He will tire of you soon enough, and I am betting he will tire of this precious bucolic doctoring life. How long will it be, I wonder, before the dynamic Dr. Byron succumbs to the pressures of boredom, of stagnation, of . . . constancy? And once he does, this mythic love you profess will make you, Miss Thackeray, ridiculously vulnerable." She paused and lifted the envelope, holding it out to Autumn. "You've earned it, dear, now try to enjoy it." Autumn stiffened. "Take it," Antoinette went on, lynx-eyed, "you may need it. Even a pittance can seem like a fortune when one's employer tosses one out onto the street. And you might not be receiving this little compensation for much longer. Once you and Cain are safely ensconced in your *affair de coeur*, no actual monies will change hands. In fact, from what I can gather, both of you will have to toady up to that eccentric old lady upstairs to realize a penny of the family fortune."

"She isn't old, Antoinette."

"My, how you do defend the poor, mad thing."

"If anyone is mad, Antoinette, it is you. How long do you intend to keep Cain on this leash you have designed? How long will it be before *you* succumb to boredom and stagnation? How long before you look into a mirror and discover that your youth and your beauty are lost to you, that your time for receiving emerald bracelets from male admirers has expired?"

"It looks as though we will both have to play the waiting game, Autumn." She tossed the envelope onto the table. "I, of course, shall be waiting in New York with my legion of friends and entertainment of all sorts. You will be waiting here with only the dour Dr. Byron and his little mother to console you. Of course, your mother's presence should afford you some comfort."

"My mother? What does she have to do with this?"

"Oh, nothing right at the moment. But she should be arriving within the week, and when she does—"

"In the name of God, Antoinette, what are you talking about?"

"You are right to invoke the name of our good heavenly father, Autumn. I think you will need all the help you can get. Your mother is coming here. Didn't I tell you I had written her?" Antoinette asked with elaborate ingenuousness.

"No. You did not," Autumn returned stonily.

"Well, I did. I penned a letter to her yesterday. It went out in the morning's mail. I advised her to catch the next coach to Cape May. I told her that, as an observer of this household, it was my duty to inform her that she ought to keep a strong matriarchal eye on the doings here. I mentioned Cain of course, and, let me see, there was something else. Oh, yes, I believe I said something about a *possible* illicit relationship between you and he—nothing libelous, you understand. But I suppose the implication was there. I really don't know how much more pain your mother can stand in this life, Autumn," she continued forlornly. "She has endured more scandal than any woman deserves." Autumn stared at Antoinette incredulously and reached out for the support of a nearby chair.

"You could not have done such a thing, Antoinette."

"You know I could and did, Autumn," Antoinette returned tightly. "Whether you acknowledge it or not, you have won, for the present. And to the victor belong the spoils." Antoinette laughed as she withdrew from the kitchen.

Autumn sat heavily in the chair. She seemed to have no strength. Cain had relinquished his entitlements for the sole purpose of eliminating Antoinette from their lives, but she was exerting more influence on them than ever. There was no point, Autumn reflected, in writing to her mother and telling her not to come; the letter would not reach Philadelphia before Antoinette's. And, she wondered, what would be the point of such a letter? Could Autumn deny the charges implied? A denial might only strengthen the accusations; denials had a way of doing that. Beyond that, Autumn had never lied to her mother, and she would not begin now. Still, she could not bear the thought of subjecting Isabel to any more pain than she had already suffered. She lowered her head into her hands. Weary and discouraged, Autumn might have allowed herself the indulgence of tears. But tears would not come; tears could not be forced. This was, in any event, no time for tears.

૭౿ ౭ઌ

Cain returned to the house that evening as Carrie and Autumn and Vanessa were taking their after dinner coffee in Vanessa's parlor. Vanessa had worn an oddly satisfied smile throughout the evening, and she had insisted that Carrie sit down with her and Autumn. Cain apologized for his intrusion; in his begrimed condition, his shirt collar loosened, his sleeves rolled up on his forearms, and his breeches stained with the day's ride, he seemed an incongruity in the neat room. But he was certain, he told the women, that they would forgive him when they heard his news. Autumn caught her breath as he strode to her and casually, almost breezily, kissed her cheek. This, then, was the way it was to be between them. There would be a new and open tenor to their relationship, it seemed. Autumn thought of Isabel and wondered how she would react to such an unconventional arrangement.

"I am too much in the grip of elation to stand on formality," Cain was telling the women. He glanced down at Autumn and his soft smile glinted in his eyes. He most definitely wanted her approval. "I have been to business all day, and part of that business concerns you, Carrie," he announced. Carrie stared without comprehension at her employer. "This day, Carrie, my life has begun—and so has yours." That woman stared dumbly at his face, framed by a tousle of black curls that brushed his forehead boyishly.

"My life has begun?" she asked.

"It has, Carrie Inman." He withdrew a sheaf of papers from his shirt and handed it to her. "This," he said warmly, "is the title to the piece of land for which you and Henry have been saving for years." He glanced toward Vanessa. "My mother mentioned to me that you had been saving long enough. And the money you've acquired can go to starting a family. I must tell you that I tried to present this to Henry today, but he insisted I bring it back to you.

The land and the house are both in your name."

"Oh, sir!" Carrie said on an astonished breath. "Oh, sir!" She jumped up and took Cain into a rough embrace. Then she turned to Vanessa and embraced her as well. "What the two of you have done for me . . . I can never thank you for it! You've given me the best gift a woman can get."

"And what is the best gift a woman can get, my girl?" Vanessa asked through her indulgent laughter.

"Why it's bein' with the man she loves," stated Carrie. There was a pause in the merriment, and Carrie moved to Autumn. "Now, Miss Autumn," she said, "if I'm movin' on, you've got to promise me you'll stay here and take care of this house for me." Autumn smiled up at her.

"I shall do my best, Carrie," she told the woman. She looked up at Cain, into the melting indigo of his gaze.

"You approve, Autumn?" he asked her.

"I do," she told him softly. Vanessa rose from her chair.

"Come with me, Carrie," she said. "Let us look over that deed to make sure it is accurate." Before the two women could leave, Cain stopped them.

"Carrie," he said, "I must ask you to stay a few days. Autumn's mother should be arriving any day, and we need to impress that lady with the best accommodations our house can provide." Carrie nodded her happy consent and accompanied Vanessa from the room.

"You said my mother is coming, Cain," Autumn ventured uncertainly.

"And so she is."

"But how did you know? Did you speak with Antoinette?" Cain's face became grim.

"Before I rode out this morning, Antoinette stopped me. She told me what she had done—about the letter she had written. I suppose she could not resist having one last triumph over us. But I checkmated her, Autumn. I wrote my own letter, and I sent it with my fastest coach and horses. Your mother will arrive very soon, and she will arrive by private coach as is her due. If we are very lucky, she will never see Antoinette's letter—and if she does, we will have the opportunity to diffuse the scurrilous message it contains. The ideal situation, of course, is that your mother will see only a loving and respectful letter, written by me, asking her to visit Byron Hall."

"Cain," Autumn said breathlessly. "I am overwhelmed by your thoughtfulness." He smiled a self-deprecatory half smile.

"My thoughtfulness, darling, is exceeded only by my love for you. Now," he asked, "why the grave expression?"

"It is only that. . . we have never really discussed what will happen next," she said. "What can I tell my mother?"

He lowered himself to her side and took her hands in both of his. "You may tell her anything you wish, Autumn." She hesitated. So many apprehensions invaded her thoughts all at once. She thought of Antoinette and the threatening words she had spoken in the kitchen. Would Cain tire of her? Would she be abandoned? Dared she give herself fully to Cain Byron? She thought of Robert, and the scene in the little room beneath the light replayed itself in her mind. Autumn shuddered involuntarily. Could she completely trust a man capable of such violence?

"Cain," she said, "I do not wish to leave my mother with a false impression—or even an unclear one. I cannot speak to her about our relationship until I understand it myself."

Cain, watching her, rose slowly, letting go her hands and allowing them, still clasped, to lie in her lap. "I thought everything was clear between us, Autumn," he said cautiously, his exhilaration of a moment ago vanishing.

"Nothing is clear, Cain. Nothing. That is what is so unsettling. Everything between us is so . . . vague. How can you expect me to live with such uncertainty?"

"We've both known all along that until Antoinette releases me from my obligation to her, we are not free to marry." When she did not speak, he moved to the French windows, opened to the wafting night breezes. Light curtains fluttered at each side of them. He stood between them, his proud shoulders drawn back. He plunged his hands into the pockets of his jodhpurs and looked out over the moon-washed lawn. "Naturally, your decisions are your own to make; I would not force you to do anything against your will." Autumn swallowed against a rising hurt. And the hurt was not hers alone. She knew she had caused Cain great injury. He turned back to her after a time. Leveling his regard, he impaled her with a stony gaze. "What is it you don't understand, Autumn?" She could not look at him, for his face, for all its rigidity, for all its hard-jawed strength, was a mask of pain.

"I am not . . . sure, Cain. I'm not sure of anything." He charged across the room in one great stride, looming over her. His demand for justice was compelling. He did not need to mention that he had given up everything for her.

"Of what are you not sure, Autumn?" he demanded. When she did not answer him immediately, he grasped her wrist and drew her from the chair to face him directly. "I asked of *what* are you not sure?"

"Cain," Autumn gasped, "let me go!" He might have shaken

her, but instead he reined the rage that threatened to overwhelm them both. He let her go.

"Answer me," he grated. Her widened gaze lifted. The color had drained from her face. "Autumn," he intoned, battling a powerful and, Autumn conceded, well-founded bitterness. "Please . . ." He paused, seeming to struggle for words. "In the name of God, why are you doing this?" The words came out in what might have been, had Cain been less angry, a groan. Autumn felt tears well up, and Cain immediately enfolded her in his embrace. "Autumn, what are you afraid of?" he entreated. "You must tell me what is troubling you. Not two days ago we were the best of lovers." Autumn drew away from him and looked up into his eyes. Their luster had dimmed to a cloudy sapphire, and torment raged behind the clouds. *The best of lovers!* The phrase caught and tore at Autumn's heart. Without a word, she reached up, wrapping Cain's neck in her arms, dragging his lips down to meet hers. She held him for a long, ravaging moment, entrapped in a kiss of such savagery that even she was astonished by the ferocity of its command. Autumn dragged herself from him and could not check the compelling impulse that made her suddenly swing back her arm and land a stinging slap on his jaw. Cain's head jerked back and his eyes widened. Tears raged now in her heart. She could not bear the hurt she'd caused him, and she could not endure the hurt he'd caused others. Robert Moffat flashed into her mind, that salty, smiling bear of a man. And now Cain was asking to be to her what he'd refused to allow his mother to be to Robert. The irony and hypocrisy of it nearly overwhelmed her. She raised her hand again, but this time Cain was prepared. He stopped the blow by grasping her wrist. "Autumn, please," he said, astounded, his own anger gone. She wrenched her arm away from his grasp and began to beat wildly at his chest. Not wishing to cause her injury, he could do no more than manage to fend off the blows. At last he was able to grab her about the waist, and with some further effort, he managed to pin her arms behind her. "Please, Autumn," he said, his breath and hers coming in harsh gasps, "tell me what enrages you so. What have I done?" Her head fell against his chest. Her fury spent, her outrage depleted, her strength deserted her. Her knees buckled beneath her, and Cain swept her up into his arms and carried her to a small sofa near the hearth. Her head fell back over his arm, and Cain noted the blue pulse that throbbed at the base of her throat, so vulnerable, so sweetly escalated by some secret wrath. He lay her down, kneeling beside her and watched her as she unclosed her eyes. Autumn looked at him for a long time. Her gaze took on a liquid, jewel-like luster.

Why, she wondered could she not say the things she wanted to say to him? Why could she not tell him of her fears? Why could she not tell him of her talk with Robert and simply ask him about his feelings for the man? Autumn knew why—she was afraid. At the bottom of all her conflicting feelings, she knew she was afraid of losing Cain Byron. He was bound to her by nothing more than an ephemeral and unfocused emotion.

"Make love to me, Cain," she said abruptly.

"I beg your pardon, love?" he responded, unsure of what he had heard.

"Make love to me," she repeated. "Make love to me forever, Cain. Let time and place be suspended. Let the heavens open to welcome us. And let us make our home there. When terrible things happen, when we are frightened or angry or disillusioned, let us always remember that we can go home—together." She raised her arms and entwined them about his neck. Cain, with unaccustomed uncertainty, lowered his lips to hers. He had no idea what had generated her anger or what had made it flow into this most disconcerting but most welcome direction. "Will you? . . . make love to me?" His muffled answer may not have served other questions, but it was plain enough for this occasion. He lifted her into his arms and strode with her from the room, up the front staircase and across the second floor gallery to his chamber. He pushed at one heavy door with his broad shoulder, sliding it open, and swept them both into the dark, moon-shadowed room.

He lay Autumn on the thickly draped bed and gazed down at her for a long incredulous moment. He realized that some terrible conflict was playing havoc with her emotions right now. Some turbulence of thought drove her to both violence and desire. He hesitated to advantage himself, and yet the lure of her sweet aggression was more than he could ignore. "Are you sure you want to do this, Autumn?" he asked her. She drew him to her.

"I am sure of only one thing, Cain, and that is our love and its most perfect expression. Nothing else makes sense to me."

"You fill me with wonder," he whispered. He pushed himself up and moved across the room to lock the doors. To his astonished pleasure Autumn followed him. She stood before him and languidly began to unfasten the lacings of her gown. A velvet heat began to flow through him, clutching and clawing at his restraint. She allowed her clothing to slide down the delicate curves of her form to fall in a frothy heap at her ankles. She was now protected only by her corset and beneath that a lacy chemise that barely concealed the upthrusting of her full young breasts. Cain caught his breath. In the moonlight she appeared to be a lustrous angel fallen to earth only to give him pleasure. She lifted her arms and loosened her hair, allowing it to cascade like liquid pearls about her shoulders. She reached out, and with the enticement of her fingertips, she divested his broad shoulders of his light shirt. Drawing and stretching the fabric tautly down his arms, she leaned to him, caressing his furred chest with her tongue. His head fell back, and he said her name again and again as the delirium of passion seething beneath his flesh engulfed him. In an agonized fever of need, he lifted her, sweeping her from her feet, and carried her to the great bed. He lay her down, tearing at the fragile lacings of her corset, rending it and the chemise from her body. Enraptured by a torrent of need, he explored and enticed her flesh. At last he took her in a towering rage of desire, pressing her to him in soul-melting undulations of ecstasy. Time became suspended. They were lifted together to a crescendo of heavenly repletion. In that moment, their souls melded in a harmony of star-kissed rapture.

Autumn's breath came raggedly, and Cain held her to him. He stroked and soothed her trembling flesh and waited for her breathing to even. At last he looked down on her in puzzled wonder. His onyx gaze held bewilderment, a certain awe, and unchecked admiration. But Autumn did not note his regard. Like a pearl, she gathered herself into his embrace as she gave herself languorously to slumber. No word passed between them.

Cain watched her as the moon passed his windows, swathing her in the luster of its light. She seemed to sleep untouched by her earlier distress, unscathed by the torture that had consumed her. She seemed so fragile in the setting of his muscled arm and so at peace as she snuggled against him. He wondered, as he awaited sleep, whether that peace would be transient or lasting.

His brows quirked as he surveyed her opaline form. She was a miracle of mysteries to him. It amazed him that this wonder of a woman, this most arresting of creatures, this most fascinating, troublesome, bewitching, adorable being had consented to be his.

Chapter 16

Within a week, Isabel Thackeray arrived one early evening. She was ushered into the mansion with a tender respect by Carrie, who left her in the front parlor—that grand and most prepossessing of rooms—while she hurried off to apprise the family of the lady's presence. Used to luxury, though she had not enjoyed such amenities for a very long time, Isabel was not intimidated by the room. Rather, as she pulled off her gloves, she surveyed it with both admiration and a cool and calculating eye. The wallpaper was a pale, shimmery topaz and was reflected in a pier glass framed in gilt, which hung above a scallop-shell mantelpiece of rare Cuban mahogany. On either side of the deep hearth were lofting French windows draped in pale lavender silk with looping valances of gold velvet. Facing the windows and hearth was a Renaissance revival parlor set in shades of purple and ivory satin. Isabel took appropriately appreciative note of the impressive chandelier that hung above her in the center of the room. It was at least three feet in diameter and glittered with hanging crystals of amethyst and topaz. Chinoiserie adorned elaborately carved etageres; the carpets were Aubusson; the ceramic was Capodimonte; the chairs were Chippendale. With a soft smile of both appreciation and melancholy, Isabel approved the obvious refinement of her daughter's employer, if not, as yet, the man himself.

"It's a . . . cozy room. Wouldn't you agree?" The voice came from behind Isabel. She glanced about the cavernous chamber to find, at one of many connecting doors, a tall, queenly woman watching her. "I am Vanessa Byron," that woman said as she approached her guest. "You must be Isabel."

"I am," said Mrs. Thackeray, extending her hand. "You are Dr. Byron's mother, no doubt." Vanessa nodded. She cast a wry gaze about the room.

"Cain's father, my deceased husband, always hoped for just the reaction you gave as you entered this room. It was designed for people who know quality." Vanessa's regard drifted back to her guest, and she smiled. "I suspect, Mrs. Thackeray, that you are one of those." Isabel nodded.

"I am so pleased, Mrs. Byron, that I was able to present you with an appropriate response." Both women laughed softly.

"Please, forgive my popping in and surprising you that way," Vanessa said as she ushered Isabel to the sofa. Before the women sat down, however, Vanessa interrupted with another thought. "I hope you will not think it impolite of me, Isabel—if I may call you by your first name—but I might suggest that we get to know each other in a more congenial setting." She glanced about reflectively. "This room was not created for cordiality."

"I do not think it at all impolite, Vanessa."

"My own parlor is not half so lavish as this, but it is not half so ceremonial." The two women passed through a series of connecting doors and finally sat together in Vanessa's more intimate, more lighthearted room on rather faded, extremely comfortable chairs. Though the furniture was of a decidedly uncertain lineage, the décor more personally than publicly pleasing, both women, though cultured and accustomed to great wealth, seemed quite at ease. Carrie brought tea, lit lamps, and announced woefully that Cain and Autumn were out for an after-dinner ride, and that one of the stablemen had been sent to find them. And he would find them, she assured the ladies, her tone implying an "or else."

"Autumn was so nervous about your arrival," Vanessa said by way of explanation. "She could not keep herself still. Carrie was appalled that Cain should take her riding with your visit imminent. Her worst fears have been realized." Vanessa laughed. "I am afraid that Carrie deems herself quite the expert on propriety."

"Proper or not," said Isabel sipping her tea, "I am very glad, in a way, that my daughter is not here to greet me. I, too, have been a bit nervous about seeing her after all these months. I sent her off as a little girl, and now she is a woman." Her words trailed off.

"She is a remarkable woman," Vanessa offered. Isabel regarded her earnestly.

"Is she, Vanessa? Oh," she said suspending her hostess's hastily advanced endorsement, "I know Autumn is a lovely woman—she was a lovely child—but time and circumstances have a way of changing people." Isabel's eyes, a remarkable brown with flecks of green, softened with a certain sadness. "Autumn had a beautiful, a most advantaged, childhood, but the last few years were a struggle for all of us. Her father, you see, was a zealous man—something of a rebel, in fact. He could never accept the status quo. In the end, he was not satisfied with his own wealth and position in the world, he desired that everyone should have a piece of that pie. He made unfortunate loans to people, backing their schemes and dreams, and he offered his own money when their designs failed. He was an optimist and a most generous man. He was the most foolishly, gallantly generous man I have ever known." She sighed. "His generosity and his optimism cost him his life, and in many ways, his daughter's life as well."

Vanessa studied the proud, petite woman sitting opposite her. While she could recognize the father's traits in Autumn, she could see the mother's, too. Isabel was gloriously feminine, with a luxurious mane of upswept chestnut curls and a perfect white cameo of a face. Yet, about her there was a lack of innocence, a spareness of emotion, a cynicism that Autumn had not acquired. Vanessa understood that cynicism but for a very different reason.

"My husband was quite the opposite," she observed. "He was not generous, either with his emotions or his money. He was, in fact, the most arbitrarily prudent of men. Nothing was ever spent unless for purposes of display. That room in there—the one in which I greeted you—is a monument to his wealth and stature. Everything in this house gave evidence to his success." She looked briefly into the deepening twilight outside the French window and watched the light lawn curtains flutter for a long moment. She glanced back at her guest. The two women were of an age, though Isabel was a few years younger than Vanessa. How pleasant a thing, how luxurious and comfortable, she mused inwardly, to have a woman who might understand long-suppressed thoughts and feelings. Vanessa sensed a bond forming between them. No truth need be hidden from this woman, no expression denied. "Oh, Isabel," she said quietly, "if your husband took your daughter's life with his generosity, mine took my son's life with his pernicious stewardship." She paused. "Cain was a most light-spirited lad. He was content to roust about the town in highest ardor. He had starch and vigor. But his father wanted him to be a proud complement to the family prestige. He insisted Cain attend the best schools and threatened to cut him out of the family entitlements unless he agreed to follow the dynastic dictates of the Byron line. There was no room for discussion—ever—on any subject. He married off our daughters to the proudest of families. He held us all up as examples of what a man can accomplish when he keeps tight control of his environment.

"When my husband died, Isabel, I felt sadness, of course, but I must add to that a certain qualification." Vanessa's tone altered. "His hand was so strong, his will so . . . crippling that I felt, almost, a sense of . . . a *terrible* sense of liberation. It is very hard to explain, but that day, the day he died, I went up into my room and . . ." She paused, looking at her guest, her expression solemn. "Isabel, I went up into my room and I laughed." The words had come out in a rush as though Vanessa was thankful to be unburdened of them. "I laughed, Isabel, for the first time in years. I could not then, nor can I now, imagine why I reacted that way at such a sad time. But suddenly the world seemed brighter. The birds' songs outside my window seemed more melodious than they ever had; the sky shone with a new luster, and the air was pure and clean. I was a child again, Isabel." And very abruptly there were tears in Vanessa's eyes. She wiped at them and took an impatient breath. "I cannot imagine why I told you such a thing," she said hastily. "You must imagine me positively insane. I thought myself insane for some time after that." Isabel set down her cup and went to her hostess.

"I understand, Vanessa," she said with a comprehension she did not completely grasp. There was a sense of wonder in her tone. She knelt close to Vanessa's chair and took the woman's hand in her own. "My husband was not cruel; he was kind. But he was controlling nonetheless. He sacrificed everything we had for a cause that *he* believed in. As in your family, everything we did and everything we had was controlled by my husband. His ideas of what was right took precedence over every other consideration. Proud men, Vanessa, whether they are openhanded or penurious, are still proud men. They destroy what should be most important to them. They place their families second to their desire to control their little piece of the world. When my husband died, though I loved him completely, I, too, felt a burdensome sense of lightness. I, too, feared what I felt. And I have never mentioned it to anyone, Vanessa, till now." They stared at each other for a long time. The silence between them was a knowing one. Isabel moved to reclaim her seat. "My greatest regret," she commented, "was that I did not take the time to teach my husband humility." She looked up to find Vanessa watching her. "Oh, my," said she, "we are a pair of the most unconventional widows, are we not?" They laughed together companionably. Isabel picked up her tea and sipped at it reflectively. "I do hope for so much more for my daughter than what we have known in our marriages," Isabel said quietly.

"And I for my son," Vanessa agreed. "You know, Isabel," she resumed after a short pause, "Autumn is very precious to me. She is like one of my children."

"I am happy to hear that, Vanessa."

"Please understand, I do not make this statement idly. I owe Autumn my life. I wish everything for your daughter that I would wish for my own. I love her dearly." Isabel cocked her head, curious at Vanessa's intensity of expression. "She came here to Byron Hall as an employee, but she remains as a beloved member of this family. I mean that quite literally, Isabel."

"I see," Isabel responded with bare emotion. "Then it is true. The letter I received from one Miss Antoinette Fraser is true." She set down her cup with a delicate click.

"Not completely," Vanessa told her. "Though I have had no access to the actual letter, Autumn told me about it, and I can only imagine that it contained jealous ravings. Antoinette is a dreadful and amoral woman."

"I suspected as much. The missive was barely coherent, the message crawling with hate. And then your son's letter was delivered. And it was most respectful."

"You may count on my son's deference, Isabel. He loves your daughter, I should say, to distraction."

"And how does Autumn feel about him?"

"She loves him, too—completely."

At that moment, Cain and Autumn burst into the room.

"Mother!" Autumn squealed in delight. She ran to Isabel and gathered her into an embrace, nearly toppling them both in the process. "We had no idea when you would arrive," she said, drawing away and examining her mother adoringly. Isabel returned the examination with an approving smile. She had never seen her daughter in riding breeches and commented on the sensible arrangement. "Cain and I went shopping in the city today. I insisted on buying them, to his discomfort." She smiled mischievously in Cain's direction and twirled for her mother's further analysis. "We made a few other purchases," continued Autumn excitedly, "not the least of which was a gift for you. We found a wonderful gold and coral necklace. I'll just go get it—" She stopped abruptly. "Oh, Mother," she gasped, "where are my manners?" She took a long calming breath, and proudly introduced her mother to Cain. Isabel extended her hand and made a brief, though most thorough, inspection of him. Silently, she pronounced him dashing, magnetically handsome, and meltingly masculine. She smiled tranquilly.

"How do you do, Dr. Byron," she said with matriarchal assurance. "Your letter and invitation were most kind." Cain bowed with courtly deference over her hand.

"And you, Mrs. Thackeray, were most kind to accept." His eyes, as he lifted his regard, glinted with a kind of knowing incandescence. *And* a rogue where women were concerned, observed Isabel wryly. Cain Byron was not unaccustomed to the art of charming a lady, and Isabel was not unaccustomed—or disinclined—to being charmed. She allowed him to usher her to her seat as she and Vanessa exchanged knowing smiles. Isabel fully understood her daughter's giddiness. Once seated, she assessed Autumn with a loving perusal.

"You look well, my darling."

"And you, Mother. Won't you come upstairs?" Autumn said hastily. "Let me show you to your room. You must be exhausted. It is not so long ago that I made that same journey from Philadelphia to Cape May. I know from experience how wearying it is."

"You forget, Autumn," responded Isabel, taking her daughter's extended hands but retaining her seat, "I came by private coach, a most luxurious private coach." She looked up at Cain. "And I would like to become acquainted with your employer. Apart from the fact that he possesses a fine coach and four and that he doesn't approve of women in breeches, I know nothing of him. Though your letters speak glowingly of Mrs. Byron—and I have seen for myself her excellent health and wit—you rarely mention her son." Cain's composure lapsed immediately. He shoved his hands into his pockets and paced to the window. "Do the two of your ride together often?"

Autumn hesitated, but Cain said quietly, "Quite often, Mrs. Thackeray."

"How wonderful for you. There is nothing like riding for fun and exercise."

"Nothing in the world," put in Autumn with an uneasy brightness. "We've ridden almost every day since . . . since . . ."

"Since the weather has been warm, I suppose," offered Isabel.

"Yes. Yes indeed, Mother. Ever since the weather has been warm."

"Since the first part of June, actually," piped Vanessa. "Wasn't it then, Cain darling, that you began to ride with Autumn on a daily basis?" Cain nodded.

"I believe it was, Mother," he offered, frowning darkly in her direction. "You see, Mrs. Thackeray, Autumn and I—I should say your daughter and I—have become . . . friends." His mother looked at him sharply. Then her eyes fell on Autumn, who said nothing. There was, however, both resoluteness and uncertainty warring in her countenance. Vanessa's regard drifted to Isabel. She merely seemed interested in what everyone had to say.

"Friends?" she asked placidly.

"More than friends, Mother," Autumn amended. "Though, you see . . . there cannot be a courtship."

Cain stepped forward, drawing his hands from his pockets, and stood before Isabel. "Mine is the regret, Mrs. Thackeray," he interjected solemnly. He lowered his onyx gaze. "I have made mistakes in my life but none so regrettable as those concerning your daughter. Assumptions have been made by others which were completely unfounded." Isabel regarded him steadily.

"I am afraid I don't understand," she said. Vanessa refrained from mentioning that no one in his right mind could possibly have understood such a fuzzy explanation. She cursed the conventions of the time that forced everyone to be so vague and roundabout regarding their feelings. Autumn sat down near her mother.

"Cain is already engaged," she explained.

"I see," said Isabel quietly. She regarded her daughter squarely. "What are your feelings in this matter, Autumn?"

"I am fully aware that, at the moment, anything other than friendship between Cain and me is impossible."

"I am devoted to your daughter, Mrs. Thackeray," Cain said, "and it is my intention to love and care for her forever." The words "marriage" and "wife" had not been mentioned, and they were conspicuous by their absence.

"Well," Isabel stated on a breath, "I believe I understand more than I did initially. You know," she added, "I am considerably more fatigued than I imagined myself to be. I would appreciate being escorted to my room." Vanessa rose abruptly.

"I shall be happy to do the honors, Isabel." As she advanced to her guest, she said, "Won't you ask Carrie to fix a light supper, Cain dear?" She cast a softer regard on Autumn. "You may bring it up to your mother later."

Once the older women had withdrawn, Cain sank heavily into the chair vacated by his mother. "Oh, Lord," he groaned, allowing his head to roll back and raking his fingers through his curls. He regarded Autumn levelly at last. "I am sorry, love. I would not have compromised you for the world."

"It is comforting to know," she said flatly, "that I have the advantage of such a protector." The last word came with a less than complimentary edge. Cain's gaze narrowed.

"Autumn," he said, clenching his words, "what could I have done? You do want us to be honest with your mother, don't you?" Autumn raised an elegantly winged brow and her chin concurrently. Her amber gaze darkened to a stygian gold.

"You might have been like other men, Cain Byron, and accepted my favors incidentally. It was not necessary for you to declare eternal devotion right in front of my mother." Cain's brows lifted, but Autumn's forbidding posture ruled out a rejoinder.

Instead, he hid a smile, observing only, "You are a most unusual woman, Autumn Thackeray."

"And one in a most unusual predicament," she returned. "If you had left it that we were merely friends, I could have simply let that suffice as an explanation for our closeness. But mothers are notoriously curious about men who say they will love and 'care for' their daughters forever without adding they will marry them, too."

"Have you no faith in the power of love?" inquired Cain. "Don't you wish your mother to know, as I do, that one day we will be Dr. and Mrs. Byron?"

Autumn sighed and averted her gaze.

"Who is being the optimist now, Cain?"

"Oh, come now, Autumn," he objected, "you cannot really imagine that Antoinette will sacrifice her whole life for the sake of wrecking ours. She will be madly in love with someone else before the season is out. In the meantime, we shall enjoy the most glorious summer of our lives, and we shall enjoy it in the fullest confidence that when autumn comes—that most magnificent of seasons—we shall be husband and wife." He paused and stood slowly, moving cautiously to her. "You look," he observed, "as though I have just sentenced you to torture on the rack." Capturing her against him, he added, "Any torture you experience at my hands, love, will be sweet, I promise you." He lowered his lips to hers and they shared a searing kiss. "Now," said Cain on a husky breath, "go up to your mother. Tell her the truth. Tell her further that you adore Cain Byron and have every reason to believe that he will make you the happiest of women. Tell her all that, my sweet. And tell her also that you fully expect that every morning of your life, from this day on, you will awaken with a smile." He pressed her to him, and Autumn felt the thunder of his heart against her cheek. "Tell her all those things, Autumn Thackeray, and believe them, for they are the truest words I have ever spoken."

Chapter 17

Few words were needed between mother and daughter, though many were spoken. Isabel counseled that Autumn must make her own decisions, and Autumn, for her part, wished that she were five years old again and might depend on her mother to tell her what to do. Isabel did warn of the pressures that would be placed on both her daughter and on Cain Byron by standards of convention manufactured and guarded by an unforgiving society. Those pressures, Autumn assured her, were already taking their toll. Their relationship would always be a stormy one, it seemed, wracked not only with external tensions but with internal ones as well.

"Cain is an entirely sincere lover," conceded Isabel, as she and her daughter strolled the meadows that surrounded Byron Hall, their wide skirts trailing deep swaths in the grasses. "But he is nevertheless only a man. He has been bred to believe that only *his* judgments are the valid ones. That is the real challenge of your relationship, Autumn."

"I can face those challenges, Mother. Failure lies in only one direction, and that would be abandoning Cain to his notions of his own infallibility."

"What then will you do about Vanessa and Robert?"

"I don't know yet. That problem seems insoluble."

"But you do know, Autumn, that no problem resides in the universe that does not have a corresponding solution."

"I do know that," Autumn responded, smiling. Arm in arm they strolled down to the sea. "And what of you, Mother?" she asked as they reached the sun-smeared water of the bay. "Have you thought of remarriage?"

"Oh, I shall never remarry, Autumn. That much is clear to me. But I have plans of a sort."

"Of a sort?" inquired Autumn.

"Right now they seem unfocused, but I dream of opening a business."

"What sort of business?"

"As you know, Autumn, I have always been a talented seamstress—or at least a patient one. I have been taking in sewing since your father's death, but now I think I should like to open a shop—a real dress shop right in the heart of Philadelphia. When you were little I designed many of your pretty outfits. I should have enjoyed making them myself, but your father didn't think it would be seemly. Our dressmaker became most impatient with me," Isabel remembered, laughing. "She always said I should leave the mundane and technical aspects of sewing to her."

"And so you should have, Mother," Autumn said.

"Why?"

"Because . . . Well, a lady of your wealth simply doesn't do her own sewing."

"I am no longer a lady of wealth, Autumn."

"But a shop, Mother, in the center of Philadelphia. At least I left the city to live out my humiliation. Please, I beg of you, think of your reputation." Isabel eyed her daughter with a tilted perusal.

"What reputation have I to protest? Friends have deserted me; invitations are nonexistent. You know how it hurt when people we had known for years passed us on the street without acknowledgment. We were not even paid condolence calls. You and I, Autumn, became invisible. In that great city of 'brotherly love' I am still invisible. Now I should like to carve out a purpose for my life. As I mentioned, I shall never marry again, I shall never turn my life over to another. And I refuse to remain invisible."

Autumn could not deny that her mother's reasoning was sound. But she had to protest that her plans were unrealistic. To start a business of one's own one needed capital, resources to which Isabel had no access. Women could not get bank loans. Women could not rent business property. "On the other hand," Autumn mused aloud, "if you could acquire some money through *private* investment . . ." She turned to her mother excitedly. "I have saved some money. I can think of no better use for it."

"I could not take your money, Autumn."

"But it would be an investment, Mother!" Isabel turned the idea over in her mind.

"An investment," she repeated quietly.

"And I am certain Vanessa would be interested in such a venture. We could be a corporation."

"If we succeed," said Isabel, as she and Autumn hurried back to the house, "we shall be the talk of every board meeting from here to Menlo Park."

Vanessa not only approved the idea, she had contributions of her own to make. She insisted that all three of them must travel to Philadelphia and choose a house where Isabel could not only live, but where she might have room to work and store her inventory of materials and equipment. Cain was apprised of their plans and was naturally dubious. His most vigorous objection revolved around the fact that none of the women knew anything about business.

"I beg to differ, Dr. Byron," put in Isabel. "I do know something about business. Quite a lot, in fact. Though I took no active role in my husband's professional life, I was an avid listener. He confided in me regularly, and I have always been a quick study." Cain eyed her in some astonishment as she proceeded to explain her plans. Autumn felt a welling pride in her mother's acumen. She displayed, as it happened, a rare and cunning understanding of the procedures and strategies involved in running a business.

At one point, Vanessa found it necessary to remind Cain that the money was hers to invest if she wished; Autumn found it necessary to remain absolutely silent throughout their talks. In many ways she understood Cain's rigorous disapproval—and it brought her closer to him. Whether he liked the notion or not, approved it or not, she, Isabel, and Vanessa were going to become businesswomen. This was not a circumstance with which Cain Byron, autocratic and proud protector of women, was familiar. Autumn recognized that in not seeking his advice, they had affronted his pride; he was probably more hurt than angry. She found his befuddlement endearing. What she did not find endearing was Cain's strenuous opposition to her accompanying her mother back to Philadelphia.

"Under no circumstances will I allow it," he told Autumn furiously.

"It is not for you to allow or disallow, Cain," she reminded him.

"Woman," he said, shaking an avenging finger at her, "you are a member of my household, and you will do as I say." Autumn bit back the obvious rejoinder that would have served to remind him of exactly whose household she was, in fact, a member. Instead she stood her ground rigidly.

"Let me tell you something, Dr. Byron, you shall have to tie me in the cellar to keep me from going to Philadelphia. . . . I can rail and brawl as well as you, sir. In the end you will gladly ship me off to Philadelphia." Cain hesitated. Autumn was nothing if not formidable when in one of these moods. He took in the elevation of her chin, the molten glistening of her eyes, the clenching of her small fists. For all she was the daintiest thing under a bonnet, she could, when she set her mind to it, give pause to the manliest of men—she'd faced down Winslow Beame fearlessly enough, reflected Cain. He was hard pressed, even in his wrath, not to smile at the memory. Still, he could not allow her and his mother to go traipsing off without male protection.

"Autumn," he said, attempting a reasonable tone, "it is not right, three women on their own in a big city."

"My mother has been on her own for more than a year, Cain, and she has survived quite successfully," Autumn reminded him.

"I shall miss you," he interjected quietly. Autumn looked at him, stunned to her bones. The sudden change in his demeanor was completely unexpected, as was the message he conveyed. Apparently, the admission was a surprise to Cain as well, for he turned from her abruptly.

"Oh, Cain," she assured him, "I shall miss you, too." Her mood had changed instantly. "Come with us," she entreated, moving to him. She lifted her hand to his proud shoulder. "Please do. The builders will be coming in to set up your office, Cain, and you won't be able to start your practice for a few weeks anyway." He turned back to her, his gaze questing. Autumn brushed at the jet curls that fell over his forehead. "I love you so much, my darling," she said gently. "And I know how difficult all this is to absorb. But please try to realize how important it is to me." Very suddenly he took her into his arms. He held her to him for a long moment. She could feel his uncertainty, his confusion. These were not emotions Cain understood.

"I can't bear the thought of losing you," he told her. "That fear haunts me every day." Again, Autumn found herself astounded by his admission. His fears were hers. She clung to him fiercely.

"Cain Byron," she told him with soft intensity, "I told you once that I would dog your every step. I told you that my soul would be yours. Remember those words, Cain, and believe them, for they are the truest words I have ever spoken."

❧ ❧

It had been decided that two coaches would be needed for the trip. While Isabel and Vanessa rode in one, the other was taken by Cain and Autumn. The baggage, hastily packed, was distributed—if a bit carelessly—between the two, and the foursome laughed in jolly acknowledgement of their rather messy departure from the proud baronial presence of Byron Hall. They arrived in the historic city of Philadelphia resembling something like a ragtag deployment of vagrant yokels. While Cain, Autumn, and Vanessa took rooms in the stately Hotel Olympus on the Ben

Franklin Parkway, Isabel went on to her small apartment over-looking the Schuylkill River on Walnut Street. Inviting Vanessa there for tea the afternoon of their arrival, she apologized for the meanness of the accommodation. Vanessa assured her that her circumstances would most assuredly change within the next few days. As they drove back to the hotel to meet Cain and Autumn for dinner, Isabel pointed out where her home had once been on the city's Main Line, a swath of majestic estates rich with prestige and—for Isabel at least—memory. She assured Vanessa, however, that she had no designs on those memories. They were for her as false and as far away as a storybook fantasy.

"I want a real home," she told Vanessa, "one in which I might map out my own future, where my own hopes and dreams might be realized."

"And that is exactly what you shall have, Isabel," Vanessa told her.

They dined that evening at one of the restaurants in the northwest section of the city called Germantown. After dinner, the mothers retired, and Cain and Autumn strolled along the city's grid of narrow cobblestone streets intersected by broad and busy boulevards. Excited and memory-charged, Autumn pointed out the sights of the city—the park where her nanny used to bring her afternoons and where later in her adolescence she would ride on Sundays; the narrow brick walks of Elfreth's Alley; the secluded courtyard of Carpenters' Hall; and the cool cavern of Old Swedes' Church where Autumn had watched with pleasure and excitement the arrival and departure of many a wedding party. They visited a bread shop and sat in the warmly lit little tavern that adjoined it as the evening ended. Cain noted that there was an air of melancholy around Autumn as she recounted the brightness with which her family's social star had shone and the rapidity with which it had faded once her father had died.

"Sometimes I think," she said quietly, "that the 'city of brotherly love' is exactly that. It doesn't care much for its *sisters*—especially its poor sisters."

It was with some surprise, then, that Autumn received word from her mother the next day that she had an invitation from one of her socially prominent former acquaintances, one Mrs. Peter Drexel IV, to attend a party at her home. Mrs. Drexel had advised Isabel that she was *praying* she would bring along her "dear, dear daughter" and their new acquaintances from Cape May. "It would seem," commented Isabel dryly, sipping coffee with Vanessa at the hotel, "that Society Hill has learned of the arrival of the wealthy Byrons. There is nothing like money to get the attention of the monied." She pleaded with Vanessa, once the invitation had been accepted, that she must promise to take on the posture of the grandest lady ever presented to the city's gentry.

"If you wish it, Isabel," said Vanessa, humorously acknowledging a certain talent for such poses. "I shall have them assuming the term 'upper crust' was invented for me."

"I should think they would all be extremely disappointed if it wasn't." They decided that a shopping trip was in order and apprised Autumn of their plans. Naturally, she was invited to join them, and she happily accepted. Cain decided he would look into the rental of a sloop for the afternoon so that they might enjoy a sail on the broad, blue waters of the Delaware.

"And see where you might rent some bicycles," Autumn threw over her shoulder as the ladies trooped from the hotel room.

"Bicycles!" Cain charged incredulously, but Autumn was gone. "Bicycles," he groused as he left the room.

Long hours of shopping and planning and much discussion prefaced their attendance at the Drexel party. It was decided that Isabel should dress at the hotel so they could all travel together. Coordination of costumes was a primary occupation of the women that long afternoon, along with the necessary exchanges of pieces of jewelry and advice on hair-dos, accessories, and make-up. Long after Cain was pacing the front parlor of Vanessa's suite and sipping impatiently at his whisky, the women were still in the back rooms, entangled in their complex preparations.

"Autumn," Cain called into that inner sanctum when a glance at his pocket watch told him it was nearly eight o'clock. "We shall be quite late if you don't hurry." Popping her head out into the parlor, she assured him that it was only a matter of moments before they could leave. A quarter of an hour later the same message was delivered, this time by Isabel. When Vanessa finally appeared it was well onto nine o'clock. Cain caught his breath at his mother's appearance, and his impatience evaporated. Vanessa was gowned in a splendid costume of royal purple grosgrain silk. The finely corded fabric hung in voluminous folds from a tightly fitted bodice, and was fringed in heavy, shimmering cerulean silk at the scalloped hem. Her hair, almost blue-gray in the reflected sheen of the dress, was swept up and caught with combs ornamented with sapphire crystals. She wore ear drops and a re-splendent roped bracelet of the real gems. She smiled at her son's gaping perusal.

"I'm attempting to look grand," she said guilelessly. "Would you say I've succeeded?" Cain nodded wordlessly. Isabel stepped into the parlor groomed with equal elegance. She wore a gown of rich cocoa-colored crushed velvet with sable piping at the hem, bodice, and sleeves. She wore the coral-shell and gold necklace that Cain and Autumn had given her and lustrous ear drops of layered coral and gold beads. Her rich brown hair with its russet highlights was coiled lavishly atop her head. But it was Autumn's appearance that sent Cain's heart racing.

She was gowned simply, but elegantly, in a clinging ecru matte silk. The empire waist, blind-stitched and almost invisible, allowed the layered skirt, hemmed in the new handkerchief fashion and trailing behind her, to lay with bold abandon about her long, shapely legs. The lightly draped bodice was deeply cut, offering a glimpse of the barest swell of innocent white flesh above it. The gown, cap-sleeved and clinging, and nearly the color of her own pale skin, though it revealed nothing, suggested quite more than it concealed. Her only ornamentation was a set of tiny amethyst ear drops on fine little chains of white gold, barely visible beneath the opaline upsweep of her moon-washed hair. She resembled a perfectly carved white cameo of femininity, an undine, or, as Cain so flatteringly put it, a "goddess."

He might have suggested that the older women attend the party without them were it not for the sudden and highly agitated bustle of activity that followed Autumn's entrance. Scarves and gloves were retrieved, fans sought out, and shawls produced. Appearances were checked in the cheval glass that stood in the little entry hall. Finally following the women out of the room, Cain determined that he and Autumn, at least, would be leaving the party very early.

The Byron party and Mrs. Emmett Thackeray and her daughter, Autumn, were announced with a flaring of nostrils and a sweeping of the liveried arm of the imperious old Drexel butler. Vanessa, Isabel, Cain, and Autumn stepped down into the gilded ballroom and were immediately received by Eugenia Drexel herself. She nearly bowed to Cain and Vanessa, who exchanged hidden smiles. She accommodated Isabel and Autumn with a canny regard, which assured them that this most favored friendship with such an esteemed—and, of course, wealthy—family would certainly put them back among the best circles in Philadelphia.

"And you deserve it, my dears," she told them condolingly. "No one was more heart-stricken than I over the way the two of you were treated by your supposed friends." The last word was said derisively and assured both mother and daughter that it was not by Eugenia's hand that they had been reduced to friendlessness. Eugenia Drexel was not one to cut a person simply because of a little thing like financial embarrassment, she assured them further. And, she added, "I plan to take Isabel under my wing now she is back." She wondered finally, eyeing Cain and Autumn, if any sort of "announcement" might be forthcoming. Isabel merely offered a mysterious smile, and Eugenia nodded in complete and solemn understanding. She had heard something, she said, of another engagement to some New York City girl, but assumed that was only gossip. "People will say the oddest and silliest things, just for the sake of saying them—especially those New York City *nouveau riche*. Those people will do anything," Eugenia confided, "to connect themselves to *real* money."

They were shepherded through the crowd by Eugenia herself, stopping briefly to exchange amenities with this group or that, and while Cain and Autumn danced, Isabel and Vanessa enjoyed their own invitations. Eugenia determined that she was personally responsible for Isabel's return to society, and each time that lady was returned to her side, Eugenia advised her protectively on which invitation to accept and which to decline categorically. "Now you must not even look at this one," she told her fervently.

She was speaking of the great, hulking, red-haired Alistair MacKenzie, who was just now striding toward them. "I just know he intends to ask you to dance, but you must pay no attention to him. He wouldn't even be here, you know, except his sister Violet's husband took him into his business. He claims—or at least Violet does—that they are descendants of Meriwether Lewis, who made that expedition to the West. Just ignore him." It was difficult to ignore Alistair Mackenzie. He muscled his way through the crush of people to Isabel's side and would accept no demurring from Eugenia that the lady was fatigued.

"Come dance with me, Mrs. Thackeray," he cajoled. "I am strong enough to hold the both of us up if you are tired." He laughed and swept her from the harbor of Eugenia's protection. The unlikely couple—the burly adventurer and the petite widow—danced a lively polka to the appreciation of the company and to the horror of their hostess. Eugenia ran feverishly to her husband and insisted that he stop the madness, but he only gave a helpless shrug and indicated that the orchestra was having as fine a time as the guests. Peter Drexel, in the meantime, kept time with the others with a sprightly clapping of his hands. A circle formed, and it was many exhausting moments before Eugenia could recapture Isabel and introduce her to the very proper and popular recent widower and bachelor-about-town, Mr. Harold P. Parker, Esquire. Mr. Parker was quite landed, according to Eugenia, and quite a catch.

Isabel suffered the man's companionship through the supper that was served in the dining hall, but found his company tiresome after only a few moments.

"I knew your husband well, Mrs. Thackeray," he told her, as he speared a slab of ham for his plate. "He was a worthy gentleman,

I should say, though I never approved of his liberal business practices."

"Isabel is so unschooled in that sort of thing," Eugenia put in hastily and with a small nervous laugh. "She can hardly be held accountable for Emmett's rather wild approach to business." Harold P. Parker nodded in agreement as he chewed doggedly at his meal. Changing the subject, Eugenia paused only long enough to catch a quick breath. "You might be interested to learn, Hal, that Isabel, like you, is of English descent. And, like you, she can trace her lineage back to the Hanovers."

"You don't say," Harold Parker replied, his brow lifting with interest. "What is your connection, Mrs. Thackeray?" Before Isabel could answer, he went on. "My own, you see, is rather roundabout, though I take some pride in saying, incontrovertible. A cousin of my grandmother's was married to an English baron. That good gentleman was instated into the Hanover line by marrying one of *his* daughters to the nineteenth Earl of Warwickshire who, as you must know, for everyone does, had a Saxe-Coburg-Gotha connection. And, obviously," he said with a condescending laugh, "when there is a Saxe-Coburg-Gotha connection, there is a Hanover connection. So you see, madam, I am, in fact, related to Queen Victoria through both her own and her husband Prince Albert's line—and that is no trifling connection."

"I should say not," Isabel commented in appropriate awe, though she'd become somewhat confused around the time of the nineteenth Earl of Warwickshire.

"And yours?" asked Mr. Parker, a challenge in his tone.

Isabel smiled meekly. "My own connection is not nearly so impressive as yours, sir," she murmured. Harold cast her a tolerant regard.

"Few are," he acknowledged smoothly.

"But yours is quite as incontrovertible as Hal's, is it not, Isabel?" put in Eugenia hastily. Though it was hardly her intention to raise Isabel's affiliation to the position of rival to the Parker alliance, Eugenia wished Harold to perceive that this woman was, in her own right, a worthy consort. "You are affiliated to the line through your father, if I am not mistaken."

"That is correct," said Isabel solemnly. "My father's great uncle Charles was married to a first cousin of George III's fourth son, the Duke of Kent, who, as you know, Mr. Parker, is Queen Victoria's father." Harold Parker, Esquire's face fell.

"That," he said with reluctant concession, "would put you in line to the throne, Mrs. Thackeray." A toast point spread with oyster pâté had been poised at his lips. It drifted untasted back down to his supper plate. Isabel smiled sweetly.

"I am probably about three hundredth in such a distinguished line," she said with a small dismissive laugh. "But, yes, I suppose it would."

"But that's incredible," said Harold, staring dumbly at her. "Quite . . . quite . . . incredible." Eugenia wondered if she'd made a terrible mistake. She hastened to mention that, naturally, Isabel would never think to pursue such a claim; she must concentrate for the moment on putting her life back together—possibly even marrying again. By that time, there were many onlookers. The exchange between the pretty widow Thackeray and the eligible Mr. Parker had been duly noted and was now being enthusiastically watched. Most of the guests had heard only a very small portion of the conversation, and it was now rumored that, somehow, incredibly, Isabel Thackeray was about to ascend the throne of England.

"One really never knows what the future will hold," put in Vanessa Byron, who was standing nearby. Everyone's attention fell to Vanessa, for she seemed to have some authority in these matters—she looked like she had a great deal of authority in a great many matters, and it was, of course, known that she had enormous wealth of her own. Vanessa nibbled sparingly on a strawberry-frosted *petit four*, and her voice held a warning. "In these unsettled times, with the boycotts in Ulster and the possible German invasions, and the aggressive imperialism of the Italians, and of course the anarchy resulting from the Taiping Rebellion in China, no one really knows what will happen to the English monarchy. 'Uneasy lies the head that wears the crown.'" She glanced at Isabel, who nodded sagely.

"You are so right, my dear Vanessa," she agreed. "But of my own ascendancy to the throne, I might say simply, it is unlikely—if . . . *possible*." If Isabel had been popular among the gathered company, she was now treated as an object of dire and menacing importance.

"You will not forget your old friends should such a thing happen," put in a lady who laughed nervously as she spoke.

"If such a thing should happen," said Isabel pointedly, "I shall treat my old friends exactly as they deserve to be treated." Small gasps greeted the remark. There were determinations among the ladies that Isabel would not be short on invitations from this moment on.

"Nothing is impossible," said Harold P. Parker fondly. His intimate smile on a face that did not smile easily was something of a shock to Isabel.

"That is quite true," she responded hastily, averting her gaze. "In the meantime, however, I shall be quite busy with a new venture." Everyone regarded her with interest, and a questing silence fell on the company. "You see," resumed Isabel, "I shall be starting my own business in the very near future—in fact it is already started." The silence deepened. "I have discovered that I am a seamstress of some faculty, and with the help of some worthy friends I shall be opening the Thackeray-Byron Dressmaking Corporation right here in the city."

"While the world is not in need of another monarch," noted Vanessa, "it is surely in need of a talented seamstress." She laughed. "I think you have made a wise choice, Isabel."

"I hope so," said Isabel, handing her supper plate to her astonished hostess. She turned back to her audience. "You may be sure, however, that as courtier or queen, I shall count on the affection and the patronage of Philadelphia's elite." In the confusion that followed, Isabel took Vanessa's arm and together they made their regal way from the room. Sending for their carriage, they hastily slipped into their capes, assisted by the now fawning Drexel butler, and left the house.

"A timely exit is an excellent thing," proclaimed Vanessa, laughing as their carriage rumbled its way across town to the Olympus.

Cain and Autumn were left to answer a flurry of questions. Autumn was urgently enjoined by several ladies to use her influence with her mother to set up appointments for immediate fittings. Once in their own carriage, Cain frowned at Autumn.

"I do hope your mother knows what she is doing," he said. "Those people seemed ready enough to accept her back into their society, and she deliberately ridiculed them—aided most unforgivably by my own mother." Autumn felt the whisper of an inward sigh and kept her gaze fixed on the gaslit streets outside the rolling carriage. She must try to remember, she told herself, that, at this point, Cain must be very tired of rebellious women. She placed her hand in the crook of his arm and smiled up at him.

"Oh, love," she said softly, "let us have a good time while we are here. Let us not allow anything to spoil our holiday."

"I have no intention of spoiling anything, Autumn," he said sternly, "but eventually the people at the party will begin to think about Isabel's behavior tonight, and they will begin, one by one, to take apart her story and examine it. Her reputation will be ruined."

"They will examine nothing, Cain, take my word for that. Wound into the social fabric of the lives of the rich is the acceptance of authority—especially of those who *seem* authoritative. They question very little, as long as their purses remain full. They live a storybook fiction, Cain, and they create that fiction themselves. They want very much to believe that living among them is a woman who might one day ascend the throne of England. I suppose," she added, "it gives their own lives some value. In any event, try to remember something else, too. My mother is a woman grown; she must make of her life what she will."

"I wonder that you take it all so lightly," Cain observed.

"You forget that I was one of them once. My own life was a fiction, a picture book fantasy. Recalling them made me happy for a while. But, like my mother, I must begin my life anew." She snuggled against him in the rocking coach. "Try not to concern yourself with my mother's reputation, Cain. She will survive, I promise you, and so will I." Autumn was not certain if that bit of philosophy comforted Cain or not. She knew that warring within him were his protective instincts and her incontrovertible logic. "It is confusing, isn't it?" she observed.

"Yes, Autumn," he said very quietly, "it is."

Chapter 18

Autumn and Vanessa accompanied Isabel to the bank the next morning to sign the articles of incorporation. They listened to the grave council of several financial advisors and generally agreed that bankers, for the most part, were pompous fools. When Autumn complained to Cain of the men's patronizing attitudes they had another near contention, with Cain, naturally, agreeing that women—even women who had their own resources—were unsuited to business. As always, when they argued, Autumn's heart became tangled in frustration. She loved Cain but despaired his lack of vision. They both agreed, at a certain point, that they were tired of confrontation.

"Let us put all this fuming behind us, love," said Cain. "As you said last night, we ought to make the most of this holiday—a much-deserved holiday. We must do everything that all the other tourists do in Philadelphia. Will you show me your beautiful city, Autumn?" She agreed with much relief. Cain promised her that this would be a time, a precious, unforgettable time, for two people, wildly in love, to make the world their very own.

The city became a playground for Autumn and Cain. All manner of diversion was theirs to enjoy. They rode bicycles in Fairmount Park, sailed on the Delaware, cheered for their favorite horses at the thoroughbred races, shopped at the merchant exchange. They dined, attended the theater, and went to concerts. They stood in awe before the historic Liberty Bell and toured the mellow majesty of Independence Hall, where crackly yellow parchments, gleaming crystal inkwells, and battered desks carried the patina of an age. In Germantown they saw a barn that had once stabled George Washington's horse. At the Museum of Art, they studied, and with much humor adjudicated twelfth-century masterpieces and Barberini tapestries and decided for themselves whether those works of art were worthy of their elevated places in history. Autumn directed Cain to stand beside a particularly ornate suit of armor. Assuming a knightly pose, he stood stiffly before her, and she walked around him assessing how he might have measured up to one of those medieval heroes.

"I would have made a splendid knight," he assured her.

"And you would," she agreed, "have been quite content to keep me securely mounted upon a pedestal." Cain's eyes, as he settled his regard on her, took on a mischievous glint.

"Securely mounted, love, but not on a pedestal." He stepped down from the dais that he had occupied and moved toward her. Sweeping her into an embrace, he bent his lips to her ear and whispered a suggestion that made her heart tip.

"Oh, yes, Cain," she whispered back. They were never far from the swelling splendor of such moments, never too absorbed in their exploration of the city's sights to become absorbed in an exploration of their love. The afternoon ended as many had before it, with the two lovers discovering the opulence of treasure to be found amid the tangled blankets of their four-poster bed at the Olympus Hotel.

Toward the end of their holiday, they strolled down Locust Street one dewy morning, toward Rittenhouse Square. The weather, always capricious in the city, turned chill, and as they reached the park a sudden squall swept in from the river. Cain protected Autumn as best he could, pulling her along in the circle of his embrace to the shelter of a tree. Looking down at her, with water dripping from the limp brim of her once pert bonnet and her heavy skirts trailing flaccidly behind her, Cain attempted, with a hopeless lack of success, to hide his amusement. He offered his handkerchief—small succor, Autumn pointed out as she mopped herself to little effect.

Cain lifted her chin with a tender forefinger, and Autumn knew she was to be kissed . . . in a public square of all places. Her alarm melted before it took hold, however. She loved Cain so. For his part, Cain could not quite understand the odd infusion of tenderness and lust that welled in his heart, but he fought neither sensation. Passersby, gentlemen and ladies all, tipped their umbrellas not in offense but in indulgent pleasure at the sight of the young couple so obviously in love. Beneath the dripping canopy of the trees, Autumn and Cain kissed, welcoming the world into the perfect circle of their love.

They spent their last day in Philadelphia with their mothers—and Alistair MacKenzie. The red-haired adventurer had quite literally swept Isabel off her feet the night of the Drexel party, and these days he seemed to be attempting the same feat. He was a robust man given to very public displays of both his strength and his affection for Isabel. Lawn bowling was a sport at which he excelled—he told them all—and invited them for a day of games in Fairmount Park. Whipping off his waistcoat and tossing off several well-aimed strikes before lunch, he quite proved his boast that day. He cheered himself unabashedly and took Isabel into his bearlike embrace with joyful self-congratulations. While the ladies found Alistair's behavior endearing, Cain remained grimly miffed. He thought it unseemly of Isabel to make herself available to such unrestrained exhibitions of public passion, and later over supper—to which Cain had purposely and quite pointedly not invited Alistair—he scolded all the women for their encouragement of such behavior. Autumn reflected wryly on how quickly Cain had forgotten his own behavior of the day before in Rittenhouse Square. And though Vanessa deemed Alistair "charming" Cain would not be moved.

"He is like a boy in his exuberance," Autumn offered.

"But he is not a boy," Cain countered over the remnants of their meal.

"That he is not," Isabel commented reflectively. Cain's brows furrowed, but he continued.

"Isabel," he argued, "how many men swing a bowling stick about their heads and hurl it to the ground triumphantly simply because they've hit a strike? He might have injured someone. A grown man ought to have more sense." Isabel cocked an oblique smile.

"No one was in any danger from Alistair's bowling stick, Cain," she pointed out.

"That is a matter of speculation, Isabel. In any event I should think twice before I accepted another of his invitations." He leaned forward across the table and confided, "In my opinion, he is a common sort—not nearly in your class. It is one thing for a man to marry 'down,' in fact it is quite the most desirable and natural of arrangements. It is entirely another matter for a lady to do the same. You must think of your reputation."

"Cain," Isabel replied, reaching out and patting his hand, "please do not misunderstand. Though I appreciate your advice, I am of an age and at a time in my life when marriage is not a consideration. I had a beautiful marriage with Autumn's father. We shared a great love and I am not anxious to see that relationship overshadowed. I shall never consider marrying again."

Cain placed his hand over hers, and said, "I am glad to hear that, at least in regard to MacKenzie. Still, you may change your mind someday, and I'd not like to think that you had sullied your reputation with the likes of that man. You must keep your options open, Isabel."

Isabel sighed. Cain had, in fact, misunderstood her. She did not bother to explain, however, that if the occasion suited her, she fully intended to take Alistair MacKenzie as a lover. Cain was bound to the role of protector, and though he seemed quite willing to forego convention where Autumn and he were concerned, he had quite a different standard for others.

She listened patiently as he continued. "Also, you must remember to take the advice of the men around you. The financial officers at the bank, for instance, are there to help you. I realize that you are astute, but it remains true that a woman of your high breeding has no true idea of what can go on in the world of business. That is a man's province." Isabel glanced to the other women, studiously avoiding any facial expression.

"Again, I thank you for your advice, Cain," she said, patting her lips delicately with her napkin.

"It will be difficult to discourage a man like MacKenzie," Cain continued, "and in the absence of a father or a brother or a son, you might wish me to speak for you."

"I believe," replied Isabel, "that I can present Alistair with a clear message of my intent." Cain nodded with satisfaction and called for the bill. As they made their way back to the hotel, Autumn refrained from pointing out to Cain that his advice of the evening smacked of the ivory-tower mentality of the medieval knights he had so successfully imitated at the Museum of Art. While that image constituted a romantic fantasy, it had little to do with real life—Isabel's life, at any rate.

The next morning, as Isabel and Vanessa continued their house hunting, Autumn and Cain left Philadelphia.

"I shall miss you, my darling," Isabel told her daughter.

"I shall miss you, too, Mother."

"Take a little advice with you back to Cape May. Love Cain enough to release him."

"Release him?" Autumn asked.

"Cain sees himself in the role of protector, custodian guardian—a knight in shining armor. Allow him to remove that armor, Autumn. I imagine it can become awfully heavy." Autumn smiled.

"I shall do so, Mother," she said.

Cain and Autumn arrived in Cape May to find that summer had blossomed fully. In their absence the Byron estate had become a bower. Flowers bloomed everywhere; green life had overtaken the lawns, vines of ivy and roses had twined along the fences and over the porch railings. Carrie greeted their arrival announcing that she had decided to stay on to see to the establishment of Cain's medical office. She accompanied Autumn upstairs—up the front stairs—to her bedroom to see to her unpacking. As Autumn pulled the pins from her wide straw bonnet and unfastened the ribbon tie from beneath her chin, she eyed the woman in some puzzlement.

Drawing off her gloves, she said, "I do thank you for staying, Carrie. I hadn't expected such a lovely surprise. We have plenty of people now to take care of the house, and I am sure you have trained them all well."

"Oh, the house is runnin' fine," explained Carrie as she began hanging up clothes, "but I wanted to stay until them carpenters left. They was creatin' an awful mess, Miss Autumn. I just couldn't stand them strangers comin' in with their dirty boots and tools and nasty cigars and nobody to tell them what's what . . ." Her voice trailed off. "The truth is," she admitted after a pause, "I didn't want to leave. I suppose in a way—a real strange way, mind you—I've gotten used to life here in this house. My Henry says it ain't my own life, but I tell him it's the one I'm used to. Sometimes, funny thing, we get real scared when we get exactly what we want. You know what I mean, Miss Autumn?"

"I do, Carrie," Autumn acknowledged sincerely. She moved to the woman, who had sunk down on the edge of the bed. "But you know your place is with your husband. He has every right to expect you to reside with him, especially now that you've been given the opportunity to do so."

"Especially now," murmured Carrie, "when I've got me a bun in the oven." Autumn's brows knitted.

"A . . . bun?"

"A baby, Miss Autumn."

"You're carrying a child, Carrie?"

"I am, miss."

"But, Carrie, that's wonderful!" Autumn knelt before the

woman, smiling up at her. "Oh, that is surely the best news in the world. It's what you've dreamed of."

"Like I said, it's one of them things that when you finally get it, it's scary."

"Nonsense," Autumn returned. "Having a baby is the most natural thing in the world." Her smile deepened. "We shall have it together." Carrie regarded her in dismay, and Autumn continued earnestly. "I want a baby, too, someday, Carrie. Sadly that is impossible right now. So, please, let me join you in your pregnancy. We shall buy new clothing for both you and the baby, and we shall scrub the nursery till it sparkles and paper it and furnish it with the very finest of baby things, and we shall pick out a splendid pram—"

"Is it true, Miss Autumn, that ladies . . . die sometimes when they're havin' their babies?"

"Of course that happens sometimes, Carrie. But it's not going to happen to you. We shall set you up with an appointment with the finest doctor in the world."

"Not Dr. Beame."

"Oh, no, Carrie, Dr. Byron!"

Autumn grabbed Carrie's hand and the two women bundled down the stairs to Cain's new office. Halting just inside the door, Autumn was amazed at the transformation that had taken place. What had once been Cain's pretentious and brazenly masculine parlor had been converted into a sterile, whitewashed harbor of doctorly order. Gone were the animal heads and brass carvings, the friezes and tasseled drapings. The only thing that was left that even remotely resembled the former ambience was the little animal horn chair, and even that had been reupholstered in a cool gray, replacing its former covering of red velvet. Cain's desk remained, but the ornate lamps and other furnishings had been supplanted by appointments of modest line and almost exaggerated ordinariness. Shelves had been built into the walls and medical books and instruments of all sorts were lined up neatly. The portrait of his father still resided over the hearth.

"I am hoping," Cain commented, "that it will inspire confidence."

"It inspires no confidence in me," Carrie said with a small shudder. Cain regarded her with a question.

"Carrie is to be your first patient," announced Autumn.

"Are you ill, my girl?"

"No . . . not ill. I mean . . . I been a little under the weather, don't you know, but it's nothin' serious." She gave Autumn a warning glance. "I ain't sick."

"Carrie's pregnant," Autumn declared. Cain merely stared. Only Autumn noted the almost imperceptible moment of uncertainty that clouded his gaze. Could it be that Dr. Cain Byron, the assured and confident Cain, was skittish about such an important first assignment? Such a familiar first patient? She moved to him, placing her hand on his arm. "Isn't that wonderful, Cain?"

"Indeed it is," he agreed, rallying. "Congratulations to both you and Henry." He glanced at Autumn then back at Carrie. "We shall have to examine you," he offered smoothly. Carrie's eyes widened.

"That'll be fine, sir. Let me just . . . I'll bring the two of you a pot of tea," she said scrambling from the room.

"She'll get used to the idea," said Autumn, smiling.

Cain folded his hands behind his back. "But will I?"

"You will, my darling," Autumn assured him, reaching up and smoothing the furrows that had formed on his brow. At this moment, she felt a well of love for him. That part of him that dominated and preached had disappeared with his uncertainty, and it was this part of Cain that Autumn held closest to her heart.

❦

Once Vanessa had arrived home and the household settled into a regular domestic routine, Autumn and Cain made a purposeful effort to keep their relationship on an apparently professional level. Neither of them wished any gossip among the people of Cape May that might jeopardize Cain's career or Autumn's reputation. The fact that Cain was still ostensibly engaged to Antoinette Fraser offered a certain protection. And Autumn's position as Vanessa's companion kept the illusion that she was an employee of the household. Still, the respectability that they were attempting to create was but an illusion and the knowledge of that lay heavily between them.

Autumn attempted to separate herself from Cain as much as possible, making a life for herself that was suited to that of any working girl. Publicly, at least, she managed an independence of spirit and a sprightly self-sufficiency. At Carrie's departure, Autumn had taken over the running of the house. She shopped daily and visited the circulating library several times a week, bicycling into town sporting her breeches—of which Cain still deeply disapproved—and making friends. She joined a literary club that met on Tuesday nights and attended local concerts and lectures. She encouraged Vanessa to come along, but that lady remained as reclusive as ever. Most afternoons Autumn spent getting Carrie's new house in order, and, as promised, preparing the nursery for the new arrival.

For his part, Cain began the business of building his practice. He received new patients every day. They were people from the town and even vacationers from the resort hotels in the city seeking the ministrations of this new young doctor. After a few short weeks his reputation began to grow, even outside Cape May. He was acclaimed as an excellent man of medicine, and he gained a reputation for gentleness and a friendly ear. He smiled easily at children who were frightened by a visit to the doctor and suggested to Autumn that she furnish the office with a few toys. Autumn noted with a jaundiced eye that Dr. Byron was especially popular with the ladies. One young woman, a Miss Rose Evert, the nubile daughter of a local businessman, came in weekly with one ailment or another. She was an attractive girl, Autumn observed, with great trusting eyes and a moist bud of a troubled pout. Through the month of July, she had one case of a pretty cough that would not go away, at least three complaints concerning an ongoing pain in her trim ankle, and several sieges of an inexplicably palpitating heart. Autumn suggested, smiling sweetly over supper, that the girl might need the attentions of a heart specialist.

Hiding his own smile, Cain commented quite forlornly, that "the poor child" was a mass of complex ailments. "A specialist," he explained, "would look to only one part of her body. Miss Evert needs someone to care for her whole ravaged self." Autumn's smile vanished and her amber gaze darkened to a copper hue.

"Miss Evert," she returned, "needs a good spanking for wasting the time of a busy doctor with her play-pretty ailments."

Cain lifted his dark brows. "A spanking . . ." he said in solemn reflection. "I had not thought of that mode of treatment."

Autumn's regard narrowed. She hurled her napkin to the table and pushed back her chair almost to the point of its falling. Without further words she made her way from the dining room across the entrance hall to the front door. Slamming from the house, she paced the wide front porch restively and noted that her footsteps sounded hollow, as hollow as her fit of temper. She chastised herself over her inability to make a joke over a silly girl's adolescent crush on a handsome young doctor. It was the stuff of which jests were made between cozy married people. But Cain and she were not cozily wed. And until Antoinette Fraser decided their future, that fact would always be a source of tension between them. She glanced up as Cain joined her on the porch. He said nothing but leaned out over the railing and surveyed the wide expanse of lawns. The evening was nearly purple in its gloaming radiance. Stars were beginning to appear overhead, and the scent of bougainvillea and the sea sweetened the warm night. He turned finally and sat on the edge of the railing. Extending his arm, his hand held out to her, he said softly, "Will you take a walk with me, love?" Autumn offered an oblique and guilty glance.

"Do you really wish to walk with me, Cain?" she asked. He smiled deeply.

"I really do," he told her. She reached out, accepting his hand, and he led her to the back of the house, past the stables, and down the narrow path to the beach.

The path to the sea at this time of year was overarched with heavily leafed trees and bordered with bushy foliage that created a shadowed, drifting darkness that seemed otherworldly. Cain and Autumn stepped carefully, their quiet footfalls descending on a blanket of pine needles and low-growing ferns. The ocean emerged, silver and placid, from the eclipse of the trees. Lapping lightly against the narrow beach, it might have been a lagoon nestled somewhere in Paradise. The couple paused before the sea and shades of light and listened, speaking not a word as they turned to each other. Cain took Autumn's face in his hands and lowered his lips to hers. Their lovemaking, always consummate, always complete, tonight would be sublime.

Cain drew the light material of her gown away from her shoulders as he unfastened the buttons down her back, slowly, languorously, attentively. Autumn shivered in the warm caressing air. Her head fell back and Cain removed the pins that held her hair, allowing its freedom, sending the pearly tresses adrift on the sea breezes. He drew her down onto the grasses that bordered the shore. The heavy, lush overgrowth embraced them. Stroking her, enrapturing her, he pressed her to his lean length, whispered her name into the shell of her ear, and she responded with a yielding hunger. As always, his desire was the lodestar to her own passion. She offered herself up to his need with a raging need of her own. Lifting her arms, she entwined them about the column of his neck, tunneling her fingers through the thick curls that abraded his collar. She longed to feel his body against hers and she divested his chest and shoulders of his shirt. Nestling herself against him, she writhed in an ecstasy of desire. He took her, arching her to him, carrying her beyond earthly boundaries. They soared together on a tide of purest rapture.

As repletion brought them, breathless, to the stygian depths of their canopied retreat, as heaven ebbed, Autumn looked into the face that smiled upon her. She had, she believed, found her heaven, and no one—not Antoinette Fraser, not an unforgiving society, not pretty girls with ailing ankles and mysterious palpitations of the heart—would ever take it from her.

Chapter 19

Autumn had become both a familiar and a notorious sight about the city, briskly pedaling her bicycle along the streets of Cape May and smiling and waving to everyone. Many people had dismissed their earlier caution and returned her greetings. For some the young and pretty companion to Mrs. Byron became a most pleasant and welcome diversion in their daily routine. For others, Autumn became the subject of disparaging gossip. Her unconformable method of transportation and her manner of dress, as well as her vigor and obvious joy in life seemed to annoy and discompose them. She became, as the summer progressed, the subject of good-humored and not so good-humored banter. Cain was not amused. He listened, tight-jawed, to the jolly chafing of some of his patients and answered in monosyllables the concerned and irritated questions of others. Tired of the gossip, impatient with invasive curiosity, he told Autumn firmly that she must dress properly and avail herself of the coaches and grooms that were always at the ready to take her anywhere she wished to go.

"You have a closet full of clothes, Autumn, and the resources to buy any dress you want," he reminded her one afternoon. "You have a battalion of servants. There is no reason on earth why you should be running about in breeches and doing your own errands—and on that bicycle no less. I will not have you chasing about—"

"I wear breeches, Cain," she told him composedly, "because my skirts kept getting caught in the wheels of my bicycle. I use the bicycle because I enjoy the exercise. I do my own errands because I want to. I've become used to taking care of my own needs, and I celebrate my ability to do so. Right now," she continued, as she stood before the hall mirror adjusting her stiff-brimmed straw hat, "I am going to the library. You will admit, won't you, that is something I *must* do myself; one cannot expect others to choose one's reading. And while I am in the city, there is no reason I shouldn't do the marketing." She drew on kid gloves and eyed Cain obliquely. His gaze narrowed.

"And that is another thing," he told her grimly, "you're always at that library. What is so fascinating there?"

"Books." She raised herself on tiptoe to kiss his cheek.

"You could buy them," Cain pointed out.

"Working girls, Dr. Byron, get their books from the library. And let us not forget," she said with a saucy smile, "I *am* what the world cheekily refers to as a 'working girl.'" Cain failed to see the humor in her little joke. He watched her as she nearly skipped from the house, her tightly breeched bottom swinging perkily.

Autumn's exit preceded only by seconds the entrance of the ever-ailing, though oddly glowing, Miss Rose Evert. Cain sighed as she entered the house, but managed a pleasant smile. "Miss Evert," he greeted her. She hastened down the corridor to his office.

"Hello again, Dr. Byron. I've told you to call me Rose, now haven't I?" She extended a delicately gloved hand that Cain took reluctantly.

"You have indeed," he said with a resigned sigh as he ushered her inside.

"Then why don't you?" she asked as she seated herself comfortably in the little horn chair. Cain regarded her quizzically.

"Why don't I what?"

"Call me Rose."

"Miss Evert," he began.

"Rose," she reminded him.

"Miss Evert," he repeated firmly. "Tell me what brings you here today."

"I'm not really sure I can explain it, Dr. Byron," she said with charming befuddlement. She drew a handkerchief from her reticule and dabbed at her eyes. Cain leaned back against his desk and crossed his arms over his white-coated chest. He regarded the young woman with a mixture of amusement and tolerance. She went on, apparently brought to tears by this latest unfocused infirmity. "I seem to be short of breath. It is just awful. One moment I am feeling fine and the next I find myself gasping for breath." She looked up at Cain piteously. "Can you help me?"

"Well, I'm not sure. Have you any other symptoms?"

"Oh, yes indeed—lots!" she returned buoyantly. "I'm flushed a great deal . . . and I have absolutely no energy. Daddy says I need a tonic."

Cain hooded his gaze. "I had no idea your father was a doctor, Miss Evert."

"He isn't," said Rose, confused. "You know very well that daddy is a piano tuner." Her brows knitted adorably. "Oh," she added in a rush of comprehension. She dimpled a pretty smile. "You're toying with me, Dr. Byron," she scolded, waving her handkerchief playfully. "How naughty of you." She regarded him through the veil of her curling lashes. Pulling off her gloves, she managed a small laugh. "You are absolutely right. From now on, you shall be the doctor and Daddy will be the piano tuner." She looked up, her clear gaze trusting. "You will help me, won't you . . . Cain?"

"We shall see what we can do, Miss Evert," Cain replied with professional reserve. As he stepped to her to begin his examination, Rose Evert seemed to gain strength. She kept up a lively monologue as she very willingly unfastened the front of her light summer frock and bared her full-fleshed bosom to Cain's rather dour perusal.

"I only wish I could be as robust a lady as that girl who cares for your mother," she remarked brightly. "She is surely the most hearty of souls. I think there has not been a day all summer that we've not seen her pedaling about the city on her bicycle. Daddy says he wonders that you allow such behavior in one of your household staff, but I say a lady as healthy and energetic as she needs some outlet for all her vigor. Daddy's such an old poop. But then, as he accurately points out, most men prefer ladies who are a bit on the . . . delicate side." Miss Evert coughed prettily to underscore her own delicate constitution. "Anyway, everyone says Mrs. Byron's good health is due to the energetic ministrations of Miss Thackeray. Mother said she was at death's door, but we both agreed she looked radiant at your engagement party." Cain's gaze shot up to find a great pair of innocent eyes looking directly into his. "It's been over a month now since the postponement of your wedding," Rose observed, "I do hope nothing is amiss."

"Nothing is," said Cain, completing his examination. Miss Evert asked for a glass of water to emphasize how grueling the effort had been for her.

"For myself, Dr. Byron," she observed, sipping daintily, "I would give just anything in the world for Miss Thackeray's hardihood—though I would never think of stuffing it all into breeches." She smiled slyly as she handed Cain her glass. "Your mother's companion is quite the talk of the town . . . and not all of it flattering."

"You may fasten your gown, Miss Evert," Cain said flatly. The lady obediently did so, but kept her eyes on the doctor's averted ones.

"Honestly, Dr. Byron—Cain—you cannot tell me that your servant's behavior doesn't give you pause." Miss Evert patted her hair and straightened her pretty lace collar. "Don't you mind that she is the subject of some extremely ribald gossip? It is said, and quite properly so, that a lady's name should never be mentioned in idle conversation and certainly not in jest. I should be distressed if *my* name were being bandied about in such a fashion. People are even starting to connect her with those literary ladies, Annie Fitzpatrick and Emma Cavanaugh." Rose lifted her brow significantly, giving dire expression to this latest information. "And you know what they say about those ladies. Daddy says they're not even ladies. I shan't tell you what else he says, but it's not nice. And who can blame people for talking, what with those two women living together and saying all those awful things about men. It's not natural. In my opinion, men are far superior to women, don't you think so, Dr. Byron?"

Cain only glanced up as he wrote out Rose Evert's prescription. "Anyway," Rose continued, "it seems to me Miss Thackeray would do well to look to her reputation. She is, after all, the employee of a respected doctor. She ought to think of *your* reputation if not her own." Rose Evert sighed. "Some people insist on living lives that compromise everyone around them. Such a shame . . ." Her voice trailed off and her eyes drifted to some sad middle distance. She glanced back to note, to her satisfaction, a troubled frown clouding Cain's countenance. "But I'm not letting you get in a word," she added, brightening. "How is my health? I have been so concerned about it."

"Your health," replied Cain evenly and with no hint of sarcasm, "has been a great source of concern to all of us this summer." He recalled the near battle he and Autumn had had over the lady's fragile state—and her constant visits. "I have written you a prescription for a tonic—as your good father suggested—but I want you to promise me you will take at least one walk every day, Miss Evert. Enjoy the sunshine and fresh air, and try not to think about yourself quite so much." Rose frowned.

"But how can I help thinking about myself? I have been so ill!"

"Miss Evert," Cain said patiently, "you are not as fragile as you imagine. You are young, and may I say, in excellent health. I have examined you thoroughly over the past few weeks, and it is my opinion that you have been blessed with a very sturdy constitution."

"You must be mistaken, Dr. Byron," she protested. "What about my shortness of breath and the pains in my ankle and my palpitations?"

"I have checked your lungs and your heart, Miss Evert, and there is no evidence of disease. For your throbbing ankle I can find no cause. There are no broken bones, no injured muscles—"

He broke off his narration at her lamentations of protest and turned to the sink to wash his hands. "Perhaps, if you insist that you are ill, we could have you looked at by a specialist," he offered. As he dried his hands, he turned and found that the color had drained from his patient's face.

"A . . . specialist?" she asked dumbly, her eyes wide and grave with numb horror. "But why, Dr. Byron?"

A smile threatened at the corners of Cain's lips; the girl was obviously not expecting such a solemn recommendation. "Dr. Winslow Beame is a friend of mine," he reassured her gently, "and a noted specialist in women's problems. He will be visiting anyway within the week, so we may as well have him look at you." Rose nodded mutely. "In the meantime," said Cain, as he led her from the room, "take those walks I suggested. Enjoy your young friends as a girl your age ought to be doing. There is no pleasure in being sick."

"Am I . . . sick?" she asked in a small frightened voice.

"No, Rose," said Cain confidently. "You are not."

"Thank God," she breathed.

"Yes," agreed Cain, "you might do well to thank God." He had not meant to frighten her, but he took a certain satisfaction in the knowledge that Miss Evert's brush with real illness—brief as it was—would most assuredly discourage any more feigning of ailments.

His satisfaction might have been premature, however, for she paused before leaving and said in a syrupy voice, "You know, Dr. Byron—Cain—when one is a lady, and vulnerably made, one must accept certain . . . dangers to one's health."

"Miss Evert," Cain remarked stiffly, "you are as healthy as . . . as Autumn Thackeray."

"No real lady is that healthy," she replied tartly. Cain cleared his throat and watched as she pulled on her gloves. "Daddy says that someone ought to talk to her and tell her that she is damaging not only her own reputation but yours, too. He says that a man who cannot control his servants is no man. And mother says that your family is headed for a scandal." She looked up, apparently recovered from her recent terror. "She says that a gentleman who allows his servants to flout his rules is doing it for a very unsavory reason."

"I think it best for people to tend to their own business," Cain returned easily.

"Oh, I could not agree more. But people will talk. It's human nature." With that warning, Miss Evert strolled languidly to her waiting carriage.

As Cain moved back into the house, he paused and looked up into the darkness at the top of the great curving staircase. Gripping the newel post, he recalled another threatened scandal, one he'd managed to avert. This latest threatened scandal would not overwhelm him, he determined, as the other one had; before it emerged, he would stop it cold. He went to his office and lit a small cigar, pacing restively beneath the portrait of his father. He glanced up, wondering how, with such a prudent patriarch, the Byron family had managed to become a magnet for scandal. He had no choice but to place the blame squarely at his own feet.

❦

"I could smell it as soon as I came into the house," Autumn commented as she entered the otherwise sterile room. Cain glanced up. He had been preoccupied with paperwork for most of the afternoon.

"What did you smell?" he asked.

"Your foul cigar smoke." Autumn stood before the mirror and removed her hat. She patted at her tousled coif. "I've told you time and again that the noxious odor of those cigars simply penetrates the entire house." Cain stood slowly and moved from behind his desk. He watched as Autumn, wrinkling her nose, opened a window and waved at the air with her bonnet. "Honestly," she continued, "driving out the evidence of your vice is a full-time job."

"My . . . vice," Cain repeated. He had never thought of his smoking as a vice.

She moved to him and stood close, regarding him with a small, condescending smile. "Do try to remember that you are a doctor, my darling," she said sweetly but with a mocking edge to her voice, as Cain perceived it. "People expect a certain restraint in the men to whom they entrust their health." She laughed and touched his chin with a delicate forefinger. "You, good sir, are not setting a very good example for your patients." Cain studied her small upturned face. He could not afford, at this moment, to be captivated by its elfin charm or even irritated by her superior tone.

"You are very quick to point out my shortcomings, Autumn. Are you as equally ready to examine your own?"

"*My* shortcomings?"

"Yours."

"What shortcomings are those?" Cain averted his eyes and tried to adopt a reasonable tone.

"It seems that people in town are beginning to make this family an object of discussion and speculation." Autumn's brows lifted. "Please allow me to finish. I must insist that you stop chasing about town on that bicycle and that you stop wearing your breeches." He glanced briefly at her, but hastily turned away. How could he look at her curving form so sweetly sheathed in her jodhpurs, so meltingly available to his perusal, and not draw her to him? He turned back to her, attempting to ignore that appealing silhouette. "I want you to avail yourself of the services of the people we've hired to attend us. There is no reason in the world for you to make yourself so visible to our neighbors. I do not approve."

"Oh, Cain," she said on a sigh, "we went through this only this morning—and a hundred times before that. I cannot just sit about the house looking pretty."

"And *I* cannot have people discussing the residents of this household. You are much the subject of controversy—some people taking your side and others falling in against you. Don't you understand that your bicycle, those breeches, your connection to those literary ladies all draw unnecessary attention to you—to us."

"I do not see how my behavior could possibly reflect on you—"

"But it does," he returned, his words biting, his tone clenched. "For all the world you are my employee. If I disapprove of your behavior and you continue it anyway, the message is that I cannot control you."

"Control me?" Her gaze darkened to a coppery glint. Cain held up a detaining hand. He knew that his use of that word had been at the very least impolitic.

"When a man allows such flamboyant behavior in one of his female staff, people might get the impression that their relationship is something other than professional. You must refrain from making yourself the subject of gossip—for your own sake if not for mine."

"I saw Miss Rose Evert arrive," Autumn returned knowingly. "I suppose she has had something to do with—"

"Rose had a great deal to say on the subject, but that—"

"'Rose'?"

"Yes *Rose*, dammit!" Cain exploded. He turned away immediately. "In the name of Christ, woman, you are driving me to distraction." Autumn drew back her shoulders and settled her hands upon her hips.

"I told you to send that woman to a specialist."

"I am going to. Win is going to look at her when he visits next week."

"Winslow Beame," Autumn shot back, "is exactly what she deserves! Now let me tell you something, Cain Byron. You are not my husband, and you have no authority over my behavior."

"Someday," Cain returned, "I shall be your husband, and I have every right to expect a compliant and respectful wife."

"When that time comes—*if* it comes—I will give you exactly the amount of respect you deserve, no less and certainly no more. In the meantime, if there is gossip, it is your fault as much as mine—"

"I am not the one riding bicycles and trooping around Cape May in inappropriate dress."

"You *are* the one, however, who happens to be harboring a mistress!"

"Yes, and I tell you that I am not happy with her behavior." Autumn stamped a booted foot.

"I suppose you would be just as pleased to have me hiding up there in the attic, clinging and possessive and wracked with cunning ailments like the oh-so-delicate Miss Evert."

"I would have you respect my wishes, madam. Is it so much to ask that I not be forced to defend your actions to every flapping gossip in the city?" He attempted to continue in what he assumed was a more reasonable tone. "I would have you know that I do not personally object to your behavior. I do not understand your need to adopt this rather . . . bohemian lifestyle, but I am not personally opposed to it. I do not even object to that curious assortment of women you call your literary friends. Though I find them rather bizarre, I can tolerate them. As a matter of fact, I went to school with Annie Fitzpatrick, and I happen to like her; I always have." He paused. When he resumed his tone was instructive and unyielding. "You have made choices that seem, oddly, to suit you. But I am by nature a private man, and I will not defend you and explain you to my patients. Do what you will, but I will continue to voice my objections. In the end, you have the power to decide whether we have a happy, contented life or a combative one."

"Thank you so much for your support of me, Cain," she rejoined, her tone heavy with irony. She brushed past him and exited the room. Cain was left in a growling bad humor. He lit a cigar, then, recalling Autumn's complaints, he snuffed it out. He glanced down at the ashy remains of his apparently stripped manhood, and tearing off his starched white coat, he stormed from the house.

ᴄ᭸᭮ᴊ

That night, very late, Cain came to bed. He slid beneath the light coverlet, his weight forcing the long wakeful Autumn to hold herself rigidly to her side of the bed.

"You are not sleeping," Cain said softly.

"No."

"Why not?"

Autumn turned to him, her face serious and searching in the moonlit darkness. "Because," she said in a solemn whisper, "my gentleman lover ran away from home. He railed a few masterful words, threw an insult or two in my direction and left."

"As I recall," returned Cain, folding his arms beneath his head, "you were not the only one insulted. I, too, took my lumps."

"Lumps?" asked Autumn, lifting her pale brows.

"You said my cigars were foul and a vice."

"I was insulting your cigars, not you," she reminded him. Looking down into the chiseled features of his face, Autumn could not contain the truth that she was glad to see him. The soft black velvet of his gaze caught a ray of moonlight and told her that he was glad to be home. "Where have you been?" she asked, taking in the very pleasing scent of him, which mingled tobacco, leather, and sea air.

"I was riding." He reached up and touched a pearlescent curl that had drifted onto her shoulder.

"All this time?"

"All this time."

"I missed you."

"I wish you had been with me." They shared a smile, but his face became serious, and he resumed as though he were describing a dream. "I had ridden very far from the house and night had fallen. I saw darkness all about me, and suddenly I was so afraid you might leave me. I felt empty. I rode home as fast as I could, in the dark, fearing all the while you would not be here when I returned." He took her into his arms. His breath was shallow, and his heart raced. Autumn held him fiercely.

"I shall never leave you, Cain, I promise." In the safety of each other's arms, they drifted into a kind of peace, but slumber eluded them both.

"Autumn," he said much later, "I have been thinking."

"As have I."

"I want you to understand something. I have faced down one scandal in my life, and I do not wish to face down another."

"Scandal," she conceded, "brings out the worst in everybody. But what if there were no such thing as scandal, Cain? What if everyone simply took your doctor's oath to do no harm and then lived their lives as best they could?"

"It would be a perfect world, Autumn."

"I agree. And if a perfect world is possible, someone has to begin somewhere to build it." He smiled.

"Are you suggesting that you and I might be those pilgrim builders?"

"We might be."

"It would be hard," he said. "We would be facing uncharted territory."

"As all pilgrims do."

"And we would have few followers. We would be alone."

"You and I," she assured him, "shall never be alone."

Chapter 20

The day was humid, hot, woolen-blanket prickly. A gas-powered overhead fan in the kitchen served only to displace the deadened summer air, not to dispose of it. Autumn worked slowly, getting in the way of the forbearing women who continued to function efficiently despite the heat. Preparing Vanessa's breakfast was a responsibility she usually cherished, for it gave her the opportunity to spend a quiet moment with the lady at the beginning of the day. This day, however, the kitchen was a runny, sticky, viscid hell. Though Autumn wore only a light summer frock, she perspired lavishly. She brushed moist tresses of her golden hair from her cheeks and neck, bumped into one of the women who was attempting to prepare corn cakes for the stable-men, apologized briefly, and made her way up the back stairway with Vanessa's tray. Her room was no cooler than the rest of the house, though every window was opened and the draperies pulled back to allow any stray breeze to enter.

"Oh, Autumn, darling," the older woman admonished her as she entered, "you really shouldn't have troubled." Vanessa had on a light morning robe, and she sat in a chair near the window. She fanned herself languidly.

"It was no trouble," Autumn lied. "I sliced a nice cool melon for us. Won't you try some of it?" In truth, Vanessa had not been eating well since her return from Philadelphia, and she had been less than communicative. Autumn sat down herself and dipped into the succulent fruit with her spoon.

"It is so hot. I don't really feel like eating."

"Vanessa, you haven't felt like eating for days. You really must try, you know; after all, I went to all this trouble." Vanessa glanced at the girl and smiled. Autumn smiled back.

"Alright," Vanessa said resignedly. "It does look inviting," she conceded. As they did every day, they chatted idly. They inquired as to how the other had slept, asked about plans for the day, talked some of Autumn's mother. "Her business is bound to prosper. We found a lovely big house for her, and she has hired half a dozen seamstresses." Autumn nodded. Vanessa had mentioned these facts before.

"And how does her social life seem?" Autumn asked as she sipped her coffee. "You will recall that her last social engagement ended in a veiled promise to Philadelphia's elite that my mother might be the next queen of England." She laughed and patted at her perspiring neck with a linen napkin. "I was wondering if the upper crust had cracked under the weight of such a possibility."

"It has not cracked," said Vanessa dryly, "but it has suffered several chinks." Though her words were heavy with droll humor, her face was solemn. She gazed out the windows over the expanse of shimmering sky and treetops. "There is a . . . situation of which you should be aware."

"What situation?" Autumn leaned forward and set down her

cup. The click caught Vanessa's attention, and she stared at the cup and saucer for a long moment. At last she looked up.

"Your mother asked me to explain it to you, but I have not had the courage."

"What is it, Vanessa?" Despite the dulling heat, she felt a sense of concern growing in her breast.

"You remember Mr. MacKenzie of course."

"I do."

"Your mother was quite taken with him. She is, in fact, in love with him."

"Her feelings for him were obvious," Autumn said casually, but her tone was wary.

"It seems," Vanessa went on hesitantly, "that your mother has taken him—quite publicly—as her lover. She has moved him into her house." Autumn stood slowly as comprehension wreathed her features.

"She is living with him openly?" Vanessa nodded. "But that is unthinkable," Autumn said. "Mother could go to jail! Illegal co-habitation carries the very stiffest penalties."

"They are both willing to take that risk. Alistair hopes, natu-rally, that Isabel will change her mind eventually and marry him, but for now, as she is unwilling to do so, he has accepted her terms. According to Isabel, they are living an *honest* life."

"But how could she do this to herself? How could she do this to my father's memory!" Autumn picked up her cup and flung it against the wall. "*Damn* her! And damn you, Vanessa, for allowing this to happen. You were supposed to be her friend. Couldn't you have talked her out of such madness?" Autumn swiped impatiently at the angry tears that had formed in her eyes. She looked up to find Vanessa's sadness and sympathy displayed acutely on her face. That lady rose and moved to the bay of windows.

"I did try, Autumn," she offered. "We discussed the matter for hours, Isabel and I, but she would not be swayed. There was no point at which we agreed . . . except perhaps at one." Vanessa bowed her head. "I understand how she feels about Alistair."

Autumn sat down numbly. "I know what it is to love a man, Vanessa, and I know what it is to be denied the fullest expression of that love. But that is no excuse for my mother's behavior. Even if she is accepted into society for her supposed link to England's throne, she will be a fool among fools, the Main Line's *all-licensed* fool. My father's name will be sullied, and I cannot forgive her for that."

"Can you not," stated Vanessa softly. Her eyes were fixed firmly on the blazing blue of the morning sky. She glanced briefly at the girl and then turned away. "Think, Autumn, on your relationship with my son. Would you, under any circumstances, let him go simply to please your neighbors?"

Autumn hesitated. "I am not making a public spectacle of our relationship," she finally insisted.

"I do not mean to be unkind, Autumn," Vanessa said moving to her, "but none of us has a right to hold ourselves up as arbiter of morality. That is probably the thing that is most wrong in the world—everyone stands in judgment of everyone else."

"I know very well about judgmental people, Vanessa, having been the victim of asinine distortions and hateful inferences. One would think my mother had had enough of censure. Why doesn't she simply marry the man and have it done? Why must she make a cause of this?"

Vanessa's tone was hard. "I don't suppose you know what your father's suicide did to Isabel." Autumn glanced up sharply.

"I know what it did to me."

"You were not his wife, Autumn. You were his daughter. His death—his . . . suicide—deprived you of a father. But it deprived Isabel of her whole identity. For you, his death was terrifying, but even without your father, you had the power to live your life, or the important part of it, as you wished to live it. Oh, granted," she went on taking a chair, "you did not have your former luxuries. You had to take a job. But you were still who you'd always been. You were still Autumn Thackeray. But when your father took his life, he took the very thing that made Isabel who she was." She looked pointedly at Autumn. "Your mother received her whole identity as a human being from Emmett Thackeray. That's who she was—Mrs. Emmett Thackeray.

"Your mother felt all the things you felt when your father died, but she felt something else, too. She felt she was nobody."

"That is ridiculous," countered Autumn. "My mother is a beautiful, intelligent human being. She is witty and vivacious—"

"She is all those things," Vanessa interrupted. "But while your father lived, she was those things as Mrs. Thackeray. She *defined* herself as your father's wife." Vanessa paused. "I believe," she continued quietly, "that Isabel will never again allow a man to imprison her identity. She will never again be merely the 'other' person in a relationship. From now on, Isabel's life will be her own, and she will allow no one to take that away from her." Autumn was silent for a long time, stunned by the revelation of feelings she'd never realized her mother had harbored.

"She is risking imprisonment in any event," Autumn mentioned finally.

"Isabel is aware of that, and she has decided to flout what she considers a bad law." As Autumn swiped at perspiration that was now mingled with drying tears, Vanessa resumed. "You cursed me for allowing this to happen," she said.

"I am sorry," murmured Autumn.

Vanessa lifted a detaining hand. "I understand, your feelings," she assured the girl, "but you must understand too, that while I would not choose such a life for myself, I do, with all my heart, support Isabel's pursuit of her own independence."

"One would think owning a business would be enough independence for anyone."

"How much independence is enough, Autumn? I lived through a long and crippling marriage to a man who held his authority like a gun to my heart. After he died, my whole existence was relinquished to the medical community in the person of Winslow Beame. Now, because of you, I have gained a modicum of independence; I have settled for the health of my body and my mind. But, I ask you, is it enough, Autumn? Is it ever enough to merely settle? Life in these times has a way of encouraging rationalization. We give in and give in—and eventually we give up. Isabel will not settle for less than she demands of life. None of us should."

Autumn felt a sudden empathy growing in her heart for her mother. She recalled her own words, spoken to Cain the previous night. She had said that in a perfect world everyone would take his doctor's oath—"first, do no harm"—and then live their lives as best they could. She had said that someone, somewhere had to begin to build such a perfect world. But why, she wondered, must that "someone" be Isabel Thackeray?

And could the world be "perfect" in any event, Autumn reflected later, as she strode out across the back lawn to the stables.

She ordered that a horse be saddled for her. Without knowing her destination or caring, she mounted the animal and spurred it to a pounding gallop. One of the older stablemen noted to himself that the young and pretty Miss Thackeray ought to be cautioned about riding astride. It just didn't look right for a young lady to be galloping about over the countryside, her light frock up there above her knees. It was bad enough she rode that bicycle. He nudged several of the younger men who were watching the departing girl with obvious admiration.

"Get back to work, lads," he groused. "Lady ought to be ridin' sidesaddle anyway, or wearin' breeches if she's a mind to ride like she is."

The golden-haired boy smiled sunnily. "You complain as loud when she does wear breeches, old man," he said laughing.

"Woman ought to stay home in the first place," the first man muttered as he returned to his work. "It ain't proper," he was heard to grumble throughout the afternoon, "it just ain't proper."

Autumn led her horse down to the narrow girdle of the beach and along the splashing shore. The cadence of hooves on the soft earth, the wind that whipped at her loosely pinned hair, and the blown spume conspired to calm her and to help her organize her thoughts. . . . She had judged both her mother and Vanessa harshly. She was as guilty as the rest of society in its desire to control the behavior of its hapless members. The horse, taking its cue from a pensive Autumn, drifted to a stop at the edge of the shore to munch on the lush grasses growing there. Autumn dismounted and wandered down to the sun-glazed expanse of the ocean. Shimmering in the blue reflection of the sky, the inlet lapped a cool invitation. On an impulse, she removed her stockings and her high kid boots and waded into the shallow water.

Relief from the humidity and the heat overwhelmed her, and she found herself heading farther into the frothy water. Wavelets played over her toes and ankles. The hem of her frock quickly dampened and became heavy. The salty cold on her legs emboldened her and allowed her to shed her inhibitions. Autumn found herself laughing as the little white capped curls reached higher— first to her knees and then to her thighs—as she became more daring, more receptive to their playful invitation.

The seabed was rocky where she waded and she tested each foothold carefully. A particularly smooth, particularly mossy little rock was, however, the instrument of both her ultimate relief and her final, literal, downfall. She fell, splashing and laughing into the water. A gull screeched overhead. Several were routed, in fact, from their languid pursuit of little fishes, and Autumn's horse lifted its head at her exclamation of surprise. Seeing that its mistress was still at hand, the pretty bay merely advanced a few steps and resumed chomping on the myriad foliage that wreathed the shoreline. Autumn seized the unexpected moment and lay full out in the undulating waters of the bay. She delighted in the happy accident and enjoyed to the fullest the sensual pleasures of the water's ebb and flow.

She was hardly prepared, then, for the sight of several ladies, parasols spread, taking their leisure on a walk along the beach. Autumn did not know whether to attempt to hide herself (that would have been impossible, since the ladies were almost upon her and had surely already spotted her) or to brazen out the confrontation. She chose the latter course, and it was with some asperity that the ladies watched her. She rose, like a mythical water goddess from the depths of the brine, and waved cheerily, ignoring her dripping gown.

"How do, Autumn," said one of the women stiffly.

"How do, Mrs. Pierce," Autumn greeted her. "Mrs. Butler," she added. "And Mrs. Harmon. Lovely day for a walk," she observed as she squeezed out the hem of her dress.

"Or a swim?" remarked Mrs. Butler dryly as she stepped back, protecting her shoes from the dribbling effect of Autumn's efforts.

"The swim was something of an accident," Autumn explained. The ladies, social lionesses all, looked down from beneath their bonnet brims and did not smile. "I was actually only intending to wade," she added lamely.

"Were you indeed," stated Mrs. Pierce with a decided lack of amusement.

"One would do well," said Mrs. Harmon, "to exercise more caution in one's spare time activities. In any event, it has been my observation that servants have entirely too much spare time in the first place." The ladies resumed their walk, whispering among themselves. Autumn had no doubt as to the subject of their conversation. And she knew it would be so for days. Cain would be furious. She sighed. As she retrieved her shoes and stockings, she realized at least some of the reason for the ladies' vicissitude. In the water Autumn's frock had become almost transparent. Her chemise and bloomers were completely visible beneath it, and beneath those, for she was wearing no corset, her "altogether" was very nearly exposed. If she had been the subject of controversy, she would surely now be the object of outright contempt. Worse than that, Cain would be forced to defend her—or maybe he would not defend her.

"Oh, Lord," she ejaculated softly. Autumn could not bear yet another confrontation with Cain. Their battles had become almost more frequent than their peaceful times together. Perhaps, she reflected, it would be for the best if she gave up her bicycle, her breeches, and her trips to the circulating library. She sat down, shifting her weight in the sand, and drew on her stockings and shoes. Vanessa's words came back to her:

"We give in and give in—and eventually we give up."

The message gave her pause. The incident for which she would surely be censured had not been her fault. On the other hand, Cain had every right to expect her not to appear half-naked before a contingent of the town's foremost ladies. As she rolled her stockings firmly around the constriction of her garters and folded the excess material securely underneath, she decided it was too bad she'd not been spotted by some of the women from her literary club. Such was the nature of those ladies, she reflected, that they might have chosen to join her—not denigrate her. But, in fact, Autumn had been seen by the standard bearers of Cape May morality. She thought, smiling broadly, it might be something of a lark to see how this little episode played itself out. Considering the well-oiled gossip mill in the city, Autumn might discover that she'd been spied stark naked, cavorting with the fishes for all the world to see. Her smile faded. She lay back on the sand, her hands pillowing her head. Eyes closed against the metallic glitter of the noontime sun she wondered at that rebellious part of her nature that would inspire such an irreverent thought. As Cain had so often reminded her—especially of late—the apple had not fallen far from the tree. The 'tree'— Isabel and Emmett Thackeray in this case—was a wild and insubordinate one, whipping its branches, refusing to be pruned. How appalled Cain would be if he knew just how insubordinate the matriarchal branch of that tree had become.

Isabel had made up her mind to flout convention, and Autumn wondered if she truly disagreed with that decision. Surely it was an extraordinary one. Surely it would cause a great deal of angst. But was it not also true that Isabel's decision had not been made lightly? According to Vanessa, it had been the subject of much discussion. It must be, Autumn determined, that her mother felt the positive aspects of such an apparently incautious move outweighed the negative ones. She opened her eyes in abrupt comprehension and winced against the brilliant sunshine. Sitting up, she realized how extraordinary a woman Isabel Thackeray really was. She was willing to risk incarceration and public alienation for the sake of her independence. If the truth be told, Isabel was something of a Victoria Woodhull—a woman of strength and decision who rooted out society's absurdities and held them up for scrutiny. She was one of those pilgrim builders of Autumn's own description, determined to help create a perfect world. It was necessary for Isabel to take a *public* stand. How otherwise was she to get the public's attention?

Autumn stood, empowered by the revelation, and brushed at her drying frock. She was about to mount her horse, when a hail from far down the beach caught her attention. Peering into the shimmering distance, she noted that Robert Moffat was striding toward her. Autumn waved a greeting, delighted to encounter him.

"Robert!" she called, advancing down the beach to him.

"How are you, little one?" he called. They met and embraced, his bulky hug enfolding her.

"I am fine. But I know I am not the one in whom you are truly interested," she told him, laughing.

"Do not be so sure, Autumn. I have missed you over these past weeks almost as much as I have pined for Vanessa." He paused, and his face became serious. "How is she?"

"She is well, Robert," Autumn returned, her tone matching his. "She is . . . physically . . . very well, in fact."

"Your answer implies a further observation. Does she pine for me, too?"

"Always." Reaching up she placed a hand on his great stooping shoulder. "Please do not despair, Robert. I have been inspired by a very special woman of my acquaintance. Your life and Vanessa's life are about to change. Will you make me a promise?" she asked. He regarded her uncertainly. "Whatever happens, and I mean that most sincerely, will you trust me?"

"I trust your motives, little one," he assured her, "but I must question your intent. And I must warn you not to put yourself in harm's way."

"You mean in Cain's way."

"Aye, little one. He is a good man, but in this instance not a clement one. There will be no charity in his heart for you if you attempt to defy him in this matter." Autumn averted her eyes.

"You must leave this to my discretion, Robert," she said with determination. "In the meantime, be of good heart."

"I shall try, Autumn," he assured her. He helped her onto her mount, and she looked down on him for a long moment. At last, persuaded of his confidence in her, she turned her horse and headed for Byron Hall. She had ridden only a few yards when she spotted Cain coming toward her on Castillo. As he approached at a gallop, she realized that he must have seen her with Robert Moffat, and her heart quickened in her breast. His facial expression confirmed what she had perceived. The lines in his gleaming countenance were hard and his eyes issued a terrible challenge.

She looked back over her shoulder to see Robert standing firmly to face what he surely knew would be a confrontation. She hastily advanced, placing herself and her mount in the path of Cain's onslaught. He merely jerked the reins, spurring Castillo around her and continuing at a pounding gallop.

"No, Cain!" she screamed.

Drawing back his rein before the lighthouse keeper, he allowed the horse to rear and claw the air violently. Robert looked up, stepping back to make room for the animal's wild prancing. It stirred sand and water into a devil-like display. Autumn's hand flew to her mouth. But she took no time to reflect. She spurred her own mount and flew wildly down the beach to Robert's assistance.

"You will leave my family alone, Moffat!" Cain was exhorting the man. His thundering rage rose above the low thunder of the ocean. "If I see you speaking to a member of my household again, I shall kill you." With the words, Cain wheeled his mount and rode off. Autumn careened to a halt.

"Go after him, girl!" shouted Robert. "Tell him the encounter was all my fault. That you didn't know who I was. Go, little one!" Autumn did so immediately. Her mind numbed, she pounded down the beach in a frenzy of determination. Desperately, she rode into the stable yard and scrambled from her horse. She ran to Cain, reaching out for him, but he threw her off.

"How dare you speak to that man!" he erupted as he continued to lead Castillo to his stall.

"But I didn't know who he was, Cain," Autumn cried frantically as she followed him. "He was only an old man on the beach!" Cain hesitated. "We made pleasantries about the day, that was all. Believe me," she pleaded through gulping sobs. Cain stopped and regarded her sharply.

"He did not speak of this family? Of this household?"

"No," Autumn lied, hating herself. The burden of that lie deepened her terror. Cain was watching her with a fierce regard. "He said he kept the light. Oh, Cain," she whispered through distorting tears, "you cannot kill a man for that."

"Not for that, Autumn," returned Cain harshly. "Not for that." Autumn was seized with a horrible premonition. She saw Cain's avenging form before her, bathed in an angry flare of light. And she knew suddenly that he would leave her. Her heart constricted, and a dizzying convulsion of breath left her lungs.

As consciousness left her, words floated in the air. "I didn't know him. I didn't know him. I didn't know him." The sky spun, the treetops whirled, and the world ended.

♋︎ ♋︎

And Cain was there, very suddenly, holding her, his strength flowing through her. She lifted shaky fingertips to her forehead. She felt cold and hot at once. "What happened?" she murmured.

Cain held her in the cradle of his arms and watched her awakening. His eyes were moist with fear and worry. "Are you alright, love?" he asked softly.

"Did I faint?" she asked.

"You did," he told her. He had called for a cold cloth and patted her face gently with it, so very gently.

"What's happened t' the little miss?" inquired a condoling stableman. There were several men about, shuffling nervously near the fallen Autumn.

"She's alright, ain't she, doc?" Autumn recognized the gruff gentleman who had stabled her horse, and attempted a smile.

"She is alright," Cain assured them all, "but I think it best if I get her into the examining room." He lifted her into his arms. "See to the horses," he said, and carried her into the house. For long moments, Cain examined Autumn, listening to her heart and taking the measure of her pulse over and over. She lay silently as he did so. At last, turning from her, he plunged his hands into a bowl of water and splashed his face and hair. He paused a long time over the bowl. "What can I say, love?" he asked her. There was a husky regret in his tone. He looked at her then, and Autumn could not tell if the rivulets that ran down his tanned cheeks were made of water or tears. He came to her quickly and lifted her into his embrace. Autumn yielded, accepting gratefully the harbor of his love.

"Cain," she said softly, "I was so frightened."

"I know," he returned. "And I am so sorry. It is not enough for me to say that, but I do say it." He looked down on her for several moments. "Oh, love," he assured her with a deepening sorrow, "I would not hurt you for all the world."

"Nor I you, Cain." Autumn held to him vehemently, vowing to keep her word even as she realized what she was compelled to do.

Chapter 21

An angry sunset had brought merciful coolness to Cape May, New Jersey. The air was dried of the day's humidity by flying night breezes. In the agitated darkness, two horses whickered nervously as they were tethered to a light wagon.

"This is ludicrous," commented a star-brushed form in the stable yard outside Byron Hall. "Why in the name of heaven aren't we taking the coach?"

"Because it might be recognized by certain of the town's gossips, and you would not want them to know you were attending a literary meeting. Now get in, Vanessa." Autumn's tone was decisive and not to be disputed. She held the reins firmly. "Come on then," she ordered tensely. With some indecision, the other woman finally climbed aboard the rickety wagon, her weight causing the old boards, unused and dried out, to creak with what seemed inordinate resonance.

"Autumn," said Vanessa, "you have nagged and railed until I am a rag of compliance, but I am repeating to you that I have no interest in attending your literary meeting. Worthy though the club may be, I have not been out in Cape May society in years. I am not anxious to socialize with the same people who have ignored me and probably tittered about me behind my back."

"These are not the same people," Autumn returned shortly, as she pulled herself up next to Vanessa.

"And why is the meeting being held so late? If my memory serves, you leave the house directly after dinner when you attend one of these meetings." Without answering, Autumn made sure that Vanessa was securely seated. "Cain's father always admonished that too much night air was bad for a lady's health."

"Cain's father isn't here," said Autumn fixedly. She clicked her tongue, snapped the reins, and led the horses from the yard at a cautious gait. And she attempted to ignore Vanessa's ongoing battery of questions.

Cain, having no afternoon appointments, had left the house after lunch to ride out to his tenant farms. He would not be back until late the next day. His absence had given Autumn the opportunity to carry out her plan. She'd taken pains to find a rarely used wagon at the back of the stables and dust it of cobwebs and accumulated leaves. She'd found a few spiders, too, and relocated them to other climes. She had discovered some abandoned tack and chosen her horses carefully. Selecting two aging, strong, but no longer producing brood mares from the far pasture, she observed that they would not be missed. As they were no longer useful, no one would question their absence. Autumn reflected as she led them in after dark that the two old girls, gentle and sassy, would serve a new and even more elevated purpose now that they were no longer doggedly propagating the proud Byron line. She had spent the rest of the day, as Vanessa had pointed out, nagging, badgering, and finally hounding that lady to acquiescence.

Vanessa watched the night pass by through the veiling that fluttered from the brim of her pretty bonnet and reflected on the fevered events of the last few hours. Autumn had supervised her preparations as scrupulously as if she'd been dressing her for a ball at the White House. It was unlike the girl to be quite so aggressive. But Vanessa reasoned this small concession might just begin to heal the little rift that had developed between them over her failure to convince Isabel to marry Alistair MacKenzie. Though Autumn had apologized for her harsh words, Vanessa had no desire to be on less than affectionate terms with her. They'd shared so much. If it pleased Autumn that she attend a meeting of the literary club—dressed to the nines, in a rackety old vehicle, in the dead of night—then attend a meeting she would. Still, Vanessa reflected, her thoughts drifting as the cart wobbled and bumped along, she would much rather be home reading the words of the sisters Brontë than spending the evening talking about them. The wagon kept up a steady, if pitching, momentum as it entered the city. Vanessa watched in some bemusement as Annie Fitzpatrick's house came into view and as quickly disappeared.

"Aren't we stopping at Annie's house?" she asked.

"No," came the tense response.

"But I thought the meetings were usually held there."

"They usually are." A silence settled on the two women. Autumn glanced briefly at Vanessa. The next few moments would either destroy their relationship or cement it. Autumn prayed, naturally, for the latter. "We're going somewhere else," she ventured. The glowing lamplit city drifted past them into darkness. The road before them became narrower and lit only by the lanterns that swung at the sides of the cart and the stars. Her heart hammering against the wall of her chest, Autumn turned the horses onto a graveled path. They came to a sudden lurching halt on a spit of land beneath the Cape May light. It rose, conic, majestic, illuminating at its topmost acclivity the star-encrusted blackness of the night. Vanessa looked up, horrified.

"Autumn," she said on a breath, "how could you."

"Go to him," that one pleaded. "I beg you."

Vanessa averted her eyes. A small silence followed. At last she said, "I can't."

"Yes you can." Autumn bounded from the wagon and ran to the side where Vanessa sat rigidly.

"I shall never, *ever* forgive you for this, Autumn."

"Yes you will. You will forgive me, Vanessa, if you will only see him—once."

"Dammit," Vanessa said, her words clenched, her tone desperate, "do you want to see the man dead?"

"He's dead now!" Vanessa looked down at her incredulously. "And so are you," Autumn continued with an intensity that startled the older woman. "You both go about making believe you're alive, you mimic the motions of living, but you are not living. You are merely existing."

Before Vanessa could reply, the door at the bottom of the lighthouse opened, drenching the space before it in light. Both women looked toward the light and saw at its center the silhouetted form of Robert Moffat. He advanced slowly, peering into the darkness.

"Who is it?" he inquired. "Autumn?"

"Yes, Robert," she answered. He moved to her and looked up. His mouth gaped. There, above him, luminescent in the starlight, was Vanessa. He said her name and glanced at Autumn quickly, the sea-glass blue of his eyes wide with disbelief, his weathered face a mask of wonder.

"Vanessa," he repeated. Autumn felt a swelling tightness in her throat as that woman reached down, offering her hand. In a fluid dream dance, Vanessa descended from the wagon. She and Robert stood before each other, facing a destiny of decision. Slowly, together in the cradle of each other's arms, they made their way up the lighted path through the door. It closed behind them, sealing up and saving forever a perfect dream.

Autumn waited only seconds before climbing back into the wagon and snapping the reins. She would return at dawn, having only imagined the happiness and fulfillment that had blossomed inside the Cape May light that long—and much too brief— night.

There was a well of tenderness between the two women as they traveled the ribbon of dawn-gray road back to Byron Hall. They wordlessly returned wagon and horses to their original locations and, once inside the house, scurried upstairs like girls. Laughing quietly, they entered Vanessa's room.

"This has been the most joyous night of my life," said Vanessa as they embraced. "I shall live on it the rest of my life."

"Oh, you don't mean that," Autumn said.

"I am afraid I do," returned Vanessa seriously.

"You *can't* mean it," Autumn entreated. She smiled as she went about the room lighting the lamps. "I intend to see that this beautiful night is repeated again and again. You don't think," she pointed out, "that I made all these plans for you only to abandon you to the sorry imitation of dreams. I am going to make it my purpose in life to see that you and Robert share many more nights together for the rest of your lives."

Vanessa smiled at Autumn's enthusiasm, but her face became solemn as she removed her bonnet and cloak. "I am only too aware of what the consequences might be if my son were to discover your intentions."

"It is time," returned Autumn, "that your son faced a few realities."

Vanessa looked up sharply. "Cain must never know about this meeting between Robert and me. You do understand that, don't you, Autumn?"

"Cain will know about it, and he will accept it."

Vanessa caught her breath and grasped Autumn's shoulders. "Autumn, please," she said urgently, "don't even imagine that you might tell Cain."

"Of course, he will be angry—"

"He will not be merely angry," Vanessa said, shaking her, "he will not be merely resentful. Do you imagine I would have lived all these years wrapped in a cocoon, steeling myself against my feelings, denying my heart, and causing myself and Robert such pain, if I believed my son would be simply angry? Understand this, Autumn, if Cain ever discovers what has happened tonight he will kill Robert Moffat. That's the reality."

"Cain will not kill anybody," Autumn said evenly.

"Think, Autumn, think about what you are saying. Robert will never defend himself against Cain's wrath. You were not there, Autumn. You don't know how it was that night." Vanessa turned away abruptly and paced the room clasping her hands and twisting them feverishly. "Cain was a madman that night. I did not even recognize him as my son. I cannot risk such a thing happening again. The only way I can protect Robert is to abandon him."

"There is another way."

"What way?"

"You can marry him," Autumn said quietly.

"That is impossible."

"Is it, Vanessa? Tell me why."

"Cain . . . he would never . . ."

"Cain has no authority in this matter, Vanessa, unless you allow him authority."

"But he is my son."

"And as such he owes you a son's respect. Don't you understand, Vanessa? Can't you see it? Cain is a grown man, and yet you have allowed him to dominate this household and to bully you as if he were an unruly child.

"If my mother has taught us nothing else, she has taught us the value of living honestly according to our own authority. It will be difficult for you, Vanessa, but once you and Robert are married, Cain will have no choice but to accept it."

"You know, don't you," Vanessa said cautiously, "that if Cain ever discovers your hand in this, it will be over for you." Autumn averted her regard.

"I cannot believe that. Cain is my heart mate. He will understand eventually . . . and eventually, he will forgive."

"Your optimism, Autumn, is born of youth and inexperience. You have no idea yet of the complexities of emotion that exist between men and women. You believe you have found perfection with Cain. You believe, in your innocence, that perfection is even possible. But even the deepest love can be flawed, because *we* are flawed. We must never trust too deeply in the indulgence of another—even the one we love most in the world.

"What your mother has taught us, Autumn, is that we must be willing to accept the consequences of our behavior, and we must accept them with grace. If I marry Robert, I may lose my son. But you might lose the deepest love you will ever know. Before we do anything, we must be very sure that we are both willing to accept the consequences. Promise me you will consider it carefully."

"I do promise, Vanessa." The two women embraced, bidding each other goodnight. They would go to their separate beds, to their separate dreams, to their separate challenges.

❦

The next morning, after only a few hours' sleep, the two women solemnly agreed that, having considered the matter carefully, they were willing to take whatever risks were necessary to see Robert and Vanessa wed.

"It is time," Autumn said, studying the contents of her breakfast cup. "Cain and I are living out a masquerade in any event." She looked up to find Vanessa watching her. "The other day in the stable yard I denied I even knew Robert Moffat. I knew then that I could not go on and possibly marry Cain with a lie between us."

"And the consequences, Autumn?"

"There are consequences in any event."

"But none so grave as those that would occur if Cain discovers that you have helped Robert and me."

"If he discovers that, Vanessa, then he will have discovered my true nature. He must either live with that or leave me. It will be his decision."

"And you are willing to accept it?"

"Yes." She looked down at the silver ring she always wore, the one Vanessa had given to her. She looked up, smiling. "This must be your wedding ring," she told the woman. And they began making plans for the actual wedding. Autumn, because of her greater mobility, would make the arrangements. Everything, they agreed, must be done in secret. Until the day that Vanessa and Robert were legally bound, they could reveal nothing of the plans. Robert's very life depended on it. Cain might well dispose of his mother's indigent lover with impunity, but he could not so easily dispose of her husband.

They determined as well that for the next several weeks, the maintaining of harmony in the Byron household must take primacy over every other consideration. They decided, first, that Autumn must make amends to the ladies who had seen her so indisposed on the beach. They decided to invite those ladies to tea. The invitation would serve two purposes. It would cloak Autumn in Vanessa's protection and offset any untoward gossip about her, and it would satisfy Cain deeply to see the women of his household acting so appropriately "womanly." Autumn set out immediately to put their plan into action.

Dressed modestly but fashionably, she arranged herself behind her driver in the ornate Byron coach. She adjusted the packages on the seat next to her with excessive care. These were gifts, wrapped and prettily beribboned. They were Autumn's way of apologizing to the three ladies. Mrs. Merriam Pierce would receive the chocolate cake as was her due as foremost lady of the town (her husband being the city's mayor). Mrs. Butler, the wife of the city's chief planner, was to be presented with the marmalade, and Ivadell Harmon would receive the berry relish as befitted her husband's more humble status as spiritual leader of the Suffering Pilgrim's church. In all cases, the gifts were to be offered at the door along with Vanessa's card inviting each lady to tea. Autumn perspired tiredly between stops, but miraculously, appeared cool and composed once she stepped from her carriage. It was not without some hesitancy that Vanessa Byron's calling cards were received, and, in fact, not till later in the day—presumably after the three ladies had exchanged views on the matter—that three notes of acceptance were delivered to Byron Hall. Autumn communicated this happy news to Vanessa, and the two were more than ready when the three ladies arrived promptly at four o'clock.

Cain arrived home to find the city's finest ladies in his parlor sipping tea, eating cakes, and generally agreeing that a hotter summer had never been experienced in Cape May, New Jersey. Autumn smiled comfortably as he entered the parlor.

"You know our guests, Cain dear," Vanessa murmured.

"I do," he acknowledged, offering a courtly bow.

"Autumn thought it time I began receiving again."

"Miss Thackeray's advice is always most judicious," agreed Cain. He glanced appreciatively at Autumn's froth of a summer frock.

"And we were only too happy to accept your mother's hospitality," Mrs. Pierce piped.

"It seems like old times, thanks to her dear Autumn," offered Mrs. Butler.

And from Mrs. Harmon, "You must be so proud of your son, Vanessa, now he has taken up practice." Vanessa nodded obligingly and expressed the expected gratitude to heaven for such a son. Cain cleared his throat and bowed himself from the room. There was general agreement all around that his engagement to the refined Miss Fraser of New York City was heaven-sent. Heaven-sent!

At supper that evening, Cain assured Autumn that she seemed on the path of a very strong comeback into the city's good graces. He approved, he told her. Vanessa, enjoying dinner with the couple, agreed. Both ladies were mightily relieved that the crisis that might have surrounded Autumn's accidental swim had been averted. The talk now in the city might well revolve around that swim, but most assuredly everyone would regard it with a softer, more gentle eye. In fact, after today's success and the approval of Mrs. Pierce, Mrs. Butler, and Mrs. Harmon, all of Autumn's misbehavior would be bound to inspire amused forbearance rather than intolerance. Harsh speculation about the Byron household was at an end.

But Autumn knew she could not rely on today's victory alone. Autumn would make herself the ornament of Cape May. She would do whatever she could to promote a harmony of the spheres both in the household and without. Her breeches had been securely tucked into a chest, her bicycle firmly abandoned in a shed, and her circulating library books returned and none checked out to replace them on her night table. From now on, she would see that the servants did the marketing and the household errands, and when she did venture out—always with the stately Vanessa at her side—she would avail herself of one of the Byron coaches. Autumn would become a monument to respectability and classic feminine obedience, and Cain and she would have no more battles over her freewheeling lifestyle. Autumn unconsciously knitted her pale brows. It all sounded so ridiculous. She looked up hastily to assure herself that Cain was not reading on her face the deceit she intended. He was, instead, smiling contentedly at the happy picture of domesticity the three of them presented sitting around the dining table.

"You will both be interested to know that Win Beame will be visiting in a few days," he said, as he sipped at his coffee. "I wrote him of our trip to Philadelphia, and he is most confident in your state of health, Mother, but he feels that he ought to be checking on you from time to time."

"How . . . kind of him," Vanessa replied, attempting to conceal her vexation.

"Yes," agreed Autumn hastily, "how . . . kind." Both women fanned themselves languidly before excusing themselves to take their evening leisure in Vanessa's parlor. While Cain took his cigar and brandy in the garden, the women passed time arranging dried flower petals and sweet-smelling herbs into little sachets for placement about the house. After a time, Autumn observed, "Cain seemed pleased with our tea party today."

Vanessa offered a wry smile and mentioned that he might not have been so pleased if Autumn had invited her literary ladies to tea. "I wish nothing more than to dig this family out of the eye of controversy right now," Autumn said seriously. "It has occurred to me to give up that society."

"But you enjoy it so, Autumn. You have given up quite enough, smoothing the way for Robert and me."

"Perhaps I shall retain my membership then, as long it does not annoy Cain or cause any gossip."

"I don't know," commented Vanessa, "how I shall ever repay you for your efforts."

"You can repay me by living happily ever after."

"This isn't a pretty fairy tale, my dear. This is real life, and in real life, scandal does not insure a happy-ever-after sort of ending. Those ladies we tried so hard to impress today will malign a union between Robert and me. It was because of the likes of them that Cain ended the affair in the first place. I've never had a use for such self-righteousness as theirs, but my son believes that the esteem of those women and people like them to be my due."

"Cain's own prejudice ended your affair with Robert. And it is his prejudice we must overcome. Whatever the opinions of Mrs. Pierce, Mrs. Butler, and Mrs. Harmon, it is Cain's opinion, his resistance, we must work on. But he loves you dearly and wants the best for you. By the time he discovers your marriage to Robert he will already have come to the conclusion that that marriage is acceptable and that it is right. That is the only way to introduce new ideas—cautiously."

❦

"Oh, hell's bells," laughed Annie Fitzpatrick, "what if she is a jailbird. I still say we ask her to speak." The meeting of the Tuesday Evening Women's Literary Club of Cape May was heartily underway.

"It's just not right," insisted Lavinia Carlson. "She isn't even, strictly speaking, a writer."

"What do you call *History of Woman Suffrage*, girl?" returned Annie hotly. "Don't you call that a book? And didn't Miss Susan Brownell Anthony write it?"

"All I can say," murmured Lavinia, "is my old man'll kill me if we invite her—"

"Aha!" put in Annie. "Now we get to the *real* objection."

"Don't be so hard on her, Annie," Autumn hastily interjected. "I'm a bit concerned myself at how the men will react to her." Annie leaned forward into the circle of women, her elbows fixed on her knees.

Eyeing her friends keenly, she said, "And don't you think that's just what they're counting on?"

"You mean the men," Lavinia clarified.

"I mean the men, Vinnie," Annie said gently. "Let's face the facts, girls, we've got us a problem here, and the only way we're going to solve our problem is to confront it." Autumn sat back listening to Annie's strong argument as her friend, Emma Cavanaugh, passed around a tray of lemonade and cakes. "I know you're all scared," Annie was saying. "Hell, I'm as scared as I can be. Those boys out there—the men—are scared, too. Everybody's afraid of Miss Anthony. But I'll tell you something else, Miss Anthony's only human, and I'll bet she's scared, too." She leaned forward, and her tone was both confiding and compelling. "But she goes out there into a hostile world every day and she says what she's got to say. Men aren't any tougher than us, they're not any more sensible or reasonable or rational than us, and they're not any brighter than us." She paused. "Men are just as crazy and feeble and ridiculous as we are sometimes, but they hide it better!" Everyone laughed, though Emma Cavanaugh cast her friend a benign, if scolding, regard. "The truth is," continued Annie seriously, "we're all human. Some of us are smarter and some of us less so, but it's not being a woman or a man that makes the difference, it's just the nature of the human animal. And that's all Miss Susan B. Anthony is trying to say. Now I say, if she's got the courage to go out there everyday and tell women what's what, we ought to have the courage to listen to her." She regarded Lavinia Carlson. "What do you think, Vinnie?"

That lady rolled her eyes. "Oh, all right, Annie," she acquiesced. "But I say we don't make this entirely public—*if* you know what I mean." She glanced about the room knowingly. "I say we don't tell our husbands."

"And *I* say," Annie interjected, "we not only *tell* them, we *invite* them." There was a round of applause, and Annie, smiling, splayed her hands. "The whole point," she said patiently, "is that there'll be no more sneaking around for us. It's fine that we keep telling each other what the problems are, but we need to start telling everybody else—including the men, Vinnie. What good is a revolution if nobody knows about it?" She offered a large laugh and patted Lavinia's hand condolingly. "Don't worry about it, my friend. They can't fight all of us. One of us at a time they can whip, but all together we're invincible!"

Chapter 22

Winslow Beame had arrived and found the changes at Byron Hall much to his satisfaction. He had some reservations however, when Autumn and Vanessa made their excuses after dinner saying that they would be visiting at the home of friends. What she and Autumn did not relate, of course, was that in fact Vanessa's "friend" was Robert Moffat. When they arrived home well after ten o'clock, they found Cain and Winslow awaiting them in the parlor.

Winslow shook an avuncular finger at both of them and said, "You two ladies had us very concerned." He eyed Vanessa curiously. "I presume that you are not tiring yourself with these forays into the night, my girl." In fact he had never seen her more aglow with health. That glow, however, might as easily be a flush.

"I wouldn't exactly call them forays, Winslow," she corrected him. "We've just been with our friends."

"Ladies of a certain age need their beauty sleep—and younger ones, too," he insisted. Autumn and Vanessa exchanged a knowing glance. No doubt Winslow Beame thought himself entirely within his rights to scold them.

"You are absolutely correct, Winslow," stated Vanessa. "You will excuse me, therefore, if I say goodnight." With those words and one last brief glance at Autumn, Vanessa withdrew. Winslow regarded the younger woman with some ferocity.

"Where have the two of you been till this time of night?" he demanded.

"It was a literary meeting, Dr. Beame."

"Surely you know better, Miss Thackeray. Literary meetings are bad business for all ladies, but especially for those who are of a particularly fragile constitution."

"Mrs. Byron enjoys them, Dr. Beame," returned Autumn respectfully, "and I cannot imagine that anything she enjoys could be harmful to her." She glanced at Cain, seeking his approval. "Don't you agree, Dr. Byron?"

"You have no idea what may or may not be harmful," Beame stated.

"Win," Cain interjected, "it is just some ladies talking. My mother has told me that getting out of an evening keeps her mind active."

"You mean inordinately *stimulated*," Winslow Beame shot back with a scalding look toward Cain. "I have told you that such stimulation could be very dangerous. I see nothing untoward in the occasional tea or afternoon social, but this sort of nighttime frivolity is unnecessary and quite, quite unacceptable for a lady who has not left her house in years." Autumn bit back a rejoinder, and looked forlornly to Cain for help. He cleared his throat.

"I see no harm in it, Win," he said carefully. His tone became firmer as he added, "As I mentioned in my last letter, our trip to

Philadelphia was extremely successful. The fact is, my mother flourished there, and you can see for yourself how composed she is now." He glanced at Autumn. "How did the meeting go?" he asked.

"Oh, it went very well. Annie Fitzpatrick is always entertaining in her observations—"

"Annie Fitzpatrick," said Winslow Beame with a narrowed regard. "I believe I met her at the engagement party. Her father is the librarian, isn't he? Unmarried girl as I recall. Talkative sort. I didn't like her." Autumn hid a smile.

"Annie is something of a bluestocking," said Cain. "She has been that way since she was a girl, but she's an interesting woman nonetheless. Very well-traveled."

"Fine thing, a woman traveling alone," groused Winslow Beame.

"Oh, but she doesn't travel alone," Autumn assured him innocently. "She takes trips with her friend Emma Cavanaugh."

"Even worse," stated Winslow. "Two women on their own. They are just advertising their availability. Why, anyone might answer that advertisement," he added pointedly, "even a Frenchman."

"I don't think there is any danger of that, Win," said Cain gently.

"No, you're quite right, old lad. That Fitzpatrick girl is quite a forceful piece of work, and even Frenchmen have their standards." He whisked fondly at his moustache and chuckled indulgently at his little joke. Autumn smiled and took the moment to take her own leave. The men remained downstairs for a last bit of brandy and a cigar.

"Let's go outside, Win," said Cain.

"Ah, yes," said Winslow Beame. "Things have certainly changed around here, Byron. Used to be a man could smoke anywhere he wanted in this house."

"Yes," acknowledged Cain as he ushered his old friend outside, "but Miss Thackeray believes that the smell of cigars is quite an unacceptable odor for a doctor's office."

"Nonsense," countered Winslow, "cigars have the odor of authority. That, in truth, is what Miss Thackeray finds unacceptable. We would all have been much better off if she had married that Fraser lad." He puffed contentedly. "Sadly—though happily for *that* family—Miss Thackeray is still wielding her considerable influence over this household." He studied the glowing end of his cigar. He continued in a measured tone. "I do not like to say it, Byron, but when a man gives so much leeway to a female in his employ . . ." Cain leveled him a brief glance. "Well, I shall not presume," continued Beame, "but think, lad, what will happen when Antoinette returns—as she surely will—to take up her rightful position as your wife? While a man's mistress is surely his own business, he might do well to consider the consequences of having her living under his own roof."

"Miss Thackeray is not my mistress," said Cain shortly.

"Yes, yes." Winslow Beame waved away his friend's protest. "I had forgotten you had become a gentleman, old lad. Still, you might consider setting the girl up in her own little house, with a small income perhaps. It is the sensible thing to do. As your friend, I might remind you that the delectable Miss Fraser is not one to—"

"As my friend," put in Cain, "you must know my thoughts on the *delectable* Antoinette Fraser."

"I can't say that I do, Cain," returned Beame tightly. "It is quite obvious, however, that there is more to your relationship with Miss Thackeray than you are willing to admit, but I cannot imagine that it would distort your sense of responsibility toward Antoinette. Consider this carefully. You cannot simply throw away an excellent marriage for the sake of one little strumpet." Cain Byron sent his cigar flying through the air like a dart.

"Autumn is no strumpet, Win, and you know it." He turned to Winslow Beame, his teeth clenched. "And how dare you presume to characterize our relationship in such a manner. I love Autumn Thackeray. I intend to marry her one day—as soon as the *delectable* Antoinette Fraser comes to her senses and sets me free."

Winslow's thick brows lifted.

"Is all this quite true, Byron?" he ejaculated. "I cannot fathom such a notion!"

"It is true, Win," said Cain, composing himself.

"But . . . then . . . the engagement."

"The engagement is and always was a sham. Antoinette has never loved me."

"What difference does that make?" asked Winslow, honestly confused. "Since when do we expect such driveling stuff of our marriages? It is enough that our wives respect us and give us our due as men—as husbands. You shall get no respect from that little—"

"Enough!" commanded Cain sharply. There was a small silence between the two men.

"Byron," said Winslow Beame after a time, "I can see you are quite at odds with yourself on the subject of Antoinette Fraser. That you have no right to be is not at issue." He splayed a detaining hand. "I shall not judge you," he said quickly. "I do ask you this, however, would you object if I—"

"I should consider it a favor," interjected Cain. "Now, if you will excuse me, I'm going to retire."

"Of course, old lad," said Beame, a question in his tone. "You won't mind, I take it, if I finish my smoke."

"Not at all. I'll see you in the morning." Winslow watched his old friend's departure with a kind of sadness welling in him. Where were the good times they'd had? Where was that kinship they'd shared? What, in the name of all that was holy, had happened to Cain Byron?

⌘ ⌘

A look of complete incredulity washed over Winslow Beame's countenance. "Birth control?" he asked blankly.

"Yes," returned Vanessa.

"Birth control," repeated Beame.

"Birth control," said Vanessa. Beame's swallow was both audible and accomplished with some difficulty.

"You cannot be serious," he said with uncharacteristic befuddlement. "You're almost fifty years old, Vanessa. Surely at your age—"

"I am quite serious," Vanessa stated easily. "I am, in fact, forty-six years old, Win, and I still menstruate on a monthly basis. I may continue to do so for another year, or two, or three—and possibly more."

Attempting to compose himself, Winslow managed a shallow clearing of his throat and addressed Vanessa's immediate question. "Well, of course, yes, there are several ways of managing that . . . particular aspect of married life. Indeed," he continued, fumbling with his words, "the most popular and safest method is, of course, the . . . um, the husband's restraint." He eyed Vanessa keenly, his brows knitted in puzzlement. "I must inquire why you would ask such a question, however. The Comstock statute outlawed contraception years ago. You aren't intending to become a criminal, are you, at your age?" He laughed nervously. Vanessa, adjusting her clothes before the mirror after Win's examination, smiled.

"At my age, Win," she said, patting her upswept coif, "I would rather become a criminal than a mother."

"But surely there is no chance of either," said the doctor with a forced laugh. When Vanessa did not join his mirth, he added stupidly, "You're not thinking of getting married, are you?"

Vanessa lifted an elegant brow. "That is none of your business, Winslow," she pointed out, ignoring a darkening of his regard. "I do want your best advice on the proven methods of birth control, and I shall pay you well for that knowledge. But remember this, as my physician, you are my employee—not the other way around. Aside from your studies of anatomy, you doctors might do well to take a lesson or two in humility, it seems to me." She turned to find that the man's face had become mottled with an unfocused anger and resentment. "Oh, Winslow," she chided, "you are the most respected women's specialist on the Eastern Seaboard. Surely this is not a new subject for you."

"Not at all," he replied gruffly. "On the other hand, I had not thought to be discussing it with you."

"Why not? You have been treating me for years. I have been a widow for ten. Surely you must have guessed the question would come up."

"I never did," Beame asserted hotly. "My God, Vanessa, such a thing never occurred to me. Such thoughts in women of your age are completely inappropriate—some might say disgusting."

"Winslow," said Vanessa tolerantly, "try to calm yourself. There is nothing disgusting about sex—at my age or at any other. Still, if you feel uncomfortable—"

"Nothing human makes me uncomfortable, Vanessa. I am a doctor." He turned to the windows and tugged manfully at his moustache, regaining his composure. "Now," he continued evenly, "what did you use while married to Cain's father?" he asked stiffly.

"Cain's father," returned Vanessa wryly, "exercised what you would call husbandly restraint, Win. At some point in our marriage he decided that I was much too much of a lady to be subjected to that sort of indignity. Cain's father took mistresses. Once that gentleman had increased himself to his satisfaction, we rarely had sexual relations. When we did, I used a pessary which I bought from a caring midwife in the city. She was a thoroughly good woman who offered counsel as well as devices." Winslow Beame sat down heavily.

"A *pessary*," he said in disbelief. "But that is a suppository, Vanessa, and quite, quite . . . immoral. Ladies do not go about sticking . . . things into their bodies."

"They do when they wish to avoid conception, Winslow."

"And they are also quite illegal," he instructed her.

"The midwife and I could have been arrested. But after Cain and his sisters were born, I decided I'd had quite enough of childbearing and quite enough of increasing the likes of Cain Byron, Sr. Beyond that, I knew of the ladies he kept in varying degrees of luxury, and I was not keen to be one in that vast number—though he kept *me* in the grandest luxury of all. Now," she said with finality, "may we get on with our discussion, or will it be necessary for me to go and find another felonious midwife?"

"I shall tell you everything you need to know," Beame said hastily. "I certainly cannot abide a patient of mine turning herself over to one of *that* sort. Those women make a mockery of everything the medical community stands for."

"They do indeed, Winslow," acknowledged Vanessa with a hidden smile. "They do indeed." Standing and tucking his hands professorially behind his back, he began. He described the period of time when a woman was most likely to become pregnant. He recommended medications to enhance her susceptibility and medications to curtail that possibility. To his credit and her relief, Winslow Beame did not question Vanessa further. He asked her if she fully understood everything he'd told her. "I do," said Vanessa. She thanked him kindly and reminded him of the confidentiality that must exist between doctor and patient. Without further words, stormily offended that Vanessa would even consider it necessary to mention such an obligation, Dr. Beame left her room.

Blessedly free of that most untoward conversation, he patted at his perspiring forehead with a large handkerchief. His first impulse was to go directly to Cain with the matter of his mother's inquiry about the new and controversial subject of "voluntary motherhood," but again to his credit, he did not. He cursed the confidentiality that Vanessa had mentioned. Cain ought to be told if his mother was thinking of taking up with a gentleman— and apparently considering marriage. And just supposing it happened to be that creature from the lighthouse again. That situation had been the start of all her troubles. Beame managed to shake off the apprehension he was feeling. If Vanessa did intend to marry, surely she would choose a gentleman who would be mature in his needs, respectful of her advanced age.

Vanessa had been right about one thing, he reflected as he prepared to meet one of Cain's referred patients, the question had come up before, and Dr. Winslow Beame was always surprised when it did. He assured most women, when they asked, to trust their husbands in the matter of birth control; if it became necessary, the husband would be informed by the lady's doctor. Beame saw no reason for women to concern themselves with such matters. Why, he wondered, did they make life so difficult for themselves? Women, he reminded himself, had a way of complicating everything.

He heard a light rap on Cain's office door. Stepping to it, he adopted his most professional demeanor. He must now face— he quickly glanced at the sheet of paper on Cain's desk and read the name "Miss Rose Evert"—Miss Rose Evert, one of Cain's most difficult cases. That lady, it seemed, insisted she had a different ailment every week, but Cain had found her healthy as a newborn kitten. Dr. Beame smiled to himself. He'd met more than a few women of her ilk. Well, perhaps to satisfy her little whimsies, he thought, he would manage to find just a little something wrong with her.

❧ ❧

If the grounds at Byron Hall had been a summer bower, they had become, by mid-September, a refulgent grotto. Big-leafed trees hung low beneath the weight of their resplendence. Flowers, in the mature stages of blossoming repletion, scented the air with their lush perfumes. The grasses grew verdant and tall. Among them, on a knoll above the sea, Vanessa and Autumn sat in sparkling white wicker chairs, sewing and talking quietly. Their hushed voices, as they discussed their secret plans, were whispered music on the air.

They turned at the insistent rustle of grass behind them. To Autumn's horror, she saw, standing tall in the soft golden green of the day, the brilliantly groomed, magnificently coifed figure of Antoinette Fraser.

"Hello, you two," chirped that woman. She made her way, dispatching grass and wildflowers beneath her heavy carmine skirts as she moved. "What is all this low, secret talking about? You sound as if you are planning some sort of conspiracy!" She trudged on forward, laughing brightly.

"Antoinette," Autumn said on a breath. Glancing quickly at Vanessa, who sat stunned and wordless, she added, "We are so surprised."

"I don't see why. You knew I would return eventually."

"But we'd had no word—"

"Yes, well, I am sometimes an impulsive creature—an original—just like you, Autumn."

"You just missed Winslow Beame," that woman said, attempting a conversational tone.

"Yes," said Antoinette, targeting Vanessa serenely, "he told me he had been visiting. He said that, with only a few very minor, if somewhat unsettling little problems, the household was running swimmingly." Vanessa sat back numbly. "He mentioned that that oafish girl had gone off to have a baby, and that Cain had referred an especially difficult patient to him. He mentioned that she may have mental problems and is thinking of sending her on to Belle Vue. Win is such a raconteur. Once he gets started with stories about his patients, he just goes on and on enjoying himself so." She noted with satisfaction the look of concern that passed between Autumn and Vanessa. "Of course, Win is ever the professional. He never gives out names and he never breaks a confidentiality, but one reads between the lines, don't you know." She paused and looked out over the ocean. "Such a pretty little view. I have missed it, in truth. But it will not be long before I have access to it every day." She glanced at the two women who watched her warily. "I intend to announce a fall wedding for Cain and me," she said nonchalantly.

"Have you consulted my son?" asked Vanessa evenly.

"Cain knows, as I do, that he has very little choice in this matter. Naturally, it is not my intention to upset a well-run household. You are welcome to stay on, Autumn, if that is your wish and, of course, Cain's desire." She gave the last word a special and highly significant emphasis. "After the wedding," she went on, "I fully intend to spend most of my time in New York. I cannot, after all, allow that pretty house in Washington Square to simply idle uninhabited."

"Cain may not agree to such a . . . sophisticated arrangement," offered Vanessa.

"Then he may certainly join me in New York," Antoinette countered flatly. "Though I must say he will not mind my absences." Autumn and Vanessa shared an oblique glance.

"How long had you planned to stay, Antoinette?" asked Vanessa. Antoinette eyed the older woman tranquilly.

"All I can say, dear Vanessa, is that without prior invitation, I shall not expect you to put me up. But I must add that I've not yet procured accommodation in town and you know how crowded are the hotels this time of year. Actually, my bags are still out in the coach, and although I wouldn't think of intruding on your hospitality, I should much rather stay here than in some nasty, cramped hotel room, with heaven knows what sort as neighbors. There are any number of foreigners about, don't you know— Irish, French, and not a few *Italians*," she said, her eyes narrowing in disapproval.

"I daresay, Antoinette," said Vanessa impatiently, "we are all fundamentally foreigners. In any event we could not think of imposing an invitation on you—"

"The other consideration would be, I suppose, how . . . odd it might seem if I were to install myself in a hotel." She glanced at her audience triumphantly. "Mightn't that cause a bit of unwelcome speculation—and gossip? Now wouldn't that give the hoi polloi something to flap about?" Autumn stood suddenly, more to stop Antoinette's babbling than anything.

"Why don't we get you settled, Antoinette," she offered quietly.

"And when will I see Cain?"

"He will be in for supper."

Antoinette smiled thinly. Without further comment and with a playful waggle of her fingers in Vanessa's direction, she followed Autumn into the house.

‡‡‡

For the evening meal, Antoinette appeared in a gown of candy apple red with black fringe layered at the deep bodice and hem. Her hair was piled almost unimaginably high, and wound among the luminous black curls was a garland of silk Le Rêve lilies. Admittedly, she was a theatrical creation and a most dramatically arranged centerpiece for the family's evening. She waved a fan of flamingo feathers languidly throughout supper and ate little, keeping up a steady flow of conversation. She regaled everyone with a vivid montage of her activities in New York since she had left Byron Hall at the beginning of the summer. She talked of the theater, the opera, the art openings and clicked her tongue forlornly at the complete lack of cultural stimulation in Cape May.

She seemed entirely unaffected by the family's silences—everyone's that is but Cain's. With the practiced artifice of an old campaigner, Antoinette made it her business to beguile him. Her soft laughter, her little jokes, her every gesture and pose were effected for his benefit and for his approval. Each time she waved her fan, the air became filled with her exotic scent. As the evening progressed, Cain seemed to relax. After the meal, she rallied them all around the piano. Cain sat with her on the bench and turned the pages of the music for her rather sultry rendition of "Put on Your Old Gray Bonnet." Vanessa and Autumn excused themselves, exhausted, before nine o'clock, and it was with some asperity that Autumn watched Antoinette lead Cain into the garden for a private conversation.

He came later to Autumn's room as she was reading by gaslight in her bed. Autumn heard his soft knock. She went to the door and protested in whispers as he took her hand and led her down the hall. When they were sequestered in his room, she told him exactly how dangerous was this little foray. He nodded but drew her to him.

"I need you tonight more than ever, love," he intoned into her ear.

"Cain," she said, pushing at his chest, "what did Antoinette say to you in the garden?"

"More of the same," he told her as he began to remove his ascot. "You must not think about it. Antoinette is—"

"Antoinette," returned Autumn, "is a practiced *cocotte*. She is a conspirator with the very basest nature of man, a trifler, a . . . tramp. She deliberately set out to seduce you tonight and she succeeded apparently. And now you expect *me* to satisfy a lust no doubt whetted by that seduction." Cain's gaze hooded as he caught her shoulders roughly.

"Antoinette is all you say she is, Autumn, and so much more. And I find her coquetry ridiculous. But right now we must both put up with it. If we want this charade to end, we must patiently and passively submit to her caprice." He let her go very suddenly. "I believe," he said quietly, "that Antoinette has no intention of marrying me. Even as she discusses the wedding and makes her elaborate preparations for, in her words, our 'lovely fall wedding,' I believe she has some other plan."

"What . . . plan?" asked Autumn, her heart suddenly going cold.

"I don't know," he said, "but in our final conversation, she mentioned my mother—and you—often. Antoinette is a dangerous woman, Autumn. For God's sake don't you know that by now?" Suddenly she was in his arms, pressed to his chest. His heart thundered, and he held her tightly, possessively. A profound and utterly horrifying notion took hold of Autumn at that moment. It had been with her all day, since Antoinette's arrival, but she had not faced it squarely. Antoinette had said once that she intended to destroy Autumn. Was that the true reason for her visit? Autumn shuddered involuntarily. If that was Antoinette's intention, she had a great deal of ammunition with which to arm herself.

Chapter 23

Another fall wedding was being planned that September. It would be a hushed affair. The Very Reverend Oliver Mombert would officiate. His wife Leslie and Autumn Thackeray would be the only witnesses.

Robert Moffat was pacing his aerie, high above Cape May harbor. "I feel like the creature that Stoker fellow wrote about—the one who comes out only at night." Vanessa and Autumn smiled.

"You mean Count Dracula," said Vanessa.

"But he drinks people's blood, Robert," Autumn put in, laughing. "He sneaks up on women while they sleep." Obviously relishing the gory image, Autumn's voice lowered menacingly. "And he sinks his fangs into their necks and drains them of their very life."

"You are very entertaining, little one," he acknowledged, cocking his brow and offering a smile. "However, you have just strengthened the comparison," he said solemnly. "We see each other only at night, and what am I in the final analysis but a con-

sumer of Vanessa's life's blood? I take all and give nothing."
Autumn bit back a hasty response and allowed Vanessa herself to
address that issue.

"We have been through this before, Robert," that lady said
gently. "I have told you and will repeat it till one of us dies, if
necessary, that it does not matter if I am rich and you are not.
You are not *taking* anything from me; you are giving me everything. You are giving me your love, Robert, and I know I can depend on that forever."

"Your love has been nurtured in shadow, it is true," Autumn
said, "but by this time tomorrow, it will have emerged into the
light of day. You may be seen together any time you wish." Robert
eyed her obliquely.

"Are you so confident that marriage will change things for
us?"

"Of course," Autumn stated with confidence. "Marriage
changes everything." The words tore at her heart like broken glass,
so hopeful were they when uttered, so despairing a notion when
viewed in terms of her own life. She forced a smile. Robert and
Vanessa were looking out at the night that encircled them. Prisms
of stars winked in the blackness of the sky, dazzlingly close. "If
the night is for Mr. Stoker's monster," Autumn observed raptly,
"it is also for lovers."

∽༄ ༄∾

As they drove home, Vanessa prodded Autumn with her own
uncertainties. "I wonder if it is not dangerous for people to be so
high above the earth as we have been. People were not meant to
soar among the stars; it gives them a false sense of their own im-

portance and makes them seem invulnerable to earthly realities."
She paused. "I would like to believe that in the end marriage will
make everything right for Robert and me, but I must remember,
and you must remember, too, Autumn, that when Cain hears of it
he will be enraged." Autumn snapped the horses to a brisk trot.

"Cain loves us both. Whatever his reaction to your marriage,
that is what we must remember."

Vanessa and Autumn entered the house through the back door
and were surprised, and not pleasantly so, to find Antoinette
awaiting them. She smiled brightly and asked where they had
"toddled off to." They each made hasty excuses for their absence,
Autumn mentioning obliquely a literary club meeting and
Vanessa murmuring something about visiting a friend. Neither
was, despite their recent deception, a particularly accomplished
liar. They doubted that Antoinette took much stock in their jury-
rigged stories, but they did not much care. The important thing
was that Cain was not there to question their absence. He had
ridden out earlier in the evening to visit Carrie Inman, who was
now far advanced in her pregnancy, and several other of his
house-bound patients.

"It's been so lonely around here," stated Antoinette petulantly.
"I've just been dallying all night trying to think what to do to
amuse myself."

Vanessa drew off her shawl as she made her way through the
kitchen and turned before exiting. "Perhaps it is time, then, that
you thought about taking rooms at one of the hotels in the city.
Naturally, we're so very pleased that you could stay with us for as
long as you have—it has been almost a week now, hasn't it?—but
we cannot, I fear, offer nearly the diversion you would find at the
Adelphi, for instance. Please do not concern yourself with our

feelings." With a quick sloping glance toward Autumn, Vanessa withdrew. Autumn watched Antoinette's gaze narrow dangerously. There was to be no more pretense, apparently, between the two women. At last she offered Autumn an altered regard.

"As Mrs. Byron seems weary of my company, I shall see about that hotel room in the morning. In case I don't see Cain tomorrow, you will tell him where I'm staying." Autumn nodded mechanically. "Thank you, dear girl. I shall retire now and you should as well. You're looking tired these days. Do try to get a good night's sleep." Her words were benign, but her tone carried a menacing weight.

In her room, undressing slowly, Autumn felt the frenzied fear that had gripped her that first night of Antoinette's arrival. Cain had made it his business to beguile Antoinette, even as she was attempting to beguile him. He had remained the courteous and politic host and fiancé. He absented himself often from Antoinette's company, but when in her presence, he accepted her chattered plans stoically. It was only a matter of time before she revealed the real purpose of her visit, he reiterated night after night. Autumn shared his certainty and deeply feared some terrible plot against them.

As she lay in her bed, hovering above slumber, she thought of Cain and felt herself returning to the days of the first budding of their love. Phantoms of their life together rose before her, harmonizing fondly with the deep well of love she felt for him, veiling discord, obscuring gloom. She saw his lips saying her name, heard her name so tenderly spoken by him. Autumn drifted into dreams . . . of Cain.

The Very Reverend Oliver Mombert performed the brief ceremony. His wife Leslie sang a lilting hymn, the strains of it echoing in the sun-dappled nave of Our Lady, Star of the Sea Church. Vanessa wore a periwinkle blue gown that matched precisely, reflected Autumn as they said their vows, the sea-glass glint of Robert's eyes.

"Is there anyone here," asked Oliver Mombert, "who knows why these two people should not be joined in holy matrimony?" The moment of quick expectancy passed, and the Reverend Mombert smiled benevolently. "Let him speak now or forever hold his peace." Then the ceremony was done. A promise . . . a kiss . . . a marriage made, thought Autumn.

The heavy door slammed open at the back of the church. Autumn and the others looked to the terrible sound. Cain stood silhouetted in the arched opening. He raised his arm, pointing an avenging finger at the figures gathered at the altar.

"Get outside, Moffat!" he roared. Horrified, disbelieving for one uncomprehending moment, Autumn felt paralyzed. Then, bolting, she ran up the aisle. Robert was upon her in several strides, drawing her back.

"Don't," he commanded. Autumn was propelled sideways into a pew.

"Robert!" Vanessa shrieked. The Momberts, having been told of the wedding's potential for discord, grabbed for her, but she shook them off. Forcing her way past Robert, she charged up the aisle. "If you touch him, Cain, I shall kill you!" she exclaimed, forcing her son back from the entrance. Arms flailing, Vanessa might have been possessed. Cain was knocked off balance, losing his footing on the steps leading down to the street. He stumbled, eyes widened, appalled, fending off his mother's wild blows.

Robert reached them. Autumn followed, running frenziedly through the church. In the sudden silence that followed, the Momberts glanced at each other, mouths agape. Never, in all their talks with Autumn about the necessity for secrecy, had they suspected that there might be a madman involved. Never in their forty years of service to the church had they encountered physical violence. They held on to each other as they made their way up the aisle to inspect the further occurrences outside.

Cain was scrambling to his feet. His face was a mask of bitterness. Brushing himself, his teeth bared, he eyed his mother scathingly.

"How dare you?" he grated.

"And how dare *you*, Cain," she shot back. "I am still your mother, and this is my wedding day."

"I do not accept that," Cain returned. As Robert appeared, Cain said, "I do not accept *you!*" His steely regard was fixed on the older man, and he grabbed for him. Vanessa immediately drove herself between them. "Get out of my way, Mother," Cain commanded.

"Get out of *mine!*" Vanessa shrilled. With a strength neither she nor her son suspected she possessed, Vanessa shoved at Cain. Once again he stumbled backwards, but regained his balance. A look of abject incomprehension crossed his face, and wrath was momentarily tempered. Immediately, however, he regained his anger.

"Go home, Mother," he clenched. "This is between—"

"*This,*" Vanessa charged, "is between you and me."

"Does the whoreson hide behind a woman's skirts?"

"Robert is not hiding, Cain. He is protecting you!"

"Protecting me?" he snarled. "In the name of Christ, how did you come up with that notion?"

"In the name of our *dear* Christ, Cain," said Vanessa raggedly, "in the name of *love*, Robert will not raise a hand to you."

"Cain!" Robert's voice filled the air as he moved forward. All eyes turned to him as he advanced. Fists clenched at his sides, he stood before Vanessa's son. The two men were of a height and their gazes met. "It is true that I shall never fight you. But I am not afraid of you. Make no mistake, I am not afraid." Vanessa tried to pull him back, but Robert held rigidly to his place before Cain. That man's black regard drifted disparagingly down the length of the older man and then back up.

"It's come to this, has it? You have driven me to physical violence and you've driven my mother to it. You've denigrated my authority, and now you tell me you will not defend yourself. Do you know what a detestable bastard your are?"

"I'm no bastard," Robert returned vengefully. "And you, boy, need a lesson in who has driven whom to what. I only wish to hell it was me could give it to you. But I've given my word," he grated, "so it won't be me. But someday—boy—someone's going to give you a lesson you won't forget. I'd like to be around to see that." His eyes glinted with his defiance, and Cain stiffened, every muscle in his body alive with the effort of restraint. Autumn stepped forward. She wanted desperately to go to him, but her movement was stilled as Cain's regard fell with horrible accusation on her. Her hands flew to her lips. She realized in the malignity of his gaze a rancor she had never thought possible between them. Stunned, sickened, she merely stared.

The Sunday afternoon quiet of Beach Street had been disturbed. People were glancing from their doors and over their fences, and they halted their Sunday strolls in their curiosity.

"Hell's bells," called a voice from across the street. "What's going on? Is somebody organizing a social and not telling the rest of us?" It was Annie Fitzpatrick. She and her friend Emma Cavanaugh strolled up the walk to the church, their parasols twirling, their skirts blowing perkily in the sea breezes. "Autumn," Annie said, smiling as she recognized her friend, "church has been over for hours. What're you folks doing here?"

Autumn cleared her throat and said gamely, "We're having a wedding, Annie."

"A wedding?" said Emma Cavanaugh excitedly. "I love weddings!"

"Who's getting married?" In the general buzz of elation that followed, people detoured their afternoon strolls to make their way up the walk to the church. Hands were shaken, and hugs were shared all around. Whispered and unwhispered exclamations were heard.

"Vanessa Byron married? Who did she marry?"

"The lighthouse keeper?"

"No!"

"Really?"

Mrs. Pierce was heard to mention that Robert Moffat was, as she understood it, said to be a descendent of Captain Cornelius Jacobsen Mey, the Dutch sailor who had founded the city. Mrs. Butler wondered how she had come by such information, and Mrs. Pierce responded that she'd heard it . . . somewhere. And, anyway, why would the very wealthy and respectable Vanessa Byron marry him if he wasn't someone terribly important? Mrs. Harmon agreed and hurried through the crowd to the newly wedded couple to tell them that she wished to be the first to open her home for a party in their honor. Not to be outdone, other ladies made it their business to ingratiate themselves with the socially prominent former Mrs. Byron and her historically prominent second husband, Mr. and Mrs. Robert Moffat were in the process of becoming the toast of Cape May.

Cain watched his mother narrowly, felt himself swept into embraces which he did not share, and finally, wordlessly exempted himself from the general congratulations. He turned and walked toward his horse that was tethered on the street. He mounted and took a last glance at the scene. His eyes met Autumn's and they shared a phantom moment of remembering. And then the world intruded. Everything that had been between them had ended. One last moment of sadness passed between them before Cain's eyes turned accusing. Autumn bowed her head and lifted it in time to see Cain's form, the broad back, the proud shoulders, the poised head, disappear from her view. Amid the cheer and high spirits, Autumn knew the truth. Everything that she had feared had come to pass. This was the one thing for which Cain would never forgive her. Annie Fitzpatrick was at her side.

"What's happened here, Autumn?" she asked gently. "Why did Cain ride off like that?" Autumn lifted her gaze. Tear-glazed, it offered a well of hopelessness.

"Oh, Annie," she said on a weary breath, "I shall never see him again." Annie took the girl in her arms as Emma Cavanaugh looked on in sympathy. "Cain was against this marriage, but Robert and Vanessa were so in love, and despite his objections, I . . ." Shamed, she could not go on.

"You did the right thing, Autumn," Emma told her. "People in love ought to be together."

"But what does it matter?" Autumn asked. "What does any of it matter if I've lost Cain?"

"You listen to me," Annie said softly, "Cain Byron isn't a stupid man—not like some I've seen. It's the stupid ones we've got to look out for. They're the ones who cause all the damage. A stupid soldier with a powerful weapon is a dangerous enemy."

"But Cain is not my enemy. Why must you turn everything into a battle of the sexes?"

"Because it boils down to that."

"Oh, Annie, don't you understand, I love Cain Byron and now I've lost him."

"You haven't lost anything, Autumn. You've won. You did what's right. As Emma says, people in love *ought* to be together. Cain knows that as well as anyone. And it's true that he's not your enemy, but he *has* lost a powerful weapon—your obedience. Like any soldier, he's got to figure out what to do next. He'll probably run and hide for a while, but eventually he'll make his way back onto the field. And, smart as he is, he'll realize how stupid and how vain his little war has been, and he'll have no choice but to make peace. In the end you'll both win. We all will."

Winner or loser, reflected Autumn, she would never be the same. Battered, bruised, aching with the wounds of battle, she must make her way back to Byron Hall to pack her things. Autumn would be heading—sadly—back to Philadelphia, back to where she'd started.

❦

The day was darkening. Sunlight gave way to cloud shadow and finally to thick twilight. Cain Byron stood by the shore, his horse's reins held laconically in his big hand. He gazed out on the dimming horizon and wondered idly what land he was viewing. Once, he and Autumn had stood on that very spot and decided it was Paris, France, they could see. They'd laughed, describing for each other the men and women and little children, berets tilted on their heads, sashaying about on the opposite shore. Cain slapped the end of the rein against his palm. He'd had enough of silly fantasies.

Antoinette Fraser, watching the dark tableau from a knoll above the sloping shore, smiled. She called to him and he glanced back over the barrier of his shoulder. Antoinette wondered if she had detected hope, then disappointment when he saw that it was she. Calling again, she moved toward him. A rigid immutability seemed to emanate from his very pores. There would apparently be no pretense between them—at least on his part. And those who lacked pretense did not expect pretense in others.

"What do you want, Antoinette?" he asked her.

Her approach must be subtle, for Cain was no pliable boy. She made a hesitant move to touch him and then drew back, pausing before she spoke. She lowered her lashes.

"I suppose, Cain, I want you." He studied her for long moments but did not speak. She looked up. "I know how . . . heartless that must sound to you. In many ways I *am* heartless—shallow you might say. After all that has happened, all I can think of is myself."

"Actually," admitted Cain quietly, "your honesty is refreshing." Her wide gaze reflecting no guile, she stepped to him tentatively, then held herself back. Lowering her lashes once again, she imagined them fanning themselves delicately over her pinkened cheeks.

"I am ashamed of what I have done. It was only that . . . well, knowing what Autumn was planning, I could not simply keep it to myself. I had to tell you of my suspicions. But . . . now, seeing you in so much pain, I wonder at my wisdom in doing so. And, Cain, I wonder at my motives."

"Don't be too hard on yourself, Antoinette," Cain returned stiffly. "I am not in as much pain as you might imagine. I pride myself on my resiliency. As for your part in this, you did what was necessary. Our motives are not always plain. In any event please don't waste your pity on me." At just that moment, a small tear appeared in Antoinette's eye and trickled daintily down her cheek.

"I don't pity you, Cain," she tossed off bravely. "I pity Autumn. What a hapless fool she was to have risked your love. I pity her for taking on a cause that would surely cost her the best love a woman could hope for. I cannot imagine what she was thinking when she decided to help Robert and Vanessa. All I can say is that she is a woman, Cain, and we women sometimes give in to terrible weaknesses—weaknesses of the flesh as well as the mind.

"You have loved two women—Autumn and, I dare to say it, me. At least I believed you loved me. And I loved you," she stated, her chin elevated. "I know that now. But I was such a reckless fool. In my youth and feminine innocence, I did not realize the value of your love, Cain. But I know that given a second chance—just one more tiny chance—I could love you as no woman ever has."

Her words came out in a gush of emotion. She had surprised Cain and even herself with their desperate appeal. She quickly lifted her hand to her lips, and the gesture gave her a vulnerability that worked very well for the moment. For the first time Cain smiled. Even when she had come to him that morning, professing reticence, Cain knew that she was quite enjoying the bitter tale she was telling him. He knew that her "suspicions" about his mother and Robert—and Autumn's involvement in their plans—

had been carefully and purposefully uncovered. And he knew that Antoinette revealed them with relish. He knew, too, that Antoinette had gone to all that trouble to discredit Autumn. Now he wondered if some of her efforts had not been on his behalf. He had not known that Antoinette harbored such deep feelings for him. He had not imagined her capable of deep feelings. His smile became regretful.

"I don't know if I can trust my own judgment just now, Antoinette, but I will concede that we really never gave each other a chance. We were always so busy showing off for each other."

"Yes," said she on a breath, as though she had just discovered something wonderful. "Showing off! I was showing off, Cain. It's what I've always done." She had not dreamed it would be this easy to portray herself as a wayward child who had finally grown up. But then, she reasoned, that is the way men wanted to see their women—as children needing an education. Her heart thundered with the victory she knew was now at hand. She barely heard Cain's next words, for she was already planning her next move.

"Despite your possible—and I must say probable—motives for revealing what Autumn was up to, I appreciate your efforts. You needn't deny that you were pleased to find Autumn in a compromising situation, Antoinette." She did not deny it. "You were always one to enjoy a hearty female rivalry." His smile deepened with approval, and Antoinette knew she was on very safe ground. Cain was now in his element, a male element. Scolding women and then forgiving them was the life's blood of their masculinity. And female rivalries always worked to their advantage. "I suppose," he was saying, "it was your very feminine nature that attracted me to you in the first place."

"Do you really think so, Cain?" she asked, lowering her eyes to preserve that perception. Her voice became childlike and filled with piquant expectation as she lifted her regard. "Do you?" He nodded benevolently. "I should simply like to die if I believed for one second that you were toying with me."

"Don't die, Antoinette," Cain said gently. "That would be such a waste of womanly perfection."

❦

And now Cain Byron was very drunk. It was a condition that had begun several days before, had intensified over the past twenty-four hours, and was relieved only when he very occasionally, though for increasingly longer periods of time, passed out. Antoinette eyed him disparagingly.

"Honestly, Cain," she said as she watched him pour himself yet another brandy, "if I'd known you were going to take on so, I'd never have told you about the wedding." Cain glanced up, his brow cocked at an untidy angle.

"An' 's a damn good thing you did, too, Nettie," he assured her. "Y'r the only frien' I've got lef'." He hiccuped sagely. Pointing at her with his glass and one forefinger, he said, "A man needs frien's. They're the meat 'n' p'tatoes of life. *You're* the meat 'n' p'tatoes of *my* life, woman, an' don't you forget it." He sat down heavily in a chair. The small hotel parlor reeked of his smell, and Antoinette waved a perfumed hanky delicately.

"I'm glad you feel that way, Cain," she remarked dryly, "but the fact is you need to *do* something. You cannot simply loll about this hotel room, seething and stinking." She'd long ago abandoned the amenities of polite remonstrance. "I went to a great deal of trouble for you. You have no idea how difficult it was keeping up with your mother and your little doxy. It wasn't easy following them about, conversing with the likes of florists and dressmakers and dull church people, and asking humiliating questions, and lying through my teeth to get information."

Cain looked up, his head bobbling, his indigo gaze bleary. "You've got good teeth, Nettie, y' know that? I don't think I ever mentioned that t' you b'fore. You've got th' bes' teeth I ever saw. I jus' wan' y' t' know how I feel." The certainty in his tone slackened, and tears formed in his eyes. "Aut'm's got good teeth, y' know."

"Good heavens, Cain," snapped Antoinette, "forget about that woman." She strode to him and snatched the brandy snifter from his stiff paw. She swore beneath her breath as the liquid from the nearly full goblet sloshed onto her gown.

"Dammit! I shall be smelling as disgusting as you," she charged as she wiped furiously at the stain. At last, giving up the effort, she faced Cain squarely. "Listen to me," she said sharply, "you are wallowing in self-pity, and I shall not endure another minute of it. I am sick to death of your intoxication. You men swear by the indulgence of drink whenever you run into a problem you cannot—or will not—face. Well, I am here to tell you, Cain Byron, you are to pick yourself up and face your problems *now*. Autumn has abandoned you, and your mother is living in *your* house with her aging Lothario. You are to sober yourself up immediately. You are to visit your lawyer and have your mother declared insane. You certainly have enough proof of that. I've told you that Win will support any claims you make against the family fortune. He agrees your mother has quite taken leave of her senses—again. I want you to take your life into your own hands, and once you've done that, I want you to come back here and beg me to marry you!"

Cain looked up, his gaze quizzical. "Marry you?" he asked. "But I love Aut'm," he told her piteously. There was one brief moment of clarity then, and he added in a slurred growl, "Th' rambun'shus chit!" He seemed about to speak further. Abruptly, his eyelids drooped resolutely, his stubbled chin dropped onto his chest, and he began to snore. Antoinette stamped her kid booted foot. Once again she cursed wrathfully. Once again her instructions had fallen on deadened senses. She looked down on Cain Byron, that standard by which, in her previous lexicon, all men were judged, and pursed her lips. Cain snorted restlessly, his head falling back. His eyes red-rimmed, his jaw nearly blue with several day's growth of beard, he seemed more beast than man.

"Hell's bells, Cain Byron," Antoinette swore softly. "You're really no better than the rest of them, are you?" A light rap on the door caught her attention. Impatiently, supposing it was yet another bellboy bearing yet more liquor in which Cain might drown his anger or his resentment or whatever it was he was battling, Antoinette swung open the door.

"Is my son here?" asked the stately figure who stood before her.

"Why . . . Vanessa."

"It is Mrs. Moffat to you, Antoinette." Vanessa smiled. "I sound rather like a nursery rhyme, don't I. 'Mrs. Moffat went to sea/A golden cat upon her knee.' I used to recite that for Cain." She moved past Antoinette and stopped before her son. "Well, well," she said softly. She glanced back at Antoinette who was closing the door. "How long has he been like this?"

"Since the wedding," the younger woman answered tiredly. "It was . . . rather planned, you see. I mean, of course, his coming here, not his drunkenness."

"I understand."

"Do you?" Antoinette asked archly.

"Yes. I do, surprisingly. Since I am not myself given to dark plotting, it surprises me that I could so easily comprehend your little scheme."

"Dark plotting . . . Mrs. Moffat? Isn't that exactly how you accomplished the marriage to your lighthouse keeper?"

"I shall not defend my methods to you, Antoinette. Nor shall I attempt to explain something you could not possibly understand. I shall say this, however, our 'plots' differ in one very important aspect. Mine was done in the name of love, while yours was done . . . well . . ." She eyed the girl quizzically. "Do you really have that much hatred in you? Does anyone?" She paused, surveying the girl in silence. "You may be wiser than I first suspected you to be, Antoinette," she said at last.

"And made wiser by your drunkard of a son."

"Cain is no drunkard," Vanessa returned mildly. "He is a man in pain. You know that now, don't you?" Antoinette regarded her steadily. "You know that Cain loves Autumn, has loved her all this time. And you know that love is not an emotion to be trifled with. That's a hard lesson to learn when you're in the business of trifling. It's painful."

"I'm not in pain," Antoinette said sharply. "If you think that, you are mistaken. But I have learned a lesson. I have learned that your illustrious son is no different from any other man. I've learned that he, like all the others, will take a woman and use what he wants of her and toss the rest onto the compost heap of his self-interest. It doesn't pain me to learn that, Vanessa. It inspires me."

"And what will you do with your lessons, Antoinette?"

"I shall do what is necessary to save myself from becoming compost. I shall marry the dimwitted Winslow Beame. He's asked me several times. And I shall become the most comfortable, the most compliant, the most callous wife that ever lived. I shall spend Winslow's money, adorn his house, bear his children . . . and hate him every day of his life. And he shall never know it."

Vanessa lowered her eyes. "Perhaps you are not so wise after all. And yet . . ." She lifted her regard. "Do you know why you were attracted to my son? I believe it was because you intuitively knew him to be *quite* different from most men of your acquaintance. You understood that with him you could never have the life you describe with Winslow. Cain would never have allowed it. Maybe some unexamined part of you hoped that somehow Cain's own honesty would uncover yours."

Antoinette smiled narrowly. "You could be right, Vanessa," she conceded with an eloquent shrug, "though I had planned to dismiss him quite harshly if he finally did profess his love. But that is moot. Cain is lost to me now." Both women regarded him obliquely. "It's not such a great loss," remarked Antoinette wryly.

"I think you know it is," countered Vanessa. "I think that's why you went to all the trouble of mounting a full scale investigation of my marriage plans and Autumn's involvement in them. I think you went to all that trouble because in your heart you know my son is indeed a very special man, an extraordinary one in fact. Maybe it's time, in light of all you know now, to reassess your future. Cain is lost to you, it's true, but Winslow Beame is not your only alternative."

"Thank you for your motherly concern," Antoinette put in, "but please don't waste it on me. Things probably turned out for the best, in any event. Winslow and I will be married. He quite enjoys my little feminine conceits. And I did succeed in sepa-rating Cain and Autumn—I believe for good, don't you?"

Vanessa shook her head sadly. "I suppose I never will under-stand the choices people make, if I live to be a hundred."

"Well, take comfort, Vanessa, for you that's not far off." Antoinette smiled deeply, her green eyes narrowing to emerald slits. "Now," she said, her tone altering, "why don't you just take your . . . resplendent, and certainly *extraordinary* lump of a son out of here." She swung open the door.

"I believe I shall do that," replied Vanessa. She moved to the chair in which Cain was sprawled. Before attempting to rouse him, she looked up. "I wish to give you one more bit of . . . 'motherly' advice, Antoinette. Please take it as a warning. Winslow Beame may not be quite as malleable as you imagine him to be. Oh, he is dimwitted enough, but even the dullest people do have moments of insight. He's going to discover your deception, and when he does, he will use every weapon at his command to get even with you. Make no mistake, Winslow has an arsenal of weapons—powerful ones. Bright people learn from the cruelty of others, stupid ones merely . . . get even."

❦

They took him home, Cain's mother and stepfather. Robert had been waiting in the Byron coach and with his help and the help of several sturdy bellboys, Vanessa had gotten Cain, stumbling, out of Antoinette's room, down the stairs, and into the carriage. She and Robert had propped him between them, but hastily rearranged themselves to accommodate his height and girth and his dead weight. He stretched and snorted and eventually spread himself full-length on one of the seats, impervious to the coach's jostling motion. Vanessa moved to the other seat, and Cain ended up with his head in Robert's lap and his feet nearly dangling from the window.

"This boy's going to feel as rocky as an old fishing boat tomorrow," Robert assured Vanessa.

"I'm sure that his rocky feelings brought him to this in the first place."

"Aye, it's true," agreed Robert. "I'm glad we found him before he did any more damage to himself." He looked at Vanessa keenly. "How did you know he was there?"

"I didn't really. I had suggested—quite impolitely, I may add—that Antoinette take a room at the Adelphi, and I just had an instinct he might be with her. Call it a mother's instinct, if you will, or a woman's. I understand that girl better than she does herself, Robert. I suspected she had a hand in Cain's discovery of our plans. She did not come here on a whim; she smelled trouble, fueled sadly by Winslow's gossip, and hoped to turn it to her own advantage. While it is true, she hoped to hurt this family in some profound way and to divide Cain and Autumn, she also, I believe, hoped desperately to win Cain for herself. Even she didn't understand that part of it. The trouble is, she wanted to win him on her terms. She hasn't learned yet that love can only be found and nurtured when the terms between lovers are mutual." She regarded Robert with a smile. Her gaze drifted then to the landscape that jogged by the rolling coach. "Now that we've found him, Robert, what are we going to do with him?"

"For the moment, my love," he said mildly, "there isn't much we can do with him."

"He did this to himself once when he was fifteen," Vanessa recalled sadly. "His father took a strap to him. He told him, in his rage, that a gentleman never indulges in spirit to the point of drunkenness. Upon his awakening, Cain had not only to recover from his overindulgence, he had to recover from his father's beating. I spread salve on the welts and offered peppermint tea. I thought it was the worst time in his life." She looked down on her son, sleeping peacefully now, his head on Robert's lap. "I am afraid that this time there is no salve in the world that is going to soothe his wounds."

At twilight Robert and Vanessa sat side by side on the wide front porch. They quietly discussed their plans. Another man had already been dispatched to keep the light, and they had decided that very soon they must leave Byron Hall. They would live out a peaceful existence on one of the many seaside farms that dotted the estate. They might find one near Carrie's property, they agreed. They both looked up when they heard the front door open. Cain came outside, awakened, recovered to an extent, and washed and combed.

"I'm sorry," he told them quietly.

"I know you are," Vanessa replied, studying him.

"How're you feeling, son?" asked Robert. "I know that's not a proper question—a gentlemen's question, strictly speaking—but I only ask it because I've got a curative in my duffel bag. An old sailor gave it me. It's a secret formula they use on the islands, don't you know."

"I do thank you . . . Robert, but," he held out the mug of coffee he'd procured from the kitchen, "I'll stick to this for now."

"And anyway," Robert observed, "you are a doctor. I guess you'd know of the best curatives."

"On this particular subject," offered Cain, "an old sailor might be better informed than a . . . foolish young doctor. But I do thank you sincerely." Vanessa knew that this was not an easy time for the two men and so she kept her own counsel. Cain's gaze drifted over the lawns. He might have been searching for something in the thickening dark. He turned back to Vanessa and Robert. "May I say that I am most grateful to both of you for bringing me home. And I owe thanks to you especially, Robert. The servants have informed me that you almost single-handedly brought me up to my bed and directed my recovery." He glanced at his mother. "I'm told you found me in Antoinette's suite at the Adelphi. I remember going there, but to be absolutely truthful that's about all I remember. I don't think I . . . took advantage."

"I don't think you did either, son," said Robert staunchly. "And if you did, and . . . if *she* did, well then it's best forgotten. From what your mother tells me, Antoinette planned this whole thing. The minx was determined from the first to cause trouble between you and Autumn."

"She accomplished that," acknowledged Cain.

"She accomplished," interjected Vanessa, "exactly what you allow her to have accomplished." Cain looked at her sharply.

"Nothing that Antoinette has done," he told her, "changes in any way Autumn's betrayal of me." Vanessa stood and moved to the porch rail.

"This doesn't have to be the end for you and Autumn. I know your pride has been hurt, Cain. I know you sincerely believe that Autumn betrayed you. No matter how you eventually come to feel about Robert and me, you think you must not forgive

Autumn for what you see as her disloyalty. You've learned your manly lessons well. You learned them at your father's knee." She swung to face him. "Let me tell you something. Your father had a way of punishing me whenever he believed I'd done something unforgivable. He stopped speaking to me—sometimes for days. His silence was as effective as a slap. While he badgered and beat you into submission, he subordinated me with his cruel silences. I'd rather've had the damned beatings."

Robert stood and hastily cleared his throat. "Silence, Cain, is golden, but it can also be deadly—especially when used as a weapon."

"As my mother has so forthrightly stated," answered Cain, "I've learned my lessons well. While I have sympathy for my mother's frustration, and . . . even a growing acceptance of her feelings for you, I can never forgive Autumn for her dishonesty and scheming."

"And what of her reason, Cain?" interjected Vanessa. "You had *lost* yours, apparently, at least where Robert and I were concerned. Autumn felt she had no choice."

"We always have a choice, Mother," stated Cain.

"Yes," Vanessa agreed sadly. "And it seems you have already made yours."

Chapter 24

Cain found himself laughing for the first time in weeks. Carrie Inman had been delivered of a little girl—"a pink and pearl darling of a colleen," as Henry stated it. The man had not been disappointed . . . exactly . . . that his wife had not presented him with a son. To prove it, he promptly invited the neighbors in to view the newborn and her illustrious mother. "She's a rare one, is my Carrie," he told everyone, toasting his wife again and again with whiskey poured freely. An exhausted Carrie mentioned to Cain that she wished her husband was not quite so proud of her efforts, but thanked the Lord he had accepted the child even though she was not a boy. She sat now in a rocking chair near the Inman hearth, cradling the babe and blessing the winding down of yet another festive evening.

"You'd think she was the only baby ever born on earth," Carrie was saying, "the very only."

"Every man feels that way about his first child, Carrie," Cain said. "A man's child is his proudest accomplishment."

"And what about my accomplishment? I'd like to celebrate it

in me own way. I haven't had so much as a dribble of time to be
proud, Dr. Byron, what with the neighbors steppin' in and
steppin' out like this was a museum where they could look at
the statues, an' me cleanin' up after their dirty boots and their
celebrations. I want some time to think about what Henry an' me
have made. I'd like to listen to the sounds of the ocean and think
about the sands of time an' all that."

"That's called 'resting,' Carrie, and you are absolutely right. I
shall speak to Henry," Cain told her, smiling.

"You'll keep an eye on them, won't you, doc?" asked an inebri-
ated Henry as, sometime later, he ushered Cain from the house.
"They're okay, ain't they?"

"Indeed they are, Henry," Cain assured him. "I've examined
them both twice now since the delivery, and I can tell you that
both Carrie and the baby are thoroughly healthy. I might advise,
however, that you make sure Carrie gets her rest. It might be wise
to postpone any more parties for a while. Carrie seems a bit
tired."

"I'll do it, doc," Henry said affably. "I'll do anything for those
two ladies. They're what I'm livin' for now, don't you know."

"I do indeed, Henry," Cain assured him, and with a wave, he
stepped down from the porch to make his way back to Byron Hall.

The nights were colder now. Winter would be setting in
soon. As the warm gaiety of the Inman party faded behind him,
as the warmth of their fire ebbed and the November night chill
invaded his woolen overcoat, Cain spurred his horse to a quick
trot. Vanessa and Robert had moved out of Byron Hall to take
their own house on a small farm near Carrie and Henry's. He
saw their cottage now in the distance, glowing softly against the
cold and the dark. And though just now he longed for warmth,

he did not stop. Seeing the two of them together reminded him of his own isolation.

It was very late by the time Cain reached Byron Hall. He looked up the road that led to the house. So often he'd wished it did not seem so imposing. This frosty night it seemed more imposing than ever. Black against the arc of the moon, it rose imperiously with only one light glowing yellow from inside to soften its somber veneer. But then, he reminded himself, the house's exterior was no veneer. It was as somber inside as out. He stabled his horse and went inside. No servant greeted him, no fire crackled in any hearth. He lit a candle and carried it up the grand staircase, his weary steps echoing hollowly in the cavernous entry hall. A fire had been laid in his room, his bed turned down, and a lamp left lit against the gloom. It was the light he'd seen from outside—small comfort in a darkened world. Cain shed his overcoat, undressing down to his shirtsleeves. He sat down on his bed, and noticed the blue envelope on his night table, encircled by the light of the single lamp. It was Autumn's stationery. It was addressed to him and marked "personal." He lifted the missive, his hand trembling. He could only stare at the characters on the envelope—his name written in that delicate and familiar hand. He lay back against the softness of his pillows, cradling his head on one arm. Dare he open it? Maybe it begged his forgiveness. Dare he risk caring once again for a woman who had scorned him? Or maybe it contained further scorn. His armor had been badly chinked, and he wished no further humiliation at her hand. Still, his mind often wandered when his rounds kept him late and he rode home in the dark, to thoughts of Autumn. And now, here was word from her. He wanted no more pain. He wanted his life to be simple, uncomplicated, ordered. And yet with a simple flourish of a letter opener, he could somehow touch her again. He rose, moving to the hearth, and lit his fire. It flared, then settled to a gently warming glow. The letter, still on his bed, beckoned him. Crossing the room in several strides, he picked it up and tore it open.

"Dear Cain," it read. "It occurred to me last week that Carrie Inman should be giving birth soon, if she has not already. I thought I would write to ask you to tell her that my prayers and fondest wishes are with her. I know you are taking very good care of her, Cain. Please express my best to Henry. I know that you will take good care of him, too. Autumn."

Cain wondered what had frightened him so? The letter was benign, conversational, sweet. He held it rigidly. He read it again and then again. He did not notice that his whole body was quaking. He did not notice that his heart thundered in his chest. He did not notice that, finally, tears, hot and stinging, filled his eyes.

༺✺༻

"What an inspired use of crow feathers!" Eugenia Drexel exulted as she stepped before the cheval glass. Autumn smiled at the lady and assured her that the dress was perfection on her. "Crow feathers, according to *Godey's Ladies' Book*," Eugenia went on as she fiddled happily with the shiny black feathers that decorated the scalloped edge of her bodice, "are being exhibited in New York City—not that any one here in Philadelphia cares two pins what *those* ladies are wearing." The several seamstresses smiled among themselves as they continued their work. Isabel sat before her sewing machine in the light of a large bay of windows and offered them a mild look of warning.

"It is true, Eugenia," she observed, "that we needn't look to the New York ladies for fashion guidance, but we must remember that *Godey's* does tend to follow the latest trends, and we do wish to keep up."

"And we certainly do, thanks to you, Isabel," agreed Eugenia. She looked about the converted third-floor parlor of Isabel's house now overflowing with the accoutrements of her trade. Dress forms were draped with velvets and damasks, and full-length mirrors were hung with silk ribbon. The two long tables were dotted with scissors, measuring tapes, pincushions, and various threads, and spread upon them were paper patterns for Isabel's own designs. As it was nearing the end of the day, Autumn dismissed the other girls and turned back to Eugenia. "What you have managed to do for yourselves is quite amazing," she told the mother and daughter. "And without the help of *men*," she confided, her tone intrigued and awe-filled. "We are all delighted for you—and some of us even a little jealous," she said, giggling. "Oh, let me just try something," she said as she turned back to the mirror. She pulled a length of black moiré from a nearby table and tied it around her waist. "What do you think?" she asked with some pride in her own inventiveness.

"I think," Autumn said gently, as she undid the large bow that Eugenia had created at the very center of her torso, "that, as you said yourself, Mrs. Drexel, the dress is perfect." Isabel eyed her daughter obliquely.

"Why you're absolutely right, Autumn," gushed Eugenia. "It's quite, quite perfect without the sash. Now, I really must have a matching hat, dear girl. And do use the crow feathers, Isabel." She turned to Autumn. "Your mother is a genius with hats—and crow feathers!"

"Yes, she is," agreed Autumn. "Now you might want to get out of that dress before you tear the basting, or discover a residual pin." They shared a knowing laugh, and Eugenia disappeared behind a screen. Autumn glanced wearily at her mother.

"Now I must have the entire outfit by Friday," Eugenia called.

"I think we can manage it," said Isabel.

"Well you really must, you know. Mr. Borodin's *Prince Igor* is being posthumously debuted in the United States, right here in Philadelphia. We cannot have those Russians thinking that our ladies are anything but the most fashionable in the world. And I shall need the *poudre* blue"—she pronounced it *poodree*—"by Saturday. We're entertaining the entire ballet company for dinner. Such a season I have never seen, Isabel." The last words were muffled by cloth.

"Step *out* of the dress, Mrs. Drexel," called Autumn in some impatience, "don't pull it over your head." Eugenia giggled sheepishly and handed the garment out to the girl.

"I am sorry, Autumn, I always forget. The fact is, I cannot keep my mind on anything these days. I hope I haven't torn any of the stitches."

"Don't bother yourself, Eugenia," Isabel said as Autumn handed her the dress with an entire seam torn.

"You know," said Eugenia, as she stepped out from behind the screen, "you and even dear Autumn could be a part of this very exciting season, Isabel. The two of you could have a raft of invitations—button me up, Autumn dear—if only you would deny those awful rumors."

"What rumors are you talking about, Eugenia?" asked Isabel, distracted apparently by the damage to Eugenia's gown.

"Oh, you know very well what rumors, my good woman." She

moved to Isabel, dragging Autumn who was struggling to fasten the woman's gown. "All you need to do is deny the rumors about you and that adventurer—"

"You mean Alistair."

"I do. You know that everyone's been saying that . . . well, I shan't go into what everyone's been saying."

"They're not rumors, Eugenia."

"Well *I* know that and so does everyone else," returned a wounded Eugenia. "Do you take us all for idiots? And we forgive you—most of us anyway. Lucy Bennet said that if it were not for the fact that you were the cleverest dressmaker in Philadelphia, she would never buy another scrap of cloth from you. Even if you are in line to the throne of England." She eyed both women knowingly. "And Lucy fancies herself one of the world's *most* sophisticated ladies." She paused. "My point, simply put, is that all you would have to do, Isabel, is deny everything." Buttoned and properly smoothed, she went to the mirror and adjusted her hat, stabbing it with a huge jeweled pin. "You must be wary of tweaking society's nose too blatantly. People are most forgiving if you just make an effort. I am sure," she stated as she pulled on her gloves, "that I could even persuade Hal Parker to call on you, if you would only cooperate. He was quite impressed with your lineage that night you met him at my party."

"First of all, Eugenia," Isabel pointed out, "Queen Victoria and half of England would have to die before I took the throne, and, secondly—"

"You are deliberately not seeing my point, Isabel. You are connected to the most respected lady in the world. All you have to do is reinforce that connection. The *semblance* of respectability is far more important than respectability itself."

"Naturally," observed Isabel, "I would have to deny that Alistair and I are living together."

"Naturally. And then send him quietly packing. Men are so gullible; you could just tell him any old thing. And it isn't only for your benefit that I am suggesting this. Think of your poor Autumn. She ought to start getting back into society. Half the swells about town are asking after her. Though sensibilities might for the moment be affronted at the thought of your both being working women, I know that I could smooth your way quite effortlessly. A little tea here, a dinner dance there, a carefully crafted explanation . . ." She waved away the effort with insouciance.

"I don't think you understand the situation, Eugenia," said Isabel genially. "First of all, Autumn will or will not make her way back into society. That is her choice, and as something of a woman of the world, even at her tender age, she may do as she wishes. As for me, I *want* people to know I am living with Alistair—I love him. And no social register in the world is going to change that."

"You are his doxy," Eugenia reproved.

"Has it ever occurred to you, dear Eugenia, that I may consider Alistair *my* doxy?"

Eugenia Drexel snatched up her reticule and pointed herself rigidly toward the door.

"You are quite, quite impossible, Isabel Thackeray," she huffed. "Frankly, I may just decide one day to stop defending you and leave you to the likes of Lucy Bennet." She lifted her formidable chin. "I shall see myself out," she said loftily, sweeping into the hallway. "And please do not forget the *poudre* blue for Saturday." Autumn and Isabel fell into an orgy of spontaneous laughter.

"Oh, Mother," said Autumn through her mirth, "Mrs. Drexel is absolutely right. You are quite, *quite* impossible. I wonder what Alistair would think of being portrayed as your doxy."

"Alistair is nothing if not a well-humored gentleman," replied Isabel, laughing. "And he is much too certain of his manliness to allow a silly label, even that one, to upset him." As she composed herself, she said with some irony and half to herself, "We are sure to get a bit of fun out of the idea, though." Autumn eyed her mother reflectively, even with a bit of envy. She'd seen the love and harmony that existed between her and Alistair. She'd seen the sharing of sentiments, the intimacy that was the keystone of their relationship.

"You and Alistair have a most singular partnership, don't you, Mother?" she observed seriously.

"Indeed we do, my darling." Isabel's eyes were the color of rosewood. They shone with confidence and love. "I am very fortunate to have found Alistair. But then," she added with elfin delight, "*he* has been fortunate, too."

"Do either of you fear the law that could imprison you for your living arrangement?"

Isabel shrugged. "The law is notoriously two-sided, Autumn. One side is for the poor and unconnected and the other for the rich. Fortunately, Alistair and I fall somewhere in the middle. I'm afraid the sheriff and his posse don't quite know what to do with us. For now anyway, Government House is turning its great head the other way. Perhaps someday the law will change, and people like Alistair and me will be able to live in peace."

"And Alistair is comfortable waiting for the change?"

"Tradition holds tightly, my darling. Alistair asks me daily to marry him. But he also understands my feelings. Given the opportunity, most intelligent people—men and women—will make a sensible compromise."

"Yes," mused Autumn. "A sensible compromise." She fiddled restively with the black moiré sash that Eugenia had abandoned.

"What is it, darling?" asked Isabel. When her daughter did not answer, she said, "It's Cain, isn't it?"

"Yes it is, Mother. It's always Cain." Her gaze dipped and then lifted. "I miss him."

Isabel set down her sewing, though she was rather seriously behind in her work. "I know." She stood and moved to her daughter. "Write to him."

"I did—"

"Oh, I don't mean that silly note asking after Carrie."

"But I really wanted to know how she and Henry were doing."

"You could have written to Carrie directly." Isabel sighed impatiently. "Benign little notes are a fine way to communicate, Autumn—*without emotional investment.* Some might call that a 'no risk' way to conduct a relationship. But *I* call it cowardice. And I would like to think that my daughter hasn't a cowardly bone in her body.

"You miss Cain. You are miserable without him. That's why you refuse to accept any number of overtures by any number of young men."

"Alright, Mother," shot back Autumn. "I miss Cain Byron. I shall *die* without him! Is that what you wanted to hear?"

"Not quite," replied Isabel flatly. She watched as her daughter fidgeted, her anger simmering. "You can go on without Cain, and you won't die of it. You are a most capable young woman, and I welcome your help here in the shop. In fact, I should hate to lose you if you ever decide to go elsewhere to look for work. But one fact remains, Autumn, you ran away. You left Cape May without even talking to Cain."

"How could I have talked to him? Cain hates me. *He* was the one who ran away. Right now he's probably laughing with Antoinette over my little note."

"What are you talking about?"

"Oh, I don't know." Autumn swiped at her tears impatiently. "I just keep imagining Cain running off to Antoinette the minute I left Cape May. She was still there, you know, when I—"

"And what if he did? Is that really the issue?"

"I shall never forgive him if he consorted with that, that—"

"Oh, honestly Autumn Thackeray," exclaimed Isabel, stalking back to her sewing machine, "you are torturing yourself so bloody needlessly." She sat down and regarded her daughter squarely. "It angers me to see you acting so . . . so . . . *ordinary*, when I know you to be an extraordinary woman. Why are you creating such ugly thoughts when you have no idea what's happening at Byron Hall?"

"But what if he married Antoinette? They were engaged, you know."

"Do you really imagine that possible, Autumn?" asked Isabel kindly. "Loving you as he does, can you really picture Cain marrying Antoinette? He gave up everything for *you*, my darling. Is it logical to imagine him throwing away his life on that silly imitation of a woman?"

"I don't know anymore," Autumn replied earnestly. "I'm not sure Cain understands his own feelings right now."

"Then you must try to help him do so. Fight with him if you must, but for the love of God, don't simply remain silent."

"Why should I help him? He has been cruel and insensitive. He has caused pain to everyone around him. Why should I coddle a bloodless male whose arrogance has made so many people miserable?"

"Because Cain Byron is not bloodless," returned Isabel quietly. "He is a decent man—one of a growing number of men who are bound by tradition, but who are trying to make their way in a changing world. Oh, Autumn, these men need our help so desperately. Cain will find his way eventually, but he will find it so much sooner and with so much less pain with you at his side." She waited for her daughter's answer. When none came, Isabel smiled ruefully. "I feel a bit like Eugenia Drexel, seeing things so clearly while the other party remains so dense."

"I am not dense, Mother, only hurt. You paint a grand Utopian picture of women helping men over the barriers of tradition, but I am one woman. And right now I feel very much alone and rejected by the man I gave my heart to." Autumn picked up a hat pattern and laid it out against a length of russet velvet. She began to pin. She was not nearly the seamstress her mother was—nor the visionary. Cain's image imposed itself on her memory. His face, the cobalt blue of his eyes, the firm mouth, the jet tousle of his curls floated before her like a watercolor mist. Before she could stop them, tears fell on the little paper pattern she held so tightly in her hands.

❧ ❧

"I'm not lettin' him in," said the little serving girl, Maura, her tinge of a brogue becoming thicker in her anxiety. The people, sitting in great wicker chairs in the back first-floor parlor of the house on Walnut Street, looked up. "He says he knows Miss Autumn, but I'm not lettin' him in."

Autumn's brows furrowed. "Who is it, Maura?"

"Says his name's *Doctor* Byron. He *says* he knows you—but I'm not lettin' him in. I told him just t' get himself down off the front stoop and wait on the street. Him comin' about this late at night, lookin' all tagrag like he does; he can't expect decent folk t' just let him in their houses on his own say so."

Autumn rose, the book she'd been attempting to read falling from her lap. "Oh, Mother," she said on a breath. "What'll I do?"

Isabel looked up from her hand stitching. "You might want to answer the door," she said mildly.

"But it's Cain."

Alistair, strumming studiously on his banjo and intermittently sounding out the tune to "Cruising Down the River," regarded her with concern. "Would you like me to go, Autumn?" Isabel placed her hand on his and offered a warning glance.

"Autumn might wish to greet her own callers," she said quietly. Both people regarded the girl. Her eyes, like Maura's, were filled with uncertainty.

"All I know," said the Irish girl, "is *I'm* not lettin' him in." She turned with a swish of her dimity skirt and bumped through the door leading back into the kitchen, her objections to such a caller fading with her progress into that part of the house.

Autumn looked from Isabel to Alistair. Then, leaning down, she retrieved her copy of Miss Austen's *Pride and Prejudice.* Wordlessly, she set it on a table and withdrew from the room.

Outside, Cain watched the house as if it might move or speak at any moment. He watched it from the sidewalk that passed along its front garden. Having been nearly bodily tossed from the stoop by a tiny wisp of a girl who seemed to have some authority in the matter, he dared not move beyond the wrought iron gate lest the girl make good her threat to "call the cops." Glancing down at himself, he realized he should have taken more care with his appearance and the manner of his arrival in Philadelphia. He'd not bothered to outfit one of the well-appointed coaches, but instead had merely saddled one of the horses for the trip. He looked up toward the porch. That snippy girl would not have treated a liveried groom as disdainfully as she'd treated him, Cain reflected. But, of course, Cain had to admit that he was not dressed so tidily as a liveried groom. His overcoat and the shirt and jodhpurs beneath it were stained with road grime, and his boots were caked with mud. He unknotted the scarf around his neck and used it to swipe at the dark curls that clung to his forehead. Despite the chill of the November night, he was perspiring—whether from apprehension or the exertion of the long ride, he did not know.

His reflections were interrupted as the door to the house swung open. A wash of warm golden light lit the steps and the garden. In the midst of the light stood that all-too-familiar, all-too-loved silhouette. Hesitantly, Cain pushed past the gate. He stood tensely for a moment in the fringes of the light, wondering whether he would be welcomed or shunned.

"You inquired after Carrie," he ventured huskily. "I . . . I thought I would deliver the message of her well-being in person." Autumn could not contain her smile. She beckoned him, her hand arching out in sweet welcome, and Cain realized the fullest relief, the fullest freedom his heart had ever known. In a few bounding strides, he was up on the stoop and Autumn was in his arms. "Oh, my love," he intoned as he clung to her. And

Autumn, yielding to the yearnings of her heart, melted into his embrace.

"Cain," she whispered, "you've come to me at last." She brought him into the house, into the lighted warmth. "I have missed you so."

"And I you, love." They stood for long moments in the front parlor before Isabel and Alistair joined them there.

"Cain," Isabel greeted him. "It is so good to see you. You remember Alistair?" The two men shook hands.

"I remember you, sir," said Cain. "How are you?"

"Better than I've been in years, lad."

"Me, too!" Cain assured him. He took Autumn into the cradle of his embrace. It seemed he could not be close enough to her, could not hold her near enough. He seemed to fear she might disappear. Autumn, too, wondered if these happy moments would evaporate. She had waited these long weeks for Cain to come to her, feared that he would not, and dreaded that he might.

It was decided that sandwiches ought to be prepared, and as everyone headed for the kitchen—and the disgruntlement of Maura—Autumn recalled those first terrible days after she'd left Byron Hall. Hanging back from the gay preparation of a late supper, she recalled her sad journey away from Cape May and her certainty that nothing would ever be right or good again. And she wondered what had changed Cain from the glowering autocrat of her recent memory to the ardent lover of tonight.

Alistair exuberantly grabbed a paper-wrapped item from inside the newly acquired apparatus called an icebox. The new contrivance offered the dubious convenience of allowing left-over food to be stored for several days. Alistair invited everyone to guess what might be in this particular package. Isabel guessed that it might be a lamb chop from last evening's dinner. Maura snatched the leftover, assuring everyone that it was, in fact, a breast of chicken from that afternoon's lunch. She then directed everyone from the kitchen, telling them that *she* would make the sandwiches.

Once back in the parlor, the couples sat laughing, Isabel complaining that she was not sure she liked being shooed from a room in her own house.

"And a fine house it is, too," observed Cain, as he glanced around. "I am glad your business is going well. I must tell you—"

"That you expected me to fail miserably," interrupted she, finishing Cain's thought. "Well, don't let it get around, but I, too, thought I'd be out on the street by Christmas."

"I assure you, my sweet," said Alistair, "that I'd never have let you starve on the street."

"A noble claim, if an empty sentiment," returned Isabel archly, "since I am not starving on the street." The couple shared a chuckle. "Actually," continued Isabel, "my business has burgeoned due to a marvelous device. It is a machine that produces an even, single-thread chain stitch."

"It is called," interjected Alistair excitedly, "a sewing machine, appropriately. It was invented by a perfectly unsavory gent from Boston by the name of Singer. He's a bigamist, you see." He sat back, laughing genially at Cain's expression of astonishment. Alistair continued with an explanation of the intricate workings of the machine, and Cain's brows furrowed.

"I'm not sure I like the idea," he said at last. "The concept of involving women with treadles, pulleys, knobs, and gears is unsavory to me." Cain regarded Autumn fondly. "I am more used to the sight of a lady with her needle and her thread, her thimble on her finger, and her work arrayed prettily on her lap. That, after all, is the point of her sewing."

"I'm afraid," Isabel said wryly, "that is not at all the point of *my* sewing. By luck or accident, the adulterous Mr. Singer and I have become irrevocably hitched." Autumn watched Cain's bemusement deepen as Maura brought a tray laden with the evening's refreshment.

"Actually," said Alistair as they ate their supper, "Isabel has become enthralled with many of the technologies that have become available to the average person over the years. We're thinking of getting a telephone, and we've already had a bathroom installed on the second floor." Cain arched a dark brow. Not only was the subject not fit for supper conversation, the idea of indoor bathrooms was something that many people considered repugnant. Imagine people attending to their most private and repulsive needs *inside the house*. Despite his happiness at seeing Autumn, Cain felt that he had entered a somewhat alien atmosphere—a place where time seemed to be speeding along at a velocity that left him mentally gasping for breath. His mental breath was to be quite taken away within minutes as Isabel and Alistair bade the younger couple good night. Together, the two people made their way to the stairs leading to the second floor. Cain watched in bewilderment as, together, they started to ascend.

"Congratulations," he said hesitantly. "I had no idea there had been a marriage."

Isabel stopped mid-ascent. "There hasn't been one, Cain," she said quietly. "And there will not be one." As Alistair continued up the stairs into the softly lit hallway above, Isabel remained to regard Cain with some sympathy. "I know all this is hard to absorb," she offered, "but the fact is, I have decided to live an honest life. And my resolve is strong as steel." Cain quirked a puzzled glance toward Autumn as Isabel followed Alistair up the stairs.

"What does she mean?" he asked.

Autumn looked up from a studious regard of the carpet to find Cain's face a mask of incomprehension. He gathered her to him, looking down at her quizzically. "She means," said Autumn, "that she and Alistair are living together openly. Mother, it seems, has decided to be one of those pilgrims we talked about so many nights ago. The ones who will help to build a perfect world. Do you recall that discussion?"

"I remember everything we have ever said to each other, Autumn."

"And everything we have not said?" she asked him.

"That, too," Cain said solemnly. "And I curse my own foolishness for the silences I have caused between us."

"We all act foolishly sometimes."

"I have acted more foolishly than you know," Cain ventured. "Antoinette, you see, was the one who told me about the wedding, and I suppose I thought for a time that she was in sympathy with me—"

Autumn shook her head and laughed softly. "Antoinette Fraser is a small piece of your history, Cain, and an even smaller piece of mine. She has no place in our future." She paused, drawing away from him. Standing and pacing, she continued. "I assume it is our future that you have come here to discuss." Cain nodded. "Then the first thing that you must know is that I would do exactly what I did before in helping Vanessa and Robert with their marriage plans. But I would not do it in secret. I want to marry you, Cain. And I shall be as proper a wife as it is within my power to be, but I am never, ever, going to hide behind a mask of dishonesty again. No matter how dangerous honesty may be, it is far less damaging than deception."

"I am not sure I understand, Autumn. You give me hope and a sense of foreboding as well."

Autumn nodded. "I know, love, I feel it, too. I wish I could promise absolute obedience to you, as the marriage vows suggest, for I know it would make you comfortable. But I cannot. You told me once that I had a choice of living with you in harmony or discord. Well, I can only make that decision day by day. I pray you will have patience with my choices; they will not always please you."

"You issue a challenge, Autumn," said Cain, rising and standing before her, "even as you offer conciliation."

"It is a challenge to both of us, Cain. I think we're up to it, don't you?"

"I don't know," Cain said quietly. "I honestly don't know."

"Well, I do. I do know, Cain." She took his shoulders in her hands. "We can face anything together. Like my mother and Alistair, we can become the pilgrim builders who take the chances, who defy tradition, who will make a tender world for both men and women."

"Your ideal is worthy, Autumn, though perhaps unrealistic. Let me tell you about the battle I fought with myself these last weeks. I have had years of breeding that told me I should not follow you here. I fought a battle against that breeding, and my love for you was my only weapon.

"If the truth be told, the traditions with which I was raised made life a simple matter, even if they made little sense. One of those traditions holds that women must obey their husbands in all things. But that is my truth, I have reminded myself, and my father's truth—not yours. According to the traditions by which I was raised, a wife lives for her husband and through him.

"But what if, I asked myself, the wife has wisdom of her own, perceptions that differ from the husband's? What if she has a searching intellect, as you have, a quick wit, as you have, and opinions and sensitivities and fundamental convictions . . . as you have? Must her intellect and her convictions be screened through those of her husband? Must her every opinion, her every response to life be approved first by her husband? Wouldn't that process tend to discourage her independent thought? Is that what we do, I asked myself, to someone we love?" Cain paused, his regard settling lovingly on Autumn.

"I have fought that battle and won, love. But it is only one battle. There are a million more questions to be answered, challenges to be met. My victory is less than secure. And I fear," he told her wryly, "loving you, I shall face a new battle every day." He smiled. "The only thing I know for certain right now is that I cannot bear to live without you. That is what brought me to you. But I don't know if I can be what you want me to be. I don't know that I can be as honest as you wish me to be, and most of all, I do not know if I have the patience to bear your honesty. All I can promise is that I will try. If that is what you require, I will try. But you must have patience with me, too, Autumn. Your expectations require much of a man."

"Not so much," returned Autumn gently. "All that's necessary is a little compromise, a bit of rearranging of one's thinking at times, and perhaps even the use of a new strategy now and then. Maybe at times we might remember to hold back judgment or the too-hasty scorn of the other's ideas. That doesn't seem so much to do for someone we love, does it? Women have been doing it for centuries." Cain reflected for a long moment, his eyes never leaving the melting amber of Autumn's. He smiled tentatively.

"Then I should be able to manage it for . . . well, at least the next fifty years."

"It won't be as hard as you think, my darling," she told him, holding his hand tenderly. "Facing challenges can be most invigorating. And winning, of course, has its own rewards."

Chapter 25

The wedding took place at the Old St. Sophia's Church on Fourth Street. Autumn was escorted down the aisle by both Alistair MacKenzie and Robert Moffat, and she and Cain stood before an assemblage of their friends and family and uttered vows as weightless as feathers, as consequential as ocean tides. The elegant simplicity of the ceremony was matched by the fluid elegance of Autumn's gown, which had been made for her by Philadelphia's premier dress designer, Isabel Thackeray. It was of a creamy satin, draped about the hem to reveal a lacy under-skirt and caught by tiny seed pearls. The bodice and skirt were appliquéd in a deeper, richer ivory. The sleeves, long and sheath-ing, were of the pristine lace of the underskirting and piped in shimmering ivory. Entwined in her upswept hair were sprays of baby's breath. She carried a bouquet of gardenias, small white hydrangea florets, and trails of tea-stained satin ribbons. For Vanessa, Isabel had made a dress of peach-patterned beige watered silk with a draping bodice that graced that woman's figure with a regal, if modest elegance. For herself, Isabel had stitched a pale bronze lace with rich coffee accents at the collar and sleeves. At the reception, held later at the Olympus, they stood together, the two women, lost in their own joyous contemplation, their men beside them.

Autumn greeted Cain's sisters, who had traveled with their families from many parts of the country. Emily Doyle, the eldest, managed to maintain her dignity even as her second-to-youngest child, three-year-old George, found his way beneath her skirts. Caroline Westervelt smiled sweetly and congratulated her brother. She took Autumn's hand and said, "Cain has never looked happier. And mother looks so beautiful. She has you to thank for that, Autumn."

"Mother is well, isn't she, Cain?" asked June McCrimmon, who had traveled all the way from Buffalo, New York. "How is her marriage to that sailor working out? I have been so frustrated," she confided to Autumn, "living so far from home." She glanced at her mother and Robert. "They seem quite happy. But I would like to have been here for the wedding." She sighed. "As you might imagine, it is difficult to travel with five children in tow."

"Is it only five now?" asked Abiah Devereaux, the youngest sister. "You'll have some job keeping up with me, June," she said heartily. "I'll be the mother of seven," she told Autumn, "come the end of December." Autumn regarded the woman's full-bellied middle worriedly.

"Should you have come all the way from Ohio in your condition?" she asked.

"For my brother's wedding?" she asked. "Of course, I should have. I wouldn't have missed meeting the girl who finally trapped him for all the world."

"Traps are for bears, Abbie," Cain put in with a small laugh. "And the woman who uses one gets exactly what she deserves."

The newlyweds left for Cape May the next morning. They had decided to delay their honeymoon till after Christmas, affording Cain the opportunity to put his practice in order. He was leaving Philadelphia with a certain understanding of Isabel's way of life. In any event, he no longer scorned the choices she had made. She and Alistair were so obviously, so completely, so composedly in love that he could admit to a confidence in their happiness and even an admiration for their abundant courage. Less consequentially, he had to admit that Isabel's sewing machine, though a mannish contrivance, was a timesaver in her work, and her icebox, if unconventional, was certainly useful. He had to admit as well, though quite privately, that the convenience of the indoor bathroom far outweighed his aversion to the idea. All in all, he felt an esteem for Autumn's mother that he had not thought possible in himself. Autumn regarded his admiration for Isabel with great hope. And the positive attitude he'd adopted toward Robert boded well for their future.

Upon their arrival at Byron Hall, Autumn's wish was to see Carrie right away. Her babe was a month old now, and Autumn wanted to make sure Carrie and the child had come through the trauma of birth well. She arrived at the Inman farm to find Carrie gaunt and tired. Henry and several of his farm hands had come in for lunch, and Carrie was busy with the preparations, the baby girl firmly planted on her hip. Even when the men had withdrawn, Carrie found it hard to relax. Autumn insisted that she would clean up the dishes and planted Carrie and her baby firmly in a chair. Carrie informed Autumn that she'd been spending much of her time helping out other farm ladies, some of whom were pregnant with second or third or fourth children.

"Since I've had me own," Carrie explained, "I've realized what a lot of work it is to run a house and look after a babe." She sipped at the tea that Autumn had made her and reflected how fine a thing it would be if those ladies had a tranquil setting in which to prepare themselves for their deliveries and recover from them. It was not unusual, she mentioned, for a woman to deliver her child at her own house, amid the chaos of older children, demanding husbands who were often intoxicated in celebration of the new arrival, and equally demanding drop-in guests. Often, the mother, delivered of her newborn, would be up within hours, feeding animals, wiping up after family gatherings, and seeing to the needs of her household. All this she did with a tiny babe at her breast.

"Imagine how exhausting that must be, Cain," said Autumn that night over dinner. "It can't be good for the mother's health, nor for the baby's. I am not suggesting that a woman must retire from life simply because she gives birth," Autumn added, "but don't you think a few days of rest are in order for such a monumental achievement? Wealthy women receive such rest, why not poor women as well? My thought is that we might turn Byron Hall into a place for the ladies."

"But if we invite women to stay here," returned Cain, "we'll have to move out."

"Precisely my thought, Cain dear," said Autumn tranquilly. "Is that really such a bad idea?" They had been to visit Vanessa's new home—a pretty farm overlooking the ocean—and Autumn had fallen in love with it. "Wouldn't Byron Hall, with all its rooms and servants, serve perfectly as a hospital for ladies in their confinement?"

"Absolutely not," said Cain, splaying an authoritarian hand. "My father would spin in his grave."

"A spinning might do him the world of good," Autumn returned brightly. "It'll clear his head. It might even change his perspective." Cain frowned and asserted that he would discuss the matter no further. Byron Hall, he said, though he had never personally loved the house, was his father's proudest accomplishment.

"That's very true," agreed Vanessa when Autumn brought up the matter at the family's Thanksgiving dinner. She looked around the dining hall, reflecting on all the years she had spent in the house. Sitting about the long, heavily laden table were Cain at its head, Robert, Vanessa, Carrie and Henry Inman, and their little girl. "Cain's father," continued Vanessa, "bought every stick of furniture in this house with an eye to its elegance. He had the house built as a showcase." She smiled ruefully. "We had many Thanksgivings here much like this one today." She glanced at her son. "Do you remember those dinners, Cain? Your father would sit at the head of the table, as you are sitting today. And I," she said, her glance drifting to Autumn, "would sit at the other end of the board, as Autumn is. Everything was absolutely perfect—except one thing. It was all show. There was never any real warmth beneath the perfection of the display." Vanessa paused. "I think it is time this house was put to some real use. It has stood long enough for cardboard lives and imitations of happiness. Don't you think so, Cain?"

Before her son had the opportunity to voice his resistance, Vanessa pronounced without fanfare, "It shall be with great pleasure that I endow Byron Hall with a fund of its own—from my share of the profits from Isabel's business—and turn it into a clinic for pregnant women." In a blaze of irony, she announced that Byron Hall would be transformed into the "Cain Byron, Sr. Memorial Women's Building."

"You cannot be serious, Mother," said Cain through Carrie's spontaneous applause.

"I am quite serious, my darling," she assured him.

"Naturally," Autumn put in, "it would be wonderful if you would stay on here to treat the ladies, Cain."

Carrie added her own encouragement. "Everyone trusts you so, Dr. Byron."

"You could maintain the same office," Autumn commented spiritedly. "And we could even introduce the new notion of voluntary motherhood. We could place reading materials about and . . ." Her voice trailed off, for Cain's regard settled on her with a withering chilliness. He stood rigidly and invited Robert and Henry to join him for brandy and cigars in the front parlor. His glare defied Autumn to scold him about it. Autumn mentioned simply that the men would find Vanessa and Carrie and her in the back parlor when they finished their cigars.

"A very nice bit of compromise," Vanessa offered when the women were alone.

"Thank you, Mother-in-law," Autumn returned, but her gaze dipped sorrowfully. "I just hope Cain is not too angry," she said. "No matter what happens, however, you have done a wonderful thing, Vanessa."

"I did the *right* thing, Autumn," Vanessa reminded her.

"Yes, you did, Mrs. Byron," Carrie affirmed jubilantly. "This is a great day for everyone hereabouts." She smiled and undid her bodice. Her baby squirmed contentedly as she began to suckle.

Carrie looked up. "In honor of this great day, I've decided to name her Vanessa."

In the front parlor, Cain offered cigars and poured three snifters of brandy from a Bristol-blue decanter engraved with a design of grapes and vine leaves. He considered the proud old piece thoughtfully before setting it down. It was the same decanter from which his father had served his own brandy. He looked up, not unaware of the discomfort of the other two men. Cain, too, felt a sense of disorientation in this overly lavish parlor with its wealth of history and pretension. He had not sat in this room in a very long time. He noted with some humor that Henry Inman searched surreptitiously for an ashtray. Cain managed not to smile as the man held an internal debate with himself as to whether or not to use a porcelain model of a human hand. He glanced up finally, sheepishly, a question in his regard.

"It's alright, Henry," Cain said, "we've used that as an ashtray since father noticed a chip in the wrist frill." They all shared a spontaneous chuckle, but Cain glanced hastily away to stare out onto the patchy lawns beyond the French windows. He felt the older men's keen scrutiny upon him.

"We have never been so companionably together, the three of us," Robert said and paused, exhaling a long ribbon of smoke. "It's an excellent thing for gentlemen to get together and share important thoughts," he said. "Don't you think so, Henry?" His eyes twinkled with merriment. Henry smiled and shrugged a bit shyly. His brows furrowed a bit, however, as he tried to focus on some "important" thought. "What, for instance," continued Robert with an oblique glance toward Cain, "did you make of Vanessa's announcement? What do you think of the idea?" Henry attempted a reply, but Cain rounded on Robert.

"I think," he said wrathfully, "that, at the age of nearly thirty, a man might expect to be out from under his mother's thumb." He tossed down his brandy and poured another for himself. "Please pardon my bluntness, gentlemen."

"Is that how you see it?" asked Robert.

"That is how I see it," he responded flatly.

"Well, now," put in Henry thoughtfully, attempting to live up to Robert's assessment of their conversation, "that's not how I see it. But, then, I'm not as smart as you, doc."

"Nor am I," Robert acknowledged. "But that's not how I see it either."

Cain smiled thinly. "Of course, neither of you are being tossed out of your own houses."

"Oh, well," offered Henry, "if you want to look at it that way . . . See," he continued, "I wasn't seein' that part of it."

Robert, stroking his beard thoughtfully, said, "Neither was I. My thoughts ran on a different track entirely. I was thinking that, in a way, Cain, your mother is forcing you *out* from under her thumb. This is her house. And the life you're leading isn't yours, it's your father's, if you'll pardon me for saying it. Of course, it's all a matter of perspective."

"And I was just considerin' everything from the ladies' point of view," Henry reflected. "It's a kind and generous thing your mother's doin', doc. Could be you don't see it that way, 'cause you didn't make the decision."

Cain sipped quietly at his drink. He watched his stepfather shift uncomfortably within the rigid planes of the chair in which he sat. He glanced about the room, realizing that it was not, after all, his taste. In his new house, wherever that turned out to be, he would demand a smoking parlor—and very comfortable chairs.

"You both make a certain sense," he acknowledged to the older men. "It is only that things happened so fast. One day, Autumn visits Carrie, and the next I'm being tossed out of the house where I was born."

"Born and bred," Robert said, toasting him and placing significance on the last word. He looked down into the swirling amber of his drink. "Change doesn't really happen all that quickly, son," he said gently, "we just think it does. We aren't always expecting change, so it catches us off guard. I've known enough change in my life to be sympathetic with your dilemma."

Robert Moffat, Cain reminded himself, had always been sympathetic. Robert had not judged him during those terrible days after Autumn had left; he'd taken care of him as a father might, as the gentle Henry would undoubtedly take care of his sons. These two men, Cain conceded, were the wisest he had ever known. Their role in their marriages, like Alistair MacKenzie's in his relationship with Isabel, was hardly traditional, and yet they seemed, like Alistair, content. He longed for their serenity.

"Let me ask you this, doc," said Henry. "Don't *you* think it's a good idea to turn this house into a hospital?" Cain nodded reluctantly. "Like I said, I'm not as smart as you, but I can't figure out what difference it makes whose idea it was in the first place."

"In truth, Henry, neither can I."

During the next weeks, Autumn and Cain searched for a new home. By mid-December, Autumn believed she'd found one. With the spicy scent of pine and old apple trees filling the frosty air, Cain led their wagon up the sun-warmed drive of a whitewashed, two-storied cottage on a knoll that sloped, tree-shaded, to the sea. It had been abandoned some years past, and the farm had been worked tentatively and with little conscientiousness. Autumn assured Cain that he could bring his horses with him to fill the stable yards, and that she would see the fences mended, the gardens cleared, and the far-flung tillage restored to its refulgent potential.

"Vanessa is determined to have the hospital opened by the end of summer. By summer," she told him with certainty, and oddly, with urgency, "this farm will be a perfect haven for you. You can go to your office at the women's building during the day and return here at night to the bosom of your little family. It will be perfect for us."

"My little . . . family?" asked Cain as they walked arm in arm over the frost-glistened lawn.

"Yes," answered Autumn hesitantly. They stopped beneath the arcing branches of a tall apple tree. "Yes," she repeated. "Your family, Cain."

"There's to be a baby?"

"Yes, love."

Cain smiled deeply and brushed her cheek with a gloved forefinger. "That is why you were so anxious to have the matter of our move from Byron Hall settled."

Autumn nodded. "I could not bear the thought of our babes being reared in that bastion of righteous disapproval. I want them raised in a new environment, fresh and sunlit, and cleared of musty traditions that may stifle and scare them. There is so much pain connected with that house." She watched Cain sober by degrees.

"Yes," he said, his response a hoarse whisper. "I know that now. And I have been the cause of so much of that pain." He placed his fingertips over her lips when she would have spoken. "It's alright, love. I can talk about it now. I must talk about it. Though I shall never completely forgive myself for carrying on those musty traditions you speak of, I understand now that I must accept what I have done and been. In order to change, Autumn, I must remember. Each time I look at you, I must remember how much I love you and how despairing my life would be without you. I can never forget how fortunate I am to have you in my life—in my arms, Autumn." He gathered her to him. "Believe me, your courage and your honesty through all of this will not have been in vain. You have taught me so much."

"And we must teach our children to be honest with themselves and others—especially with those they love. And we must teach them to have courage, Cain. We must make certain they are never afraid to do what they know is right."

Cain nodded his agreement. "We rail and brawl and make animal noises in our pain, but, optimists that we are, we produce ourselves all over again. I suppose it is because, optimists that we are, we believe we can make the world better."

"Oh, Cain," said Autumn earnestly, "we have been given a great responsibility and a most glorious challenge."

He took her face in his hands, and said, "I believe we're up to it, Autumn. Don't you?"

Afterword

CAPE MAY, NEW JERSEY

1905

For the most part, the little whitewashed two-story cottage on a knoll sloping toward the sea is quiet. All about, the world is dark, slumbering in the cricket song and peaceful scents of night. Inside the cottage, a little boy, his eyes heavy with inter-rupted sleep, pushes open the door to his sister's bedroom. He stands for a moment in the soft glow of the light from the hallway.

From the toasty nest of her blankets, the sister asks, "What are you doing up, Bobby?"

The lad rubs his eyes. "I had a dream," he whispers.

"A bad one?" asks the girl.

"It was awful."

"Want to climb into bed with me?" The boy nods sleepily and shuffles across the room to his sister's bed. She makes room for him beneath her quilt. When they are cuddled together, she croons their grandmother's version of a familiar nursery rhyme:

"Bobby Byron went to sea
A golden cat upon his knee.
He found a treasure in the deep
A child fair who would not sleep.

Bobby Byron closed his eyes
Rubbed his cat and heard her sighs.
'Little friend be kind to me
Take me further out to sea.'"

"Tell me about your dream," the girl says gently.

"It was about you climbing that tree this afternoon, Isabel," he says with soft accusation. The little girl laughs, the sound rippling in the darkness. "It's not funny," the boy scolds her. "I was scared you'd fall. Pa's told us a million times not to climb that apple tree."

"It hasn't been a million," the girl corrects him sagely.

"Then . . . a trillion," the little boy returns with a yawn.

"A trillion is more than a million," instructs his sister. There is a silence. "I did it, though, Bobby," she says quietly, with wistful wonder. "I tried to climb that tree all summer, and I finally did it." The boy nods, his golden curls tousled on the pillow, his thumb tucked firmly in his little bud of a mouth. "Don't be scared for me," she says. "It wasn't that hard, and it was worth it once I got to the top. The world is beautiful from way up there."

The little boy looks over at his sister. In the dark, her gaze glints indigo. Taking his thumb from his mouth for a breath of a second, he asks, "Can I do it tomorrow?" Isabel shakes her dark curls.

"Maybe you'd better not, Bobby. Pa'd be mad." The boy accepts her judgment; she is, after all, nearly seven and a half, two years older and far wiser than he.

"But promise me," he says drowsily, his words muffled by his thumb, "you won't do it again either."

"Oh, I won't climb that tree," the girl assures him dreamily. "I've already done that. Tomorrow, though, I'm going over to visit Grandma Vanessa and Grandpa Robert." The little boy makes a questioning sound. "I'm going over there, Bobby," she explains softly, "'cause they've got a bigger tree."